Operation Wrath, Mahoney had called it. A plan for preemptive nuclear strikes on the capital cities of Syria, Iran, Iraq, and Jordan.

"If this does get out, it will be suicide." Wasserman, the Mossad chief, was deeply frightened.

Wallace Mahoney nodded tiredly, feeling his years and wounds. "One does not set out to catch a panther with a mousetrap."

THE HOLLOW MEN

SEAN FLANNERY

CHARTER
NEW YORK

A Division of Charter Communications Inc.
A GROSSET & DUNLAP COMPANY
51 Madison Avenue
New York, New York 10010

THE HOLLOW MEN

An Ace Charter Original
First Ace Charter Printing: January, 1982
Published simultaneously in Canada

Manufactured in the United States of America
2 4 6 8 0 9 7 5 3 1

This book is for Lorrel Elizabeth . . . a very special lady.

We've got ourselves a mole, gentlemen. Not the queer little creature that hides from the sun as it burrows underground, but a rodent of a person who has burrowed within our organization, selling us to the enemy while telling us he's our friend.

> *From a talk at Wormwood
> Scrubs by an assistant
> director of the British
> Intelligence Service, October
> 9, 1954.*

Principles are such lovely things, too bad they're wasted on the human race.

> *Anonymous*

THE HOLLOW MEN

The fog that obscured the mountains was beginning to lift when the tall, impeccably dressed man arrived at the nondescript stone building on Geneva's banking row. He surrendered his Citroën Ds 19 sedan to the attendant and took the elevator to the fourth floor.

He was tired and somewhat discouraged. Too many people had died in the strike on Israel's spy satellite receiving station at al Qaryūt. And yet the strike had been absolutely necessary. They all had agreed to that.

The bank's president met him as he stepped from the elevator. "Good morning, sir," the smaller man said.

"Good morning. I have a financial statement to send to my stockholders."

"Of course," the banker said, his voice soft. Everything in Geneva was soft and subdued. Especially in the financial section of the city. "A Telex arrived for you just this morning."

"I see," the tall man said. After his labors of the last days he wanted nothing more than to take the first flight home and rest during the coming weekend.

Depending upon what was in the Telex, however, he might have to change his plans. He had an odd, gut-level feeling that al Qaryūt, despite the projections, could very well blossom into a major problem. A very major problem indeed.

PART ONE
HARES AND HOUNDS

I

NORTHERN MINNESOTA . . . MONDAY

On the morning that the woman arrived, which was a full nine months after Margery had died, Wallace Mahoney got stiffly up from the wicker chair in the screened-in porch where he had spent the night, and stretched.

Somehow, God help him, he had made it through another night without blowing his brains out. He looked down at the loaded .38 revolver on the table and shook his head in sadness.

Through the screen he could look across the once well-tended lawn, which had not yet been mowed this summer, to the dock where his small fishing boat was tied, and beyond, to the lake itself.

The water that morning was glass smooth, as it was at most dawns. Across the lake he could see a thin curl of smoke rising from a chimney on one of the cabins, and he imagined for a moment that he could smell the wood burning, could smell the bacon frying.

The pines that grew close along the shoreline were reflected in the water, making a pattern away from the docks, and out near the middle a large ripple was spreading from where a fish had jumped, feeding on the water bugs that skimmed the surface.

"Christ," Mahoney swore half to himself as he picked up the pistol, turned, and went through the cabin to his study. He locked the gun in the top drawer of his desk, then went back into the house to the bathroom where he stripped off his sweat-soaked clothes and climbed carefully into the shower, letting the hot water take away the aches and pains in his old body.

At 64, Wallace Mahoney felt that he had done too much, had been too many places, and had seen too many things for any six men. Unlike most men his age who have an edge of sorrow for all the things they had never done, Mahoney felt that he had been dealt more than his share of living.

He was a man of medium height—something under six feet—with heavy shoulders, a thick neck, and a paunch that contributed greatly to his 220 pounds. During the past few years he and his wife Margery had fought a constant battle against his weight, and what he called the "ravages of gravity" on his frame, to little or no avail.

The only two physically redeeming factors—three if you counted Marge's insistence that he had a handsome face—were the facts that he had not lost his silvery white hair, and that two years ago the doctors at Bethesda Naval Hospital had stripped the varicose veins from his legs.

Now there were ugly scars spiraling from his thighs around to the backs of his calves nearly to his ankles, but the constant pain was gone.

As the water drummed on his face and chest he let his mind relax from the terrible pounding he had given himself during the long night. He was feeling guilty, and he knew it.

Although his doctor would tell him he had nothing to feel guilty about, Mahoney could not shake the feeling that had gradually come over him during the past few weeks.

He was no longer devastated by the fact that Margery was dead, nor did he have the pains, the shortness of breath, the constriction in his throat that had plagued him for the first months. No longer did he sigh so much, nor did he feel the vast emptiness in his gut.

The sleepness nights and the loaded pistol had become nothing more than symbols now. They weren't the threat that they had been at the beginning when one night he had raised the gun to his temple, had cocked the hammer, and had begun to squeeze the trigger.

A few nights after that incident, he had stumbled and fallen on his way to his study to get the gun, and had been unable to get up or even crawl. He had lain there in the middle of the living room floor whimpering like a baby, unable to do anything for two hours.

Then he had gone through a two-week period of not eating. He lost forty pounds, and the skin hung slack on his face until he finally realized that if he was going to die, it was not going to be that way.

He had gone through another phase of hating everyone, especially his old cronies from the Company, and even his son and daughter-in-law. But, like the other stages of his grief, those feelings had passed as well.

Then, for a few weeks, he had sat in front of the blank television screen day after day, watching his entire life with Marge unfold. The time after the war. The harsh life they had led in New York City when the CIA had first been formed and he worked out of a tenement apartment as an analyst. And then Germany, and fatefully Moscow and the operation with Zamyatin which ended in the death of his son Michael.

He also relived his own personal failures and triumphs, always measuring them against the life he had had with his wife.

Finally there had been one piece of unsettled business. One year ago he had come out of retirement when a high-ranking Soviet officer had defected from Beirut Station and he was needed on the debriefing team. He did not want to think about it, but his thoughts were being dragged back, almost against his will.

When he was finished in the shower, he shaved and then dressed in a pair of lightweight khaki slacks, a short-sleeved khaki safari shirt, and a pair of soft, slip-on shoes, amazed with himself that he was thinking about the Company again.

Back in the living room he poured a stiff shot of Kentucky sour mash whiskey, took a cigar from the humidor on the sideboard, and went outside where he settled down on one of the lawn chairs overlooking the lake.

A year? A year and a half ago? It seemed like centuries in the past, not only because his memories were fading, and not only because of Marge's death, but also because he had been so unsure of himself at the time.

Jada Natasha Yatsyna, chief of station for the KGB in Beirut, had defected, and in her debriefing she had told Mahoney the story of how the Soviets had attempted to sabotage the Americans' first test of the atomic bomb in New Mexico.

It had been a strange, twisted tale of espionage, deceit, and brilliantly planned operations that had very nearly succeeded. But there had been something else as well. Something that the Soviet woman had hinted at, something that had ended in her murder in San Antonio.

Mahoney rubbed at the scar on his left side, just below the armpit, where the bullet had entered and exited, as he thought about that day. He too had nearly been killed, but had managed to call the CIA's duty officer in Langley. The mess had been picked up, and Mahoney had been hospitalized. All very quietly.

According to Jada there could have been some kind of collusion then between the American and Soviet governments. At Langley they were calling it the "delusions of a sick old woman."

"And besides," McBundy, the missions and operations chief, had told Mahoney, "who gives a damn? It happened thirty-five years ago."

"I give a damn," Mahoney had said from his hospital bed. "They killed her and Lovelace, and they tried to kill me."

But by then Margery had gotten sick, and he had forgotten about it all until now.

He picked up the glass of whiskey and sipped it, the liquor burning his throat but instantly warming and loosening the tight knot in his gut.

The telephone in his study rang, jerking him out of his morose contemplations, and he turned to look toward the house, but he did not immediately get up.

John? he asked himself. It was probably his son calling from California to check up on him again.

The telephone rang a second time, its bell strident and somehow out of place amid the serenity of the lakeside, and Mahoney put down his glass, got to his feet, and shuffled into the house.

He got to the phone on the fourth ring and picked it up. "Yes?"

"Wallace, this is Darrel Switt."

Mahoney sat down in his desk chair and pocketed the cigar he had not lit yet. "Good morning, Darrel," he said his voice hoarse. He had not spoken with anyone for at least four days, and his throat seemed dry.

"I hate to be a bother like this, Wallace, but there may

be some trouble brewing for you. And it'll break fast."

The old familiar pang of expectation grabbed at him, and he sat forward, the appropriate responses coming back immediately. "What have you got, Darrel? Spell it out."

"Do you remember a woman by the name of Sonja Margraff?"

For a moment Mahoney drew a blank, but then it started to come back to him in bits and pieces. "Berlin Station. The seventies. Her brother was killed on an eastward operation."

"That's the woman. She quit the Company and emigrated to Israel a short time after that."

"I had her figured for marriage. White picket fence, two cars, kids, a dog. Bethesda, perhaps."

"Negative. Try Tel Aviv. Try single. And try Mossad."

"Israeli intelligence?" Mahoney asked, his interest piqued. "Is she here?"

"On her way out to see you, we're assuming."

"Why?" Mahoney asked, looking out the rear window toward the dirt road that led back to the county trunk highway.

"No way of knowing for sure," Switt said. Mahoney had worked with the young man in Moscow at the time Switt had been assigned as a case officer attached to the embassy. He had been the OD at Langley on the day Mahoney had nearly bought it in San Antonio. And it had been Switt who had cleaned up the mess for him.

He was continuing. "We took a quick peek at the case files to see if we could come up with any connection. You were the signing officer on her brother's mission."

"I see," Mahoney said, the Berlin days coming back a little more clearly now. Suspected missile installations near Leipzig. They had to be sure. Her brother had been shot coming across near Helmstadt. "Is she on a diplomatic passport?"

"No," Swift said. "Which has us a bit stymied here. She's traveling on a legitimate civilian passport. A tourist. But how many tourists come from Tel Aviv to Duluth?"

"Where is she now?"

"Republic Airlines from Minneapolis. Should be touching down within ten minutes or so."

"And?" Mahoney asked.

Swift was silent for a moment, and Mahoney could almost see him playing with the ends of his long, luxurious mustache. He could also see the blue jeans that Swift always wore. "Do we get the FBI in on this, Wallace? Do you think you need them? Is she harboring a grudge?"

"I don't think so," Mahoney said, thinking as he spoke. He tried to recall what he knew about the woman, but it was very little. He had a picture in his mind of a small, petite girl who had been almost completely destroyed by her brother's death. "Senseless," she had called it. Now he could sympathize with her feelings.

"I don't think so," he repeated. "I have a gun, and my eyesight is still pretty good, but I don't think it'll come to that."

"You're sure?" Swift said.

Mahoney could hear the uncertainty in the younger man's voice. "Not completely, but I don't think we have to call in the cavalry just yet. How'd you pick her out?"

"Someone happened to see her boarding at Lod. One of the diplomatic corps, I guess. It filtered downstairs to Larry Triggs in Intelligence-Watch, and he flagged it. We picked her up in New York where she had connections to Chicago. At first we figured the Israeli consulate there, but Triggs was curious so he stuck with it. She

spent an hour in Chicago, never leaving the airport, and
took off for Minneapolis. Triggs sent one of our legmen
along with her, and he called a little while ago to say she
was heading to Duluth."

"He isn't on the plane?"

"No," Switt said. "He thinks he may have been
spotted. Triggs told him Minneapolis was the end of the
line. He remembered that you were in the vicinity and
asked me about it not more than five minutes ago after
he had pulled the case files."

"Mossad," Mahoney said, thinking out loud.

"That's right. Arab operations. Lebanon mostly.
Which is why Triggs flagged her. What the hell is she
doing here?"

"Don't do anything rash," Mahoney said. "Maybe
she's just come for a visit."

"Unlikely."

"Give me a few hours with her. If I haven't called
you, give me a ring. Then you can break out the troops
if there's trouble."

"Be careful, Wallace," Switt said, his voice guarded
now. "She's gone through our school, and presumably
the Mossad has trained her."

"We're allies."

"With Israel," Switt said. "Not necessarily with Miss
Margraff."

"One other thing," Mahoney said. "Find out who the
receiving officer was on the flag, will you?"

"What's that got to do with anything?" Switt asked.

"I don't know," Mahoney replied. "Just curious."

The cabin was set a hundred feet from the water's
edge on the acre and half of heavily wooded property.
Behind the house, to the left of the driveway that led to
the dirt access road, was a boathouse in which was

stored fishing gear, gardening tools, old clothing, news-papers and magazines, and a potpourri of other junk accumulated over the years. To the right of the drive-way, set behind a garden, was a small ramshackle green-house, many of its windowpanes cracked or broken, two of them stuffed with rags.

The trays of plants inside suffered from neglect, most of them brown and shriveled now that Marge was no longer alive to take care of them, and the vents had not been opened yet this summer so that the glass was filthy and steamed up.

Mahoney sat in the greenhouse, the loaded pistol stuffed in his belt beneath his shirt, and waited for Sonja Margraff to show up.

He had left a radio playing in the house and had brewed a pot of coffee that was clearly visible on the kitchen counter through the back screen door. His car was parked near the boathouse. Nothing was out of place, nothing would spook the woman into thinking this was a setup. But Mahoney wanted to see what her first moves would be from a position of relative safety. She would not spot him through the dirty glass.

The atmosphere in the greenhouse was thick and warm, and Mahoney had begun to sweat when the car nosed around the corner and came down the driveway, its tires crunching on the loose gravel. He stiffened and carefully leaned forward so that his nose was just inches away from the glass.

There was only one person in the car. Mahoney could see that much from his vantage point, and he could see that it was a woman, but he could not recognize her.

The car pulled up and parked next to his, and a mo-ment later the door on the driver's side opened and Son-ja Margraff stepped out.

She was a small woman, thin with short hair in a pixie

cut. She was dressed in a fashionable, lightweight beige suit and wore high heels and nylons. Definitely not the sort of outfit a Mossad agent would wear on an elimination operation. Nor was it the kind of clothing a woman bent on revenge would choose for the moment she confronted the man she believed sent her brother to his death.

He could see that she could hear the radio playing, and as she walked from the car and mounted the steps to the back porch, he could also see that she was being very cautious. She was frightened of something.

At the back door she knocked once and then looked inside. "Mr. Mahoney?" she called out, and when there was no answer she turned, stepped down from the porch, and went around out of sight to the front of the house.

Mahoney let himself out of the greenhouse and hurried across the driveway to the car. A bright yellow disk with the word AVIS printed on it dangled from the key still in the ignition. On the front seat was the woman's purse, and on the back seat was a small, brightly colored canvas overnight bag.

Mahoney silently opened the car door, reached in, and grabbed the purse, then quickly went through its contents. No weapon. The usual makeup, a small wallet with several hundred American dollars and some change, as well as an Israeli plastic identification card with her photograph and thumb print. Sonja Margraff, born October 11, 1945, in Copenhagen, height 167 centimeters, weight 55 kilos, eyes brown, hair brown, address 15 Hadeganin, Apt. 7, Tel Aviv. Her passport was there, as well as the return halves of her airline tickets from Duluth to Minneapolis to Chicago to New York and finally back to Tel Aviv by tomorrow. She was not planning on a long visit.

In the back seat Mahoney quickly went through overnight bag, which contained only a few clothes and no weapons.

When he had replaced the bag and had closed the car door, Sonja was coming back from the front of the house. When she saw him, her eyes flickered to the car and she smiled.

"Did you find what you were looking for, Mr. Mahoney?" she asked. Her voice was soft, with a slight accent.

"I didn't find what I thought I might," Mahoney answered. She seemed very feminine and could have passed for a woman much younger than thirty-six except for the lines around her eyes and at the corners of her mouth. Her face had the character built of stress over a long period of time.

"I haven't come to kill you," she said, the slight humorless smile coming back to her lips. "How did you know I was coming?"

"I didn't," Mahoney lied. There was something about her that he could not quite put his finger on. It was disturbing. "I was in the greenhouse when you showed up. I was curious. I don't get many visitors."

She seemed to think, and then she shrugged. "My plane leaves in a couple of hours, so I have very little time. I've come to ask for your help."

Mahoney came across the driveway to where she was standing by the corner of the house. "Coffee?" he asked her.

She shook her head. "Perhaps a little cognac, and then I must be quick"

Mahoney nodded and showed her into the cabin where he poured her a brandy and himself another whiskey, and then they went out to the front lawn where they sat in folding chairs.

"It is lovely here," she said, sipping her drink. She looked at Mahoney. "I was sorry to hear that your wife had died. I remember her from Berlin. She was a lovely woman."

"Thank you," Mahoney said. "What are you doing with yourself these days? I lost track of you after Germany."

Again there was the same faint trace of a humorless smile on her lips. "I emigrated to Israel as you no doubt saw from my passport. I'm working with the Mossad."

Mahoney arched his right eyebrow.

She set her glass down on the small redwood table between them and then sat forward. "I don't have very much time, Mr. Mahoney, so I'll come immediately to the point, if I may."

Mahoney took a sip of his whiskey and set down his glass also. He nodded.

"As I said, I've come to ask for your help."

"Officially?" Mahoney asked. "Or is this a personal request?"

"A little of both," the woman said. She seemed to have an athletic grace that was evident even as she was sitting. "We need help. I know that you retired from the Company a couple of years ago. I mentioned your name and was given the go-ahead to contact you."

"By whom?" If she was for real she would tell him the one name he wanted to hear. The CIA had been wrong before with its agent identification procedure.

"Ezra Wasserman will meet you in Athens on Wednesday if you agree at least to listen."

Mahoney nodded. Wasserman was the head of the Mossad. That in itself wasn't significant. What was important was the fact that Sonja spoke his name out loud. Among Israel's many state secrets, one of the most closely guarded was the identity of the Mossad chief.

"What kind of help?" he asked, his interest even more aroused now that he knew she was probably for real.

"There is a mole in our service," the woman said. She was obviously nervous. "No one is aware of the investigation except for myself, Wasserman, and General David Ben Abel who is chief of Aman, our military intelligence. And, of course, Begin."

"That's a select list. Why have you been included?"

Sonja smiled, this time with some humor. "Uncle Ezra and my father are close friends. He's almost like family to me. I suppose he needed a trusted messenger."

Mahoney nodded. It was very much the kind of answer he had expected. "You need an outsider for the investigation," he said. "Your double agent must be someone at high levels, and very deep."

"Yes," Sonja said. "Will you help us?"

Would he accept? he asked himself. He was thinking about Darrel Switt and wondering who the diplomat was who had flagged her at Lod Airport. If he did accept, the leaks would have to be plugged immediately.

"What precipitated this?" he asked.

Sonja's eyes narrowed. "I'm sorry, I don't understand."

"How long has the existence of the mole been suspected? Why did you come to me now?"

Understanding dawned on her face. "Uncle Ezra will explain everything to you on Wednesday. Will you at least agree to meet with him? Talk to him?"

"Where in Athens?"

"If you agree at least to listen, arrangements will be made."

II

LOD AIRPORT . . . TUESDAY MORNING

Now that it was morning, David Ben Abel turned off his desk lamp, noisily sucked the last of his now cold tea from his glass, and then got up from his desk. He went to the window and looked out across the airport which was beginning to come alive.

He wasn't really seeing the increasing activities on the field, however. Instead he was still grappling with the problem that had occupied him all night.

"Schweine," he said with feeling in his native German. The streets will run red with the blood of every Jewish man, woman, and child. That was what they were promising.

For several moments he had an intense vision of a chimney rising stark into an overcast sky, spewing its sickly sweet smoke into the leaden air while a terribly off-key orchestra played a waltz.

He shuddered, then forced his mind back to the problem he had worried about throughout the night.

Al Qaryūt. There were only two possibilities, he had reasoned in his precise fashion. The first was that the raid had been nothing more than a random act of terrorism by the Jordanians against a radar installation. But if that was the case, why hadn't they hit the radar installation at Rafid, or the one at Bar'am, or Argaman, or even En Gedi? They were more accessible than al Qaryūt, more strategically located.

The second possibility, however, the one that Ben Abel suspected was the truth, was that somehow the Jordanians knew that the installation at al Qaryūt was not a radar station, that it was in actuality the receiving center for Israel's new spy satellite system.

If that possibility was a fact, then it admitted a traitor, which meant Wasserman was correct.

Although Ben Abel had a deep respect for the Mossad chief, and in fact genuinely liked the man, they could not have been more opposite, not only in physical appearance, but in their backgrounds, their philosophies, and most importantly in their methods.

Ben Abel was a bear of a man; tall and very husky with a thick mustache and hair that was only slightly gray, belying his 68 years.

He and four other men had sailed a small boat across two hundred miles of Mediterranean from Cyprus to Palestine late in 1948, arriving half dead from exhaustion, exposure, and thirst. They were immediately recruited by the Haganah, and had been fighting ever since.

His promotion to officer status came almost immediately once it was recognized that his was a natural military mind. From that moment on, his career was nothing short of distinguished.

Ben Abel's military philosophy had always been: "Never send your men into a situation you would not gladly and willingly go into yourself." And on more occasions than anyone could count, Ben Abel's superiors had tried everything short of a firing squad to keep him out of the thick of things.

Two attitudes, neither of them totally unexpected, had arisen from his propensity toward involvement in the "thick of things." The first was the generally held attitude of his superiors that once Ben Abel got something into his mind there was no swaying him. It wouldn't matter if you were the Messiah himself, finally come down to Earth, he would do what he felt was right, with absolutely no compromise.

And the second attitude, the one held by any man who had ever served under him, could best be described by a single word: love. Ben Abel was not merely respected by his men, although he was feared by those who would not or could not measure up to his strict standards, he was genuinely loved.

Throughout all of Israel's struggles beginning with her War of Independence in 1948, through the early years, through the "Hundred-Hour War" with Egypt in 1956, the Six-Day War in 1967, and the Yom Kippur War of 1973—through all of that—Ben Abel had fought gladly and willingly.

And he would have continued to fight except that in 1977 Begin had asked him to take over the Aman, Israel's military intelligence service, which was sinking rapidly into oblivion for lack of strong leadership.

For several days the old general had stormed around Tel Aviv, talking with friends, meeting with his officers, and then he had spent a week "in the bush," as he called it, reviewing defensive measures along the Syrian and Jordanian borders.

Finally, however, Ben Abel could not say no to his leader, and he tackled his new job with the same dogged determination and organization he had brought to everything he had ever done.

"Think of it as war," Begin told the aging general.

"Hell, I know the value of military intelligence," Ben Abel had replied. "You don't have to coddle an old fool. Just point me in the right direction."

But now, Ben Abel thought as he turned away from the window, the war he had been fighting for the past four years was coming to its first major campaign. Wasserman would be fighting the battle on his own terms, terms that Ben Abel violently disagreed with. But it would not stop him from doing his own fighting.

He went back to his desk, picked up the telephone, and buzzed for his ADC, Captain Zepharim Kominski, but there was no answer. Next he dialed the number for Base Operations, housed in the building just behind this one. The OD answered.

"Base Ops, Sergeant Elias."

"Has Captain Kominski arrived yet?"

"Yes, sir," the sergeant said crisply, recognizing Ben Abel's voice. "Would you like to speak with him, sir?"

"Send him up here on the double."

"Yes, sir."

"How's your wife?"

"Sir?"

"Your wife, Sergeant. She had the flu. Is she feeling any better?"

"Yes, sir," the man said. "Much better. I'll tell her you asked."

"Do that," Ben Abel said, and he hung up the phone and went back to the window. It was a trick of command he had learned years ago. Find out about your men, know about their personal lives. If you ask about their mothers or sweethearts or wives, they'll appreciate the interest, and follow you to hell and back without question because they'll know you care.

As head of the Mossad, Ezra Wasserman had done a good job—he had done a tremendous job. But in this instance, Ben Abel was of the firm belief that the man was wrong in his methods.

Ben Abel figured if it could be wrapped up in a few days and delivered to Ezra on a silver platter, the Mossad would have to abandon any plans to bring in an outsider. Wasserman would also have to abandon his patently absurd suspicions.

Ben Abel had to smile as he thought about Wasserman's chief suspect. Foolishness. It was nothing but foolishness.

Someone knocked at the door, and Ben Abel turned away from the window. "Come in," he called out.

Captain Kominski, his ADC for the past ten years, entered the office and closed the door behind him. "Have you been here all night, sir?" he asked, coming across the room to the desk.

Ben Abel nodded.

"Why the hell didn't you call me or something? I could have helped with whatever you were doing."

"Take it easy, Zeph," Ben Abel said easily. The relationship between the two men in private was relaxed and friendly, almost the same relationship as a father and son. Only while others were present did either of them observe proper military custom that the disparity in their rank demanded.

"Well, you look like *drek,* sir."

"And I feel that way too. But I want you to go out and get us some breakfast, and when you get back we've got some work to do."

"What kind of work, sir?" Kominski asked.

"Intelligence work. We're going to find out who the hell ordered the raid on al Qaryūt."

"I thought the Mossad was covering that."

"They are," Ben Abel said. "But so are we. Now get down to the mess hall and bring me something good to eat. I'm starved."

* * *

TEL AVIV . . . TUESDAY EVENING

Ezra Wasserman looked up from his work as the door opened and his secretary stuck her head inside.

"They're here," she said. "But you have a T-I call on the Green Line."

"Who is it?" Wasserman replied, his voice very soft.

"Sonja."

"I'll take the call first," he said.

"Yes, sir," his secretary replied, and she withdrew, closing the door softly behind her. Ever since Wasserman had taken over the Mossad, its headquarters off Allenby Street had taken on a very quiet and subdued air for the simple reason that he could not abide loud noises of any kind.

He reached across his desk, picked up his telephone, and depressed the lit green button. It was a phone number known to very few people even within the Mossad and was changed on an irregular basis, sometimes as often as three times in a week. Its real designation was Tactical Operations Input and was used only in emergencies when direct communication with Wasserman was critical.

"Troubles?" he asked without preamble.

"Not with him," Sonja's voice came over the line. It was obvious that she was telephoning from out of the country. "He agreed after some hesitation."

"Where are you?"

"Paris. Charles de Gaulle Airport."

It didn't make any sense. She should have been on her way in. He had shoved aside his bleak thoughts, his fears and suspicions, but they all came bubbling to the surface now, and his stomach flopped. "Why Paris?" he asked.

"I think I've picked up a tail."

Wasserman had been sitting back in his desk chair, but he sat forward now, something else clutching his gut. "Hold on a second, Sonja," he said, and without waiting for her to reply he hit the hold button for the Green Line and buzzed his secretary.

"Yes, sir," her voice came over the intercom.

"Get me Max in Paris on the double. Put him on one."

"Yes, sir," she said, and he punched the Green Line again. "Where are you at this moment?" he said.

"Phone booth on the mezzanine," she said, and Wasserman could hear a slight catch in her voice. She was frightened.

"All right," he said, his mind racing. "When we're finished talking I want you to take a cab to the Gare du Nord. Have your dinner there at the station and then purchase a one-way ticket, first class, for Berlin. There should be an overnighter you can catch."

"Is Athens still a go?" she asked.

"Never mind that for now. When did you spot the tail?"

"That's just it, Uncle Ezra," Sonja said. "I think I picked one up out of New York and again out of Chicago. But I lost him at Minneapolis."

"New York?" he said. "Impossible."

"I thought so too. But I'm sure he was following me."

"Can you come up with an Identi-kit on him when you get back?"

"Definitely. I got a couple of very good looks at him. One in profile."

"Why'd you divert to Paris? Did he pick you up again?"

"No," Sonja said. "It's become a little more sophisticated. They have at least two pairs. Alternating. I picked out the one pair in Chicago and another at Kennedy, so I diverted to Paris. The first pair was on the plane with me."

"I see," Wasserman said, although he didn't. Why had she been picked out? What the hell was happening? For a brief moment he considered canceling his meeting with Mahoney in Athens. But it had already been set up. Foolproof. Or was it?

"What about after Berlin?" Sonja was asking.

"Come home," Wasserman said, and the light on line one began to flash. "Got to go now. Take care. But whatever you do, try not to spook them any further. Just cover yourself."

"All right," she said, and she hung up.

Wasserman punched the button for line one. "I have a job for you, Max."

Max Rheinhardt had been the Mossad's man in France for the past seven years, operating a moderately successful import/export and freight forwarding business with offices in Paris and Le Havre. He was a highly efficient, very dedicated man who had been a youngster of fourteen fighting with the resistance in Austria during the Second World War.

Wasserman outlined the problem for him in a few concise words, ending with the instructions that Sonja wasn't to know that Max had become involved.

"*Mon dieu,* what do you want me to do then? Simply take a train ride to Berlin and back?"

"Not quite," Wasserman said dryly. "I want to know who they are."

"Any ideas?"

"A couple. They may be CIA."

There was a silence on the line for several seconds. "Can you tell me what Sonja is up to for you?"

"Not yet, Max. But it's important."

"Good enough for me. It will be as you ask."

"I'll telephone in twenty-four hours for your report."

"*Bon,*" Max said and hung up.

Wasserman released the line and buzzed his secretary. "Give me a couple of minutes and then send them in."

"Yes, sir," the woman said, and Wasserman replaced the phone on its cradle and sat back in his chair.

Three things were bothering him at the moment. The first was the Central Intelligence Agency.

Two days earlier he had spoken with Begin about the problem, and they had both come to the conclusion that if their American friends were officially informed of what was happening, of what *had been* happening, relations between them and the Mossad would be irreparably harmed.

Begin had put it quite succinctly when he said, "You don't share a secret with your neighbor, no matter how friendly he may be, if the neighbor is going to tell it all over town."

The Mossad had a leak. A terribly large leak. If it became public knowledge, there would be big trouble from it.

The second worry that occupied Wasserman's beleaguered mind was Ben Abel. The old fool was up to something, and whatever it turned out to be it would be spectacular. Ben Abel never did anything by halves.

He made a mental note to call in David's ADC, Kominski, as soon as they returned from Athens and pry it out of him. He and Ben Abel were close, almost like father and son. And although the man had an undying loyalty to his general, he could be made to understand that Ben Abel would be jeopardizing not only his career by a foolish move at this point, but Israel's security as well.

Finally, Wasserman was worried about Mahoney. He had met the man once, briefly, at Langley some years back, and from that first impression, plus Sonja's recommendations and his own research, he had come to the conclusion that the man was good enough for the job, or at least had been good enough. But whether he would take the assignment, and whether or not he was any good now, were two very large questions.

"He's worth a try, at least," Wasserman had told Begin after they both had had a little time to digest Sonja's startling suggestion to bring in an outsider.

The door opened and Wasserman looked up from his thoughts as the four men who would be going to Athens with him filed in. He shoved his concerns aside for the moment and rose to greet them.

III

ATHENS . . . WEDNESDAY

During the long flight from Duluth to Chicago and then Athens direct, Mahoney worried about Darrel Switt. The young man was the sharpest individual he had seen in the Company's ranks for as long as he could remember, and he had simply not bought Mahoney's explanation for Sonja's visit.

What he was doing, or at least what he was contemplating doing, was illegal. American law strictly forbids its citizens from involving themselves in the activities of foreign governments without the express approval of the State Department. And to work for a foreign intelligence service was even worse.

After Sonja had left him, Mahoney had made reservations for the flight to Athens leaving Chicago late Tuesday and then had called Switt, who was relieved that everything had turned out well, yet was peeved that Mahoney was obviously lying.

"People don't fly halfway around the world to spend a couple of hours chatting and then return home," Switt snapped.

"We rehashed the old Berlin days. It's something she

said she had to do.''

"So she came to kiss and make up?" Switt asked, the sarcasm heavy in his voice. "Forgive and forget?"

"Not quite. She said she wanted to understand.''

"Understand what?" Switt said sharply.

"About what happened in Berlin with her brother. She admitted that she had wanted to kill me. That she had thought about it for a long time.''

"But no longer.''

"That's right, Darrel, no longer. She didn't take any potshots. No hand-to-hand combat. Not even a slap in the face.''

Switt was silent for a long moment, and when he came back on the line his voice was very low and guarded. "That woman is a Mossad agent, and something is probably going on that I don't want you involved with, Wallace. Do you understand what the hell I'm saying? You're retired. Stay that way.''

"Forget it," Mahoney said. "Lose the file.''

"I can't and you damned well know it. Even if I wanted to do it, I couldn't. The unit was flagged. Remember?"

"Then bury it. You damned well know you can do that.''

Switt sighed in frustration. "If you get yourself involved in something, I'll be looking over your shoulder every step of the way.''

"Bury it, Darrel, and I'll promise you one thing.''

There was another moment's silence on the line. "What's that?" Switt finally asked.

"If I should happen to hear of anything of interest, you'll be the first to know. But I don't want any Peeping Toms, passport flags, shadows. Nothing.''

"Wallace—" Switt started to object, but Mahoney cut him off.

"Who was the diplomat who flagged the woman?"

"I don't know," Switt said.

"How about the receiving officer?"

"McBundy," Switt said, and for a moment Mahoney was seeing McBundy at the hospital talking to him about the Russian woman.

"I'm going to have to log this," Switt was saying.

"Go ahead," Mahoney said, his mind still elsewhere. "But I'm not going to create a fuss, you know me well enough."

"That's the trouble, you ruthless sonofabitch, I do know you too well."

Ruthless sonofabitch. Those words kept coming back to Mahoney as the 747 came majestically in for a landing at Athens Hellenikon Airport with a sharp bark of its tires and then the thrust of reversing jets.

Single-minded he had always thought of himself. He turned to look out the window at the white runway lights flashing by in a blur. Perhaps even devoted. Or to a lesser degree, unwavering. But ruthless? And a sonofabitch? It all depended upon the point of view. There were probably some Germans still around from the war who thought of him in those terms. And perhaps a fairly large number of Soviets at Dzerzhinsky Square who might use the Russian equivalent. But it hurt that Switt would say such a thing.

The aircraft turned onto a blue-lit taxiway and bumped slowly toward the modernistic terminal building as the passengers began unbuckling their seat belts and retrieving their carry-on luggage from the overhead compartments.

Mahoney was one of the last passengers off the airplane, and by the time he retrieved his single suitcase from the incoming baggage turntable, the customs hall was crammed to capacity, and it took him nearly half an hour before he was checked through.

It was just 8:00 P.M. by the time he made it up to the main hall in the terminal, which was busy with arriving and departing passengers, the announcements over the loudspeakers in Greek, French, and English, and redcaps everywhere. As he headed for the bank of doors out to the street, he let his gaze roam around the huge hall, finally spotting the luggage lockers along one wall, and then he was outside.

The night was warm and humid, with only a light breeze that brought to him the smells of diesel exhaust from the buses, gas fumes from the cars, and burned kerosene from the huge jets. There was a lot of traffic, and cabs were constantly pulling up, disgorging passengers, taking on new ones, and with a blare of horns and screeching tires heading into the city.

For several moments he stood watching the comings and goings until a cab pulled up at the curb, and the driver leaned across the front seat. "Hey, you," he shouted through the open window.

Mahoney ignored him. Instead he turned to his right and walked over to where several boys dressed in ragged white shirts, dirty white slacks, and rope-soled shoes were hustling the tourists for money.

When he approached, several of them broke away and surrounded him, all jabbering for money. One of them carried a shoeshine kit.

"Shine, mister? Buck? Shine, mister?" the boy said in heavily accented English.

Mahoney pulled out a five dollar bill and the luggage locker key that Sonja had given him. "I forgot my bags," he said. "One of you boys want to go back for them?"

One of the boys grabbed the key from Mahoney

and darted through the doors into the terminal. The others scattered as Mahoney hurried after him, and just inside the doors he stepped to one side and watched as the boy raced across the large hall to the bank of luggage lockers and searched for the proper number.

Sonja had given him the key with the instructions that the method of contact with Wasserman would be in writing in an envelope in the locker.

As far as Mahoney could tell, no one was paying any attention to the boy who almost immediately found the correct locker and inserted the key.

Over the years Mahoney had learned not to trust third party instructions for blind drops. Too much could go wrong. Too many people would be involved.

The boy was opening the locker. If there were people watching, they'd be wondering what the hell was going on. They'd soon be looking for him in the sidelines. Mahoney hoped he would be able to spot them first.

The explosion was short and very sharp, almost like a high-caliber rifle shot, directed out from the open locker door, flinging the boy about twenty feet.

For a long, pregnant second, everything in the terminal came to a stop, and amid a rising babble of voices, screams, and shouts, Mahoney turned and went back out to the street. He walked nonchalantly to one of the airport buses that would take him downtown to Syntagma—Constitution Square—and boarded, a deep, dark vengeance rising up in his heart.

Ezra Wasserman's thoughts were on Max Rheinhardt as he stood on the second-floor balcony of his hotel room that overlooked the city. In the distance was Mount Lycabettus, the highest point in Athens, and in the opposite direction he could just make out a portion of the Acropolis. Below it were the city's slums.

There had been no answer that afternoon at Max's Paris number. Although it was too early to begin inquiries, Wasserman was starting to get a little nervous. It was unlike Max not to at least leave a message with his office if he was delayed.

The trouble with intelligence work, he had decided long ago, was that unlike the movies and novels, the real thing was never quite so well defined or wrapped in such neat packages. Real life was decidedly more sloppy and infinitely more complex.

If anything could go wrong, it would and usually did. Mechanical troubles with cars, missed schedules, overbooked hotels, lies and double lies, shades of meaning interpreted as many different ways as there were individuals dealing with it.

"Intelligence goals, not specific missions—those are your bread and butter," Isser Harrel, Wasserman's predecessor had told him several years ago.

And indeed Wasserman could only think of a half dozen missions, as such, that the Mossad had been involved with over the past ten or fifteen years. Among them was the kidnapping of Adolph Eichmann, the hijacking of the missile boats from Cherbourg, France, the stealing of the maintenance plans for the Mirage jet fighter from Switzerland, and the release of the hostages at the Entebbe Airport in Uganda.

The vast majority of the Mossad's time, money, and manpower was spent fielding agents who became friends with people in foreign countries. Gossip from a thousand sources, added together, was the usual means of satisfying an intelligence goal.

He finally turned from his musings and went back into the hotel room. Kedem was slouched by the door, his shoulder up against the wall, smoking a filter-tipped Time. Berne was relaxed in an easy chair facing the television set. And Rotsinger was just coming out of the bathroom.

They all looked his way. "He hasn't called yet, Ezra," Berne said. He glanced at his watch. "It's only eight-twenty. The first try is only five minutes overdue."

Wasserman hated lying to his own people, but there was no help for it. He crossed the room and poured a glass of ouzo at the sideboard, adding a little mineral water to the sweet liquor, which turned cloudy.

"If it's a no go, I want you three at the alternates," he said, turning back to face them. He sipped at the drink. "Gently, though—I don't want him spooked."

The telephone rang. Rotsinger was the closest to it, and Wasserman nodded for him to answer it.

Berne jumped up and turned off the television's sound as Rotsinger picked up the phone.

"Yes?" he said. Wasserman was watching the man's face, and after a moment Rotsinger took the phone away from his ear and covered the mouthpiece with his hand. "Ben-id didn't show. Do you want David to stand by?"

Wasserman nodded. "Midnight will be long enough."

Rotsinger nodded, spoke briefly into the phone, then replaced the receiver on the cradle.

"Do you want us out until midnight as well?" Kedem asked.

"Yes," Wasserman said. He hated to waste his people like this. "There are a couple of things I'll follow up with in the meantime."

"That could be dangerous, Ezra," Kedem said. "Do you want one of us with you?"

"No." Out of the corner of his eye he noticed that Berne was suddenly concentrating on the television and he turned that way.

It was apparently a news broadcast, and the scene was at the airport where a body was being loaded on a stretcher by two white-coated men. It was a small body covered by a sheet.

"Turn it up," Wasserman said sharply.

Berne complied, and the announcer's voice came on. None of them understood Greek, but Wasserman was staring at the rows of luggage lockers beyond the stretcher. No explanation was needed. An explosion had ripped apart one of the lockers and had damaged a half dozen others.

Mahoney, he thought, but the body on the stretcher that was being wheeled away through the crowd was too small.

But who? And how had the connection been made so quickly? And who had booby-trapped the locker? And why?

He thought instantly of a half dozen names stretching back to Tel Aviv. But all of them who had handled the envelope with Mahoney's instructions, and the locker key, were low-level hacks. None of them had been told a thing. Not a thing. How in hell had the connection been made? How?

Rotsinger was staring at him, and Wasserman forced himself to grin.

"The Greeks are blowing themselves up now," he quipped.

There was a possibility that the explosion at the airport had no connection with Mahoney's arrival. But it was too coincidental for Wasserman to realistically consider it.

For a moment a sharp stab of real pain coursed through his body with the thought of Sonja. Could she be the mole? Damn. Was it possible after all?

"What is it, Ezra?" Berne was asking, and Wasserman focused on the man. "Do you think there's a connection with Ben-id?"

Wasserman forced his mind to slow down. Forced the worry about Sonja into another compartment and shook his head. "No," he said, then he looked at the television. "It just reminded me of home. Of our own troubles."

The other three men nodded their silent, tight-lipped agreement, and after a moment the mood lightened although it did not pass.

"Midnight," Wasserman said. "Then I want you all back here."

"What if he doesn't show?" Kedem asked.

Wasserman shrugged.

Kedem nodded. "The bastards," he said.

Mahoney had checked in at the King George Hotel across Constitution Square from the airline offices where the bus had dropped him off. He registered under his own name, taking absolutely no precautions to hide or mask his presence. He wanted someone to come after him. He wished for it.

After he had taken a quick shower, he changed his clothes and then left a message at the desk for anyone inquiring about him that he would be spending the evening at Papaspirou, which was the most famous of Athens's sidewalk cafés. It was located in front of the American Express offices just across the park from his hotel.

As he headed across to the restaurant, his step firm and purposeful, a scowl on his face, he kept seeing the little boy snatching the key from his hand. He kept seeing the locker coming open, and hearing the explosion.

Wasserman had not been behind it. There would have been no reason for it. Perhaps it had been Sonja. Or more likely this entire Athens thing had been an incredibly sloppy setup. If that was the case, there need not be a mole within the Mossad. It could be that the service was just incredibly riddled with leaks, like an ancient ship in a storm.

Papaspirou was crowded, but he managed to get a table for two away from the sidewalk, so he could sit with his back to the building, and ordered a coffee. When it came he lifted the cup to his lips with shaky hands and sipped at it, not really tasting the thick, strong, heavily sugared brew.

He was just as angry with himself over the young boy's death. He should have rejected Sonja's instructions, setting up a much safer procedure instead. There could have been another way.

Christ. He hadn't accepted this job, let alone even started it, yet already he was making mistakes. Big mistakes.

Wasserman showed up a couple of minutes past ten, a flushed, worried expression on his face. He spotted Mahoney almost immediately and threaded his way between the tightly packed tables.

Mahoney had never had any dealings with the

man, although he had met him once several years ago during an interagency briefing at Langley. He remembered the Mossad chief as a small, dark, very intense individual who listened more than he talked. In appearance, at least, he had not changed much.

He sat down across the small table from Mahoney without a word, and when the waiter came, ordered an ouzo and water. When his drink arrived he mixed it, took a sip, and then leaned forward.

"It was very foolish of you to check into the hotel so openly," he said.

"If I hadn't, you wouldn't have found me."

Wasserman shrugged. "I'm sorry about the airport," he said. "Who did you send to the locker?"

"A little boy," Mahoney said sharply. "Who the hell knew about it besides you?"

Wasserman flinched. "A half dozen of my people. Low-level. They had absolutely no idea what was going on."

"I'll want their names," Mahoney said. Wasserman nodded. "Who else?"

"Sonja," Wasserman said, a pained expression in his eyes.

Mahoney looked past the man for a moment, across the Leoforos Amalias at the ugly Parliament Building. Without turning back he said, "What's her position within the service? Could she be the mole?"

Wasserman didn't answer at first, and Mahoney respected his silence. She had called him "Uncle Ezra." It had to be painful.

"I thought it was likely," he said finally. "Or at least I did at first, which is why we decided to include her."

Mahoney looked at him. "You told her you suspected a mole, and you asked for her help?"

"Something like that. She mentioned your name. Said we needed an outsider."

"Which either clears her, or she's much shrewder than you give her credit for being."

"I've known her since she was born," Wasserman said in some anguish. "I changed her diapers, wiped her snotty nose, bought her a toy when she had the measles."

"And grieved for her when she went to the States?"

"That too," Wasserman said.

Mahoney thought of his own children, which led him instantly to Marge. He clamped off that line of thinking. "When she came to me I wasn't sure I'd accept your proposal. I'm still not sure. Nor am I quite sure exactly what is it you want me to do."

"Find out who our traitor is," Wasserman said.

Mahoney shook his head and wondered just what the hell was going on here. Either Wasserman was a fool, or he was holding something back. The latter was the most likely. "First of all, I know nothing about the Mossad. It could take months, even years, for me to wade through your personnel and operational files. Secondly, the whistle has already been blown on me. Someone knew about our meeting and wanted it stopped. And finally, I don't think you could cooperate with me at the level I'd require."

"I know what you're thinking, but I've been given a carte blanche on this."

"Could Sonja have booby-trapped the locker?"

"I don't know."

"You haven't been watching her?" Mahoney asked incredulously.

"No one else is in on this," Wasserman said defensively. "I've kept watch on her physical movements. But if she's the mole, she's not working alone.

She could have gotten a message off."

"How'd you cover your tracks tonight?" Mahoney asked.

"I set up a bogus meeting with a Syrian—Amahel Ben-id—who supposedly has high-level military planning secrets to sell us. A primary location and three alternates. I brought four people with me. They'll be roosting on their perches until midnight."

Mahoney could find no fault with it, but he sipped his coffee a moment in silence, still wondering if he would take the job or not. Still angry about the death of the young boy. Still upset with his own mistakes. Still distrustful.

"We need your help," Wasserman was saying. "We simply cannot do it without you. If Ben Abel had his way he'd shake up the entire structure—top to bottom—to see what fell out. It would ruin us."

Everything, of course, pointed to Sonja. At least at this stage. The fact that she had been flagged getting on the plane in Tel Aviv could have been her own doing. And now the bomb in the locker. But it was too pat and yet too full of holes.

"No one knows you have been asked to help except Begin, Ben Abel, Sonja, and myself," Wasserman was saying. "You'd be coming to Tel Aviv primarily as a tourist as a cover for an arms deal you're trying to negotiate."

Mahoney looked up at him, and he had to smile. "None of that is really necessary. Your mole knows I'm coming, and exactly why I'm coming."

IV

BERLIN . . . THURSDAY

Ezra Wasserman was a short man, standing under five-feet-six. His face was round, his ears and nose large, but his eyes were small, dark and very intense. To a casual observer it might have seemed that Wasserman had shrunk ever further into his diminutive figure as he trudged along the boarding tunnel from the Lufthansa airliner into the terminal at Tempelhof Airport. But whenever he was deep in thought, as now, he seemed to draw inward. It was as if he pulled a shell around himself to fend off the world while he thought.

He was passed immediately through customs without a fuss on the strength of his diplomatic passport, which identified him as a member of the Israeli Foreign Office. Within ten minutes from the time his plane had touched down, he was climbing in the back seat of a taxi that immediately headed into the city.

Max's message had been as short as it was cryptic. He had sent a telegram to the office at Tel Aviv that said: HOTEL STEINPLATZ, BERLIN, COME AT ONCE, MAX. The message had been relayed to the hotel in Athens, and early this morning Wasserman had dismissed his four agents who would return home on their own.

He had a fair idea what it was all about, and it was one of the many reasons he was deeply disturbed at this moment.

He was almost certain that Max was going to tell him that the two who had followed Sonja from New York were CIA legmen. If that was so, Mahoney would have to be called off.

Wasserman had thought long and hard about that, and about his meeting the previous night with the man, finally coming to the conclusion that it had been a mistake to even consider hiring an outsider.

The American had put it quite aptly when he warned that the Mossad's doors would have to be thrown open very wide if any results were to be expected. It was something, Mahoney had said, that he did not feel the Mossad was capable of doing.

Yet without a free hand, a totally free hand, Mahoney would be shackled even before he began.

The weather in Berlin was pleasantly cool after the oppressive heat and humidity of Athens, and for a while Wasserman was able to relax in the cab and let his mind go blank. But it didn't last long, of course. His thoughts kept straying back to Sonja, and to Mahoney who said he would hang around Athens for a few days, delaying his arrival in Tel Aviv until Sunday.

"It'll give us a chance to disconnect ourselves from each other," he had said.

Which, on reflection, Wasserman thought now, translated to mean that Mahoney wanted to do his own investigation into the explosion at the airport. It fit with his overall impression of the American as a man of long experience and great competence, yet a man with a chip on his shoulder.

Depending upon what Max had to report, Wasserman decided that he would telephone Mahoney at his hotel in Athens and tell him thanks but no thanks. Which left Sonja. But that was a problem not only to Israel, but to her friends and family as well. As physically ill as it made Wasserman feel when he thought about it, he resolved that he would step out of his role as Mossad chief—something he had never done before— and handle this on a personal level.

Sonja could not lie to him. She had never been able to lie to him in a face-to-face confrontation. And he was amazed with himself at that moment that he had not had the courage earlier to confront her point-blank with his suspicions.

The Hotel Steinplatz was a five-story edifice that fairly exuded peace and restfulness, and as the taxi pulled up in front of the building, Wasserman had to appreciate the irony.

Max Rheinhardt had probably killed several dozen men since the Second World War, and yet he was a man of great peace. This was exactly the kind of hotel Wasserman had expected his operative would select.

After he paid the driver he carried his single suitcase into the hotel and across the lobby to the desk, where he set it down on the threadbare carpeting.

A young clerk, dressed ludicrously in an ill-fitting tuxedo, came from the alcove where the hotel's switchboard was located, a fake smile on his face.

"You have a reservation, Mein Herr?" the man asked.

Wasserman shook his head. "No. I have come to meet a friend of mine who is a guest here. Herr Max Rheinhardt. I'm afraid I don't know his room number. . ."

The smile left the clerk's face, his eyes went wide, and a moment later, as if he were recovering from a stumble, he looked over Wasserman's shoulder and nodded.

Wasserman's breath caught in his throat, and as he was about to turn around, there was a movement behind him and strong hands gripped his arms just above the elbows.

"We wish you no trouble, Mein Herr," someone behind him said, and Wasserman turned his head to look up into the face of a young, blond, blue-eyed man who looked more like a mountain than a person.

For the briefest of moments Wasserman was back forty years as a second man quickly and efficiently frisked him, but then it was as if the scene came back into focus and he remembered who he was and when it was.

"I'll look at your identification now," he said in rapid-fire German.

The big man released his grip and stepped back.

"Macht schnell," Wasserman barked.

A slight humorless smile came to the blond giant's features, and he produced a wallet that he flipped open and held out for Wasserman's inspection. It identified him as Detective Lieutenant Gunther Heilbronn with the Berlin Police Department, Homicide Division. The other man was Sergeant Dieter Wolffe.

"Max Rheinhardt is dead?"

"Yes, sir," the lieutenant said. "May I see your identification please?"

"Of course," Wasserman said, and he pulled his passport from his breast pocket and handed it over.

A number of people had gathered in the lobby to see what all the fuss was about, and Wasserman was again having trouble keeping this place in any kind of focus. From the moment Sonja had suggested calling in Mahoney, things had gone from bad to worse. First the explosion meant for Mahoney at the Athens airport, and now this. What had Max stumbled onto that cost him his life? Surely the CIA had not ordered his elimination.

There was an explanation, but Wasserman didn't want to dwell on it in too great detail for the moment. But Sonja could have diverted to Paris not because she was being followed, but because she was meeting someone. She could have spotted Max, and . . . killed him?

"I'd like you to come to headquarters with us, sir," the lieutenant was saying. "You can identify the body, and there are certain questions."

"Certainly," Wasserman said. He picked up his suitcase and went with the two police officers out the front door and around the block where they got into a plain black Mercedes sedan.

Sergeant Wolffe drove while Lieutenant Heilbronn, who was clearly agitated, rode in the back seat with Wasserman.

"Before we get downtown I'm wondering if you wouldn't mind answering a couple of questions. Totally off the record."

Wasserman pulled himself away from his thoughts about Sonja and looked at the cop. "Max Rheinhardt and I were old friends, if that's what you mean. We were going to meet here for a short holiday together. It's something we've been doing for years."

"His office in Paris expected him back later today," the lieutenant said. "Strange of them to say such a thing if Rheinhardt was planning on a vacation."

"Max always operated that way," Wasserman said. "If an important client were to call, his office would contact him, and he'd return from wherever he was." He turned and looked out the window at the passing scenery.

"I have a feeling that Max Rheinhardt was more than a simple businessman."

Wasserman turned back. "Why do you say that?"

"His murder was the work of a professional. Before he was killed he was interrogated."

"I see," Wasserman said. If it was Sonja she had help.

"We'll never solve this murder, you know," Heilbronn said. "Rheinhardt checked into the hotel last night. No one saw or heard a thing until this morning when a maid entered his room with her passkey. She wanted to make up his bed. She found him."

"Arrangements will be made to transport his body back to Paris."

"Not to Tel Aviv?"

"Paris was his home, Lieutenant," Wasserman said sharply. "And this conversation has been off the record. We'll leave it at that. I'll want to see him, though."

"Of course," Heilbronn said. "As I said before, we need a positive identification."

Sergeant Wolffe knew the city well and was an excellent driver. Within a few minutes they had pulled up into a parking lot behind a large, modern building in the heart of the city. Out front, stainless steel letters spelling POLIZEI HAUPTQUARTIER were stuck in the lawn like an ornament.

Inside, Wasserman was made to wait in Heilbronn's fifth-floor office while his credentials were being checked by telephone with the Foreign Office in Tel Aviv.

It took less than a half hour before a now very deferential Lieutenant Heilbronn returned. With him was the Chief of Police himself. The Foreign Office, in cases like these, always identified Wasserman as a special governmental envoy from the Ministry of Finance. Although he was not listed as an investigator as such, he was identified as a very important money man. And money was power anywhere in the world.

"We're sincerely sorry that you had to learn of the

death of your friend in this manner," the police chief said. He was a man of medium height, with steel gray hair cropped very short, and deep, penetrating eyes.

By the respect Heilbronn paid the man, Wasserman suspected he was a very harsh, unforgiving boss.

"If there is anything we can do to facilitate this matter for you—" the man began, but Wasserman broke in.

"I'll want to see his body, the police report, and the photographs of the room. I understand he was interrogated."

"Lieutenant Heilbronn will see to everything for you."

"Has an autopsy been performed?"

"Under these kinds of circumstances it is required by our law."

"I'll want to see that report as well."

"Certainly," the chief said, a bit of his previous amiability leaving his manner. "In return we will expect a complete statement from you."

There were contingencies for this sort of thing, of course, with cooperating governments. Max's background story as an importer/exporter would hold. The motive for his murder would be listed as simple robbery.

Wasserman nodded.

"Then I'll leave you with Lieutenant Heilbronn. If there is anything else you need, don't hesitate to ask."

After the chief had left, Wasserman prepared a brief statement for the police files that included Max's background as a businessman, and the planned holiday.

The police report and photographs, however, showed that Max's hotel room had been thoroughly searched.

"What were they looking for?" Heilbronn asked.

"Money?" Wasserman suggested. He had no idea what they could have been looking for. Perhaps written orders.

Heilbronn shook his head. "His wallet contained a

thousand francs or so, and a couple of hundred marks."

"That's it, then," Wasserman said. "He would have had several thousand marks for our holiday. Evidently he hid the bulk of his money somewhere and was murdered for it."

Heilbronn smiled sadly and shook his head. "Your friend must have been an exceedingly *geizig* man. He allowed himself to be tortured to death without revealing the hiding place of his money. Otherwise the search would not have been so thorough."

Wasserman got to his feet. "I'd like to see him now."

"As you wish," Heilbronn said, and together they went to the morgue in the basement of the building, where an attendant brought the body out on a stainless steel rollabout table.

Wasserman had not yet been shown the autopsy report, so he asked the cause of death before the attendant threw back the sheet.

"Suffocation," the man said.

Wasserman flinched.

"The subject was tortured extensively. There are small circular burns—probably from the tip of a cigarette—inside his nose, in his armpits, between his toes, and at the tip of his penis. A small bath towel was stuffed in his mouth to muffle his screams, and he swallowed it. More than half the bulk of the material was actually in his stomach."

Wasserman took a deep breath, nodded at the attendant, and then steeled himself as the sheet was thrown back.

V

TEL AVIV-JAFFA . . . SUNDAY

Tel Aviv, or more properly Tel Aviv-Jaffa, welcomed Mahoney as it would any other tourist—with indifference. And during the long cab ride into the city from Lod Airport, he had to ask himself again what the hell he was doing here.

He had absolutely no business mixing in the affairs of any foreign country. He was retired. And yet he was like a general going into battle against an unknown enemy. But in this war his only allies were the prime minister of the country, an aging general, the head of the secret service and Sonja—one of whom, at least, was suspect.

Wasserman had not given him very much comfort in Athens, but he supposed the man was under a two-way pressure and it could not be helped. In the first place, there was a mole in his service.

He had not been quite clear about just how he knew a mole was operating, telling Mahoney that explanations would be forthcoming. Nor could he shed any light on what damage the deep-cover agent had already done.

And secondly, Wasserman was under the pressure of having to live a triple life instead of his normal double in which he was the secret head of the Mossad while still maintaining a respectable middle-class existence as a minor government clerk. Added to that now would be his secret dealings with Mahoney.

Mahoney had spent most of Thursday and Friday at the English-language library in Athens, looking up and reading as much about Israel's history as he could digest in such a short time. The library had an excellent back file of *Time* and *Newsweek* magazines, probably sent over from the embassy, from which he gleaned most of his knowledge.

Still, it was going to be a difficult business for the first days, if not totally impossible. He felt as if he were a blind man in a chess tournament expected to do well when no one had bothered to tell him the rules.

The airport was located thirteen miles to the southeast of the city, and as the driver expertly dodged the heavy traffic along the Derech Hashalom, Mahoney tried to pick out some of the sights described in the news magazines, but nothing seemed to be where it should be in the tangled urban sprawl of stark whites and soft browns.

Tel Aviv, the largest in Israel with its population approaching the half-million mark, was founded in 1910 as an adjoining city to the seaport of Jaffa. The port city, itself an ancient settlement dating back to before the birth of Christ, was joined officially with Tel Aviv in 1949, shortly after the State of Israel was proclaimed.

Earlier that morning he had checked out of the King George, confirmed his reservations at the Dan Hotel in Tel Aviv, and then had taken a cab out to the airport for the choppy two-hour El Al flight over the Mediterranean.

All during the weekend he had been very careful with himself, doubling up on cabs, taking buses for a couple of blocks, and then walking down deserted alleys before backtracking.

But no one was following him, and no other attempts were made on his life.

He knew he was being foolish in accepting the assignment, but despite Darrel Switt's warning to him, and despite the explosion at the Athens airport, he felt that there was still a chance he could be effective.

Friday night at his hotel he had gone over all the options. First of all, if Sonja Margraff was the mole, she could have suggested bringing him in to throw everyone off the track. Once he showed up in Athens, she could have engineered his elimination.

But Wasserman had assured him that Sonja had been nowhere near Athens. Which meant that if she was the mole, she had help. A network of some kind in order to penetrate Wasserman's system of low-level legmen who had placed the instructions in the locker.

Fighting one person would be difficult enough. Going up against a network would be next to impossible, especially if the mole was reporting to Moscow, in which case the helpmates would be KGB-trained.

Another option that Mahoney had come up with was that the mole had become suspicious of Wasserman's and Sonja's comings and goings, had traced her movements to Mahoney, and had put it together. The mole could have found out about the locker, made a quick trip to Athens, and after Wasserman's people had placed the instructions, had set the trap.

In that case the mole could be working alone—the safest alternative—but strongly suspected that Mahoney had been called in for an investigation. The mole would be on his or her guard. And it would take some prodding for that person to make a mistake.

The cabby dropped Mahoney off in front of the Dan, which was a large tourist hotel directly on the Mediterranean. He paid the affable driver and carried his bag into the lobby where he checked in and was assigned a luxurious room overlooking the sea. The bellboy checked the bathroom, opened the curtains and the sliding glass doors to the balcony, letting in the fresh air, and offered to help Mahoney unpack.

"Thanks, but I can manage," Mahoney said, tipping the young man, and then he was alone.

Ostensibly Mahoney had come to Israel as a tourist, but that weak cover was nothing more than a smoke screen for his primary cover as an arms salesman.

Wasserman, with Begin's cooperation, had let it slip in the proper circles that Mahoney was coming to Tel Aviv as an unofficial emissary from the U.S. government to discuss the terms of a large arms sale.

The weapons—which were the latest assault hardware in the U.S. inventory—would be surplus units funneled through a machine parts manufacturer in New Jersey.

Wasserman had given him enough preliminary background material to make this story plausible under all but the most stringent questioning.

"You'll be expected to be rather closed-mouthed about your comings and goings, of course," Wasserman had said. "If anyone tries to get too close, you can shove them off without too many questions."

The setup was all right and would probably convince everyone except the mole, who had only three courses of action open. The first would be to lie very low and do nothing, making no mistakes, in which case it would be damned difficult to pry him or her loose. The second wuld be to arrange Mahoney's death, setting it up as either a simple accident or as the result of someone upset about his weapons negotiations. And the third, which for the mole would be the most extreme, the most desperate, would be to run.

He stood by the open glass door looking down at the beach filled with tourists enjoying the warm day, and beyond, at the Mediterranean with its sailboats and, out near the horizon, a large steamer of some sort.

Nothing seemed to be the same as it had been in the old days, he thought morosely. The entire affair with Sonja and Wasserman and Athens seemed somehow cold and empty, if personal dealings could be compared with temperature or quantity. Everything seemed senseless yet somehow contrived.

For instance, he did not believe he was actually in Tel Aviv. Nor did he believe that Margery was dead.

It was silly of him, this sense of unreality, but he could not help himself. He felt as if he were sliding down a meaningless tunnel toward nowhere in particular. It was as if he were being held in suspended animation.

Because of the unexpected trouble at the Athens airport, Wasserman had cut his briefing short, returning, he had told Mahoney, to Tel Aviv early Thursday, promising a fuller briefing as soon as Mahoney arrived.

"I've set up a safe house in Tel Aviv," Wasserman had said. "You'll need it as a clearinghouse anyway, as well as a source of contact with me."

"And Sonja?"

Wasserman hadn't answered at first, but he looked definitely uncomfortable.

"Sonja is in on it?" Mahoney had prodded.

Wasserman nodded. "It was her idea."

"Great," Mahoney said sourly.

Wasserman had left Papaspirou after that, and on parting neither man was at all sure he'd ever see the other again.

The telephone by the bedside table rang. Mahoney turned away from the open door, went across the room, and picked it up.

"Yes?"

"Now," Wasserman's voice came over the line.

Mahoney held the receiver to his ear and when

Wasserman hung up he strained to hear the secondary click that would mean someone had monitored the call from the local switchboard. But it never came, and after a few seconds he hung up the phone.

Wasserman's safe house was at 2-B, Kfar Saba Street, which was about three blocks to the south of the thirty-five-story Shalom Mier Tower, the tallest building in the Mid-East and the new center of Tel Aviv's business district.

After Mahoney had cleaned up and changed into a lightweight summer suit with an open collar, he took a cab to Shalom Mier and spent nearly an hour looking through the many shops, finally taking the elevator to the observation level on the top floor.

After leaving the building fifteen minutes later from an emergency exit near the public restrooms, he nonchalantly strolled along Hatalmi Street, coming at last to the narrow intersection of Kfar Saba and Pines.

It was an area of small shops with apartments above, and like the other sections of Tel Aviv Mahoney had seen this day, was busy with traffic of all kinds.

He walked past number 16, which housed a tobacconist, and at the corner he crossed the street and headed back, crossing again in the middle of the block and quickly ducking through the doorway that led upstairs to the apartments.

For several minutes he remained on the first floor landing, watching the entrance at the foot of the stairs. But no one came after him, and finally he turned and trudged to the second floor where at the end of the narrow, dimly lit corridor he came to 2-B.

As he raised his hand to knock, the door opened and Wasserman was standing there with an intensely worried look on his face.

"Were you followed?"

"I don't think so," Mahoney said, and Wasserman stepped aside to let him in.

The apartment was small, consisting only of the sitting room that overlooked the narrow intersection of Kfar Saba and Tzedek, a tiny bathroom, and an efficiency kitchen tucked into one corner. A broken-down couch along one wall folded out into a bed, and in the corner near the kitchen was a small table and two chairs. By the window were two dilapidated easy chairs, a small coffee table between them.

"I wasn't sure you'd come," Wasserman said as Mahoney poked around the room opening drawers, lifting the cushions from the couch and chairs, and peering down lampshades.

He turned. Wasserman had locked the door and had gone to the kitchen where he was pouring them each a glass of brandy. He came back to where Mahoney stood by the window.

"We're quite safe here," Wasserman said, handing one of the glasses to Mahoney.

"What did you find out?"

"My people delivered the envelope on Friday, and by Saturday the key was back here for Sonja."

"She didn't backtrack?"

Wasserman looked away for a moment. "She didn't go anywhere near Athens."

Mahoney took a sip of his drink. Wasserman was holding something back. He was certain of it.

"Begin wants you out of the country," Wasserman said. "And I agree with him. You can stay here until we can arrange something for you."

Mahoney had half expected that, and in fact had been surprised that Wasserman himself had not pulled the plug in Athens. Again he debated with himself whether he should go home or continue. But he did not like it when people started taking potshots at him. For the rest of his life he would have the little boy's death on his conscience.

"The locker was left unattended from Friday until I showed up on Wednesday?"

Wasserman inclined his head in a barely perceptible nod.

Home or continue?

"What did you find out on your six legmen who handled the instructions and the key?"

"Nothing yet. I'm working on it, but it's very slow. I don't want to spook anyone."

Mahoney had to laugh at that. "Someone is spooked already," he said. "Girlfriends, wives, mistresses? Anyone with a dubious connection?"

Wasserman shrugged. "As I said, it will take time."

"I want their files."

"Begin wants you out."

Mahoney set his glass on the table. "You've already said that, Ezra. You've also said that *you* want me out. Will you kick me out of the country?"

Mahoney waited, watching Wasserman who stood silently, staring into the street, as if the answer were down there. Finally, the Israeli said, "No."

"Then do I still have your cooperation?"

"We can't guarantee your safety—" Wasserman started to say, but Mahoney cut him off.

"Let's do without the bullshit, Ezra. The fact of the matter is, you have a traitor working either in your Mossad, the Aman, or in the government itself, and it has you people scared silly. But there's more to it than that, isn't there?"

Wasserman said nothing.

"The mole is high-placed, which is bad enough, but there's even more," Mahoney said. He turned away momentarily to look out the window at the busy intersection below. "It's my guess that you people feel particularly vulnerable right now, which is the only reason you're asking for my help. You're doing something or planning something that's extremely sensitive, and a mole in your midst could ruin everything."

Wasserman didn't say a thing.

Mahoney turned back. "I told you in Athens that if I accepted this job you'd have to be open with me. I'll have to know everything. No secrets."

Wasserman seemed to carefully weigh Mahoney's words, and then he set his untouched drink on the table. "The Mossad is a very efficient service."

"It has the reputation of being among the best in the world," Mahoney admitted.

"We would kill you if you betrayed us," Wasserman said, his hesitant manner suddenly gone, his voice hard.

"But you still need my help."

"Yes," Wasserman said. "From what we know about you, you are a man to be trusted."

"Then trust me, or send me home, but don't threaten me."

Again Wasserman seemed to weigh Mahoney's words with great care. "I want your word on this. Your word that you will never discuss this operation with anyone at any time. Not even with your own government."

Mahoney thought about Darrel Switt. "What's the word of one spy to another?"

"Nothing if the circumstances change," Wasserman said. "But I want it anyway."

Mahoney nodded. "You have it."

"Good," Wasserman said. "It began ten days ago at al Qaryūt."

Mahoney sat down in one of the overstuffed chairs, took a sip of his brandy, and then pulled out a cigar and lit it as Wasserman paced the room while he talked.

Al Qaryūt was built as a receiving station for a new
weather satellite system, put up by ComSat, Ltd, a British company. At least that is what the world was led to
believe.

In reality the satellite, parked in a stable orbit over the
Mediterranean, contained electronic surveillance equipment. Al Qaryūt was the receiving center for information the satellite gathered.

"A small force of Jordanian terrorists crossed our
border and attacked the station, killing all 27 of its operating personnel and completely destroying the equipment.

"You must understand one other thing," Wasserman
said, stopping in front of Mahoney. "Paranoia is the national sport of Israel. Al Qaryūt was supposedly a
weather station, but it was disguised as an ordinary
radar squadron, indistinguishable from any of a dozen
others. So why was it attacked?"

"How secret was the real purpose of the station?"
Mahoney asked.

"Very," Wasserman said. "There weren't too many
people who knew its real purpose."

"Then your mole is among them."

"Presumably," Wasserman said. He turned and went
across the room to his briefcase and took something from it. "They tried to kill you in Athens. They
might try again," he said, coming back to Mahoney. He
was carrying a shoulder holster that contained a .380
Beretta automatic. He held it out.

"What good would that have done me against a
bomb?" Mahoney asked. He made no move to take the
gun.

"Absolutely none, but if they've tried once they'll
probably try again. Maybe their methods will change."

"And we'll have a shoot-'em-up," Mahoney said,

smiling wryly at the thought. He never did like guns, and during the months since Marge's death, he had developed a real aversion toward the things. "How do you know I won't get nervous one night and shoot an innocent bystander? How would that be explained?"

"We're not playing games here," Wasserman said angrily. "Your life is at risk. I don't want it thrown away for nothing."

"If I'm assassinated, you'll have your conduit back to the mole."

"I'm serious about this."

"So am I," Mahoney said, but he reached out and took the weapon. Without pulling the gun out of the holster, he knew by its weight that it was loaded.

Wasserman went to the radiator in one corner where he bent down and did something with the valve. "One full turn to the left, then lift up," he said. He straightened up and pulled the radiator away from the wall to reveal a safe. "Right, left, right, 9, 17, 31."

A moment later he stepped aside so that Mahoney could see into the empty safe. "We call these sort of things *sliks,*" he said. "In the old days we used to hide weapons and ammunition in them. And later, the entire filing system for Shai, the Haganah's intelligence service, was operated out of these ratholes."

"Does Sonja know about this one?" Mahoney asked.

"Only you and I, although Sonja of course knows about this apartment, and she will guess there is a *slik* here."

Mahoney thought a moment. "After today I'll put my reports in writing here, and you can bring the files and other material I'll need. I don't think we should be seen together, or even come here together unless it's an absolute emergency."

"Agreed," Wasserman said, and he gave Mahoney a

telephone number. "It's my home phone. If you need anything, or if you're in trouble, call there and say Larry will be coming home. No matter where I am I'll get the message and come here immediately."

Mahoney nodded.

"I'll have the dossiers and contact sheets on my six legmen who handled the Athens deal for you tomorrow. What else will you need?"

"A list of possibles," Mahoney said softly. He suspected there would be trouble over this request.

"I've already worked up a suspect list," Wasserman said, but Mahoney was shaking his head.

"You can redline the suspects for me, but I want a list of the *possibles*. That means anyone and everyone who knew what al Qaryūt really was, or who might even have guessed."

"No," Wasserman said firmly.

"Why?"

"It was a closely guarded secret, but the list would be large. Many of the people on it are my closest friends. I don't want you prying into their lives and affairs needlessly."

"One of those people is a traitor."

"I have a list of suspects—" Wasserman started, but Mahoney didn't let him finish.

"Then take your goddamned gun and let me go home. You don't need my services."

Wasserman was stunned by the savagery of Mahoney's tone.

"Put a watch on your list of suspects. Sooner or later the traitor will make a mistake and you'll have him. If he or she is on the list."

"We can't do that, and you know it."

"Then cooperate with me, for chrissake. You want help, get the hell out of the way and let me help."

Wasserman sighed. "It will take time."

"Give me the dossiers as you get them, but don't stop until you've covered the entire list."

"All right," Wasserman said. He closed the *slik* and slid the radiator back in place. Then he went to the table by the window where he picked up the brandy glasses, took them into the kitchen, and rinsed them out. "What's your first move going to be?" he called.

Mahoney got up, went to the window, and looked down at the traffic on the street. There was no one lounging there. No one out of place. No suspicious cars parked along the curb.

"Hares and hounds," he said half to himself.

"What?" Wasserman said, coming from the kitchen. "I didn't quite catch that."

Mahoney turned away from the window. "My methods may be a little unorthodox, but no matter what happens over the next few days or so, I want you to give me plenty of elbowroom. I don't want the cavalry called out."

Wasserman nodded uncertainly.

"You've heard of the old gumshoe game, hares and hounds?"

Wasserman nodded again. "Send a top-notch legman out on the streets, and have your trainee try to stick with him."

"Exactly," Mahoney said. "It's usually a one-on-one exercise. I'm going to develop it into a team sport."

VI

EN GEDI . . . SUNDAY NIGHT

The military jeep carrying David Ben Abel was admitted through the main gate of the 217th Surveillance Squadron on the west shore of the Dead Sea a few minutes after eleven in the evening.

Kominski was driving, and during the long trip out from Tel Aviv neither man had spoken more than a half dozen words, both of them lost deep in their own thoughts.

The guards had been alerted to the general's arrival and merely waved him through once they had gotten a good look at his face. Under normal circumstances he would have stopped and chatted for a moment with the men, but that evening he was tired from the day's hectic events, and the strain of the past seventy-two hours was beginning to tell on him.

He was also angry that Ezra had sunk so low as to call Kominski in and try to browbeat him. He knew that his ADC had felt badly about the entire affair—a sort of guilt by association—but Ben Abel's acceptance without question of the man's written report had done little to assuage his apparently battered conscience.

Wasserman himself had done little to ease the tension between the two services either, refusing to apologize for his maneuver.

During the fifties and sixties a rivalry had developed between the two intelligence services that had deepened into mistrust at times. In the old days, accusations of incompetence and bungling flowed faster and thicker than shared information. It was one of the reasons that Begin had asked him to head up the Aman.

"You and Ezra are friends," the prime minister had said at that first meeting. Perhaps your mutual trust will filter throughout the organizations."

And it had. Until now.

To top it all off, Ezra had called earlier that evening with the news that the American Sonja had spoken of had accepted the assignment and had arrived that afternoon.

That, almost more than anything else, had sent Ben Abel into a deep funk. Not only was there dirty laundry in the service—within the Mossad Ben Abel was certain —but now they were holding it up for public inspection and ridicule.

Ezra had been guarded with his comments, however, mentioning something about the "exigencies of the situation," whatever the hell that meant, and asked for a meeting on Monday afternoon.

There'd be a meeting all right, Ben Abel thought. And at the meeting he would personally lay the entire thing in Wasserman's lap—the problem, the action (which would be culminated that night), and the solution. Neat and simple. The American could go home. Wasserman could mind his own business. And he could get on with his job.

Lieutenant Colonel Elihau Esserman, the squadron commander, was waiting for them outside the Operations hut, and even before Kominski had brought the jeep to a complete halt Ben Abel had leaped out.

"Have they come across yet?" he said as he strode up the gravel walk.

The squadron's ongoing mission was to monitor Jordanian activities on the far side of the Dead Sea, which included photographic flyovers, electronic monitoring, and an occasional foray.

Esserman, a young man of less than thirty with thin boyish features and long, gangly legs, saluted. "No, sir, not yet. But something's come up that you'd better take a look at." Despite his tender age, he was very good.

"So you said on the telephone," Ben Abel said. "Here I am."

"Inside, sir," Esserman said nervously. "I can't explain it because I simply don't know what it means. You have to see for yourself."

Kominski had shut off the jeep and he came up the gravel walk. Esserman nodded at him and then led the way into the Operations hut, down a narrow corridor, and into the dimly lit Staging and Analysis Center. It was a large room, dominated in the center by a table on which was a relief map of the Dead Sea and the shoreline around it to a depth in most places of twenty-five miles within Jordan.

A half dozen men and women stood around the map table, while along one wall several men and women manned the communications and monitoring equipment. At the far end of the room a plotter was marking aircraft positions on a clear plastic analysis board. Aircraft in the vicinity, no matter at what altitude, were plotted on this board, while on the situation map, ground and sea activities were displayed.

The Center was an exact copy of a dozen others around Israel's borders, the standardization one of Ben

Abel's innovations during the past four years. A team
member from any surveillance squadron could, without
retraining, go to work at any other squadron.

"Anything yet?" Esserman said, crossing directly to
the table.

A young lieutenant looked up and shook his head.
When he spotted Ben Abel he stiffened slightly but
smiled.

"Good evening, General," he said.

"What's the present situation?" Ben Abel said sharply, coming to the table and looking down at the displays.

Although Ben Abel was usually congenial, it was well
known that he alone was the one to set the tone of any
meeting.

"They have only two patrol boats out tonight," the
lieutenant said crisply. With his pointer he indicated the
models that showed their positions. "They've crossed
again, and at this moment one is heading south toward
Cape Costigan, and the northern unit is passing the Hot
Springs."

"No signals yet from our people?"

"No, sir, we haven't seen a thing."

"Weather's clear on the other side? Coordinates correct?"

"Yes, sir," the lieutenant said.

"What have we got out?"

"Two units shadowing theirs."

Ben Abel looked up at the lieutenant, then over at
Esserman. "Put a third boat out. Have them standing by
a hundred yards off the line."

"There's something else you'd better look at first,
sir," Esserman said.

Ben Abel ignored him for a moment, turning back to
the lieutenant. "I want two fighter-interceptors from
Har Raqiq standing by as well."

Nearly everyone in the room looked up at that, and

Kominski stepped forward.

"We can't do that, General," he said softly.

Ben Abel ignored him as well. "I gave an order, Lieutenant."

"Yes, sir," the man said, and he reached beneath the table and grabbed a communications handset from its cradle.

Ben Abel turned to Kominski.

"We have people coming across. I don't care what it takes, we'll get them back. Do I make myself clear?"

"Yes, sir," Kominski said, and Ben Abel looked at Esserman.

"Now what have you got to show me that's so important?"

"In my office, General," the squadron CO said, and without waiting for Ben Abel's reply, he turned on his heel and stalked across the Center and entered his office. which was beyond the aircraft plotting board.

"Stay here," Ben Abel snapped at Kominski. "If the signal comes, order the aircraft up."

"Target, sir?"

"Ataruz," Ben Abel said, and he went across the room and entered Esserman's office, closing the door behind him.

The CO was standing behind his desk looking down at a number of air reconnaissance photographs. When Ben Abel came in he glanced up.

"Your ass is going to be in a sling when they find out about this in Tel Aviv, General."

Ben Abel came across the room to the desk. "You let me worry about my ass, Eli," he said. "You're just following orders."

Esserman nodded. "Can you tell me why you sent six of your people to Ataruz?"

"It's been identified as a missions strike center." For a moment Esserman seemed confused, but then sudden understanding dawned on him. "Retaliation for the strike on al Qaryūt? It was only a weather station."

"A half dozen men do not make a strike force, Eli. I sent them over to take a look around. Infiltrate. Information gathering, nothing else." The plan had been much more daring than that, but Ben Abel had no intention of sharing the real intent with Esserman.

"Well, it looks as if they accomplished more than that, although how they did it is beyond me at the moment."

"What are you talking about?" Ben Abel asked. He had a sudden premonition of disaster.

"These," Esserman said, indicating the photographs. He selected one from the pile and handed it to Ben Abel along with a large magnifying glass. "Ataruz Thursday about 0200."

Ben Abel laid the photograph on the desk and bent over it with the magnifying glass. The compound, enclosed behind a high wire fence, was less than a thousand yards square. There were trucks and jeeps parked at various spots throughout the base, and near the main gate there were four soldiers evidently being spoken to by a fifth. Some of the windows in the buildings were lit up. Nothing unusual.

He looked up. "What are you trying to show me?"

"Bear with me, General," Esserman said. "Three more and it will become evident." He handed across another photograph which Ben Abel laid atop the first. "Friday 0330."

The photo showed much the same things as the first. A few lights on in some of the buildings. Two men at the front gate this time, probably guards. One man entering a building near the east fence. Business as usual and as expected for an installation of this kind at that hour.

"Saturday 0210," Esserman said, handing Ben Abel another photograph.

Again the picture was much the same, and Ben Abel could feel his impatience rising.

Esserman had selected another photograph from the pile, and he came around the desk and laid it next to the others Ben Abel had looked at. "This one is for tonight. A little over an hour ago at 2150."

Ben Abel bent down and studied this last photo. At first it looked the same as the others, and yet there was something different about it. Something odd.

Esserman had caught Ben Abel's momentary confusion. He took a pencil and pointed at two buildings near the center of the base in the Saturday morning photograph. "Notice which windows are lit up," he said.

Ben Abel studied the photo for a moment, and then moved to that evening's shot. The same lights were on.

In quick succession then, Esserman pointed out other direct matches. Other lights. Jeeps and trucks in the same positions. A door in a shed near the back of the base left ajar in both photographs.

"The only difference between the two are the soldiers," Ben Abel said, looking up. "In tonight's shot there are none."

"We thought so at first," Esserman said. He pointed with his pencil to the front gate house. "Look toward the bottom of the door. What do you see?"

Ben Abel studied the spot. "A smudge. A shadow. I don't know." He looked up.

Esserman reached across his desk for a large manila envelope from which he extracted three photographs. "These are enlargements of three different spots on the base." He handed the first to Ben Abel. "The front gate."

It was clear now that the smudge in the larger photo was a booted foot jutting out of the doorway.

Esserman handed him another shot. "Near the motor

pool. Front seat of a jeep."

This enlargement showed a man lying against the steering wheel of the jeep. He was asleep or dead.

The last photograph was an enlargement of a window. A number of indistinct shapes could be seen within the building.

"I can't make it out myself," Esserman said. "But my photo lab people assure me it is their mess hall. Fifteen bodies."

"They're all dead," Ben Abel said, his mind spinning.

"Yes, sir," Esserman said. "Sometime between 0210 yesterday and 2150 tonight. We're guessing it happened this morning."

Ben Abel studied that night's photograph a few seconds longer. "No damage whatsoever," he said at last. "Gas perhaps?"

"I had hoped you could tell us that, sir."

Ben Abel shook his head. "It was not my people," he said. He had sent them over to kidnap the Ataruz commander, or at least one of its officers. From that man he had hoped to learn the source of the al Qaryūt strike orders. But this was stunning.

"I have no idea what to do next," Esserman said, breaking into Ben Abel's thoughts.

"We're going to wait until dawn. My people still may be coming across."

"And then?"

"And then we're going to run a daylight recon operation."

"There could be some shooting."

Ben Abel nodded tiredly. "I'll inform Mr. Begin immediately," he said.

TEL AVIV . . . MONDAY

Chaim Malecki came as a complete surprise to

Mahoney, who had planned on spending the morning resting up from the ordeal of travel and then settling down for the next couple of days at the Kfar Saba apartment to do his homework.

He had risen early, had taken a hot, leisurely bath, and by eight o'clock sat sipping his first coffee on the balcony overlooking the sea, when Sonja Margraff telephoned from the lobby.

"I know you're up—room service told us you were having your coffee," she said brightly. "The question is, are you dressed and ready to go?"

"Us?" Mahoney said, trying to catch his balance.

She laughed. "This is Sonja. I told you I'd call as soon as I could. But I suppose you wouldn't know about Chaim. We live together. He's here with me now. Insisted we come over and welcome you to Tel Aviv."

Mahoney silently cursed Wasserman for not telling him about this, but he didn't want to go off half-cocked, unprepared. "I'm a bit tired, Sonja," he said. "Perhaps we could get together later this evening, or even better, tomorrow."

Someone said something in the background; Mahoney could hear the muffled voice. "Just a moment," Sonja said, and a second later she was back. "Chaim would like to talk with you."

Before Mahoney could object, a smooth, well-modulated man's voice came over the line. His English sounded definitely American East Coast. Boston?

"Good morning, Mr. Mahoney," he said. "I'm Chaim Malecki. Sonja has told me quite a bit about you, and about the real reason you're here in Tel Aviv. I'd like very much to meet you face-to-face. I think I can help. And I have a proposition to make you."

"I don't know what to say," Mahoney mumbled.

"Say yes," Malecki said. "When I came in late last

night, Sonja told me that you were here."

Whatever she had told him, the hares and hounds were beginning, but Mahoney had the uncomfortable feeling that he was one of the rabbits. "Give me fifteen minutes," he said. "I haven't bathed yet."

"Fine," Malecki agreed. "Let's say eight-twenty in the coffee shop downstairs?"

"See you then," Mahoney said and hung up.

For a moment he stood looking down at the phone, his mind seething with a dozen different thoughts, none of them very pleasant. He picked up the phone again, got an outside line, and dialed the number that Wasserman had given him. A woman answered on the first ring.

"Hello," Mahoney said. "I'm calling to tell you that Larry *has* come home. He's at the Dan Hotel."

"I see," the woman said, and she hung up.

Mahoney put the phone down, went across the room to the bureau, and opened the top drawer. The gun Wasserman had insisted he take was stuffed beneath several shirts; only the edge of the shoulder holster strap was visible. As he looked at it he thought about Athens and the several possibilities the bomb presented.

If the mole had placed the bomb, or had ordered its placement, it would have been a large mistake. Would other mistakes be made?

He shoved the shirts aside at last, pulled the gun from the holster, then closed the drawer. From the closet he took out his sport coat and put the gun in the breast pocket, not at all happy with his decision to carry it, and then he laid the coat on the bed.

He glanced at the phone, checked his watch—which showed less than two minutes had passed since he had made his call—then went out to the balcony where he forced himself to sit down, relax, and try to clear his mind. But it wouldn't happen.

What the hell was she trying to do? The question kept running through his mind. If she was the mole, she'd be trying to keep him off-balance by staying a step or two ahead of him; by doing the unexpected. If she was not the mole, if she was innocent, and truly trying to help with this investigation, she was making a large error.

Finally, he wondered, just who the hell was Chaim Malecki?

The telephone rang a couple of minutes later, and Mahoney jumped up, rushed into the room, and picked it up. "Yes?" he said.

"What the hell is going on?" Wasserman shouted. He sounded highly agitated.

"Sonja called a few minutes ago. She's with a man she calls Chaim Malecki. Says she lives with him. They're here to welcome me to Tel Aviv. Who the hell is he?"

"Damn," Wasserman swore. "I didn't expect this so soon. What exactly did she say?"

"I spoke with him on the phone. He said he knew all about me. The *real* reason I was here. Who is he, and what the hell does he know?"

"He works for me," Wasserman said, the news completely stunning to Mahoney. "Or I should say he's what you might call an ex-officio member of my staff."

"What does that mean?" Mahoney asked, his voice low, his mind racing.

"He was born in Boston, came here about fifteen years ago. His family still lives in the States, although there is a branch in England. They're mostly in the newspaper business. Loads of money. He went to Northwestern, then was a Rhodes scholar, finally ending up with the Washington *Post* before he came to us. Very big then in government circles."

"I'm listening," Mahoney snapped.

"He's turned into a money man for us, that's all. With his family background, his government connections, as well as the connections he made in college, he developed a specialty of raising money. Unofficial money. Anonymous money."

"What does he do for you?"

"He travels almost continuously. Washington, San Francisco, Paris, London, Berlin. Wherever he goes he comes up with money as well as gossip. He's invited to all the right parties and soirées."

"Washington, San Francisco, Paris . . . perhaps Athens?" Mahoney suggested.

Wasserman was silent for a long time. "Definitely not," he finally said.

"What does he know about me?"

"I don't know. Whatever Sonja told him, I suppose. He didn't get it from here," Wasserman said. "But whatever it was she told him, it dealt with your cover as an arms salesman. She wouldn't have told him the other."

"Who else does she discuss her business with?"

"Come on, Mahoney, she could hardly avoid telling Chaim about you. They've been living together now for five years. They're practically husband and wife. She'd have to come up with some kind of an explanation for you if she was to have any dealings in this thing."

"One more question," Mahoney said. He was angry. "Is his name on your list of possibilities?"

"No," Wasserman snapped. "I trust him more than I trust you."

"Then he did not know about the incident we discussed. The truth about it?"

"No," Wasserman said, but this time his voice was weak.

"No possibility? Not even the faintest possibility? He had no glimmers?"

There was a silence on the line.

"The truth," Mahoney said.

"It's possible," Wasserman replied finally.

"I want his dossier, and I want it fast."

"He's a friend of Begin's and Dayan's. Hell, they have dinner together at least once a month."

"I don't care whose friend he is," Mahoney said, and he didn't. If Malecki knew what the station at al Qaryūt had really been, he was a suspect.

"It'll be there later this afternoon, along with the others," Wasserman said. "Is there anything else?"

"Not for now," Mahoney said.

Malecki was tall and good-looking, with bright eyes, modishly long hair, and an impeccable wardrobe. He stood up from where he and Sonja were seated at a small table overlooking the pool, and waved when Mahoney stopped just inside the doorway of the busy restaurant.

The hostess had come up to Mahoney, several menus in her hand, and she offered him a smile. "Good morning, sir, table for one?"

"No," Mahoney said. "I'm with Mr. Malecki and Miss Margraff."

The woman looked over her shoulder to where Malecki was standing, and her attitude suddenly and dramatically changed from one of polite interest to one of deference. "Yes, sir," she said crisply, and she led Mahoney across the dining room. "Would you care for a menu, sir?"

"No, thanks," Mahoney said. "Coffee will be fine."

When the hostess left them, Malecki extended his hand, and Mahoney took it. The man's grip was pleasantly firm.

"Welcome to Tel Aviv, Mr. Mahoney," he said. His smile seemed genuine. "Sonja has told me a lot about you, and frankly I was very eager to meet with you."

"I'm afraid you have me at a disadvantage, Mr. Malecki," Mahoney said. "I don't know a thing about you."

Malecki laughed. "We'll rectify that this morning," he said, and he and Mahoney sat down.

"Chaim has a proposition for you," Sonja said. The nervousness and apprehension she had exhibited at the cabin were gone now, replaced by a radiant look. It was obvious at first glance that she was in love with Malecki.

The waitress came with Mahoney's coffee. When she was gone, he sat back and allowed a slight frown to come across his features. "Actually I'm a little disappointed in myself."

Sonja's smile disappeared, and Malecki looked quizzical. "Why is that?" he said.

"Obviously my ruse as a tourist hasn't been particularly effective."

"Sonja's uncle works in the government. When your name was casually mentioned she told him that she knew you from the U.S. Trade Mission in Berlin."

"Are you still working in the intelligence service?" Mahoney asked, turning to her. She colored slightly.

"We don't talk about things like that here," she said.

"I just wondered," Mahoney said. "You were working for the CIA in Berlin, weren't you? I believe your brother worked for them too."

The jab had hurt her deeply, and he knew it. But his job here wasn't to act pleasant. And if hares and hounds it was to be, he was going to start with her and Malecki.

"You seem particularly well informed," Malecki said, a coolness in his voice.

Mahoney turned to him. "A man in my position has to be, Mr. Malecki."

"Please call me Chaim."

Mahoney inclined his head. "Do you work for the government as well?"

"As a matter of fact I do, in a sort of unofficial way. I'm what you might call a project money man."

"Sounds intriguing."

"It keeps me busy as well as informed," Malecki said, and he leaned forward a little closer to Mahoney. "I know exactly why you're here, Mr. Mahoney. Begin spoke about you a week ago."

Mahoney said nothing.

"Once the deal is concluded I'll be called in to raise the money for it. You understand we can't divert government funds for the project. Too many watchdogs."

"And your proposition?" Mahoney asked. "You mentioned something like that earlier."

"I think we'd better establish you as a bona fide tourist before too much attention comes your way, if you understand what I mean."

"We'd like you to move out of the hotel and come stay with us," Sonja blurted.

"It'll be a week, maybe longer before we can arrange a meeting for you with Begin," Malecki said. "He's been very busy. And you must know the delicacy of this situation for us."

Both of them were looking at Mahoney, waiting for him to say something. Waiting for him to see the logic in what they were saying, and gracefully accept.

Mahoney sat forward in his chair, took out a cigar, and carefully unwrapped it. When he had it lit he blew the smoke directly across the table.

"Exactly what the hell is going on here?" he said harshly. Sonja reacted almost as if she had been slapped, and Malecki's eyebrows rose. Mahoney waved the cigar in Sonja's direction. "I knew Sonja only slightly when she worked in Berlin, which was what . . . ten, fifteen years ago? And suddenly she's my long, lost friend. And then there's you, the mystery money man. Frankly I've never heard of you, Malecki, and I've suddenly become damned suspicious. Just where *do* you come up with your information? From Sonja?" Mahoney puffed on his cigar again. "I'd bet my last dollar that she works for the Mossad. You both probably do. I want to know why the hell you've contacted me. The *real* reason."

Sonja started to say something, but Malecki cut her off.

"You're right, Mr. Mahoney, Sonja and I both do work for the Mossad. And you're also right in your suspicions. Actually we're worried about you. We've been assigned to make sure you don't bungle this. The deal is too important to us."

"I see," Mahoney said, the cigar clenched in his teeth. "Begin is spooked and wants the dust around me to settle down before he agrees to talk. Doesn't want to get his hands dirty."

"Something like that," Malecki said. "It'll make our job easier if you move to my home. I have plenty of room, and—"

"You can keep a close watch on me," Mahoney said. He took the cigar out of his mouth and shrugged. "Fine with me. Saves on my hotel expenses. But I am going to check you out."

"How would you do that?" Malecki said.

Mahoney laughed. "Trade secret," he said. "But don't worry, I won't upset the applecart."

After they had finished in the restaurant, it was decided that Mahoney would move his things over to Malecki's immediately, and then the three of them would do some sightseeing.

"Just like the tourist you're supposed to be," Malecki explained.

For a moment as they were leaving the coffee shop, Malecki was slightly ahead, and went through the doorway first, giving Mahoney just a brief instant alone with Sonja.

"Set up a meeting with Ben Abel for tomorrow," he said softly, and then they were in the lobby.

VII

Ezra Wasserman was an orderly man, and yet everything around him seemed to be going to hell in a basket, and he was not able to do a thing about it.

He was deeply worried that the entire operation was going to blow up in their faces at any moment, putting them into the same kind of position the CIA had found itself in a few years ago. The American intelligence service had not yet recuperated from the devastating blows it had received at the hands of Congress, and perhaps never would.

It was about three o'clock when he returned from the Kfar Saba apartment where he had placed a number of dossiers from the suspect list in the *slik*. As he shuffled from the parking lot to his office near the Central Telegraph office downtown, he was deep in thought.

Ben Abel had telephoned in the early morning hours, and all through the day Wasserman had tried his damnedest to figure out what the old fool had gotten himself into now.

From what he could piece together, it seemed that some kind of a mission had been run across the Jor-

83

danian border near Ataruz, and it had gone sour.

Ben Abel had made it clear that it was an Aman operation, but he had promised to be in Tel Aviv later in the afternoon to lay it all out.

There were men in Israel, Wasserman mused, who still hearkened back to the old days, who still felt the tug of their memories for the roughshod camaraderie of a unified Israeli population standing alone in defense of her freedom. They forgot, of course, the dissention between the Haganah and the Irgun and the Army itself that on more than one occasion had led to mass arrests and even fighting. But they were the ones for whom time had stopped, or at least had stagnated.

As he turned onto Allenby Street and crossed at the corner, Wasserman remembered in vivid detail how it had really been in those years. The lack of weapons, the lack of ammunition, the lack of food, of fuel. In fact everything they needed, not only for defense but for the sustenance of life, had been in critically-short supply. And the fear, the ever present fear that they would be overrun and slaughtered.

No, he thought, he had no romanticism, if it could be called that, for those times. No nostalgia for the daring missions, for the triumphs over impossible odds.

Those times were gone. Dead and gone. Best left buried in the history books along with Moses, the Masada suicides, or even the Holocaust. It was a view that was arguable, he knew. But he had his hands full with here and now.

As he walked he found himself thinking with considerable pain about Ben Abel, one of those hearkeners of the past. And about Mahoney, who was of the same generation as Ben Abel but was one of the most pragmatic men he had ever encountered. About Max Rheinhardt, once a dangerous man whose loyalty to Israel had only been an accident of birth. And finally about Sonja and her incredibly confused existence.

It was all so muddled, and somewhere within the tangled morass was a traitor to Israel.

He turned down a narrow alley that opened onto a spacious courtyard, pleasant with trees and well-tended flowers. A number of gift shops fronted the mini-park on three sides, while a door on the fourth was marked in Hebrew and English on a brass plaque: MINISTRY OF FINANCE: ANNEX.

Wasserman crossed the courtyard and entered the Annex, which was a front for Mossad's operational headquarters, signed in with the security guard, and took the elevator to the fourth floor.

A young woman seated behind a desk in the tiny reception room looked up from her typing as the elevator doors opened and Wasserman stepped out.

"Good afternoon, sir." She smiled. Wasserman returned the smile and stepped across to the plain metal door opposite the elevator.

The woman buzzed the lock, and Wasserman went inside to the narrow corridor that ran the length of the building.

There was a muted buzz of conversations behind closed doors, clattering typewriters, and ringing telephones that never faltered but only rose and fell in accordance with the business of the day. Although Wasserman disliked discordancy of any kind, this business-as-usual patina of ever present sound on the fourth floor was comforting. Somewhat like a ship's engines at sea.

At the end of the corridor he entered his outer office just as his secretary was hanging up the phone. It was a large room, couch and chairs along one wall, a huge desk and a bank of file cabinets opposite.

She got up and followed him into his inner sanctum, waiting until he had taken off his coat and hung it neatly on the back of his chair, loosened his tie, and sat behind his desk.

"Tea?" she asked. She was a large, raw-boned woman, with a beet-red complexion and a huge bosom, who never seemed to smile. But she was efficient and discreet. She was holding a sealed manila envelope.

"Later, perhaps," Wasserman said. "Something for me?"

"Quite a lot, actually," she said. She handed the envelope to him. "Saul sent this up from research. It's 'Eyes-Only' so I didn't get a chance to screen it."

Wasserman laid the envelope on his blotter but made no move to open it at that moment. He knew what it contained.

"General Ben Abel telephoned while you were out. Said he would be here at four sharp," she was continuing. "Sonja needs a minute of your time, and Mr. Malecki arrived five minutes ago and said he has to speak with you."

"Where is he now?" Wasserman asked.

"Downstairs in the commissary."

"Fine," he said. "I'll see Sonja first."

"Yes, sir," the woman said, and she left, closing the door softly.

Wasserman slit open the envelope with a penknife and extracted the five Identi-kit drawings that Sonja had made up last week. He had sent them down to Saul Breitlow, Chief of Research, for identifications.

Breitlow had attached a short note to the drawings identifying one man as John Miller, CIA legman from New York, and the other four as unknowns.

Miller was the one who had followed Sonja from New York to Minnesota. The other four had followed her to

Paris, and presumably to Berlin.

For an instant, Wasserman had a sharp, clear picture in his mind of Max Rheinhardt's body in the morgue. It had not been a pretty sight. Max had died very painfully.

Despite his fears and suspicions, he still found it nearly impossible to believe that Sonja could have had anything to do with Max's death. And yet so many things pointed in her direction.

His secretary buzzed him and he flipped the switch on the intercom. "Yes."

"Sonja is here."

"Send her in," he said, slipping Saul Breitlow's note beneath his desk blotter. He had a feeling that now would be a good time to confront her point-blank with his suspicions. Tell her about Max and ask her straight out what she knew about it. But that resolve faded the instant she came in the door.

"Chaim is here and wants to talk to you," she said, coming across to the desk. She was wearing sandals without nylons, a knee-length khaki skirt and a short-sleeved blouse.

"I know," Wasserman said, looking at her. She seemed somewhat haggard, as if she had not gotten enough sleep lately; as if she was worrying about something. And yet she had a freshly scrubbed, healthy glow about her.

"I've just got a minute," she said. "We're going over the weekly summaries so I'll have to get back."

Business as usual, Wasserman thought. Was it a sham, or was she innocent? He could not bear the thought of her being the mole. And seeing her now, he could not help but envision her as a young girl.

"I told Chaim that Mahoney was here to work out an arms sale. We've got him out at the house now, but

Chaim doesn't trust him."

"I expected something like that," Wasserman said. "But Mahoney is going to have to work it out himself. You haven't told Chaim anything else, have you?"

She shook her head. "No," she said in a very small voice. "I hate lying to him, though."

"I know. I don't like it either. But it's going to have to stay that way, at least for now."

She nodded. "One other thing. Mahoney said he wants a meeting arranged with General Ben Abel as soon as possible. I thought I'd better clear it with you first."

"I'll take care of it." Was it all an act? Did she have a control somewhere? Moscow perhaps?

Sonja was looking past him, a pensive expression on her pretty face. "Is this really happening, Uncle Ezra?"

Wasserman got up and came around the desk to her, his stomach suddenly tied in knots. "Hang on a little longer, Sonja," he said, taking her by the shoulders. She was tiny.

She looked up at him. "Maybe we jumped to the wrong conclusions about al Qaryūt. Maybe it was just a coincidence."

"Mahoney will find out."

She flinched. "I don't like him," she said. "He doesn't trust me."

"He doesn't trust anyone."

She started to say something but then clamped it off, her eyes straying to the Identi-kit drawings on the desk. "Have they been identified?" she asked.

Wasserman glanced down at the drawings. "Not yet," he said.

She nodded absently. "I have to get back."

"I'll set something up for Mahoney with Ben Abel and get back to you later today."

* * *

After Sonja had left, Wasserman buzzed his secretary and asked her to have Malecki come up, then stuffed the drawings and the note back in the envelope and put it in a desk drawer.

Five years ago when Sonja first started seeing Chaim, her father had made several trips into Tel Aviv from his kibbutz near Beersheba to see what was going on. He was deeply concerned that his daughter had gone off on another of her tangents.

At the time Wasserman had told him that he had nothing to worry about with Chaim Malecki. And the five years had justified his assurances.

Malecki was a gentleman in the finest sense of the word, and had done more for Israel than many dedicated men twice his age.

David Ben-Gurion, in a speech to the Knesset in the late fifties, had told the parliament that what Israel needed most were dedicated men and women; men and women who held truth and freedom above all else.

They were almost the same words that Rabin had used during a Sons of Israel ceremony in which Malecki was presented with the medallion struck in gold.

And the words were repeated once again, almost verbatim, a few months ago by Begin during a state dinner when Malecki was introduced to the new U.S. ambassador.

Like Sonja, Wasserman hated lying to Malecki, but it could not be helped. The man was too publicly visible to become involved in this investigation. If he started poking around, all hell would break loose. He wondered, though, if Malecki had any suspicions about Sonja.

His secretary buzzed a few minutes later, and Wasserman reached out and flipped the intercom switch.

"Yes."

"Mr. Malecki is here, sir."

"Send him right in," Wasserman said, and he got up and came around the desk as the door opened and Malecki, dressed in a beautifully tailored summer suit and silk shirt open at the neck, came in.

"This is a surprise, Chaim," Wasserman said, shaking the younger man's hand.

"Sorry to barge in on you like this, Ezra, but something is going on that needs your attention."

There was a troubled expression on the man's face. Wasserman motioned him to a chair.

"It's Wallace Mahoney. He's staying with Sonja and me at the house."

"So I've heard," Wasserman said, going back around his desk and sitting down. He did not trust himself to say anything else. He wanted to tell Malecki what was really going on, but aside from the fact that he did not want the man involved in this investigation, he could not predict how he would take the news that the woman he loved was suspected of being a traitor.

"He's supposed to be here to sell us weapons," Malecki was saying. "Or at least that's the story I've been told."

"But?" He was going to have to play this very low-key. He reached out and buzzed for his secretary.

"Yes, sir?"

"We'll have that tea now, Shiela."

"Yes, sir. Right away."

Malecki seemed impatient. "Dammit, Ezra, don't shuffle me off like this. Mahoney is ex-CIA, I know that much. But I have a hunch he isn't so 'ex.'"

Wasserman let his eyebrows rise. "You think the CIA has sent him here to spy on us?" He had a brief thought about the legman who had followed Sonja to Minnesota, and he wondered if Mahoney was aware of it.

"It's a possibility," Malecki said.

"Anything is a possibility," Wasserman muttered, thinking that even this could be so. "But not very likely. Mahoney was a CIA analyst. Been retired for a couple of years. He is a legitimate arms representative. Works for State, unofficially."

Shiela came in with a small tray containing two glasses of tea, already laced with sugar and lemon.

Malecki looked up and smiled at her. "How are you this afternoon, Shiela my love?" he said lightly.

The hint of a smile crossed her features. "Fine, sir, just fine," she said, and then she turned and left.

"I've never seen that woman smile in the ten years I've known her," Wasserman said, looking after her.

"I told Mahoney that Sonja and I both worked for you, and were assigned to keep him out of trouble."

"We've already run a background check on him, but if it would make you feel better, I can send a twix to our people in Washington to have another look."

Malecki took his tea and sipped at it, then set the glass back on the tray. "Let me know what you come up with, would you Ezra?" he said, getting to his feet.

"Don't worry about Mahoney," Wasserman said, getting up as well. "He's a little odd, but he is who he claims to be."

Malecki grinned. "Paranoid would be closer to the truth," he said. "We'll talk again when I get back."

"You're leaving?"

"Washington first thing tomorrow morning. Probably won't be back until late in the week. The Stewart Graham will is being contested, so I have to speak with the attorneys. We might just come up with a couple of million."

"Good luck," Wasserman said warmly.

Ben Abel showed up precisely at four o'clock, out of

breath, red-faced, his hair disheveled, and dark sweat stains at the armpits of his khaki uniform.

Shiela had barely buzzed to announce his arrival when he barged into Wasserman's office, slammed the door, and stalked across to the desk.

Wasserman was shocked by his appearance. He was 68 years old, but at this moment he looked like a man in his nineties, on the verge of collapse.

"Good God, what has happened, David?" Wasserman said, getting to his feet.

"First al Qaryūt, and now Ataruz," Ben Abel shouted. He was carrying a briefcase, and he set it on top of the desk, scattering some of the papers there. "In a few minutes I'm going over to see Begin. I'm done playing your little games."

Wasserman had the terrible, sinking feeling that he was witnessing the disintegration not only of a dear friend but of the entire operation. He sat down.

"Late last week I sent six of my best people across from En Gedi to infiltrate Ataruz."

"Why Ataruz?" Wasserman heard himself asking.

"The raid on al Qaryūt was a Jordanian operation. Ataruz is—or I should say was—their staging base for such operations."

"What did you hope to accomplish by that, David?"

Ben Abel leaned forward over the desk, one hand on his briefcase, the other in a fist, knuckles white. "I instructed my people to kidnap the post commander or one or more of its officers and bring them back alive."

Wasserman could not believe what he was hearing. The old fool. The incredible fool.

"Everyone at Ataruz—the men, the officers, and even two dogs—everyone is dead."

As if in slow motion Ben Abel was opening his briefcase and pulling out a dozen air reconnaissance photographs and spreading them out on the desk.

Something was going to have to be done, and done quickly, one part of Wasserman's brain was figuring, while with another part of his mind he was looking down at the photographs which showed bodies, everywhere bodies. Unmarked as far as he could see. Perhaps sleeping.

He reached out and buzzed his secretary.

"Yes?" her voice came over the speaker.

He looked up into his old friend's eyes. "Telephone Mr. Begin, and ask him . . . no, tell him, that General Ben Abel and I have to meet with him immediately."

VIII

TEL AVIV . . . TUESDAY

The cab dropped Mahoney off at the Dan Hotel, and after he had paid the driver he went inside, crossed the lobby, went through the coffee shop, and nonchalantly left the hotel by a side entrance.

A young Army corporal was seated behind the wheel of an open military jeep across the driveway from the side door, and he looked up as Mahoney approached.

"Mr. Mahoney?" he asked.

Mahoney nodded. "Good morning."

"Good morning, sir," the corporal said, starting the engine as Mahoney climbed in beside him.

The young man pulled out of the parking lot and, driving well within the speed limit, headed north along the Hayarkon, which loosely followed the shoreline, turning inland a few blocks north of the Sheraton Hotel complex, then crossing the river.

During the ride Mahoney looked back several times, but as far as he could tell they were not being followed. He had no idea where the meeting with General Ben Abel was to take place. Last night after dinner Sonja had only told him that a jeep and driver would be waiting for him at the side entrance of the hotel. They had

had little time for any further conversation.

He had not informed Wasserman of the meeting, although he was certain Sonja had. Nor had he managed the time to go to the Kfar Saba safe house to look at the dossiers. They would have to wait.

The driver turned north on the Ibn Gvirol and sped up as they left the city behind. The day was bright and very hot, and even the wind from their motion did little to afford any cooling.

To the west he could see the stacks of what appeared to be a power station, and to the east was the suburb of Ramat Aviv, beyond which was Tel Aviv University.

About a mile farther, the driver slowed and turned onto the entrance road marked Sde Dov Airport. The airstrip paralleled the highway, and in the distance Mahoney could make out the hangars beside which was parked a military helicopter.

The driver headed directly for the hangars, and as they got closer Mahoney could see two men in Air Force uniforms lounging next to the machine.

"Are they waiting for me?" Mahoney asked.

"I believe so, sir," the young man said, keeping his eyes on the narrow access road.

They pulled up behind the helicopter, and one of the Air Force officers walked back to them.

"Mr. Mahoney?" he asked as Mahoney climbed out of the jeep.

"That's right."

"If you'll follow me, sir, we can get started."

"Just a minute," Mahoney said, and he turned back to the driver. "Thanks for the ride, son, but I'd like to ask a favor of you."

"Sir?" the corporal said, obviously confused.

"I'd like you to return to the hotel where you picked me up, then wait there for a half hour before reporting back to your duty station."

"I don't know—" the young man started to say, but

the Air Force officer stepped in.

"I'll clear it with yur CO. Go ahead and do what he asks."

"Yes, sir," the corporal said. He put the jeep in reverse, backed away from the helicopter, and headed back toward the highway.

"Thanks," Mahoney said brusquely to the officer, and he followed the man to the helicopter's side door where he climbed aboard. The officer helped him strap himself into the canvas-webbed bucket seat.

"It'll take us about forty-five minutes to get there," the officer said. He was young, not more than thirty, and smelled faintly of after shave lotion.

"Where is there?" Mahoney asked, looking up at him.

"One of our Forward Command Posts near Asha. It's about a hundred yards back of the actual cease-fire line. Golan Heights."

"I see," Mahoney said.

The officer hesitated a moment, then said, "May I ask why you wanted your driver to return to the hotel?"

"You may not," Mahoney snapped, and the man backed away.

"Yes, sir," he said. He went forward to where he climbed into the pilot's seat next to the other officer who had already strapped in. A few moments later the engine kicked to life, the rotors began to spin, and the machine slowly lifted off, accelerating to the northeast.

As far as everyone except Sonja, Wasserman, and Ben Abel were concerned, he was nothing more than an arms dealer. His services were needed, but no one had to like him for the excessive profits he was expected to make.

He smiled sadly to himself as he watched the barren countryside unfold below him. Here and there were areas of green, cultivated fields that stood out in sharp contrast with the dull browns and soft grays of the desert.

The Israelis had done much with this land, but as a

people they were mostly young in spirit and brash in deed. Much like his son Michael had been.

He clamped off that thought in his mind, preferring not to allow himself any more grief, and turned instead to the problem he had been hired to solve.

ASHA—OCCUPIED GOLAN HEIGHTS

From the air, the Forward Command Post at Asha looked like a gigantic spear poised to strike east across the Syrian border. At the point was a squat, solidly built observation tower, the blue and white flag of Israel flying from its sharply peaked roof. Behind it were several dozen barracks and Quonset huts, and farther back, in a large bowl-like depression, were row upon row of tanks, rocket launchers, trucks, jeeps, and other military hardware. Bringing up the rear, in two solid lines, were at least twenty howitzers, stockpiles of shells beside each gun under camouflaged netting.

The helicopter set down on a circular landing pad behind the barracks, and immediately a jeep came out from the compound as Mahoney unstrapped and climbed down out of the machine.

It had been hot in Tel Aviv, but here the sun beat down like a blast furnace, and Mahoney immediately took off his jacket, feeling somewhat light-headed.

The pilot and copilot climbed down as the jeep pulled up. An Army captain was behind the wheel.

"We'll be standing by in the Ready Room to take you back to Tel Aviv whenever you're finished here, sir," the pilot said.

"Thanks," Mahoney answered, and he climbed into the jeep. The driver turned the jeep around and sped off across the compound toward the observation tower. "The General is waiting for you at the lookout."

"Are you expecting trouble out here, Captain?" Mahoney shouted over the noise of the jeep's engine.

The officer glanced over and grinned. "We're always

expecting trouble, Mr. Mahoney," he said.

Mahoney estimated that the population of the installation was at least a thousand men and officers. He wondered how many other camps like this were set up along the forward lines. With places like this, and with the highly effective Israeli Air Force, the Syrians would never have a chance of regaining as much as a foot of lost territory.

The driver pulled up at the base of the observation tower. "The General is waiting for you up top," the officer said.

Without a word Mahoney got out of the jeep, crossed to the stairs, and trudged up to the platform.

General David Ben Abel stood looking toward the east through a set of large binoculars. No one else was on the platform, which was equipped with cameras, radio equipment, and in one corner what appeared to be a very large infrared night scope.

The general was a large man. Graying hair, thick mustache. His khaki uniform was stained with sweat, the sleeves rolled up and buttoned above the elbows.

Mahoney came across the platform to stand next to the general, and he looked out across the barren landscape. A couple of miles away he could make out a similar structure. The Syrian observation post. Behind it, he supposed, was their stockpile of men and weapons.

The general lowered the binoculars and turned to Mahoney. "Welcome to the Syrian desert, Mr. Mahoney," he said. His voice was soft, almost gentle. His English held a slight British accent.

"Why in God's name would anyone want such a place as this?"

The general laughed. "Inadvertantly you have stumbled upon the truth. In God's name. This is the Promised Land."

"Or is it *lebensraum?*" Mahoney asked.

Ben Abel's complexion turned a pasty color. For a

long while he stared at Mahoney, raw hate in his eyes. "Don't speak to me of the German ideals of *lebensraum* or *weltreich*, Mr. Mahoney. I could easily take my gun out and shoot you here and now. My wife and I spent eight years in Nazi concentration camps. She did not survive."

"I'm sorry," Mahoney said, disliking what he had done. But there was something deep within Ben Abel's eyes that he had detected almost immediately. Something disturbing. Mahoney had seen it before in another pair of eyes. In the eyes of a Russian he knew during the war.

"Why did you come here today? What do you want from me?"

"There are only three people in Israel with whom I can speak the truth," Mahoney said. "One of them is suspect."

"I know. Ezra picked her because he suspected her. Wanted to see what her reaction would be," Ben Abel said. Now his eyes were wide, guileless. And yet Mahoney still had the feeling that the old man was a lot shrewder than he let on. And that he was definitely hiding something. Something painful.

"What about you, General? Who do you think is the traitor?"

Ben Abel seemed to think about the question for a moment. "I am an honorable man," he said. "Sneaking down back alleys informing on my own people . . . these are despicable acts."

"Perhaps necessary given the proper circumstances."

"No," Ben Abel said, shaking his head. "Your kind of people disgust me."

"Odd talk for the head of Aman."

Color came to Ben Abel's cheeks. "If you are referring to al Qaryūt, or—"

"Or what?"

Ben Abel said nothing.

"I'm referring to the fact that a traitor is at work here. I've been hired to uncover him or her. I cannot do it alone. I need help."

Still Ben Abel held his silence.

"What do you think about Sonja?"

"She's an old family friend. Wasserman is a fool."

"How about Chaim Malecki?"

"You're barking up the wrong tree. Go home."

For some reason Ben Abel was playing games with him, and it did not make sense. What was he trying to hide? "Were you told about the incident at the Athens airport?"

"Yes," Ben Abel said. "You were lucky."

"What did it mean to you?"

The general sighed impatiently. "It told me that you are a foolish man, as well as lucky. But I am glad you came here after all. I wanted to meet you. I wanted to tell you to leave Israel. Let us solve our own problems."

"How would you do it?" Mahoney asked. He was getting tired of the game.

"That is none of your business. None of this is. Go home," Ben Abel said. He turned to look toward the east again, and he stiffened. He raised the binoculars to his eyes and intently studied something across the desert.

"What is it?" Mahoney asked. He could see nothing out of the ordinary.

"You just may get the chance to see what we're really up against here," Ben Abel said. He turned to the radio, picked up the microphone, and keyed the transmit switch. "Operations."

"Yes, sir," the loudspeaker blared.

"Looks like something happening at one-oh-one . . . ." He raised the binoculars to his eyes with one hand. "One-oh-one-baker. Send up a spotter."

"Yes, sir," the speaker blared.

"I'm not going to leave, General," Mahoney said,

sorry now that he had come out here. It had been for nothing. "Someone tried to kill me, so I have a personal stake in it now."

Ben Abel glanced at him. "Am I on your list of suspects as well?"

Mahoney smiled. "Everyone is, General, including you."

"And you think you can be effective here in a country of which you know little or nothing?" Ben Abel said, his voice rising. "What have you accomplished so far? What have you learned of significance? Are you closing in on our traitor?"

Mahoney said nothing. The man was possibly right.

"Or are you just stumbling around through our dirty laundry?" the general shouted. He waved his arm toward the Syrian position. "We're fighting for our lives here. This is no exercise. They're waiting out there with atrocities that would make Hitler's madness seem mild by comparison. 'The streets will run red with the blood of every Jewish man, woman, and child.' That is what they are promising, Mr. Mahoney. What have you to offer—"

An artillery shell came in high and burst with an ear-splitting explosion about a hundred yards to the south of the observation tower. A klaxon started up somewhere behind them, and a moment later a second shell whooshed in, bursting about seventy-five yards to the north.

"Call the three-oh-eighth for an air strike," Ben Abel said calmly into the microphone. He was studying the Syrian position through the binoculars.

A third shell came in, this time close to the north, rocking the observation tower to its foundations.

"Get out of there, General, they're bracketing you," the loudspeaker blared.

Ben Abel dropped the microphone, set the binoculars down, and shoved Mahoney toward the stairway.

"Move!" he shouted.

The thought that Sonja, Wasserman, and Ben Abel all knew he would be here this morning flashed through Mahoney's mind as he hurried down the stairs.

Answering fire started up from behind the barracks and supply dump area, and as Mahoney reached the ground a fourth Syrian shell burst less than twenty yards to the north, partially collapsing the observation tower and knocking him to his knees.

Ben Abel was directly behind him, and a second later a half dozen soldiers were hustling them both away from the tower.

They had gone less than fifty yards when there came a deep-throated whine, and the two men who were helping Mahoney shoved him to the ground. "Now!" one of them shouted.

An unbelievably harsh *whump* seemed to rock the entire earth, and a split second later dirt and pieces of wood and metal were flying everywhere.

IX

TEL AVIV . . . WEDNESDAY MORNING

If Mahoney's mood could have been set to music it would have been funereal. He stood at the window of the safe house looking down as Kfar Saba Street came alive with the dawn.

Behind him were the stacks of personnel dossiers that Wasserman had left for him in the *slik*. Beside them was a coffee cup and an ashtray overflowing with cigar butts. The atmosphere in the apartment was closed and stale, a thin blue haze hanging near the ceiling.

He had finished his reading an hour ago, about the same time he had run out of cigars; since then he had stood at the window waiting for the morning to come.

Lately he had felt somehow safer in the light of day, as if he had regressed back into his early childhood when the night held hobgoblins and bogeymen. But this morning the bright sun in the pale blue sky did little or nothing to dispel his apprehension or his dark feelings.

The spy novels would have termed this a dirty business. The weather would be filthy. And the characters in the drama either a holy white or a brooding black.

But people were mostly invisible, their lives, their

emotions, and their basic motivations hidden. People, what little you could see of them, were mostly gray.

Mahoney turned away from the window and absently patted his breast pocket for a cigar as he went to the piles of dossiers and began gathering up the folders to relock them in the *slik*.

Wasserman had included his own dossier as well as Ben Abel's and Sonja's.

The Mossad chief was a dedicated, conscientious man. Public service all of his life. Wife. Three children, all grown. Perfectly clean record. Highest recommendations.

Ben Abel was honorable. Nearly the prototype for the aging general who had lived his life well despite adversity, had fought hard despite overwhelming odds, and when peace came, treated his former enemies with tolerance for the error of their ways. He would go to Valhalla when he fell. The hero transported upward in a chariot drawn by winged horses, while bearers brought up the rear with his weapons and armor to the blaring of trumpets.

Wasserman's and Ben Abel's dossiers had been monochromatic. As had the personnel files for the others Mahoney had read.

But Sonja . . . .

He backed away from that thought for the moment as he stuffed the files back in the thick metal safe behind the false radiator.

The "incident" along the Syrian border, as the news media would be calling it this morning, Mahoney supposed, had lasted less than fifteen minutes. Four Israeli Phantom F-4's had crossed the border, inflicting heavy damage on the enemy's forward post at Rafid. Two Israeli dead, eleven wounded; Syrian casualties were reported heavy. The U.N. Security Council would meet soon and would strongly censure the brief breakdown in the cease-fire agreement.

Wasserman knew that he would be going out to see the general. Ben Abel himself knew, of course. And Sonja.

Mahoney closed and locked the safe door, then shoved the radiator back in place. He gathered up the ashtray, the coffee pot and cup, and brought them into the kitchen where he rinsed them out and laid them on the drainboard to dry.

When he was finished with those housekeeping chores, he washed his hands and splashed some cold water on his face. In the mirror over the sink he studied his reflection. His cheeks were puffy, his complexion pale, almost sallow from too much smoking, and his eyes were red-rimmed from lack of sleep.

Years ago Marge had started calling him Old Man as a term of endearment. He could not quite recall how it had begun, but at this moment he definitely felt old.

After a while he turned, went back into the tiny living room, and sat down tiredly in the easy chair by the window, laying his head back and closing his eyes.

Wasserman would be showing up soon and would no doubt have plenty to say because of yesterday's incident, and because Mahoney had simply disappeared on returning to Tel Aviv.

No longer did he believe that the terms of his employment were as simple as they had been presented to him both by Sonja and then later by Wasserman. No longer did he believe he was essentially alone in this investigation. There were other watchdogs.

Wasserman, Ben Abel, and probably Begin strongly suspected Sonja. Mahoney had been called in to confirm or disprove their suspicions, but he had also been called in to act as bait.

The scenario was actually quite simple. If Sonja was the mole, and she knew that someone was here to investigate, she would try to kill the investigator. It did not really matter whether she succeeded or not. The only important point would be linking the assassination or assassination attempt on her.

And yet, Mahoney thought, there was one major anomaly in that line of reasoning. If Sonja was the traitor, why in hell had she suggested an outsider for the investigation?

She had not struck Mahoney as a person of that enormous an arrogance, neither in person nor in her dossier. She did not seem to be a person so cocksure of herself that she could risk bringing in an outsider for the investigation and then killing him, thumbing her nose at everyone.

But everything, large and small, pointed her way. Her obvious nervousness and uncertainty when she had come to the States to enlist his aid. The explosion at the Athens airport. Her maneuvering of Malecki so that he would invite Mahoney to his home. And finally, yesterday, the attack on the Asha Forward Command Post. The risks of that move were monumental. The attack could have begun an all-out war.

Her dossier had been no less damning, no more helpful in her defense.

Mahoney opened his eyes, momentarily surprised with himself that he could still think in terms of Sonja's "defense."

Forty-one years ago. The beginning of World War II. It seemed like such a terribly long time ago, and yet it had all happened less than a lifetime in the past.

Sonja's parents had fled Germany shortly before the Nazis invaded Poland in 1939, and they took up residence in Denmark. When the Germans finally occupied that country, and Jews everywhere were required to wear the Star of David on armbands, Sonja's father joined the Danish underground, and somehow he and his young wife survived.

Sonja was born shortly after Europe was liberated, and her brother Peter was born a few years later.

Despite the work her father and other Jews did, Denmark was no place for him, nor was the destroyed, resentful Germany. Since no trains or very little other transportation was moving across Europe, Sonja's parents went on foot across the continent to northern Italy, where they secured passage aboard a ship bound for Palestine. They were on their way to Israel—to the Promised Land—but the British stopped them and forced them at gunpoint to Cyprus where tens of thousands of displaced European Jews were trying to make it to Israel.

There they remained until the British relented and allowed the Jews into their homeland.

Her father joined the fledgling Israeli military intelligence group called Shai, and later he worked for Shin Beth, which was responsible for internal security, and finally Aman, which had taken over military intelligence activities from the Haganah.

Those first years had been terrible. The war with the Arabs had been a nightmare coming so closely on the heels of the Holocaust in Europe. And yet Mahoney had trouble understanding what had happened next in the Margraff family.

When Sonja's brother Peter turned eighteen he came to the United States where, with the help of an uncle living in New York City, he became an American citizen, joined the U.S. Army, and later worked in military intelligence.

The family must have been terribly upset by Peter's

decision, and yet a couple of years later Sonja did exactly the same thing.

She finished college as a political science major at New York's City College, applied for and was accepted by the newly formed Central Intelligence Agency as a translator and low-level analyst, and finally after a few years of experience and training was attached to the CIA's Political Services Division.

The CIA had made other mistakes in its history since the early fifties, but Mahoney had always felt they had blundered badly by posting a brother and sister to the same station.

Yet, incredible as it seemed, it had happened. Sonja's brother had been killed, which nearly unhinged her, and within a few months she had quit the Company, and, Mahoney had always presumed, moved back to the States to find a comfortable marriage.

All that was in Sonja's personnel file that Wasserman had brought to the *slik*. But except for a few comments from her various supervisors, that data was raw, little more than dates, places, and assignments.

Added to her files, however, were the results of a rather extensive psychological study done on her by the Mossad. When she had returned to Israel she had applied to work as an agent with the secret service. Before she had been accepted, she had been the object of a very detailed debriefing, due in part to her experience in Germany, and in a large part to the fact that she had left her own country and had worked for several years for a foreign intelligence agency.

Her Rorschach and Minnesota Multiphasic Personality Inventory tests showed that she was of normal mental health, considering what she had been put through, except for a rather strong father fixation. She needed a father image close at hand. It was one of the reasons, Mahoney supposed, that she was so attached to

Wasserman, and one of the reasons she was now so much in love with Malecki, a man nine years her senior.

Although the tests did not discuss her real father, who was still living, Mahoney was reasonably certain that Sonja no longer felt close to him, if she ever did.

But—and this was the big *but* in Mahoney's mind—if the father thing with her had been nothing more than a part of her normal development, and had nothing to do with her brother's death, it would provide no basis for the case against her.

But, if she had somehow changed because of the terrible ordeal she had gone through in Germany, she might have changed enough to become a traitor.

Mahoney heard someone on the stairs and he opened his eyes. It was a man, and the step was heavy. Probably Wasserman.

He sat forward, took the Beretta out of his coat pocket, levered a round into the chamber, and slipped off the safety.

The footsteps stopped at the second-floor landing, just down the corridor from the apartment door. He was probably standing there, holding his breath, listening for sounds, any sounds.

Mahoney could hear the noise of traffic below on the street, and somewhere in the apartment building a baby was crying. Then the footsteps came along the corridor and stopped at the door.

Mahoney raised the Beretta with a steady hand as the door came open.

Wasserman stood there, a strained look on his face, and his eyes flickered from the gun to the radiator that covered the *slik,* and then to Mahoney's eyes.

"I didn't know what to expect," he said softly. "Sonja was worried when you didn't show up last night. I had to cover for you."

Mahoney lowered the weapon, flipped on the safety,

and pocketed it as Wasserman came all the way into the apartment and closed the door behind him.

"What message have you brought me from Mr. Begin this time?" Mahoney asked.

Wasserman came across the room and slumped tiredly into the easy chair across the small table from Mahoney. "He hasn't been told that you were out there. Ben Abel is furious, though. Your meddling is going to start another shooting war, according to him."

"It may," Mahoney said.

Wasserman flinched, and he glanced over at the *slik*. "Have you looked through the material I left for you?"

"Yes," Mahoney said, offering nothing else.

Wasserman turned back. "Well?"

"Two questions, Ezra. What is Ben Abel hiding, and why didn't you bring me Malecki's file?"

"I discussed it with Begin. He thinks Chaim should be asked to help with the investigation."

"No," Mahoney said sharply.

"He would have nothing to gain," Wasserman answered just as harshly. "For God's sake, his father is still in the States. He came to us by choice, and he's been doing a brilliant job. Everything is going for him."

"I want his file."

Wasserman was silent for a moment, and when he spoke he seemed to be choosing his words very carefully. "He came to me yesterday. Said he didn't think you were really here to sell us arms. He thought you were still working with the CIA, here to spy on us."

"Because of al Qaryūt?" Mahoney asked.

"I don't know. But it isn't the action of a traitor."

"I don't understand you," Mahoney said. "On the one hand you suspect a woman who has been almost like a daughter to you. Yet you cannot bring yourself to doubt Malecki. What is it, Ezra?"

Wasserman seemed genuinely distraught, and Mahoney stood up and stretched.

"Is it just the money thing?" Mahoney asked. "Is it because Malecki has the talent to raise money for your little projects? Is that why he's untouchable?"

"Your innuendo is way off," Wasserman said, looking up at him. "Malecki himself first suggested an installation such as al Qaryūt. He had the connections with ComSat in England. It was he who approached them. It was he who came up with the money. What reason would he have for destroying his own project?"

"The plot thickens," Mahoney said, turning away.

"What the hell do you mean by that?"

"When I first asked you if Malecki knew about al Qaryūt, you gave me a song and dance about how it was possible he might know. Now you're telling me it was his idea. I want his file."

"No," Wasserman said.

"It's a condition of my continued employment . . ." Mahoney started to say, but then it struck him. The entire incredible thing struck him, and he looked at Wasserman in open amazement and had to smile. "You took a large chance, Ezra, telling me about al Qaryūt in the first place, didn't you? It must have given everyone fits."

"I don't understand."

"Sure you do," Mahoney continued, now in a soothing tone of voice. "No one knew about al Qaryūt. Not the Syrians, not the Jordanians, not the Lebanese, not even the U.S. State Department, which probably would not have allowed such high technology into the Middle East." Mahoney looked out the window, across the rooftops of the lower buildings on the other side of the intersection. "You know, I was so damned caught up in trying to figure out who the hell your mole was, that I completely bypassed al Qaryūt. Amazing.''

Wasserman was staring down at his shoes, his hands folded together in his lap.

"It does put you in a bind now, Ezra. At this point you've only two choices. Eliminate me, or trust me completely."

"What do you take me for?" Wasserman said defiantly.

Mahoney smiled again. "You established that for me earlier when you gave me your mini-lecture on the Mossad's efficiency and the necessity of maintaining a strong defense posture. You mentioned something about killing me."

Wasserman held his silence, but so did Mahoney, and finally the Mossad chief relented.

"His file will be here this afternoon."

"Good," Mahoney said. "How about Ben Abel? What is he hiding?"

Wasserman rubbed the bridge of his nose with his thumb and forefinger. "I'm going to arrange a meeting for the three of us tonight in David's office. It's in the Military Records Building at Lod. Seven o'clock be all right?"

Mahoney nodded. "What has he done?"

"It's quite incredible, actually. But it will have to keep until tonight."

"Why?"

"Because I said so," Wasserman snapped. "Because we don't know what it means yet ourselves."

Mahoney sighed. There was so much here that he wasn't being told, and yet he was expected to do their dirty work. "Seven o'clock," he said at last, and he headed for the door.

"Where are you going?"

Mahoney looked back.

"Beersheba."

"I see," Wasserman said, and the same expression of anguish as before clouded his features.

X

GAN HAIFIZ KIBBUTZ . . . WEDNESDAY

The kibbutz at Gan Haifiz, just outside Beersheba, consisted of several dozen neatly maintained buildings located on a slight rise. The compound was surrounded by farm fields, lush green at this time of the year. But beyond them, in all directions, stretched the desert, bleak and forbidding.

At the kibbutz office a young girl, fairly bursting out of her short shorts and khaki short-sleeved shirt, had run to fetch Carl Margraff, and when the man arrived Mahoney was not the least bit surprised by his appearance.

In stature he was a head shorter than Mahoney, but his body seemed rock-hard, the muscles bulging at his calves, upper arms, and bull-like neck. His face was heavily weathered, his hair thick and only slightly graying, and his eyes were held in an apparently permanent squint. He was dressed in khaki shorts, a short-sleeved military shirt, and thick-soled boots, the tops of his heavy wool socks rolled neatly.

Mahoney stuck out his hand. "Mr. Margraff, I'm Wallace Mahoney."

Something flashed in the man's eyes, but he shook Mahoney's hand, his grip strong, his hand rough. "We'll go for a walk," he said, his English sounding very British. He turned and at the door grabbed a pith helmet from a peg and tossed it to Mahoney. "You'd better wear this. The sun gets mean out here."

Outside Margraff started away from the office building at a brisk pace, Mahoney following much more slowly. After a couple of yards, the man realized he was walking too fast, and he stopped until Mahoney caught up.

"Everything is done in a hurry around here," Margraff said by way of apology. "There never seems to be enough time in the day."

"How long have you worked this kibbutz?"

"Since '65."

"You've come a long way."

Two canvas-covered trucks passed through the central square and ground their way toward one of the larger buildings on the other side of the compound.

"The desalinization equipment—finally," Margraff said. "Our number one and three wells have been pumping up salt water."

"It must be difficult here," Mahoney said as they headed across the square toward a line of trees below, which marked the edge of the fields.

Margraff looked at him. "No more difficult than raising children," he said. "Do you have any?"

"A married son. Three grandchildren. They live in Southern California."

Margraff started to speak, but Mahoney held him off.

"We had another boy, Michael, who was murdered a few years ago. My wife has been dead for nine months."

"You're no stranger to tragedy then," Margraff said softly.

"No," Mahoney agreed. The sun was hot and he was sweating hard. He found himself anticipating the relative coolness in the shade of the trees below them.

"You worked with Sonja and Peter in Berlin, didn't you?"

"Yes, I did."

"I imagine old Wasserman has asked you here on something or another. *Gespenste,* perhaps?"

Mahoney allowed a momentary expression of surprise to cross his features, which Margraff caught.

"Ezra and I are old friends. He and I and David Ben Abel and a few others used to get together for a not-so-friendly game of poker in the old days."

"Does Wasserman often chase *Gespenste*—ghosts—as you say?"

They were walking slowly down a gravel path, and Margraff stopped. "Look, Mahoney, I know you work for the Central Intelligence Agency."

"I'm retired. But I'm curious as to why you brought up Ezra Wasserman's name."

Margraff seemed to think a moment. "Why *are* you here?"

"I wanted to talk to you about your son."

They started walking again. "There's nothing to say unless he wasn't doing his job properly, or unless someone made a mistake." He looked up. "Did you make a mistake?"

"No."

They were almost to the line of trees, and Mahoney spotted two flat rocks across which a stout board had been laid as a bench. It looked like an inviting spot.

"Have you seen Sonja in Tel Aviv?"

"Yes, I have. As a matter of fact I'm a house guest of her's and Chaim Malecki's."

"He's a good man," Margraff said. "The best."

"I was surprised to learn she had quit the Agency and returned to Israel."

Margraff said nothing, and they walked the rest of the way down the hill in silence. Under the trees Mahoney gratefully sat down on the bench. It was cool here in the shade, and a light breeze was blowing. Beyond the trees were the farm fields, and Mahoney could hear the sounds of cultivators working the crops.

Above them, in the compound, Mahoney could suddenly hear a group of young children singing an Israeli folk song. It was pleasant.

"When Sonja and Peter were little, my wife and I used to tell them about Germany, and about our days with the resistance movement in Denmark," Margraff said. He was standing, staring up the hill toward the compound. "They used to ask to hear the same stories over and over again. Never seemed to get tired of them." He turned to look at Mahoney. "I suppose we instilled in them a spirit of adventure. They were always going off by themselves."

"Wasn't there adventure enough for them here in Israel?"

Margraff laughed, but it was humorless. "Your American writer Mark Twain once wrote that as a young boy he thought his father was an ignorant man. As he himself grew into a man and left home for a time, however, he said that he was amazed at how much his father had learned in those years."

Mahoney managed a smile.

"I was very much involved in the defense of my country, Mr. Mahoney. For Peter and Sonja I was Israel. They had to leave it to understand what it was all about."

"Which is why Sonja returned?"

Margraff seemed to be listening to something, but Mahoney supposed he was remembering the old days.

"Peter was always an impulsive boy. His one weakness was that he thought he was immortal. But he was also very much like his sister in another respect."

"What was that?" Mahoney prompted after a moment.

Margraff looked at him. "They both, once they were convinced in their hearts that something was correct, would fight for it to the death. Bar no obstacles. Peter evidently thought his mission was important."

"It was vital."

"Like Peter, Sonja was, and still is, a very headstrong individual. A fighter. She'll defend to the death whatever she believes in."

"Were you close?" Mahoney asked. "Sonja and you?"

The question seemed to anger Margraff. "At first," he snapped. "But those were difficult times for us. During the late forties and early fifties our backs were to the sea. We were fighting for our lives."

"Who did she admire in those days?" Mahoney asked as gently as he possibly could.

"What the hell kind of a question is that . . ." Margraff started, but then he cut himself off. "Her brother," he said instead. "When Peter left for the States I knew it would only be a matter of time before she'd follow him. He could do no wrong in her eyes. He was a combination of Gandhi, Hercules, and David."

"Do you see her often now that she's back?"

Again the question seemed to anger Margraff, but as before, his irritation quickly passed. "Not nearly enough," he said. "But ever since she moved in with Chaim she's been coming out here more often. Talking over the old days."

Mahoney stood up after a while, with some difficulty. It was as if a gigantic weight had been placed on his shoulders. "I have to leave now," he said. "But thank you for taking the time to talk with me."

"Peter's mission was important, wasn't it?" Margraff asked. "You did say that."

Mahoney nodded. "We suspected that the East Germans were building a missile base near Leipzig. We had to know."

"Were they?"

"No," Mahoney admitted. "But we had to be sure."

"How did you learn that?"

"Peter radioed us the information before he tried to get across. They pinpointed him, and at the border they stopped him."

"Thank you, Mr. Mahoney, for your honesty," Margraff said. "I'd like to repay it."

Mahoney sighed. "There is no need."

"Ezra and I are old friends," Margraff started as if he had not heard Mahoney. "He told me that you had come here to work out an arms deal."

"If that is true, you'd understand why I couldn't confirm or deny it."

"I understand," Margraff said. "But I won't tell Sonja that you were here to see me."

"Why not?" Mahoney asked to cover his complete surprise.

Margraff smiled sadly. "There are a couple of reasons, neither of which we have to go into," he said. He glanced up the hill toward the compound. "I've got to get up there; to help with the desalinators." He shook hands with Mahoney. "Have a good trip back."

LOD AIRPORT . . . WEDNESDAY EVENING

It was early evening by the time Mahoney came into the suburbs southeast of Tel Aviv, and he was tired and discouraged. The seventy-mile drive to Beersheba in itself had not been unpleasant. The four-door Chevrolet the Hertz agency had supplied him with had done fine on the wide, well-paved highway. There had not been much traffic, and the automobile's air conditioning had kept him comfortable.

But he felt battered. Mentally worn-out. At Gan Haifiz he had found what he was looking for, and more. It was depressing.

Sonja's father was a shrewd man who had evidently put much of what was happening together quite accurately. His two reasons for not telling his daughter about the meeting with Mahoney were quite simple. In the first place, if Sonja was innocent of whatever Mahoney was obviously here to investigate, her father did not want to hurt her by mentioning the visit. In the second place, if she was guilty, the investigation would be spoiled.

Which indicated nothing more than the fact that Carl Margraff suspected Mahoney was here on something other than an arms negotiation mission. But so was Malecki suspicious. The common denominator was Sonja.

Mahoney had spent very little time at Malecki's palatial home near the university in Ramat Aviv since he had moved from the Dan Hotel on Monday.

Early Tuesday Malecki had informed Mahoney that he would be leaving the country on one of his trips later in the day, and after he had gone, Mahoney had telephoned Wasserman, asking him to keep Sonja busy during the next few days.

Before Malecki had left, however, he had taken Mahoney on a tour of the house, which contained at least twenty rooms and seemed more like an embassy of some sort than a residence. Young people were everywhere, many of them living at the house, and all of them busy with paperwork.

Malecki explained that with his family connections in the States, the connections he had made in college and with the newspaper, he had developed the specialty of raising money. Money from U.S. federal sources—such as for explorations and scientific digs—from businesses, and from wealthy individuals. But the paperwork was mountainous. Thus the young people, who were mostly business and economics majors at the university.

Sonja had proudly told Mahoney the night before, over their first dinner together, that in the past eight years since Chaim had started in earnest here, he had raised more than fifty million dollars to begin new kibbutzim, and to do relief and desert reclamation work.

Mahoney had been given free run of the house, and was told that he could consider it his home for as long as he wanted to remain in Israel and generally use the place as his headquarters.

On Tuesday, before he had left to see Ben Abel at Asha, he had told Malecki's rotund housekeeper, a stern woman of at least sixty, that he would be sightseeing in Haifa for at least a day, perhaps longer, and not to worry if he did not return that evening.

The woman had seemed indifferent toward him, and the young people who worked around the clock paid him absolutely no attention. But Mahoney was sure that a detailed accounting of his comings and goings would get back to Malecki.

He supposed that he should return to the house that night and check in to allay any suspicions, but he didn't want to be with anyone at the moment. He wanted to go directly to the Kfar Saba apartment and sleep for a couple of days after his meeting with Wasserman and Ben Abel. To rest his weary body as well as his troubled mind.

It was nearly seven o'clock by the time he made it to

Lod Airport for the meeting with Ben Abel and Wasserman. Across the field from the civilian terminal he came to a security gate.

A military guard came out of the gatehouse and walked back to Mahoney who rolled down his window. The air here smelled strongly of burned kerosene.

"Mr. Mahoney?" the man asked.

"Yes. Do you need some identification?"

"It's not necessary, sir," the soldier said. He half turned and pointed through the open gate toward a large, four-story building three hundred yards away. "That's the Records Center, sir. It's room four-oh-seven. You can go right in."

"Thanks," Mahoney said, and he drove through the gate to the building where he parked near the front doors beside which a flag of Israel flew from a tall pole, illuminated by two strong lights.

He got out of the car, mounted the three steps to the glass doors where he went inside, and signed in with a young woman in an Air Force uniform who was seated behind a narrow counter. She gave him a plastic pass that he clipped to his lapel, and directed him to the elevators across the hall.

Wasserman, a deeply troubled expression on his face, was waiting by the elevators on the fourth floor. When the doors opened and Mahoney stepped out, he seemed greatly relieved.

"Thank God you're here," he said, obviously straining to keep his voice low.

Something clutched at Mahoney's gut. This *was* trouble. "What's happened?"

Wasserman looked both ways down the deserted corridor. "I didn't touch a thing. I wanted you to see this for yourself. We're going to have to do something."

Mahoney followed Wasserman to the end of the cor-

ridor where they entered a tiny office furnished with a
desk and typewriter, a couple of locked security file cabinets, and four chairs.

"Ben Abel's ADC left at five," Wasserman said.
Across the room was another door which the Mossad
chief stared at. "He's in there," he said softly.

Mahoney crossed the room, opened the door, and
looked in. General Ben Abel was slumped facedown at
a large desk, the back of his head blown nearly half
away. Blood, bits of bone, and white matter were splattered across the desk, over the carpeting, and on the
wall.

There was a lingering odor of perfume or after shave
lotion, as well as the faintly metallic smell of blood that
Mahoney could nearly taste at the back of his throat.

He stood in the doorway for several seconds mentally
cataloguing the scene. There were two bookcases to the
right stuffed with what appeared to be military manuals.
To the left was a leather couch and two chairs grouped
around a coffee table. Behind the desk was a large window, open, the curtains rustling slightly in the breeze.

Ben Abel's desk was loaded with file folders, several
of which had been knocked to the floor. A coffee cup at
his right hand had also been knocked over, spilling its
contents across the blotter, some of it soaking into the
old man's right sleeve.

He went all the way into the office, careful not to step
in any of the mess on the thick carpet, and behind the
desk he touched the side of Ben Abel's neck with the
back of his hand.

The skin was still slightly warm to the touch. The general had been dead no more than one or two hours.

Wasserman had come into the office, and Mahoney
turned around. "Did you discover the body?"

"Yes," Wasserman said. He was having trouble

speaking, his complexion was pale, and tiny beads of sweat had formed on his upper lip. "I got here at six-thirty."

"I thought our meeting wasn't until seven?"

Wasserman licked his lips. "He called this afternoon. Asked me to come out half an hour earlier than you. He said he could prove now who our traitor was."

"Good Lord," Mahoney said half under his breath. He looked down at the body. "That's what he was hiding from us. He was running his own investigation."

"It's more complicated than that," Wasserman said.

Mahoney looked sharply at him.

"The raid on al Qaryūt was a Jordanian operation."

"You told me that."

"David believed that the raid was staged from a Jordanian base at Ataruz on the east bank of the Dead Sea. He sent some people over there last week."

"Why?" Mahoney snapped, his mind racing.

Wasserman looked at the dead man. "He told me that he wanted to kidnap the Ataruz commander, bring him back, and interrogate him."

"Christ," Mahoney swore, but Wasserman wasn't finished.

"His people didn't return. A recon flight was ordered over Ataruz, and—"

"And what?"

"Everyone is dead over there. The entire base. We found out this afternoon that they were gassed. Labun. It's an American-made nerve gas."

Athens, Asha, and now Ataruz. Was someone playing an alphabet game?

"All hell is going to break loose now," Wasserman was saying. "We won't be able to hide this."

Mahoney looked at him. "Does anyone in the building know about this yet?"

"I haven't spoken with anyone," Wasserman said. "But no one has reported anything. Whoever it was had access to the building, and knew him well enough so that he didn't raise an alarm."

"Where were you when he telephoned?"

"At home. I left early."

"I see," Mahoney said, his mind seething as he tried desperately to focus on the one elusive concept that would tie everything together.

He turned away from the desk and looked out the open window. Ben Abel's office was at the rear of the building, and two hundred yards away were two other structures, one of them a sprawling single-story building, the other a two-story cube, its flat roof bristling with antennae.

"What are the two buildings across the parking lot?" he asked.

"The big one is Base Operations, the one with the aerials is the Communications Center," Wasserman said without coming further into the room.

It would have been a hell of a shot from out there, Mahoney thought, but not impossible. Which meant Ben Abel's murderer need not have signed in with the security clerk downstairs.

He turned around. The mole was becoming increasingly desperate. But why? The thought was almost painful in its intensity. Why not run for the nearest bolthole? Why do things like this?

Because the mole was not finished here. A glimmer of an idea began to form in Mahoney's beleaguered mind. Desperate people, when pushed, make mistakes. If the push was strong enough, compelling enough in its concept, might not the mistakes become correspondingly colossal?

Al Qaryūt was a push. Destroying it had been a mistake. Ataruz had been destroyed to try and cover that mistake.

Mahoney came slowly out of his thoughts, the idea he had come up with too frightening to dwell on for any length of time, and yet there was no other choice.

"I know how to expose your traitor," he said softly.

Wasserman turned a shade paler, if it was possible, and he took a half step closer.

"But I'll need help. A lot of help."

"Is it Sonja?" Wasserman asked, his voice strangled.

Mahoney came around the desk. "I don't know," he said. "Where is she at the moment?"

"At the office," Wasserman said.

"Is she alone?"

"No. She's working with an operational analysis team. She's been at it all day."

And Malecki?"

"Washington."

"I see," Mahoney said, and he turned to look back at Ben Abel's body. The secret of al Qaryūt had been tempting for the mole. What he was contemplating now would be impossible to ignore. But dangerous. Very dangerous.

He turned back. "I'm going to disappear for a few days, Ezra. I don't want you to look for me."

"What are you going to do?" Wasserman asked.

Mahoney shook his head. "When I'm ready I'll contact you and we'll meet. But I'll want you to bring along one of Ben Abel's aides. Someone low-ranking. Someone you can trust."

Wasserman was having difficulty in accepting what Mahoney was saying. "What the hell are you planning?"

"You don't want to know. Not yet."

"God—" Wasserman started to say, but Mahoney cut him off.

"You're going to have to pull yourself together. I can't do this alone."

Wasserman turned away and walked slowly into the outer office. "What am I to do?" he said in real anguish.

Mahoney followed him. "Help me find Ben Abel's murderer."

"I don't want it to be Sonja, but I'm afraid," Wasserman said. He turned around. There were tears in his eyes. "What is it you want me to do for you?"

For one last moment Mahoney's resolve for what he was contemplating weakened, but he took a deep breath and let it out slowly. "Number one," he began. "I want you to have your phone line swept for a tap. If there is one, remove it and sweep every day."

"It's done as a matter of routine," Wasserman said.

"Then do it twice a day," Mahoney said. "Or better yet, put some kind of a continuous monitor on it. And check the downtown terminal as well."

"My phone isn't being tapped."

"Maybe," Mahoney said. "Number two. I want all the files in there on Ben Abel's desk bundled up and sent over to the Kfar Saba apartment. Somewhere in that pile Ben Abel evidently figured he could find the mole. I'll also want the recon photos of Ataruz."

Wasserman nodded.

"Third. I want you to call in a low-ranking military doctor as soon as I leave here. I want the cause of death listed as a heart attack. Arrange for a full military funeral. Closed coffin."

Wasserman agreed after a hesitant, obviously painful moment.

"Fourth. I want Sonja sent away for a few days. I don't care where. I just want her out of Tel Aviv for as long as Malecki will be gone. And I do not want her tailed."

"Chaim will be back next week sometime, I think."

"That's plenty of time," Mahoney said, his mind now racing ahead to everything he was going to have to do. "And finally I want some stationery."

"I don't understand," Wasserman said.

"I want a supply of letterheads. Yours, Ben Abel's and Begin's. I'll also need a typewriter, documentation stamps—an entire set of them—a clear series of classification indexes, routing slips, operational folders, and if you're using the microdot system, a For-Your-Eyes-Only magnetic label kit."

Hares and hounds, Mahoney thought, not really seeing the strange expression that had come over Wasserman's features. For the biggest stakes of all.

XI

Tel Aviv University was mostly quiet at this hour of the evening. In a few of the buildings night classes were just winding up, and in the dormitories lights were already beginning to go out.

As Ezra Wasserman drove onto the rambling campus he tried to put his mind at ease. Yet he could not help but think that he had failed. That he had made some very crucial errors in judgment, and that Israel's security might best be served by his resignation.

He turned in at the Political Science Laboratory and, spotting four automobiles near the rear of the building, swung that way. He parked next to a plain gray sedan with military plates, but even before he had shut off the ignition, his door was jerked open, and he was looking into the barrel of a large-caliber pistol. A second later a strong light was shined in his eyes.

"Good evening," he said softly, holding himself perfectly still.

The light was taken away almost immediately, but it left spots before his eyes. "Sorry, sir," a man said. "We had to make sure."

133

"It's all right," Wasserman replied. He shut off the car but left the keys in the ignition, then grabbed his briefcase and slipped out from behind the wheel.

"Mr. Gezira asked us to keep watch, sir," the man said as he holstered his weapon. He was a large man, dressed in civilian clothes. Behind him and to the right, another equally large man was holstering his gun as well.

"I appreciate his concern, but I'll ask you to keep out of sight now."

"Of course, sir," the man said, and he stepped aside as Wasserman crossed the parking lot and entered a back door of the building.

Another plainclothes security guard was posted just inside the stairwell door and he nodded as Wasserman came through the door.

"They're on the second floor, sir. To your right."

"Thank you," Wasserman said politely although he was seething inside, and he trudged up the stairs.

When Begin had ordered this meeting he had suggested the Political Science Laboratory building because it would not be in use at this hour, and because Defense Minister Levi Gezira and Foreign Minister Mahman Shapiro had both conducted workshops on campus many times before. Their presence, if discovered, would not be considered too far out of the ordinary.

No one knew Colonel Emil Heilmann, who had been appointed interim head of the Aman just this morning, nor would anyone recognize Wasserman.

Who else would be at this little nocturnal gathering was anyone's guess, but Begin had been very specific in his instructions and the reasons behind them.

"I've been fielding some pretty embarrassing questions over the past few days," he had said without much of a preamble. He had telephoned on the Green Line.

"We're going to have to put a lid on it, Ezra."

"The opposition party?"

"Not yet, but it's coming if we allow it."

Begin's position within the government was shaky enough as it was, but if his political enemies got hold of the fact that an American was involved in Mossad business, they would have a field day.

"What can I do?" he had asked.

"Could you be prepared to conduct a briefing tonight?" the prime minister asked.

"What kind of a briefing, and to whom?" Wasserman replied. His hand holding the telephone shook.

"I haven't decided yet, beyond Levi and Nahman, but the group will be small and absolutely trustworthy."

"I thought this was going to be kept totally quiet."

"I had hoped for that, Ezra. Honestly, I had hoped for that, but I'm under a lot of pressure up here. I received a call just this afternoon from the American ambassador. Wanted to know if there was anything he should be made aware of."

"In regard to what?"

Al Qaryūt."

"Good God."

The prime minister was silent for a moment. "We've got to begin covering ourselves, Ezra," he said finally. "In case this thing should blow up in our faces."

"I understand," Wasserman had said. "What do you want me to tell them tonight?"

"Everything, Ezra."

Those two words echoed in Wasserman's mind, giving him a chill as he reached the second-floor corridor.

Colonel Heilmann, who was a younger, less harsh rendition of Ben Abel, was waiting by an open door a few spaces to the right of the stairwell. When he spotted Wasserman he beckoned.

"Down here," he said.

Wasserman shuffled down the dimly lit corridor toward the man. Heilmann and Ben Abel's ADC Kominski had both been included in covering up the fact that the general had been murdered, and both had taken it very hard. The strain was evident on Heilmann's face.

"The funeral has been set for Sunday," the man said half under his breath.

"I know," Wasserman said, looking toward the open door. "Am I late?"

Heilmann shook his head. "We only just arrived," he said, and he stepped aside to let Wasserman in.

The room was small and book-lined, used, Wasserman supposed, for graduate seminars. It was furnished with a long conference table around which were positioned a half dozen chairs. Venetian blinds on the two large windows had been drawn closed.

In addition to Gezira and Shapiro, the Knesset's firebrand majority party leader, Zvi Andabo, was present; all of them were seated around the table. They looked up when Wasserman came in. No one smiled, and the tension in the room was so bad it was almost a physical thing.

They would have even less reason to relax or smile when he was finished briefing them, Wasserman thought as he went to the head of the table where he put down his briefcase. Heilmann closed the door and took his place at the table beside Andabo.

Where to begin, Wasserman thought.

"I presume you all know why you are here this evening," he said.

"We do not, which is precisely why we are here," Andabo said, his voice nasal. He was a thin man, very short, with wide eyes beneath thick glasses. His manner was abrasive, but he was brilliant.

Wasserman found the man distasteful, but Begin swore by him. "Then, Mr. Andabo, if you will do me the courtesy of listening, I will proceed."

Defense Minister Gezira, who cut just as dashing a figure as Moshe Dayan had in the old days, rapped the knuckles of his right hand on the table top. "No rhetoric," he snapped. "Not tonight."

"I just want to know who murdered David Ben Abel, and why it's being covered up," Andabo said irritably.

Foreign Minister Shapiro, who had come to Israel from England in 1951, was packing his pipe. "Hear, hear," he said softly, not bothering to look up.

Everything, Begin had said.

"David was murdered by a traitor to Israel. We're covering it up because we feel it is in the best interest of our investigation."

No one moved a muscle in the stunned silence that followed.

Heilmann had probably told them about the murder, contrary to Begin's warning to everyone concerned, and Wasserman had to wonder how much of what he was going to tell these men would find its way into public knowledge. Begin had said brief them, and brief them he would, but he was going to cut off any interference right now, even before it began.

"I'm going to tell you gentlemen at the outset that this is an extraordinary business, and our methods, of necessity, are extraordinary as well."

"Is this another Israel Beer mess?" Gezira asked.

Beer had been the most infamous of spies. During the mid and late fifties he had been privy to Israel's most closely guarded secrets. Finally, in 1961, it was discovered to everyone's horror that the man had been reporting to Moscow all along.

"We hope it does not develop into that," Wasserman said. "But it is very possible." He passed a hand over his forehead. It had been a busy day, filled with worry about what Mahoney was up to. "If, when I'm finished here this evening, you do not approve of my methods, you will have my resignation."

"Don't threaten us," Andabo said.

"No one is asking you to step aside, Ezra," Gezira said. "Begin has every confidence in you. So do we." The man glanced at the others who all nodded in turn. "But we have to keep our lines of communication open if we are to do our jobs effectively. You understand that, don't you?"

It was more like a group of old ladies at tea wanting to be privy to the latest gossip, Wasserman thought, but then he immediately felt bad about it. These men had every right in the world to know what was going on. Their confidence in him, however, would not be so strong when he was finished.

"It started about four years ago," he began.

"Can you be a little more specific than that?" Gezira asked.

"Unfortunately not. We'll probably never know how long the traitor has been sharing our secrets."

"With whom?" Andabo asked. "Perhaps if we knew who the traitor is working for—where our secrets are being sold—perhaps it would give us a clue."

"We don't even know that for sure," Wasserman said.

Shapiro, who was called The Professor, laid his pipe in an ashtray and leaned forward. "Just what is it you do know, Ezra?" he asked.

Wasserman opened his briefcase, took out the several file folders, packets of photographs, and Identi-kit drawings, laid them on the table, and set his empty briefcase on the floor.

"As I said, it began about four years ago. It was a particularly quiet time for us. Mostly we were digesting data and summaries from Cairo prior to Mr. Begin's real work on the peace accord. Most of my heavy load had tapered off, leaving me with little more than day-to-day routine housekeeping chores."

He sat down as he continued with his little narrative. The softening up for the big blows, one part of his mind was thinking as he took them through the preliminary steps of his discovery.

Like secret services the world over, the Mossad's procedure for handling incoming data from whatever source was to funnel it down two distinct paths after initial screening. If the information was of immediate value, such as for the running of agent networks, for inclusion in summary reports that would be sent to the government, or for specific missions, it would be acted upon immediately. Analysis would worry the bits and pieces. Records would cross-check for duplication. Verification teams would often be sent out on reliability checks. And finally appropriate actions would be recommended and taken.

The vast majority of data gathered, however, took another much less glamorous path. Canceled airline tickets, telephone logs, menus, photographs, weather reports—a thousand and one details of no immediate or singular value—were sent, after screening, down to Record Keeping where a horde of clerks would pigeonhole each bit into an appropriate niche.

Personal jackets absorbed much of this "junk mail" of the Service. Foreign government indexes, foreign personality files, geographical data atlases, commercial establishment projections—an unbelievably vast collection of files and cross-indexes—absorbed the rest.

"Actually quite an interesting collection if it's taken in

large enough pieces," Wasserman said. "Looking through it all is somewhat like browsing through an encyclopedia."

"I'm sure that's all well and good, Ezra, but get on with it," Shapiro said, puffing on his pipe.

"It was a slack time four years ago, so I went browsing."

"With what object in mind?" Gezira asked.

Here Wasserman had to smile despite himself. "Curiosity and boredom, to tell the truth, Levi. Or at least that's how it began. Later, as I got warmed up, it became a sort of challenge to me. Since I took over the Mossad I've made it an objective to reorganize and streamline our operations. Up to that point I had completely neglected Records Keeping. I thought it was time to put them through their paces. See if the right hand knew what the left was doing down there."

"I don't see what that has to do with anything," Andabo said almost petulantly.

"I'm coming to it," Wasserman replied, remembering exactly how it had been. "I started out by wading through the Foreign Personnel Register for the Libyan, Lebanese, and Syrian intelligence units. The important people we knew about had their own red-flagged jackets in the organizational charts we keep, of course. But this group I looked at consisted of the clerks, legmen, and minor department heads.

"You have to understand that just like any other government agency, there is a constant shuffling of personnel within any secret service. And after a couple of days of reading I was beginning to get a picture of how the lower-ranking Libyan, Syrian, and Lebanese were moved about like game pieces. I was getting another impression as well, though, and that was the timing of those promotions, demotions, and lateral transfers."

He stopped a moment, as he had on that day four years ago, to consider the mental leap he had made that had quickened his pulse and sent him into a flurry of work that for weeks kept him in his office through the night.

"And?" Gezira prompted.

Wasserman looked up out of his thoughts. "It struck me that every time I made a structural reorganization within our service, a similar reorganization was made in the other three services. Usually within weeks of our changes—in some instance within days."

"What?" Andabo said.

Wasserman turned his attention to the majority party leader. "The other three secret services went through the same reorganization and streamlining process that I took the Mossad through. Out of the clear blue sky they began to get efficient."

"So you suspected a traitor. Someone at an administrative level passing on the information," Gezira said. He seemed intrigued.

"I wasn't sure at that moment. They watch us just as we watch them. It could all have been a coincidence, so I went further. I started looking at cement and steel."

"Now you've lost me," Gezira said.

"I had to fix the back step of my house. The concrete had chipped so I bought a bag of cement. It got me thinking, so I ran a request through Records Keeping to summarize the quantities and dates of orders for building materials the Jordanian and Syrian secret services were ordering."

"More coincidences?"

Wasserman nodded. "I'll take our forward post at Asha and the Aman's surveillance squadron at En Gedi as examples because they're both new and because we'll speak about them later.

"Whenever we build such an installation near a

border, the enemy soon finds out about it and builds something to counter the effect of what we've done. Across the border from Asha there is a Syrian outpost. Across from En Gedi is the post at Ataruz."

Gezira broke in. "You're going to tell us that in those two instances, the Syrians and Jordanians ordered up the cement and other building materials for those bases even before we had begun work on our own?"

"Exactly," Wasserman said, and he could see finally that what he was saying was beginning to sink in. Even Andabo understood what had happened.

"Any other examples?" the defense minister asked.

"Too numerous to mention."

"Why wasn't something done about it?" Andabo said.

"Done about what? They could all have been the product of a Syrian and Lebanese agent network here in Tel Aviv and in Jerusalem. But then when al Qaryūt was attacked on the night before it was to go operational, I knew for certain that we had a traitor at very high levels passing information to our enemies."

"It must be someone who knew what al Qaryūt really was," Gezira said. "That's a small list."

"Large enough and important enough so that we cannot investigate each and every one on it without creating a very large fuss," Wasserman said.

"That kind of an investigation would topple this government," Andabo said.

"Exactly," Wasserman agreed. "Which is why I went to Mr. Begin about this three weeks ago."

"Did you share your suspicions with David as well?" Gezira asked.

Wasserman nodded. "The afternoon he was murdered we spoke on the telephone. He asked me to meet him in his office later that evening. He said he knew how to find out who our traitor was."

"His phone lines were monitored, and he was murdered before you could get to him" Gezira said softly. "Is that what you're implying?"

"It may be more complex than that, Levi," Wasserman said. "David's own investigation started last week. He figured that the raid on al Qaryūt had been staged from the Jordanian post at Ataruz—it's just across the Dead Sea from En Gedi.

"He sent six of his people across with the orders to kidnap the commanding officer. He wanted the man brought back alive for interrogation, feeling that there was an excellent chance he could find out who ordered the raid, and therefore have at least a clue as to how the information conduit worked."

"Was it successful?" Gezira asked.

Wasserman took the packet of Ataruz photographs, including several from a reconnaissance flyover early that day, and handed them down the table. "Everyone at Ataruz, including David's six commandos, were killed. Labun. It's an American-made nerve gas. A Jordanian medical unit showed up this morning and began picking up the bodies. They'll undoubtedly pin it on us, and either make a stink in the U.N. or mount a retaliatory raid."

Gezira and the others were looking at the photographs. "Why the hell wasn't I told about this sooner, Ezra?" he demanded angrily.

"Until today Mr. Begin and I both felt that the Jordanians would not take any military action."

"I didn't know anything about it," Colonel Heilmann was saying.

Gezira got to his feet. "I'm going to have to alert our forces along the Jordanian border immediately."

"Five more minutes, Levi, and I'll be finished here," Wasserman said.

The color slowly drained from the defense minister's

normally placid face, but he sat down. "There's more?"

"Yes. And I'm afraid it's not going to be much to your liking."

"I don't like this already," Andabo said. "Who else did you share your suspicions with? Other than David Ben Abel and Mr. Begin, that is."

There was an ache centered in Wasserman's chest, and the room seemed closer than before. "Sonja Margraff," he said.

"Carl Margraff's daughter?" Shapiro asked.

Wasserman nodded.

"Why?"

"She heads up the Arab division, I believe," Heilmann said.

"Is that correct, Ezra?" Shapiro asked.

Wasserman squared his shoulders as he gazed down the table at the four men. "That's correct," he said. "But I shared what I knew with her because I suspected her of being our traitor."

Andabo started to sputter, but Shapiro looked at him with contempt. "Shut up," he said, and he turned back to Wasserman. "Does Carl know?"

"No," Wasserman said.

"What was her initial reaction?"

"Much the same as yours," Wasserman replied, thinking back to the conversation he and Sonja had had. "She agreed that if we mounted a full-scale investigation of everyone who had knowledge of al Qaryūt, the consequences would be disastrous. She suggested we bring in an outsider to do the job."

Andabo had gone pale. "I sincerely hope that you're not going to tell us what I think you're going to tell us."

Everything, Begin had said. The words kept echoing and rumbling through his mind. Yet he didn't know everything. Who killed Max, and why? And where had

Mahoney disappeared to? What was he doing?

"Tell us the rest," Shapiro said. "We've come this far. Let's have it all."

Slowly then, as if in a dream, Wasserman took the four men through the next steps. The suggestion of Wallace Mahoney, retired Central Intelligence Agency analyst, with whom Sonja and her brother had worked in Berlin. The meeting in Athens and the explosion at the airport. Sonja picking up a tail and Max Rheinhardt's murder.

He took them through all of it, passing down the table the drawings, Mahoney's dossier, and the reports on the artillery attack at Asha while Mahoney and Ben Abel were meeting.

In the end, he recounted in detail for his audience the moves Mahoney had made already, the materials he had been supplied with just that morning, and the fact that he had completely disappeared.

"Amazing," Shapiro said softly.

"Insanity is more like it," Andabo snapped.

Gezira got to his feet. He looked old and tired at that moment. "I've always liked you, Ezra. Always have had a great respect for your abilities and judgment. But I think you've gone too far this time. I intend discussing this with Mr. Begin."

"In the meantime," Wasserman said, getting to his feet and gathering up the files and photographs spread over the table, "I'll ask you not to discuss any aspect of this situation with anyone."

"You presume to tell us—" Andabo began, but Wasserman cut him off.

"Indeed I do, Mr. Andabo. Indeed I do."

XII

TEL AVIV . . . SUNDAY

The Scotch House, as innocuous a hotel as it was, became Mahoney's citadel cum operational headquarters. From his room on the fourth floor overlooking the ornate St. Peter's Church a block and a half away, he could almost believe he was not in Israel. From his balcony, with the soft Mediterranean evening breezes rustling his hair, cooling him from his labors, he could almost forget why he had been called here, what had already happened to him, and what he was about to unleash on the world.

His hotel was in Jaffa, or Yafo if you looked for it on an Israeli map, and in the early evenings of his first days of self-imposed confinement, he had gone for walks through the ancient seaport town. Down the block past the Coptic church, around the corner to the Yehuda Haymit past the Greek embassy, and then on to the corner of St. Antonio's Latin Church. Across Yefet to the Yugoslavian embassy, then past St. Peter's and finally back to his hotel.

The previous night—Saturday—however, he had not left his room. He was too nervous to leave unguarded the thing he had created. Instead he had sent down for several sandwiches and a bottle of American bourbon, all of which had cost him forty-five dollars, American, plus a tip for the aging bellhop who had fetched the items for him.

"You must be a Christian," the bellhop had guessed when Mahoney had first checked in on Thursday morning.

By the second day the man, who dressed in a hideous green uniform with tarnished brass buttons, confided in Mahoney that Joppa (which is what the place had been called in the ancient days) was the very seaport from where Jonah departed for Tarshish and was subsequently swallowed by the great whale.

On the third day the bellhop, whose name Mahoney learned through no fault of his own was Simon, told him that in the ancient days Joppa was a battleground. The Egyptians had made war here, followed by the Persians and later the Greeks.

Mahoney supposed this plethora of information, this outpouring of Jaffa trivia, came in response to a sort of pity for him. The aging Christian on his deathbed come for the last pilgrimage.

Before he had checked into the hotel he had stopped at Malecki's home where he picked up his suitcase and informed the dour housekeeper that he would be gone again to Haifa and points beyond for perhaps as long as a week.

Then he had gone immediately to the safe house at Kfar Saba where in the morning he left to do some shopping. By eleven o'clock Wasserman had shown up with the requested materials, and when he had left a few minutes later Mahoney had prepared himself for his sojourn both mentally and physically.

During his busy shopping spree he had purchased a

prosthetic left shoe for a man with a clubfoot. He had purchased a pair of thick spectacles from a junk shop, and from a secondhand store had bought a threadbare suit of clothes, all in black as if he were in mourning, which in a way he was, or as if he were an ascetic, which he had become.

Suitably attired, he had limped from the taxi into the lobby of the Scotch House, a weary traveler who wanted nothing more than peaceful bed and board so that he could presumably settle the affairs of his soul in a quiet atmosphere.

The first night he had gone out for his walk, he had noticed on leaving the lobby that the garrulous bellhop was speaking with the old woman who managed the place. On his return she had changed her indifferent attitude to one of solicitude. Thereafter everyone in the hotel treated him with respect and deference. A pilgrim in the Holy Land.

He finally turned from the balcony and went back into his tiny room where he finished packing the bulky documents he had written into a shopping bag. The rest of his things, along with the microdot kit, the various rubber stamps, and three different colors of ink pads, had already been bundled up in his suitcase.

From beneath his pillow he took the Beretta and shoulder holster, strapped it on, and then pulled on the black coat, buttoning every button.

The suitcase was already by the door, and with the shopping bag and typewriter case in his left arm, he made a quick survey of the room, making sure he was leaving nothing behind.

Satisfied with his perusal, he donned the thick spectacles, opened the door, hefted the suitcase, and limped along the corridor to the stairs, and then slowly, and apparently painfully, down to the lobby.

The bellhop spotted him first, and he raced across the lobby taking the suitcase and typewriter from Mahoney's hands.

"Mr. Wallace," he said reprovingly, "you should have rung for me. You shouldn't be carrying all this by yourself."

The manageress had come from her office behind the counter and scowled across at them. "Did you walk all the way down those stairs carrying that heavy suitcase?"

Mahoney nodded, a guilty expression on his face, and he approached the counter, his limp worse than ever. "I didn't want to bother anyone," he said, his voice hoarse.

"Are you leaving us today?" the woman asked.

Mahoney nodded again and cleared his throat. "Jerusalem . . ." he started, and then stopped as if he was embarrassed. "I must . . ."

"There, there," the woman said, reaching out and patting his sleeve. "We understand. I'll have your bill for you. Can we call you a taxi?"

Mahoney nodded a third time, his head bobbing as if on a rusty spring. "Please . . . if it's not too much trouble."

"Posh," the woman said, and she turned and scurried back into her office, where through the open door Mahoney could see her using the telephone. A few moments later she returned with his bill, which he paid in American dollars. A couple of minutes later the cab had come, the bellhop had helped him into the back seat, stuffing his suitcase in the front, and Mahoney told the driver that he wanted to go to the Central Railway Station, making absolutely sure the bellhop overheard.

Then he laid his head back and closed his eyes as the cab sped across town through the heavy traffic.

Much of what he had written had been relatively easy. The overall assessment files, although by far the bulkiest, had been the simplest for him to do because essentially they contained the same kinds of material he had worked on during his entire career with the Central Intelligence Agency.

The assessments, contained in three thick file folders, all marked with triple red stripes denoting critical matters, all marked For-Your-Eyes-Only and S-1 distribution, and all heavily marked with authorization stamps as well as TOP SECRET in red, top and bottom, were in support of the two critical files. The first was a brief letter from Menachem Begin to General Ben Abel, with a numbered copy to Wasserman, asking for recommendations to a number of sweeping defense and political posture questions.

From a superficial standpoint, the Begin letter would have been suspect as a phony. Such questions were not usually asked of intelligence departments, especially not military intelligence units which often tended to be self-serving. That is unless the head of state had a specific objective already in mind and was looking for the kinds of answers he already expected. On second reading then, the deeper significance of the letter became apparent, raising the likelihood that it was genuine.

The second critical file, which was actually in two parts, consisted of a recommended line of action and a specific implementation timetable.

That second critical file was a summary, in part, of the bulkier assessment units, and was backed in full detail by budget lines, personnel allocations, field effect reports, and hardware data.

Finally, as a sort of pin-the-tail-on-the donkey file—something that Mahoney strongly suspected Ben Abel might have initiated if he were alive and had been a party to this—was a request for a Mossad political repercussions analysis.

The prime question had been: What shall we do? Ben Abel's answer had been clear, concise, and to the point. His counter question: If we do it, what can we expect by way of retaliation?

The Central Railway Station was busy, and no one paid the slightest attention to the old man who climbed out of the cab, paid the driver, and limped inside carrying a suitcase, a typewriter case and a shopping bag.

Nor did anyone pay any attention to the old man as he went into one of the public restrooms, otherwise they might have wondered why he never came out.

Mahoney, dressed in his own clothes now, the prosthetic shoe, dark suit, and thick glasses in his suitcase along with the shopping bag filled with reports, hurried from the restroom across the depot to a telephone kiosk where he called the number Wasserman had given him. He told the woman who answered that Larry would be coming home immediately.

Then he took a cab to the Histadrut Building on Arlozorov, walked two blocks, took another cab to the El Al Building on Hayarkon, and finally boarded a city bus which left him three blocks from the Kfar Saba apartment.

During each transfer Mahoney had kept a sharp watch on his surroundings, and by the time he had made it to the rear of the apartment building, he was reasonably certain his movements had not been traced. He entered by the back door, and trudged up the stairs to the second floor.

He listened at the apartment door for a moment, then let himself in with his key, closing but not locking the door behind him.

For several seconds he stood just within the living room listening to the sounds of the street, of the apartment, and of his own heartbeat, and then moved across the room, gently placing the suitcase and typewriter on the dining table, almost as if they were bombs.

Careful—for some strange reason that even he couldn't define—to make no noise, he opened the *slik* and withdrew the single file that it contained. Across the room he sat down in one of the overstuffed chairs by the window and began to read what meager information Wasserman had brought him on Chaim Malecki.

Beyond a birth date, college and work experience, as well as immigration data, the file contained very little information of any real value. Five minutes after he had begun his reading, Mahoney was finished, and he re-locked the file in the *slik*.

Lily-white. That's what Malecki was. Lunch with Begin who wanted him included in this investigation. Wasserman not wanting his file dirtied by Mahoney's interest. Loved by Sonja, respected by Carl Margraff, and trusted by General Ben Abel. Lily-white. No one was that perfect.

Mahoney turned away from the false radiator and stared across the room, not really seeing what he was looking at. Was there anyone on this earth so perfect he never cheated on his taxes, never had a speeding ticket, never even flirted with his neighbor's wife? Was there anyone so good that his life was free of black marks?

He thought about Marge and wondered if he had become overly skeptical about human beings and their motivations. Then he thought about himself and the things he had done in his life that he was ashamed of, things he had done that he still thought of with regret from time to time. Where were Malecki's little faux pas?

From a distance he heard the downstairs door open and two men start up the stairs. He started to reach for the gun beneath his jacket, decided against it, and then countermanded his own decision, finally pulling the Beretta out and checking to make sure the safety was fully off. If the thing in the suitcase were to get loose, uncontrollably loose, the results would be disastrous.

He stepped backward into the kitchenette and waited until the two men reached the second floor and came down the corridor to the door. A key grated in the lock, and the door swung open.

Wasserman, a much larger, huskier man behind him, stepped into the apartment and stopped when he spotted Mahoney in the kitchen, gun in hand. He seemed nervous, ill at ease. The man behind him was frankly curious, although he looked as if he hadn't slept in a week.

"One of General Ben Abel's aides?" Mahoney asked, holstering the gun.

They came all the way into the apartment, and Wasserman closed the door. "His ADC," he said. "Captain Zepharim Kominski, Wallace Mahoney."

The man was dressed in civilian clothes that didn't seem to fit either his frame or his personality. He came across the room and shook Mahoney's hand.

"We met," he said. "At Asha."

"You picked me up at the helicopter pad," Mahoney said. "I didn't recognize you out of uniform."

"We just returned from the funeral," Wasserman said.

"How much has he been told?"

"Nothing, except that David was murdered, and you are helping with the investigation. He helped us cover it up."

Kominski had watched the exchange, his jaw tightening. "Look to Germany," he said. "I'll bet my life's savings my general was murdered by an ex-Nazi."

"No," Mahoney said. "Your general was murdered

by a traitor to Israel. I was hired to find the person. That's why he was killed."

Kominski's reaction was startling. His complexion instantly turned white, his eyes widened, his nostrils flared, and his mouth opened, but no sound came out.

"Can he be trusted?" Mahoney asked.

"Completely," Wasserman said.

"I'll help you," Kominski said. "Was it a Syrian or a Lebanese?"

"A countryman."

"No," Kominski said. "No one in Israel would murder David Ben Abel. He meant too much to us."

"His murderer probably works for the Mossad," Mahoney said. "Your general figured out who it was, and he was murdered for it."

Kominski was having trouble accepting what Mahoney was telling him. In that respect, at least, he was very much like the general he had served. Direct and forward, with a lack of understanding about people who were the opposite.

"I'll talk to Colonel Heilmann. We'll get the staff on it—" he started to say to Wasserman.

"No," Mahoney snapped, cutting the man off. "The general's murder was only one of many things this person has done to your country. There has been more, much more. And there will be other terrible things if the traitor is not stopped."

"Who the hell are you anyway?" Kominski said, his voice rising, the terrible anger inside of him showing in his eyes.

"A friend," Mahoney said.

"Then let me put the staff on it!"

"It's either my way or you will be reassigned, Captain," Mahoney said, his voice harsh. He turned to Wasserman. "Embassy duty in Argentina?"

"It can be arranged," Wasserman said, not understanding exactly what Mahoney was doing but going along with him anyway.

Kominski looked from Mahoney to Wasserman and back again. He wanted to argue, he wanted to lash out at something he could not understand, but he held himself in check with great effort.

"All right," he said, his voice tight.

XIII

HAIFA . . . MONDAY

Haifa, as far as Mahoney was concerned, was a city of unpleasant extremes. To the west was the Mediterranean, serene and blue, puffy white clouds hanging low to the polluted horizon. Inland, to the east, was Mount Carmel, dug into and built upon like any Southern California abomination. In between was the city itself, spewing its smoke and ash and chemical wastes into the air and land and water from its three major railroads, from its Iraqui pipeline, from its refineries, and textile plants and cement works, and soap factories, and flour mills.

The people, too, seemed more strident than in Tel Aviv. Less conscious of the history around them than in Jaffa, and apparently much less aware of the struggle their country was engaged in than the troops at Asha or even than men like Margraff at Gan Haifiz kibbutz.

But the city suited his mood, even though he knew he was being grossly unfair to its people by his assessment. On Sunday afternoon he had checked into a shabby hotel near the waterfront commerical district, parked his rental car in a parking garage one block away, and began walking. By early evening, tired and disgusted with himself more than anyone or anything else, he had taken his dinner at a seaman's bar and had retired early, although he had not gotten to sleep until well after two in the morning.

He had risen by six and had again walked. Determined, an onlooker might suspect, to walk himself into the ground, to beat his sensibilities into submission by touring the grossest sections of the city, to flounder in a morass of factory wastes without ever admitting their products. Determined, those few who might know him would be led to believe, to convince himself of the goodness possible in the world by seeping himself in her cesspools.

Contrast. Positive could not be positive without a strong negative. The ends justify the means—cause and effect. But were the means justified by nuclear weapons and napalm bombs, by deceit and murder, by mendacity and evil?

"Number one," Mahoney had singlemindedly begun his preamble back at the safe house once he was assured that Kominski had calmed down enough to listen and cooperate. "Your phones are clean? No one intercepted my call?"

Wasserman nodded. "No taps."

"Two. Sonja is out of the city?"

"She's in Athens running down leads on the bombing."

Mahoney's eyebrows rose, but he made no comment. As long as she was out of Tel Aviv for the moment it didn't matter where she was.

"Malecki?"

"Still in Washington."

"The files from Ben Abel's desk?"

Wasserman seemed suddenly uncomfortable. "There were too many of them to simply drop off here. You set a time and they'll be delivered."

"Fair enough . . ." Mahoney started to say, but Wasserman, who had become more and more agitated during all of this, interrupted him.

"What the hell have you done? What have you come up with? Four days ago you told me you could find Ben Abel's murderer. The next day you disappeared. . . ." Wasserman's agitation suddenly seemed to disappear, as if he had just realized he had gone too far.

Mahoney brushed past the bewildered Kominski to stand directly in front of Wasserman. "What is it, Ezra? What have you found out? Is it Sonja?"

Wasserman hung his head. "It's her. I'm almost a hundred percent convinced now."

Mahoney nodded. "She didn't stay at the office that night?"

Wasserman looked up. "She was gone nearly an hour. They had no orders to hold her or follow her."

"The hour matched?"

"Perfectly. Her name is in the building register. She stayed less than five minutes."

"What's going on," Kominski asked. "Sonja who?"

Mahoney ignored him. "We've got to be sure, Ezra. It's too pat."

"I'll do anything, go to any lengths to prove it's not her."

Mahoney stared at the Mossad chief for a long time. The man had had a rough life; nearly everyone in Israel had been touched in one way or another by the struggle. But he was about to receive one of the biggest shocks of his life. Mahoney wondered how the man would handle it. How any of them were going to handle it.

"I think you'd better have a seat, Ezra," Mahoney said. "You too, captain."

Wasserman and Kominski looked at each other, then

went uncertainly across the room where they sat down by the window.

"What is it?" Wasserman asked.

Mahoney went to the dining table where he opened the suitcase and withdrew the files he had worked on. For several seconds he clutched them to his breast almost like a mother might hold her babe, afraid for the moment to let it go; afraid now that the time had come to give it birth.

Finally, however, he turned and, dragging one of the chairs with him, went across the room to the curious Kominski and the clearly apprehensive Wasserman. He sat down, the files in clear view on his lap.

How to soften the blow, Mahoney wondered. Or did it matter?

"How much has Captain Kominski been told about my presence here in Israel?" he began.

"Nothing other than the fact that you are working for me with the direct approval of Mr. Begin. That and what you've told him yourself today."

"But my extent or purpose?"

"We didn't touch on that," Wasserman said. He could not meet Mahoney's eyes, his attention riveted on the red diagonal stripes across the bulky file folders.

Mahoney turned his gaze to Kominski. "What I'm about to share with you, Captain, is of vital importance to your country. I want you to understand that at the beginning."

Kominski nodded uncertainly, the fire about his murdered general still smoldering deeply in his eyes.

"How well did you actually know General Ben Abel?"

"I was his ADC, for God's sake—" Kominski began, but Mahoney interrupted.

"How well did you know him as a man? Personally.

As a fellow human being?"

Kominski colored slightly, curiously offended by the question. "He was a general; I'm only a captain."

Mahoney didn't say a thing, and Kominski fidgeted for a few seconds.

"I don't know what you mean. Tell me what you want."

"Was he an habitual man? By that I mean was he strong on routine? Did he have a daily schedule that he stuck with?"

"To a degree," Kominski said. "Over the past few years he had become—"

"Forgetful?" Mahoney finished.

Kominski nodded. "It wasn't anything serious."

"I'm sure it wasn't," Mahoney said. Kominski had recognized in his chief the very point that Mahoney had picked out of the general's dossier. The point upon which he had begun to build his plan. "Was the general's forgetfulness something of public knowledge?"

"Certain jokes were made," Wasserman said, and Mahoney turned to him.

"Jokes?"

Wasserman's eyes came up from the file folders and met Mahoney's. "The man was getting old. He was past retirement age. His subordinates did not find him any the less effective, however."

Kominski seemed to flare, but Mahoney held them both off. "I didn't mean to imply a thing, gentlemen, on the contrary." Again he turned his attention to Kominski. "You are quite familiar then, with the general's day-to-day routine? His comings and goings, including the kinds of things he might be forgetful of?"

"I don't understand any of this, sir," Kominski said. "What do you want?"

"There is a traitor within your government, Captain.

A person at the very highest levels. I have been hired to ferret out this person. I'll need your help."

"We've already gone over that," Wasserman said impatiently, but Mahoney held him off.

"Just a bit longer, Ezra, and it will all become clear to you. Crystal clear. I assure you."

When Wasserman had again settled back, Mahoney turned to Ben Abel's ADC. "Several days ago, armed with suitable materials, I hid myself here in the city and invented an introductory to an operational plan. It's a For-Your-Eyes-Only, to Mr. Begin and his War Council, from General Ben Abel."

Kominski's eyes were drawn, like Wasserman's, to the stack of files on Mahoney's lap.

"These are in English. They would have to first be translated into Hebrew. Then it would be up to you, Captain, to plant this material in such a fashion that it would appear to have been misplaced by the general before his death. Once that was done, the documents would have to be treated as if they were real."

The apartment was suddenly quiet. There was no noise from anywhere within the building, and outside there seemed to be a lull in the traffic as Mahoney continued.

"You're a loyal soldier, Captain. You were close to General Ben Abel. Very close. You could not allow anything to besmirch his memory."

Kominski wanted to say something. He wanted to lash out. Mahoney could see it clearly. But the man kept his silence.

"You'd make inquiries. Very quiet inquiries as far up the chain of command as you dared. Not in any direct reference to lost documents, of course. But the hint would be strong. You might even go so far as to speak with Ben Abel's old friends like Ezra Wasserman. These documents you'd be looking for are so important that you'd gladly turn the entire country upside down to find them. To save your general's reputation."

"The mole will find them first," Wasserman said.

"Yes," Mahoney replied. "When the information these documents contains surfaces, we will have found not only the traitor, but we will also have found his or her path. The conduit. The control."

"How can you be so sure the information will surface?" Wasserman asked. "Whoever gets this material could not act on it. With everyone looking for the files that Ben Abel supposedly misplaced, the mole would have to sit on it until the search died down."

Mahoney shook his head, gathered the files from his lap, and passed them over to Wasserman. "Operation Wrath," he said. "It's too important to sit on."

Wasserman took the files, studied the routing and documentation stamps, and then opened the top cover of the first unit. Kominski had gotten up from his chair and moved over beside the Mossad chief so that he could read over his shoulder.

Mahoney got up from his chair, went into the tiny kitchenette, and poured himself a brandy, then lit a cigar.

It was late afternoon by the time Mahoney had walked himself out, but before he returned to his hotel for a few fitful hours of sleep he stopped at a tourist kiosk and purchased a guide to Haifa along with a map of the "Key Sights of the Port."

He wasn't hungry, so he went directly up to his room, where he took a bath, poured himself a stiff shot of whiskey, and then sat by the window looking toward the harbor at the lights on the ships anchored there.

The documents and all the supporting data had been

nothing more than an outline of a plan of action strongly recommended by Ben Abel and supported by Wasserman in an offhand way. The general recommended that they make preemptive nuclear strikes on the capital cities of Syria, Iran, Iraq, and Jordan.

"Israel must not only be guaranteed her borders," Ben Abel had presumably written, "but she must also have control over much of the Middle East oil fields if she is to gain a permanent place of world prominence, and therefore safety."

Operation Wrath, Mahoney had called it.

"If this does get out, it will be suicide," Wasserman breathed. He was deeply frightened.

"One does not set out to catch a panther with a mousetrap," Mahoney said from where he stood at the kitchen door.

Time, a much shaken Wasserman had pleaded at the end. They would need time to digest the material and then decide if they should or could implement his plan.

XIV

TEL AVIV . . . TUESDAY

"That's it, then."

Zepharim Kominski wound the last sheet of paper out of his typewriter, looked over his work, then glanced up at Wasserman.

It was shortly after five in the morning, and a thin blue haze of cigarette smoke filled Kominski's apartment. They had worked through the night, as they had the previous night, translating the documents Mahoney had written.

"Go ahead and put the stamps and routing markers on that last batch, and then I'll get out of here," Wasserman said. "It's been a long night." He stood with his back to the room, staring down at the sparse, early-morning traffic along La Guardia.

He had a headache, and his stomach was acting up from the tea he had drunk all night and from the cigarettes he had smoked. Several years ago he had all but given up the habit, only smoking one or two now and then during periods of heavy stress. That night he was sure he had smoked at least a pack, perhaps more.

Mahoney's Operation Wrath was nothing short of

brilliant. What few changes he and Kominski had made during the translation only amounted to adjustments in the wording here and there to suit General Ben Abel's particular style.

The budget lines Mahoney had cited had come from the operational files he had looked at; the personnel allocations from the same group of dossiers. But the hardware data had come as a very large, unpleasant surprise. Mahoney, and therefore the CIA knew in great detail just what nuclear weapons and delivery systems were in the Israeli arsenal. That fact alone was going to make Begin, and especially Defense Minister Gezira, very uncomfortable.

But that bit of knowledge would elicit only an after-the-fact discomfort. The operational documents themselves were going to produce the biggest stir of all. And the curious part of it, Wasserman thought, was that he himself was convinced that Mahoney's methods would work, if handled with care. Despite the danger then, he had resolved to argue on Mahoney's behalf.

"You know, the crazy thing about it all, is that this is something the general might have suggested," Kominski said softly.

"Not a word about this to anyone," Wasserman warned, turning back. In addition to the headache he had an ache in his gut from thinking about the documents. Kominski had easily forged Ben Abel's signature, and with Begin's the files would become indistinguishable from the real thing.

"If the Americans ever got hold of this there would be big trouble."

"They won't," Wasserman snapped in irritation. "I'm not going to let this get out of my sight, not to mention out of the country."

Kominski had finished marking the last page, had inserted it in the final file folder, and he stacked it with the others in a neat pile on the edge of his dining table.

"What's the next step?" he asked.

"I'm taking the entire works up to Mr. Begin this morning. The final decision is going to have to be his, thank God," Wasserman said. "Have you thought about where we can plant these things?"

"I've got a couple of ideas."

"Fine," Wasserman said. He came across the room to the dining table and stuffed the files in his briefcase, then locked it. "Burn the English originals this morning along with your typewriter ribbon."

"Right away," Kominski said tiredly. "Do you want some breakfast?"

"No, I'm going directly up to Jerusalem."

Something had obviously been troubling Kominski, and it came out now. "What does Sonja Margraff have to do with all of this?"

"None of your business at this moment," Wasserman snapped. He grabbed his coat from where it was draped over the end of the couch, put it on, got his briefcase, and headed for the door.

Kominski got to his feet. "There is one thing we're forgetting here. And that is, if we grab whoever lifts the documents, we'll never know where they were going."

Wasserman stopped, his hand on the doorknob, and turned back. "What are you suggesting?"

"I think we should follow whoever picks up the files and find out who he—or she—delivers them to."

"And after that?"

"What I'm trying to say is that as long as we can maintain control we should let the files go as far as they will. I mean if we know who has them at all times, and can jump in and arrest that person, why not let it run?"

Wasserman thought about what Kominski was saying

but then shook his head. "Too many chances for a slip-up. Somewhere along the line we might miss a contact. Or the files could be duplicated." He shook his head again. "No. We'll just grab whoever makes a try for these."

"How far do you trust Mahoney?" Kominski asked, his voice very soft.

Wasserman was startled by the completely unexpected question. "We don't have much choice in the matter at this point, do we?"

"I guess not," Kominski said. "But he's maneuvered us way out on a limb. We can either trust him completely, and do whatever he suggests, or you can send him home."

"I want you to stay clear of Mahoney," Wasserman said. "Let me handle him. I don't want you running any operations on your own. Do I make myself perfectly clear?"

Kominski nodded.

Wasserman turned, left the apartment, and downstairs exited the building by a back door where he climbed into his car.

The dawn was breaking, but Wasserman, who generally was a morning person, was not looking forward to what the day would bring. Not looking forward to it at all.

XV

TEL AVIV . . . WEDNESDAY

They were at the Savoy Hotel dining room on Yona Hanavi, a block and a half up from the waterfront. Mahoney was seated across the table from Malecki and Sonja, wondering if they felt the least bit embarrassed after the incident the night before. He knew he probably would if the positions were reversed. And yet he wondered just how it was they could live together; one of them so apparently lily-white and the other so apparently a traitor to her country.

He had returned from Haifa early Tuesday, moving back into his old room at Malecki's home in Ramat Aviv. He had a spacious bedroom, a small but well-appointed bathroom, and an airy sitting room that looked across a wide field toward the university. His quarters were on the second floor of the far wing of the huge house, and unless he went downstairs for a meal, or crossed over into the central courtyard wing to look in on Malecki's excellent library, he could feel like the only guest in a very secluded hotel.

Sonja had returned Tuesday morning from Athens but had been immediately called to the office, so they hadn't had a chance to talk. Later in the day Mahoney had spoken to Wasserman who promised not only to have a decision on the nuclear strike documents soon, but also to have the dossiers they had found on Ben Abel's desk brought over to the Kfar Saba safe house.

Mahoney could understand the man's hesitation in the first instance, but he wondered why he held back with the files.

Later Tuesday evening Malecki had returned from Washington totally unannounced a couple of hours after Mahoney had retired to his own quarters for the night.

The incident, as Mahoney thought of it now, had occurred around midnight. Unable to get to sleep, he had slipped into a bathrobe and had padded softly down to the library in the central wing intending to find something to read.

The lights were out in the large room, but the curtains had been left open, the moonlight brightly illuminating Malecki and Sonja in each other's arms, naked on the carpeted floor. They were making love and would not have noticed Mahoney backing out the door except that he brushed up against the jamb in his haste.

Malecki looked over his shoulder and then rolled over, exposing Sonja. She had relatively large breasts for her body size, flattened out now because she was on her back. Her legs were spread.

Mahoney could feel a warmth in his neck and ears. "Excuse me," he mumbled.

Malecki said something, but Mahoney didn't quite catch it as he turned and hurried down the corridor to his own rooms.

For a long time that evening he could not get to sleep. Seeing them making love like that, and seeing Sonja's body, caused conflicting emotions. On the one hand he felt dirty; like a voyeur, while on the other hand the scene reminded him strongly of himself and Margery. Especially in their early days when the concepts of love and sex were nearly synonymous. For the first time in more than a year he felt a sexual stirring; an awakening to the warm and satisfying relationship he had had with his wife.

Well into the early morning hours he felt a deep aching need for a woman; and he felt an acute sense of loss not only for his wife, but for their youth together.

The next morning he had missed them at breakfast and had spent the day touring the city, not able to proceed until a decision was made about the nuclear documents, or until Wasserman finally relented and supplied the dossiers from Ben Abel's desk.

Malecki had telephoned around three, while Mahoney was still out, leaving a message with his housekeeper that the American guest was to meet him and Sonja at seven at the Savoy Hotel.

It was only ten minutes after that hour now, but already Mahoney was disturbed with their blithe optimism apparent not only in their carefree actions but in the inconsequential nature of their conversation.

Arrogance, confidence, or ignorance. Which?

Malecki had just ordered their second round of cocktails, and he turned to Mahoney, a pleasant smile on his face.

"Sonja and I have been so busy this past week or so that we've neglected you, I'm afraid."

"Still no word from Begin?" Mahoney said half under his breath. The dining room was crowded.

Malecki seemed to ponder the question for a moment, but then he shook his head. "Possibly sometime next week. Are you terribly anxious to speak with him?"

Mahoney smiled wryly. "I'd like to finish my business

here and return home."

Sonja's expression darkened, but Malecki did not catch it. "When you first arrived I told you that Sonja and I had been assigned to watch you. I have an admission to make. I wasn't quite telling you the truth."

Mahoney chuckled but said nothing as he unwrapped a cigar and lit it.

"Ezra Wasserman has a high regard for you."

"That you don't share?"

Malecki seemed startled. "What in heaven's name gives you that impression?"

Mahoney shrugged. "In any event I'm sure your staff has kept you well briefed on my comings and goings. I'm afraid, though, that I have an admission to make."

"Oh?" Malecki said, leaning forward slightly.

"I've been lying right along as well. I haven't been playing the tourist role, although I did spend a couple of days in Haifa."

"Extraordinary," Malecki said. "What have you been doing with yourself?"

"I spoke with General Ben Abel for one," Mahoney said, pausing a moment. "At Asha."

"Were you involved in that fray up there?" Malecki asked.

"Right in the middle of it," Mahoney said. "The old general wasn't too fond of me and my methods, but he performed magnificently under fire. No fear. Cool head."

Sonja's complexion had gone pale.

"Then he had to die. Overwork, I suspect," Malecki said. "I was sorry I couldn't make it back from Washington in time for the funeral."

The waitress came with their drinks, and a moment later another waitress came with menus.

Before Mahoney opened his, he laid down his cigar.

"I want to apologize for last night," he said.

"Last night . . ." Malecki started to ask, but then he understood what Mahoney was referring to, and he glanced at Sonja. "No apology is necessary on your part. In fact, we should be the ones to apologize. We weren't exactly discreet."

"It is your home."

"With dozens of semipermanent house guests," Malecki said. He was somewhat embarrassed now. "We do get a little carried away at times. I hope it didn't cause you too much discomfort."

Mahoney waved it aside.

"You spoke with General Ben Abel, for one," Malecki said, bringing them back to the pertinent topic as Mahoney had hoped he would.

"I also went to Beersheba. Gan Haifiz, to be more specific. I spoke with Sonja's father."

"Why?" Malecki said, his voice harsh, the single word very sharp.

Mahoney took his time answering. "I spoke with Ezra Wasserman and he mentioned his name. I thought Sonja's father might be able to help me."

"In what way?"

"It's quite simple. Without information I would not be able to do my job. Mr. Margraff is a wellspring of useful facts and figures." He smiled. "He mentioned you in the warmest of terms."

"He's a good man," Malecki said, grim-lipped.

Sonja had said nothing through all of that, nor did she say anything now. There was a look of surprise and hurt in her eyes, directed at Mahoney. Malecki caught the expression this time, and it seemed to anger him.

Mahoney deliberately averted his gaze, picked up his menu, opened it, and studied it for a long while. When he had finally made his selection he closed the menu and laid it back on the table.

Malecki was staring at him as he had when Mahoney had looked away.

"You're not ordering?" Mahoney asked as if nothing had gone on previously.

"I always have soup and a salad."

"Nothing more?"

"I'm a vegetarian. And you?"

"Steak. Rare. I'm a carnivore."

There was a tension around the table that was nearly a palpable entity; almost like an expanding balloon surrounding them all that finally burst when the waitress came and they busied themselves ordering.

When the young woman, dressed in a black uniform with frilly, starched white cuffs, collar, and apron, left them, Mahoney raised his glass.

"I'd like to propose a toast," he said mildly.

Malecki lifted his glass, and a moment later so did Sonja. Her hand shook slightly.

"To men of high principle. General Ben Abel was one."

They all sipped at their drinks. Hares and hounds, Mahoney thought. He wondered how much more of this they would be able to handle.

"Do you admire men of principle, Mr. Mahoney?" Malecki said, setting down his glass. Sonja had again shrunk back in her seat almost as if she were ready to bolt at a moment's notice and wanted to be as far away from their grasp as possible when she jumped.

"That would depend, I suppose, upon what set of principles you're speaking of," Mahoney said breezily. "I mean Yasser Arafat is a man of principle, isn't he?"

"Point well taken," Malecki said. "But not quite the one I was aiming at."

"What are you aiming at? Exactly."

"The concept of rigidity, Mr. Mahoney. Quite simple, actually. Don't you find that principles inject an almost moribund inflexibility in the people who subscribe to them?"

Mahoney laughed out loud, and a number of people at other tables around them looked their way. Sonja seemed confused.

"A strange view for a man of your social position and background. I would have expected you'd be a traditionalist."

"I make use of it."

"A dangerous philosophy."

Malecki smiled. "I'm not speaking anarchy, Mr. Mahoney, on the contrary. This is a modern world we live in. Fast-paced, uncertain. I'm suggesting flexibility over dogma, nothing more."

"What do you think, Sonja?" Mahoney asked, turning to her.

She looked up, her eyes wide. "I don't know what you two are talking about."

"Principles and the men who subscribe their lives to them," Mahoney said. "Was Ben Abel a man of principle?"

"He was a lovely old man," she said, averting her eyes again. "He believed in order and in the free State of Israel."

Mahoney turned his questioning gaze to Malecki who responded.

"Exactly what I was saying."

"Which is?"

"Ben Abel was a man of high principle. He died because of his inflexibility."

Even Sonja bridled at that remark, and she turned to Malecki. "What are you saying, Chaim?"

"Simply this, darling: Ben Abel was a lovely old man who worked himself to death for his principles. Had he been more flexible he would have understood delegation of power and responsibility. He would have understood that he had gone as far in the fight as humanly possible for him. That it was finally time for him to step down and enjoy what he had already accomplished. What did you think I was saying?"

Guilty or not, they both seemed like terribly lost souls to Mahoney. Like two people playacting at being real. And he hesitated again from continuing with his little game that surely was hurtful but that was carefully calculated to dislodge the truth.

"Your brother was a man of principle, wasn't he, Sonja?" Mahoney said.

She flinched.

"Yes, he was, Malecki answered for her. "I did not know him, but from what I've heard from Sonja as well as from her father and others who knew him well, he was very definitely a man of principle who gave his life for your country."

Mahoney ignored the man, directing his gaze and his comments toward Sonja. "You and he were very close, weren't you?"

Sonja turned to him, tears beginning to well up in her eyes. "Yes, we were," she said.

"What are you trying to do?" Malecki interjected.

"I was always afraid for him," Sonja continued. "He was so . . . so reckless most of the time. Even when we were kids he'd try things that none of the rest of us would dare."

"Were you surprised when he went to the United States?"

She thought about the question for a moment, then shook her head. "Not surprised. Hurt, maybe, but not surprised."

"So you followed, to look after him."

"What do you want, Mr. Mahoney? What are you driving at?"

"The truth," Mahoney said softly. "I'm here on a very sensitive mission. One that my own government isn't aware of for the most part. I have to be very careful with whom I'm dealing."

"Are you too a man of principle?" Malecki asked, and now there seemed to be a dangerous edge to his voice.

"Most definitely," Mahoney said.

A startled expression crossed Malecki's features, and a moment later someone called out from behind Mahoney.

"Hello, there."

Malecki rose as Mahoney started to turn in his seat, and Sonja looked up.

"This is a rare surprise," Malecki said woodenly as if he really didn't mean it.

A tall, stern-looking man in his late forties or early fifties came up to the table and shook Malecki's hand. He wore a lightweight gray pin-striped suit, the knot of his wide tie perfect, and a diamond ring of at least a full carat on the little finger of his right hand.

"I'd like to present Miss Sonja Margraff," Malecki said.

The tall man turned and took Sonja's hand. "I've heard a great deal about you, Miss Margraff, all of it in the finest of terms, but none of it doing you any real justice."

Sonja smiled demurely.

"This is Roger Hannon," Malecki explained to her. "I've seen him at the last two fund raisers in Washington."

"Just a minor contributor, I'm afraid," Hannon quickly added. "I'm what you might call a fixture on the

Washington social scene. They tell me I dress well and tell a good story. Apparently I look good hanging around with a cocktail in my hand."

Sonja laughed. "It's a pleasure to meet you, Mr. Hannon."

"Please," he said. "Roger sounds so much better, especially from a lovely young woman such as yourself."

"You'll have to attend one of our dinners," Sonja said.

"As much as I'd love to, I'll have to postpone. I'm just passing through Tel Aviv on my way home. Visited with an uncle in Athens."

"Next time," Sonja said.

"Of course," Hannon replied, and he turned and extended his hand to Mahoney who had gotten to his feet.

"Roger Hannon," the man said.

"This is Wallace Mahoney, here on vacation," Malecki said, and for the briefest of instants Mahoney was dead certain that Hannon had recognized the name. The man's eyes flickered reflexively toward Malecki and his grip tightened. But then the instant passed.

"Pleased to meet you, Mr. Mahoney," he said politely, and then he turned back to Malecki. "Spotted you from the door on my way out and just had to come in to say hello."

"You have to leave?"

"Unfortunately," Hannon said. He shook Malecki's hand. "Nice seeing you."

XVI

TEL AVIV . . . SUNDAY

Zepharim Kominski sat half reclined in a steel-framed easy chair in the Ready Room, his feet up, a morose expression on his face. He stared past the television set and out the windows toward the Lod Airport civilian terminal across the field. His eyes were nearly shut, open just barely enough to see, his hands were folded across his stomach, and his flight suit was unzipped halfway down his chest.

He had been sitting like this since ten the night before, asleep for all intents and purposes as far as an outsider might guess, but wide awake and very alert to the comings and goings from the busy Operations and Briefing Center across the corridor to his right.

The only way in or out of the Center was through a set of swinging doors, and for eight hours now he had watched men go in, noting what they carried with them, and then watched them come out. He was looking for the brown, standard issue briefcase with the tarnished brass corners and large scuff marks on both sides that had been General Ben Abel's.

The previous evening Wasserman had given the go-ahead. Kominski had placed himself on his monthly forty-eight-hour Flight Ready status, had set the general's briefcase next to a file cabinet in the Ops Center, and had begun his vigil.

He was not sleepy, although under ordinary circumstances he would have dropped off immediately despite the hustle and bustle of the Ready Room. Instead his mind was seething.

Every now and then, feigning a restlessness in his sleep, Kominski would shift his position in the chair so that his right hand or left elbow would just brush against the snub-nosed .38 revolver he carried in a zippered side pocket of his uniform. It gave him confidence.

There had been two times in his life that qualified as genuinely bad periods, he had decided during the night. The first was when his parents had been killed during the Six-Day War, nearly fourteen years ago.

They had fought the Nazis in 1939, and had survived. They had been herded into the ghetto in Warsaw, and had survived. They had escaped to Denmark and then Sweden, and had survived. They had endured the British blockade of Palestine, and the War of Independence, and every other skirmish and scuffle, and had survived. They had managed the hardships of kibbutz life—the desert and the Arab snipers their constant grim companions. They had survived that too. Then came the 1967 war, when they were both killed. Not by artillery fire or by any sort of military action. They had lost their lives in a bus crash while on their way to Tel Aviv to round up supplies for the kibbutz.

During that dim period in Kominski's life he had felt totally helpless. Totally unable to do one thing about the circumstances.

Then came Ben Abel. Over the years he had worked for the general, he had come to love and respect the old man, almost as he had loved and respected his father.

When his parents had died, it had been fate. Nothing more. But Ben Abel's death had been murder, and he had been led to believe that the murderer would be the same person who might come looking for the general's briefcase.

On the heels of this, the second of his life's disasters, he felt he could do something positive to tip the scales of justice back toward the positive. There would be no plea bargaining. There would be no deals. No prisoner exchanges. None of that. The person who had killed Ben Abel was going to die this day.

Wasserman sat in the passenger seat of the nondescript rented Opel, leaning back against the headrest as he smoked a cigarette. They were parked in the Operations parking lot a half dozen rows back from the front doors. The window on Mahoney's side was open, and although the evening had been unpleasantly warm, there was a slight chill in the morning air that smelled faintly of burned kerosene from the airstrip behind them.

The green light had filtered down from Begin Friday at noon, and it had taken them the weekend to get it all sorted out and running.

"If we queer this," Wasserman had said, "there'll be no turning back. The mole will either bolt or go so deep we'll never dig him out."

"Him?" Mahoney had asked, understanding full well why the Mossad chief had preferred to use the masculine pronoun.

Wasserman knew that Mahoney understood, and had not bothered to answer.

Friday afternoon, before Sonja or Malecki had returned from the office, Mahoney had told the housekeeper that he was going away again, this time to Bethlehem. He even went so far as to drive the forty miles southeast to the city, check into a tourist hotel, and then race back to the Kfar Saba apartment very early Saturday morning.

Wasserman had finally come across with the dossiers that had been stacked on Ben Abel's desk the night he had been murdered, and Mahoney had gone through them, the most indecisive bit of work he had done so far.

There were dossiers on everyone, including Sonja's dead brother, her father, Sonja herself, as well as dozens of others. It meant absolutely nothing. And in fact, comparing the list of dossiers with Wasserman's suspect list —the list of those who knew the existence of the al Qaryūt station—proved nothing either. The lists did not match. Nor were the differences significant.

By early Saturday evening Mahoney was finished with his reading and when Wasserman showed up with the operational plan he was ready to get out and begin doing something constructive.

The general had become somewhat absentminded over the past few years. The afternoon of his death he had spent an hour at the Operations and Briefing Center, as he did on many afternoons, waiting for recon planes to return. It was a busy place. People were coming and going twenty-four hours a day, all of them with flight cases, so that the extra briefcase sitting in a corner by a file cabinet would not be noticed by anyone unless they knew the general's habits, and knew the general might have left it somewhere. Ben Abel often took classified documents with him.

Finally, early Saturday afternoon Wasserman had gone out to Ben Abel's home, feigning a very worried, preoccupied look, and went through the old man's study. When he was finished it was obvious to the general's family that the Mossad chief had not found what he was looking for and was plainly upset about it.

"The word," Wasserman had explained to Mahoney, "will spread from there via my staff."

It had been a particularly difficult thing for Wasserman to do, since he had been friends with Ben Abel and the family for years. And when Mahoney had acknowledged the fact, Wasserman had barked, and Mahoney had dropped it.

Kominiski was in the Ready Room, Begin was at home awaiting word, and they had sat here in the parking lot since ten the night before.

A light tan Mustang II convertible pulled up at the front entrance of the Operations building. Chaim Malecki, wearing a flight suit, got out, mounted the single step, and entered the building.

"Tell me about Kominski," Mahoney said as he reached into his breast pocket, took out a cigar, and lit it. He glanced at his watch. It was ten minutes after six.

"What do you want to know?" Wasserman said languidly without sitting up.

"How close was he to Ben Abel?"

"David was like a father to him. His own parents were killed in '67 or '68, I think. A bus crash."

Mahoney thought about Sonja and her father fixation. Perhaps it was a national neurosis. "Were they close enough that Kominski might consider revenge?"

"It's possible . . ." Wasserman started to say, but then he sat up with a start. "What is it?" he said.

Mahoney pointed his cigar toward the Mustang II. "Malecki," he said. "He was dressed in a flight suit."

"Not Chaim," Wasserman said, staring at the car.

Mahoney shrugged. "What's he doing here this morning, then?"

Wasserman reached around into the back seat,

grabbed the antenna with its magnetic mount, stuck it out the window on his side, and slapped it on the roof. He reached back again and grabbed the microphone from the portable radio. "Ops One, this is Mobile Alpha."

"Mobile Alpha, this is Ops One. Go."

"Need a quick check with Air Traffic for Chaim Malecki. What's he flying this morning, and what's his destination and ETA?"

"Be right back," Mahoney said, and he got out of the car and went across the parking lot toward the Ops building as he pulled the Beretta out of his shoulder holster, levered a round into the chamber, clicked off the safety, and stuffed the gun in his jacket pocket, his finger on the trigger.

Malecki, he kept thinking. Lily-white Malecki. But why, for chrissake? The man had everything going for him, why sell out his own country? Certainly not for idealism. He had made that patently clear the other evening at dinner in the Savoy Hotel. Principles were a thing of the past. Roll with the punches. Why?

Mahoney approached the front door with caution and peeked inside. Kominski was lying back in an easy chair in front of a television set, his eyes closed, apparently asleep. His right hand, however, was in the pocket of his flight suit. Probably a pistol. No one else was in the room at the moment.

Across the room Mahoney could see the doors of the Operations and Briefing Center. If Malecki came out now, the operation would definitely be ruined. And yet Mahoney felt he had to take the chance.

He opened the door, went into the Ready Room, and crossed quickly to Kominski.

"Our man just went into the Operations Center," Mahoney said, and Kominski opened his eyes.

"Malecki?"

Mahoney nodded. "You have a gun in your pocket. If you kill him now we'll never know why he killed your general, or who he works for."

"I—"

"I'm going to leave now. But if you shoot him, I'll be coming after you," Mahoney said. He had been keeping an eye on the Ops Center door. He turned and hurried across the Ready Room, out the front door, down the step and across the parking lot where he slipped back into the driver's seat of the Opel.

Wasserman was agitated. "He's ferrying a Lear to Brussels. Scheduled to leave at 0700."

"Is that normal?" Mahoney asked, keeping an eye on the front entrance.

"He's done things like that before, if that's what you mean. Someone probably donated the Lear, and he's found a buyer for it."

"Then we're going to let him go."

"Not if he takes Ben Abel's briefcase."

Mahoney turned to the Mossad chief. "Let's say Malecki does take the briefcase. Then what if you stop him?"

"Then we've uncovered our traitor, and we've stopped the documents from leaving the country."

"And that's all, dammit," Mahoney snapped. He was agitated now. "Who the hell is Malecki working for? Who is his control?"

"I don't care . . ." Wasserman started to say, but then he stiffened, and Mahoney turned back to look across the parking lot. Malecki had come from the Ops Center and was climbing into his car. Mahoney picked up the binoculars lying beside him and brought them to his eyes.

Malecki was carrying a briefcase. Ben Abel's.

"Get the car going and pull up to the front entrance," Mahoney said, and he climbed out of the car as Malecki took off.

Kominski was waiting at the door, his hand in his flight suit pocket, as Mahoney came across the parking lot.

"The sonofabitch killed General Ben Abel," he said loudly. Much more and everyone in the building would know that something was going on.

Mahoney pulled the man away from the door. "Listen to me, and listen to me closely, Kominski, because I'm only going to tell you this once. Malecki is a traitor to your country. He killed your general and he's tried to kill me twice. More than that he's sold your country down the tubes and has been doing so for the past several years. But he's only an employee. If we're going to stop this once and for all, we're going to have to find his boss. Find him and stop him. Do you understand what I'm saying? If you go after him now, we'll never find out who's running him."

Kominski said nothing.

"Goddammit, Captain, I want your word you'll do nothing and go no further with this. At least for the time being."

Kominski finally nodded. "Yes, sir," he said. "I'll give you a chance. But I'm not going to wait very long."

"Good enough," Mahoney said. He turned and went out of the Operations Center building and climbed into the passenger seat of the Opel that Wasserman had brought around to the front entrance.

"Well?" the Mossad chief asked harshly. The radio antenna was still on the roof, and he had the microphone in his right hand.

Mahoney nodded. "He's got Ben Abel's briefcase."

Wasserman paled slightly. "That's it, then," he said,

and he keyed the microphone. "Ops One, this is Mobile Alpha."

"Mobile Alpha, this is Ops One, go," the radio speaker blared from the back seat.

"Wait a moment," Mahoney said sharply. "For God's sake think of what you're doing, Ezra."

Wasserman looked at him for a long moment.

"Mobile Alpha, this is Ops One, go."

"Can you arrange a jet for me to Brussels? Something that would get me there before Malecki touches down?"

"Mobile Alpha, this is Ops One, do you read? Go."

"Ezra?"

Wasserman keyed the microphone. "Ops One, this is Mobile Alpha, stand by a moment."

"I can get you there ahead of Malecki's Lear. But it's too damned dangerous, Mahoney. Those documents . . . if they got out we'd be in big trouble. Not only would everyone know that we had a traitor in our midst, they'd censure us for playing with fire. My God, threatening nuclear war?" Wasserman stopped, awed by the immensity of what could happen.

"I know," Mahoney said. "But if you stop Malecki now, you'll never know who was running him. Sooner or later they'd place someone else here. You'd never be able to trust anyone. And besides, I think Sonja may be involved too."

Wasserman shook his head.

"Malecki was in Washington when Ben Abel was killed. You said so yourself. Which leaves Sonja. You must let me do this my way, Ezra. You must."

"I'd have to talk it over with Begin."

"There's no time."

It was a terrible burden for the Mossad chief. Mahoney knew it intellectually, but he could also see it written all over the man's face.

"You hired me to do a job. Let me finish it. Get me to Brussels ahead of Malecki."

"Damn," Wasserman swore. He keyed the microphone. "Ops One, this is Mobile Alpha."

"Mobile Alpha, this is Ops One, go."

"Have Mr. Gezira telephone me on the flight line."

"Yes, sir. Exactly where will you be?"

"AF one-oh-one."

"Yes, sir."

Wasserman laid the mike down beside him on the seat, put the car in gear, and headed away from the Operations Center toward the Air Force flight line. "There'll be no time to get your things," he said.

"That's all right," Mahoney replied, his heart starting to slow down now that Wasserman was cooperating and Kominski was calmed down at least for the moment. "If I have to stay overnight, I'll buy some things. Just don't send any of your people after me, whatever you do. We're close now—I don't want to screw it up."

"I'm allowing this against my better judgment," Wasserman said.

Mahoney said nothing. He was trying to figure out just why Malecki was involved in something like this. It did not make any sense whatsoever. What in hell did the man have to gain? And how did Sonja fit into it all?

"If those documents of yours fall into the wrong hands . . ." Wasserman started, and Mahoney looked up. "They simply cannot," the Mossad chief said. "It could mean an all-out war."

XVII

TEL AVIV . . . SUNDAY

Malecki's Lear jet accelerated down the runway of Lod Airport, lifted off in the last thousand feet, then was quickly lost into the pale blue morning sky to the west.

Mahoney turned away from the window in the maintenance office of Air Force Hangar 101 as Wasserman was finishing his conference call with Defense Minister Gezira and Begin.

When he put down the telephone and turned around he seemed to have aged by at least ten years in the last few minutes. He rubbed his eyes and the bridge of his nose and then looked up.

"We'll get you there," he said softly.

Mahoney glanced toward the door into the hangar where Gezira's Mirage fighter-interceptor was being prepared for departure.

"Malecki just left," he said.

Wasserman looked toward the window. "We'll get you there on time, but we may run into trouble with the Belgian authorities."

"We can't be held up at the airport," Mahoney said. "If there's any fuss, Malecki will be sure to notice it. If

189

he sees an Israeli military aircraft on the ramp, he'll know that we've tumbled to him."

"I know," Wasserman shouted. "For God's sake, I know!"

Mahoney stood stock-still. Wasserman had been pushed as far as he was going to be pushed. Another word, a motion, anything, and Mahoney was certain the man would blow. And he could not blame him.

Mahoney and Wasserman stood facing each other for a long time until someone came to the door and they both looked that way.

"Come," Wasserman snapped.

The young line chief stuck his head in. "Oh-one is ready whenever you are, sir," he said.

"Be there in a minute, Sergeant," Wasserman said, and he turned back to Mahoney as the young man withdrew. "From this moment on you are not alone in this. I'm alerting our Brussels Station to be on the lookout not only for Malecki, but for you as well."

"It won't work," Mahoney said. He had half expected something like this.

"We're not letting those documents of yours out of our sight."

"And if Malecki gets wind of it? What then? You have to admit that whatever you tell your people in Brussels it will have to be extraordinary. Put a tail on Chaim Malecki, the fair-haired boy of Tel Aviv?"

Wasserman said nothing.

"What about Sonja? Have you given her any thought? Malecki was in Washington the evening Ben Abel was murdered. So who killed him? Sonja, or some other accomplice?"

"You don't understand—" the Mossad chief began, but Mahoney cut him off.

"I think I do. If the documents are taken for real, it

would put Israel in a very difficult spot. I'm sure that Mr. Begin has made that patently clear to you."

"You *don't* understand," Wasserman said with no trace of rancor. "Our allies are more than that term implies. Without the United States or France, let's say, we would not be able to defend ourselves. The airplane out there is a French design, the blueprints are from Switzerland, and the thing was paid for, at least in part, with American dollars. Do you understand that?"

He turned away without acknowledging the fact that Mahoney had nodded.

"Your countrymen have a curious shortcoming in their viewpoint of this part of the world, you know. For an American, a nuclear weapon, a fighter-interceptor, or even an assault rifle is always looked upon as a defensive weapon," He turned back. "Defensive, Mahoney. To even suggest the word preemptive is anathema to your people."

The man was correct as far as he went, Mahoney thought. So what would move him? "I've been out of the intelligence community for some time now, and even during my career I never dealt directly with the Israeli desk."

Wasserman smiled weakly.

"What are you telling me, Ezra? Are you saying that Israel has contemplated using her tactical nuclear weapons? Are you telling me that my funny papers aren't so far off the mark and therefore would be welcomed with open arms as the real thing?"

"How in hell am I supposed to answer that kind of a question?" Wasserman shouted. It almost seemed that he welcomed Mahoney's diversion.

"After al Qaryūt and Ataruz? With the truth."

"Damn," Wasserman swore, turning away. He walked over to the desk, picked up the telephone, held it up to his ear for a long moment, then slammed the instrument back down on its cradle so hard that everything else on the desk jumped. "I didn't want you in on this in the first place," he said.

Mahoney glanced out the window. The updated Mirage that was designated by the Israelis as Kfir (Young Lion) had been pulled out to the ramp. The pilot was standing on the wing getting ready to climb into the cockpit. "Then fire me," he said softly.

Wasserman didn't answer.

"Alert your people in Brussels, and arrest Malecki as soon as he lands. You've got enough evidence on him for a conviction. Then you can pull Sonja in. My guess is that she's done whatever she has out of love for him."

The sun was coming farther into the sky, and as Mahoney stared out the window, an El Al airliner came in on its final approach toward a landing across the field at the civilian airstrip.

"I do have your word, don't I?" Wasserman said almost pathetically.

Mahoney turned around. "You do," he said. He sympathized with the man. This had come as a big blow to him. If Begin himself had been the quisling it could not have been worse.

"Then go," Wasserman said.

"No interference?" Mahoney asked, almost hating the necessity of the question. From across the field he could hear the roar of the reversing jets as the airliner touched down for a landing and started its braking.

"Just be careful. That's all I ask. We're playing with fire here."

BRUSSELS . . . SUNDAY

It took them something under an hour and a half actual flight time to make it the twenty-one hundred miles from Tel Aviv to Brussels, and during that time Mahoney felt he had gotten a handle on Malecki's apparent motivation for selling out his adopted land.

Money.

Brussels was an ancient city that dated back to before the seventh century A.D. when it began in the marshes of the Senne River from a series of Gallo-Roman settlements. By the tenth century, commerce dominated the scene, setting the pace for the city of more than a million. Since that time Brussels had been at the hub of European finances and struggles.

If Geneva was the center of the world economy, then Brussels was at least its counterpart on the European scene.

Sonja had bragged that in the past few years Malecki had raised more than fifty million dollars for Israel. How much of that money had come from selling secrets? And to whom?

When Mahoney had left Tel Aviv the weather had been bright, not a cloud in the sky. But fifty thousand feet over the Swiss Alps, he had seen the first of the frontal system below them. It was like an advancing horde of soldiers assaulting the mountains that at this altitude could be judged only by the deep shadows on their leeward side and not by relative size.

True to his word, Wasserman, through Begin's office, had arranged the landing at Brussel's Zaventem Airport so that absolutely no fuss was made. At least none on the outside where anyone who cared to watch could see.

The Israeli war plane was cleared into Belgian airspace without question, the pilot was given his landing instructions, and the young man rode the invisible electronic beams down through the thick overcast, breaking into the clear less than a mile from the end

of the runway which rushed up to meet them at nearly two hundred knots, the rain spattering against the
windows like a machine gun attack.

They turned off near the end of the runway into a
blue-lit taxiway, away from the civilian terminal. A
bright yellow pickup truck, with a large sign on its
roof that read FOLLOW ME, pulled out in front of
them and led the way at a rapid pace past the private
aviation hangars and onto the government section of
the field, finally slowing down to a bare crawl before
it turned off.

A man dressed in a set of white coveralls, sound-
deadening ear protectors on his head, appeared out
of the mist and waved a set of paddles at them, guid-
ing them into one of the military hangars.

Once they were fully inside, the guide waved the
paddles in a crossing motion, and the young pilot
flipped a number of switches, the jet dying with a
high-pitched whine, and the canopy came open.

The hangar doors were rumbling closed when a
ground crewman shoved a boarding ladder in place
against the Mirage, then scurried up to the open
cockpit where without a word he helped Mahoney
undo his straps and then step over the edge and climb
down to the floor.

Several men, one of them in military uniform,
came from the back of the hangar, and Mahoney
turned toward them as they approached.

"Mr. Mahoney," one of the civilians, an older man
in a severely cut dark suit, said. His voice held a very
heavy French accent.

Mahoney held out his hand but the man ignored it.
The others just stared at him impassively.

"You have been allowed here in our city at our
sufferance for twenty-four hours, not a moment long-

er. It is a personal favor to Mr. Begin."

"On his behalf I would like to thank you, Monsieur—" Mahoney started, but the official ignored his words.

"Your pilot and this aircraft will remain under quarantine in this hangar. A guard will be posted. Once you return here your immediate departure will be required. Are you armed?"

The last question was spoken very harshly, and for a moment Mahoney debated lying to the man. But if they searched him, they would immediately kick him out of Belgium.

"Yes, I am," Mahoney said. "Would you like my weapon?"

The man stepped back and said something to one of the others in a very rapid-fire language that Mahoney took to be Flemish. When he turned back the expression on his face was even more stern.

"We wish only to know the make and caliber."

"It is a .380 Beretta automatic."

"I see," the official said. "While in the city—you may not leave the area without our permission—you will be accompanied at all times by Monsieur Rabinét. He is from Interpol. He will act as your driver and your guide."

"I understand," Mahoney said. This was going to be very delicate. "Do you wish to know the nature of my visit here?"

"I do not," the official said, puffing up. "Suffice it to say, we expect no trouble. Especially none involving any citizen of Belgium or of the North Atlantic Treaty Organization. Do I make myself perfectly clear?"

It was as if someone had just pulled the rug out from under Mahoney. He heard himself answering yes it was perfectly clear, but his thoughts were very far away. He was running down a series of dark, twisted corridors that led from Wasserman and the Mossad, to Malecki and Sonja, and finally to Darrel Switt and the diplomat who had flagged Sonja's departure from Tel Aviv and her subsequent visit to Minnesota.

NATO. Whenever he approached that thought it was as if someone had switched on a blinding light directly in his eyes. He knew that the light should be illuminating something for him. Something deeply hidden, but he could not see it. Yet.

A small, dapper man with thinning gray hair and pince-nez had stepped forward and was introducing himself.

"Pardon me?" Mahoney said, coming out of his momentary shock.

"I said I am Emile Rabinét, monsieur. If you tell me what you require, we may begin at once. Would you like food and drink first?"

Mahoney shook his head. "No. Do you have a car nearby? And is it equipped with a radiotelephone?"

The Interpol officer's eyebrows rose. "Yes," he said.

"With care," the official said to Rabinét in French.

The little police officer turned to him. "Perhaps you wish someone else to handle this, Monsieur Minister . . ." he said softly.

Mahoney had to suppress a smile. Whatever Begin had told the Belgian authorities, there were going to be repercussions, especially if Mahoney lost Malecki and the documents. And now it seemed as if Rabinét was caught in some kind of a power play as well.

"Of course not," the official said. He glanced at

Mahoney, a deep hatred in his eyes, and then he and the others turned and stalked off across the hangar.

"Trebault, I'm afraid, does not like Jews," Rabinét said; watching the others leave. Before Mahoney could comment, he added, "As for me, I am indifferent, although I am frankly intrigued by your presence here. My car is just outside."

Mahoney inclined his head, then followed the little man across the hangar and out a side door into the windblown rain where they climbed into a black Citroën sedan parked in the shadows.

Rabinét started the engine, switched on the windshield wipers, and then turned to Mahoney. "So, monsieur," he said, a slight smile on his lips, "how may I be of service?"

"A man will be landing here soon in a Lear jet. I want to follow him, to see whom he has contact with. Beyond that I cannot tell you a thing."

"I understand," Rabinét said. "For me, my instructions are threefold but simple. To assist you in any way you may require. To make sure you stay out of serious trouble. And when it is over to make a report." He smiled again. "What you do not tell me, I cannot report, n'est-ce pas?"

Mahoney liked the man, and in some respects his help was going to make things somewhat easier here in Brussels.

"If you have the tail number of the aircraft, I will find out when it is due," Rabinét said.

Mahoney gave it to him, and the little man got on the radiotelephone. In a few moments he was speaking with the Zaventem Air Traffic Control supervisor in the tower across the field.

NATO, Mahoney thought again as he half listened to what the policeman was saying. He wanted to back away from that thought, but he could not. Yet it made even less sense than anything else he had come up with on this case.

If—and Mahoney had to admit it was a very large *if*—Malecki was passing Israel's secrets to someone on the NATO staff, what could it possibly mean?

Although Israel was not a member of the North Atlantic Treaty Organization, most of its thirteen member countries were at least sympathetic with Israel's aims. Who then in the alliance would benefit most by knowing Israel's secrets?

"Twenty minutes," Rabinét said, and Mahoney focused on him.

"Through which customs will he be processed?"

"None," Rabinét said. "It seems Monsieur Malecki is merely delivering an airplane. He has already been cleared for the commercial terminal and is booked on a return flight to Tel Aviv which leaves one hour from now."

"He will be restricted to the terminal building then, won't he?" Mahoney asked, trying to think this out.

"*Oui.* As a matter of fact he will be required to remain in the VIP lounge until departure."

"Is there any way you can find out to whom he is delivering the airplane?"

"Not easily," Rabinét said. "Not without attracting a certain amount of attention."

"I see," Mahoney said, not so much because he really did see, but because he needed to think. "Is there someplace where we can watch Malecki get out of the airplane?"

The little policeman shrugged. "The observation deck."

"Have you a pair of binoculars?"

"In the trunk."

"Let's go."

Rabinét drove them across the field where he parked the car in one of the airport's officials' slots, and he and Mahoney went up the stairs to the outside observation deck on the third floor.

The airfield seemed curiously flattened and elongated from this angle, the blue taxiway lights, and the double rows of white runway lights describing odd, angular patterns in the overcast, rainy day.

Mahoney picked out the landing lights of the Lear as it broke out of the overcast to the south, and he watched as the jet slowly touched down for an expert landing, finally identifying the tail numbers when it turned onto a taxiway.

"Is it him?" Rabinét asked.

Mahoney looked away from the binoculars. "Yes."

"Are you expecting trouble?"

"I don't know," Mahoney said. He looked across the field as the Lear came slowly down the taxiway, its strobe light flashing sharply in the mist.

"You're not Jewish, are you," the policeman said.

Mahoney smiled. "No, I'm not," he said. He moved to the left toward a thick stanchion on top of which was a strong light. The detective followed suit, taking up position slightly behind and to the left of Mahoney.

The Lear whined slowly around the east wing of the terminal building, and a ground crewman waved it to a parking slot next to an Icelandic Airways DC-10.

The engines died, the lights went out, and a couple of minutes later the side door opened, and Chaim Malecki stepped down to the tarmac, strode purposefully across the ramp, and entered the building below them. He carried no briefcase.

"Is that your man?" Rabinét asked.

"Yes," Mahoney said absently as he spotted a pair of headlights coming toward the aircraft. It was an automobile, he could see that after a moment, and finally he looked away again from the binoculars as the small gray Opel two-door pulled around behind the Lear and parked near the open hatch.

A short, heavyset man with a thick shock of light-colored hair showing beneath a stocking cap got out of the Opel and climbed aboard the jet.

Mahoney turned the binoculars back to Rabinét. "I want you to take a close look at the man when he gets out of the airplane. See if you recognize him."

Rabinét took the binoculars, but he stared at Mahoney for a long time.

"What is it," Mahoney said. "Do you recognize him already?"

Rabinét shook his head stiffly, almost as if he had a sore neck. "The license plate," he said.

"Yes?" Mahoney asked.

Rabinét turned and brought the binoculars up to his eyes. A few seconds later the man in the knit cap came back out of the airplane, got into the car, and drove away. He was carrying the briefcase.

"Who is it?" Mahoney shouted.

Rabinét seemed to take a long time to lower the binoculars and turn to Mahoney. When he finally did there was an odd, thoughtful expression on his face.

"I do not know what you are involved with, monsieur, but I think you should leave Belgium at once."

Mahoney watched the car disappear into the distance, the nuclear strike documents gone. "Are you going to tell me who he is?"

Rabinét was silent, and Mahoney turned to him.

"Who is he?"

"I do not want this kind of trouble, monsieur. I will not include this in my report," Rabinét said. "His name is Per Larsen. He is a Dane."

"NATO?" Mahoney asked.

Rabinét hesitated a moment longer. "More than that," he said at last. "He is the chief of operations for ININ. Inter-NATO Intelligence Network."

The sun was just beginning to wreath the uppermost Gothic spires of the Church of St. Gudule in a pink glow, when the short, heavyset man threw open the front windows of his apartment. Overnight the cold front had passed, leaving the air of downtown Brussels with a scrubbed smell.

Per Larsen breathed deeply of the fresh morning air as if the action could in some small measure relieve the unbelievable tension he felt.

He had worked through the night on the Israeli documents, painfully translating a line here, a snatch of a phrase there, a key word in another section.

Larsen was not a stupid man; on the contrary, he was quite intelligent. However, translating something as complex as the documents he had been given from one very difficult language foreign to his own into another foreign language was decidedly taxing.

With a horror that had mounted through the night, the man had begun to get a glimmer of what he had in his hands. And minutes ago, when he finally got up from his work-laden desk, he knew full well what he had and was deeply disturbed.

The very thing that had frightened and changed the world since 1945 appeared to be on the verge of actually *happening. It was incredible. Almost too incredible.*

Larsen turned away from the window after a time, went back to his desk, and picked up the telephone. When he had the long-distance operator on the line, he gave her a number in Geneva, Switzerland. The connection was made quickly, because at this hour the trunk lines were not busy, and the number was answered on the third ring by a soothing, well-modulated voice.

"*Yes.*"

"*This is Wildflower,*" *Larsen spoke softly into the mouthpiece.*

"*Yes.*"

"*Something very extraordinary has happened. We must meet.*"

PART TWO
THE GENEVA COVENANT

XVIII

LOD . . . SUNDAY

It seemed to Mahoney that he had gone from day into night when he had flown to Brussels, and now that he was returning to Tel Aviv, it was as if he had made a second transition, and yet it had all happened in the same day. He was hungry, he was tired, his mouth tasted of rubber from the oxygen mask, and most of all he was awed.

God help him, but all of this time he had thought of Israel and her problems as small stuff. A spy in the middle of the government giving or selling secrets to the Arabs, or perhaps even to the Soviets, was small potatoes by comparison to the problems faced by the United States. But it wasn't so. It had never been, he could see that now.

Mahoney let his thoughts wander back and forth: to Rabinét, the little Interpol detective the Belgians had sent out as his watchdog; to how Malecki had appeared as he strode across the tarmac and entered the terminal building; to the frigid reception he had received in the hangar; and finally to NATO in the person of Per Larsen, chief of ININ.

NATO. The entire concept and its blinding ramifications were nothing less than stunning. Lily-white Malecki passing Israel's secrets to a man who was privy to the secrets through routine channels anyway. Where was the flaw?

The Mossad and the CIA had always maintained a warm liaison that if not totally open, was nearly so. Through the quarterly summaries, NATO ministers were advised of the Mid-East situation, the information used in their war games and strategy sessions. Per Larsen was a vital part of those gatherings.

Exactly what was it that Malecki was passing to the man? Where in God's name was the flaw? The incongruity?

The grinding of the landing gear motors brought Mahoney out of his thoughts, and he looked up as the Mirage slid down the invisible electronic beams toward the end of the main east-west runway at Lod Airport. Tel Aviv was below and behind them now, sparkling in the bright afternoon sun.

Wasserman would have to be made to understand that this business was not finished yet. There were too many questions that would never be answered if Malecki was simply arrested.

He could see a commercial airliner waiting on the taxiway for its turn to pull out on the runway and take off.

Had Per Larsen ordered the bomb in the luggage locker at the Athens airport? Had he engineered the murder of Ben Abel? Or the killings at Ataruz?

The fighter-interceptor crossed over the string of approach lights and, just beyond the end-of-runway marker stripes, touched down with a sharp bark of its tires.

Lily-white Malecki. Perhaps the secrets he gathered were offered up to the highest bidder. NATO would be interested in Israel's plans for preemptive nuclear strikes —something the Mossad would have shared with its allies. A nuclear war in the Mid-East could drag the entire world down the drain. The Lebanese, of course, would have been interested in al Qaryút as a spy satellite receiving station. And then there was another tantalizing thought. How about the U.S.? What secrets might his own government have purchased this way?

They turned down a taxiway and bumped across the field toward the military hangars as the young pilot opened the canopy, letting the hot, dry outside air fill the cockpit.

In the distance, Mahoney could see Wasserman's car parked in front of the hangar, and as the Mirage approached, the car door opened and Wasserman got out.

They pulled across the parking ramp, and just in front of the open hangar doors a ground crewman waved his paddles, and the young pilot killed the engine. A moment later two other crewmen shoved a boarding ladder to the side of the jet, and one of them scrambled up and helped Mahoney undo his straps and then helped him step over the edge of the cockpit and down the ladder.

"Thanks for the ride," Mahoney said as his pilot was climbing out of the cockpit. The young man grinned down at him.

"Any time, sir," he said.

Mahoney turned and went across to where Wasserman stood by his open car door. His suit looked rumpled, as if he had slept in it, his open collar exposing a tuft of white chest hair. His eyes were red.

"You didn't bring it back," he said softly.

"No," Mahoney said. They stood a couple of feet apart, facing each other.

Wasserman visibly paled, and for a second it seemed as if he was going to collapse. "You lost him?"

"Malecki is on his way back here aboard a commercial airliner."

"With the briefcase?"

"No. He delivered it."

"Who has the files, Mahoney? Where did they go?"

Wasserman seemed like a man on the verge of drowning, holding his hands out for a rope or at least a life jacket.

"Lets go someplace where we can talk, Ezra."

"Where are the files? Who has them?"

"He left them on the plane. Someone came a minute or two later and took them. It was all arranged. Very neat . . ."

"For God's sake, who has them?"

"Per Larsen, the chief of NATO's intelligence network."

The play of emotions across Wasserman's face was so intense it was almost frightening. It was as if the man had just been told his wife and child had been murdered.

"You didn't follow him? You didn't try to stop it?"

"I couldn't. I was ordered to leave the country."

Wasserman passed a hand over his eyes. "Someone else is in on this? Someone else knows?"

"An Interpol detective. But he only knows that I was there following Malecki. He has no idea what the files contain."

Wasserman turned away and looked at his car. "You've blown it, Mahoney. You've put us into an untenable position." He turned back. "You do realize that, don't you? I mean, you do understand what you've done, don't you?"

"Yes, I do, Ezra. But I don't think you understand the significance of what is happening here . . . what has been happening."

Wasserman tried to wave it off, but Mahoney continued.

"Malecki is reporting not to a Russian, or a Syrian, or a Lebanese. He's not reporting to one of Israel's enemies. He's reporting to the chief of NATO's intelligence unit. Doesn't that tell you anything?"

Wasserman blinked. "You don't really give a damn, do you?" he said. "I mean, when this is all over with you're going to waltz back home and you're not going to have to worry about it."

"Listen to me, goddammit," Mahoney snapped. "Larsen is only a buffer. A messenger boy. I'm sure of it. Who does he report to?"

"It doesn't matter," Wasserman said.

"You're wrong—it *does* matter! Damn! Use your head, Ezra. Malecki didn't kill Ben Abel, and neither did Per Larsen. So who?"

Wasserman was silent.

"Who ordered the attack on al Qaryūt, and why were the troops at Ataruz murdered? That's not the work of the chief of NATO intelligence."

Wasserman turned without a word and climbed into his car.

"I'll need a place to work," Mahoney said. "Somewhere other than the safe house. Someplace where you can come and go without questions being raised."

Wasserman started the engine as Mahoney hurried around to the passenger side and climbed in.

"It's over, Mahoney," the Mossad chief said, his voice now deadly calm. "Pack your bags. You're leaving on the first available flight out."

"And then what?"

"And then we're going to lick our wounds. Try to pick up the pieces. I'm sure Mr. Begin will be in contact with your president. We'll have to tell him everything now."

"And Malecki?"

"Will be arrested and tried as a spy."

"Per Larsen?"

"The United States *is* NATO. They'll handle it."

Mahoney closed his eyes for a moment as he tried to put it all together, as he tried to make some sense of it. Something was missing, something very vital that would tie it all together. It was just below the surface, and he could almost see it, could almost reach out and touch it.

"The CIA knew that Sonja was coming out to see me," Mahoney said after a moment.

"I know that," Wasserman replied. "They followed her to Paris and then on to Berlin. They killed one of my investigators."

Mahoney snapped around. "What?"

"There were five of them. Sonja came up with Identi-kit drawings on all of them. One of them has been nailed as an Agency legman."

"How about the other four, Ezra?"

"Two teams. One followed her as far as New York, the other on to Paris."

"But they haven't been identified yet?"

"No," Wasserman said. "But the transition between the single legman and the two teams was too smooth not to be coordinated."

Mahoney's mind was racing. "Three days, Ezra," he said, focusing on the man. "It's all I'm asking."

"To do what?"

"To finish what you hired me to do. To pick up the pieces for you."

Wasserman shook his head. "You've already caused · enough damage."

"Three days, Ezra. I'll agree to any conditions you impose on me, but just give me three days."

Wasserman said nothing. He was obviously under a great strain. Mahoney could see a small blood vessel throbbing at his temple.

"You have nothing further to lose, and possibly everything to gain," Mahoney said. "And besides, there's Sonja to consider."

"What about her?" Wasserman almost shouted.

"She's almost certainly involved in this thing. You do want to know for sure, don't you?"

Wasserman's head dropped. "You're a ruthless sonofabitch, Mahoney," he said.

TEL AVIV . . . SUNDAY NIGHT

Wasserman's unpretentious home in Kfar Shalem, a pleasant suburb in Tel Aviv's southeast quarter, became Mahoney's new operational headquarters. It was situated a few blocks off the busy Derech Lod in an area of peace and solitude, exactly the kind of place that suited the Mossad chief's personality. The house itself had been reconstructed a few years earlier to Department of Defense specifications for any new building in the city, with a thick roof and twenty-four-inch-thick courtyard walls to withstand mortar and automatic weapons fire. Each and every new building in Israel was being constructed to serve as an individual fortress in case the country was ever overrun. Each building had its own supply of food, water, weapons, and ammunition for a very long siege.

This insulation from the outside world was perfect for Wasserman. When he was home he could feel snug and very safe from his outside worries.

Wasserman's wife, Elizabeth, fit the house very well, almost as if she were one of its installations. She was a quiet, soft-spoken woman who doted on her husband, but never to the point of distraction. She was there whenever he needed a comfort, but absent or silent whenever that was his need.

If the woman knew or suspected that something extraordinary was afoot between her husband and his guest, she made no mention of it. Not even the tiniest hint that she found Mahoney's sudden presence unusual. It was as if Mahoney were a favorite uncle who had shown up after a long absence from a household that he was expected to treat as his own.

The Wassermans' two daughters were married, and their only son, David (named after David Ben Abel), was a captain in the Air Force and would not be home on leave for months. And, since Ezra and his wife seldom if ever entertained, there was little likelihood that Mahoney's sojourn would be disturbed.

His room was at the back of the house, a single window overlooking a pocket-size rose garden that Wasserman tended during his off-duty hours. A narrow bed with a clothes trunk at the foot of it took up one wall, and along the opposite was a small desk beside which was a bookcase. Model airplanes hung from the ceiling over the desk, and sports trophies gathered dust in the bookcase.

Later that first afternoon, while Mahoney was eating a light lunch, Wasserman went downtown where he purchased a few items of clothing and a number of toilet articles. Mahoney's suitcase was still at Malecki's home, and there was no way at the moment of retrieving it without causing too much suspicion.

At Mossad headquarters, Wasserman pulled out the entire series file on Malecki, including the master index of his operations but not the operational files themselves.

Back at the house he dumped the pile on the bed in Mahoney's room, and offered only three conditions.

"You'll have to do your studying at night; these files have to be returned each morning. You're not to leave the house without first informing me. And finally you're not to use the telephone."

"Fine," Mahoney said absently as he picked up the bundle of files from the bed and brought them over to the desk.

"Are you going to need help with this?" Wasserman asked. Now that he was committed to going along with Mahoney at least for three days, his anger seemed to have evaporated.

"Not for now," Mahoney said, looking up. "But what about my absence from Malecki's house?"

"No one but Mr. Begin will know where you are or what you're doing. We're going to keep it that way for the moment. If either of them ask me, I'll simply tell them I don't know."

Mahoney looked at his watch. It was just a few minutes after eight in the evening. "Get some sleep tonight, Ezra. You look as if you could use it. If I have any questions, they can wait until morning."

Wasserman looked at the stack of file folders on the desk. "This batch is in English. The analysis and specific operational jackets are in Hebrew."

"Why is that?"

Wasserman had to smile. "Hebrew is too unwieldy a language to be used for Records Keeping, no matter what the Information Ministry says to the contrary."

"How about the operational jackets?"

"Tomorrow night," Wasserman said. "I'll have to go over them with you."

Malecki, Chaim Dennis. Background Investigation completed 23 November 1966, the index tab on the first file read. Inside the front cover the buck slip was covered with a dozen different sets of initials and dates ranging from early February of 1966 until mid-November of the same year.

The second file, marked *Malecki, Chaim Dennis,* carried the subtitle *Personality Profiles From Field Investi-*

gations. A third and fourth were marked *Educational Contact Summaries* and *Work Experience Contact Summaries.*

Other files in the stack Wasserman had brought contained detailed psychological test and interview results, records of Malecki's financial holdings and dealings, commendations from a large number of high-ranking Israeli government officials (including Wasserman himself), and a very detailed accounting of his fund raising activities from the very beginnings in 1967 until as recently as the Stewart Graham will last week.

Mahoney had to admit to himself that he had no real idea what he was looking for other than a clue as to Malecki's motivation for turning traitor to his adopted country. But he had the vague hope that somewhere in the pile would be a hint of why Per Larsen was his contact. Perhaps they were old school chums, perhaps family friends, perhaps it was deeper than that.

At first, in his reading, Mahoney picked and chose the topics he pursued, much like a man at a smorgasbord might sample the dishes in order to find the few most appetizing to him. Later he delved more deeply into the specifics of the man's life.

Malecki had been born into wealth but of the self-made, shirt-sleeved variety that apparently did not sit well with the rank and file Boston monied set.

His father, Levi Malecki, had emigrated from England in 1920, worked as a common laborer in a number of factories in New Jersey until 1924 when he invented a new process for manufacturing wire racks such as the ones found in iceboxes or kitchen ovens.

Malecki Wire Rack Company flourished, and in 1927 Levi married Deborah Bernstein, they bought a house in Queens and, for an investment, a small weekly newspaper in Brooklyn. In 1928 their first child was born dead, in 1929 a second child was stillborn, and 1931 the Maleckis, now millionaires, moved to Boston from where they began buying as many newspapers as they could with the profits from the wire rack company.

When the electric refrigerator began to replace the ice-box, Malecki's racks made the transition, and Levi bought more newspapers. When wood-burning kitchen stoves disappeared, totally replaced by gas or electric ranges, Malecki's racks made the change, and Levi bought even more newspapers. The company had weathered the Depression and seemed to thrive on change.

By 1934 Levi and Deborah were sustaining members of a number of symphony orchestras, libraries, and Gifted and Talented Youth Centers across the eastern seaboard, and in addition to the wire rack business, owned 17 newspapers mostly in the Midwest and East.

In 1936 Chaim was born, his mother dying on the table giving birth to him. From what Mahoney could gather from his reading, Chaim's father put the same amount of energy into raising his son that he was putting into the creation and maintenance of his business.

At the age of four young Malecki could read and write, and at five, after only one year of public schooling, it was decided to place the boy in a special school in New Hampshire.

There was little information for this period of Chaim Malecki's life, other than the fact that he apparently did outstandingly well. His father's business continued to grow during the war because of government contracts. His company supplied all the wire racks for military field kitchens, and his newspapers supplied the war news for a hungry public.

In 1952 Chaim graduated from the New Hampshire School for Gifted Children and was immediately accepted as an honors student at Harvard where he studied political science, graduating three years later in 1955, summa cum laude.

The next year he was accepted as a Rhodes scholar at Oxford where he studied history and law at All Souls College, returning to Boston in 1957.

One month later, Levi Malecki suffered a near fatal heart attack, and for the next three years Chaim ran the wire rack business, going public with it in 1959, and turning over its complete control to a board of directors in 1960. That same year his father, fully recovered, returned to the newspaper business.

At five o'clock in the morning Mahoney got up stiffly from the desk and went into the bathroom where he splashed some cold water on his face. Then he went to the window and stared out into the predawn darkness.

Lily-white Malecki. In 1960 he went to work as a political science reporter for the Washington *Post,* and for the next six years he covered not only the Congress but was also accredited as a foreign correspondent, spending a few months in Berlin, six months in Paris, nine months in South Africa, and briefer stints in a half dozen other cities around the world, including ninety days in Moscow in 1965.

Boston society had never accepted his father and mother for a variety of reasons: they were nouveau riche, hardly better than common workmen; Levi was an immigrant; and, worst of all, they were Jews.

Chaim, on the other hand, was accepted in Washington as well as back in Boston, in part because he had been a Rhodes scholar, in part because of his connections with the government, and in a large part because he was young, handsome, and rich (now that the money was at least second generation, never mind where it came from).

Mahoney turned away from the window and went back to the desk where he neatly stacked the files for Wasserman, who would be returning them to Mossad archives in a few hours.

Something happened in 1966, something that had not been explained in any of Malecki's records, that changed his entire life.

Suddenly, and for no apparent reason, Chaim applied for and was accepted as a landed immigrant in Israel. Up to that point his life had been outstanding. What had happened to him to suddenly and so dramatically make him change his mind about the United States?

Mahoney went to bed where he lay on top of the covers and closed his eyes. Where were the inconsistencies in Malecki's life that caused him to become a traitor to Israel? Or, Mahoney wondered as he dropped off to sleep, had Malecki come to Israel in 1966 for the specific purpose of spying?

XIX

TEL AVIV . . . MONDAY NOON

Mahoney had awakened briefly at 6:30 when
Wasserman entered his room to retrieve the Malecki
files, and they had spoken for a couple of minutes.
Wasserman had promised to return the financial eval-
uation folders as well as a large sampling of Malecki's
operational files this evening. And then he had left.

Someone was at the door in what seemed like only a
few seconds later, and Mahoney opened his eyes assuming it was Wasserman again.

"Come in, Ezra," he said, sitting up.

The door opened, but it was Wasserman's wife, a
troubled expression on her face. "I hate to disturb you,
Mr. Mahoney but you have a visitor."

"What?" Mahoney said, confused. He wasn't quite
awake yet. "Has Ezra already left for work?"

"Heavens, yes," the woman said. "Hours ago. It's
nearly noon."

Mahoney looked at his watch which showed it was
just a few minutes before twelve, and the sleep finally
began to clear from his befuddled brain. "A visitor?" he
asked.

"It's Sonja. She's waiting in the courtyard for you."

Mahoney swung his legs over the edge of the bed and got to his feet, fully awake now, the news of Sonja's presence disturbing.

"Have you telephoned Ezra?" he asked.

"He's in conference, but I left a message for him to call."

"All right," Mahoney said, trying to organize his thoughts. How in hell had Sonja found out he was here? And what did she want? "Tell her I'll be with her in a minute or two. But don't make any further telephone calls, and don't leave the house."

"I don't understand," the woman said. "It's just Sonja."

"Your telephone may be monitored, Mrs. Wasserman, and there is a good chance that this house is under surveillance."

Her right hand went to her mouth. "Oh," she said, and she turned and left the room.

Mahoney went into the bathroom where he washed his hands and face, combed his silvery white hair, and then back in the bedroom put on his jacket, first making sure the Beretta was still in the pocket before he went out.

Sonja was waiting in the courtyard just inside the front gate, but before Mahoney went out he watched her for a few moments from a small window beside the door in the front hall.

She was wearing sandals with no nylons, a plain khaki skirt and blouse, her hair was done up with a bright red band, and she carried a moderately large shoulder bag. She was clearly nervous, and as he observed her she fumbled in her purse for a cigarette, which she lit with shaking hands.

Wasserman's wife came from the back of the house.

"Will you be going out, Mr. Mahoney?" she asked soft-ly.

Mahoney turned away from the window. "I may," he said.

The woman seemed embarrassed. "I'll have to inform my husband when he calls."

"By all means," Mahoney said, smiling. "Tell him I'll be back as soon as possible."

The woman nodded, and Mahoney turned and went out to Sonja who spun around at the sound of the door opening.

"Thank God I've found you," she said, coming across to him.

"How did you know I was here?"

"I didn't," she said. She was on the verge of tears. "You weren't at the Kfar Saba apartment, and your things are still at the house. This was the only place I could think of here in Tel Aviv."

"What's happened, Sonja?"

"We've got to talk. You've got to help me."

Mahoney reached for her arm. "Come inside. Ezra's wife can fix us some tea."

"No," she said, shrinking back. "She'll call Uncle Ezra, and he'll come right home to find out why I'm here."

"He'll find out anyway," Mahoney said.

"I know," she said, distraught. "But first you have to listen to me."

"All right," Mahoney said. "Where do you want to go?"

"My car is out front. We'll go for a ride."

Mahoney's eyes narrowed. "Where is Chaim right now?"

Sonja reacted almost as if she had been slapped. "Please," she said. "Not here."

Mahoney hesitated a moment longer, but finally he nodded and went out the front gate with her where they climbed into her open-topped Triumph sportscar. Something obviously extraordinary had happened to put Sonja in such a state, and the only thing Mahoney could think of at this moment were the Operation Wrath documents, and the fact that they now knew Malecki was the traitor. Had Sonja somehow found out about all that?

She drove at a reasonable speed south of the city, through Jaffa, and then down the seacoast highway toward the resort town of Palmahim. They had been gone for nearly half an hour before she finally spoke.

"Chaim is working at the house. He's been there since he returned from Brussels," she said. She seemed somewhat calmer now that they were away from Wasserman's house.

Mahoney had a queer feeling at the pit of his stomach. "What was he doing in Brussels?"

Sonja glanced at him. "About a month ago he was given a Lear jet as a contribution. He had a buyer for it in Brussels, so he had to ferry it there."

"But that's not what you came to tell me," Mahoney said, his heart slowing down.

She shook her head without taking her eyes off the road. "Someone tried to kill him."

For a seeming eternity Mahoney just stared at the young woman, what she had just said hanging in front of him like a dark cloud of smoke. It was as if he found himself in suspended animation for those seconds. His heart seemed to have stopped.

"When did this happen?" he heard himself asking, as if his voice were coming from a distance.

"This morning," Sonja said, apparently not understanding his shock. "We were having breakfast in the garden. Someone fired at him. Chaim said it was a rifle, and he thinks the shots came from one of the dormitory rooms on the university campus."

"How many shots?"

"Three . . . we think," Sonja said. "The first hit the table just an inch away from Chaim. The second hit his chair an instant after he had jumped away, and the third ricocheted off the patio blocks. But by then we were safe, behind the wall."

"What happened next?"

"I wanted to call the police, or at least Uncle Ezra, but Chaim wouldn't hear of it. He said he would handle it himself. He said he had a good idea who might have done it."

"Did he tell you who?"

"No," Sonja said in a small voice.

"And you haven't discussed this with Ezra?"

"No," she said. "There was no one else for me to turn to except you."

Mahoney had a very good idea who had attempted to kill Malecki, and why. But he wondered who Malecki's chief suspect was, and how it would affect the investigation. If Malecki became spooked now, he might run, and then they would have trouble picking up the pieces.

"I'll help you," he said after a few moments of silence. "But you'll have to promise me that you won't tell Chaim that you came to see me today."

"Why would someone try to kill him?" Sonja asked.

"I don't know for sure," Mahoney said, thoughtfully. "But I have to ask you something."

She said nothing, waiting for him to continue. They were well south of Tel Aviv now, the Mediterranean to their right.

"Why did Chaim quit his job with the Washington *Post* in '66 and emigrate to Israel?"

Sonja looked at him with new fear in her eyes. "You've been in Chaim's records. Why—" She broke it off in mid-sentence. "My God, you suspect him of being the traitor."

"I suspect everyone, Sonja, including you," Mahoney said. "Can you tell me what happened to Chaim in '66 to suddenly make him pull up stakes and come here?"

It took her a long time to answer, but Mahoney had no way of knowing if her hesitation was because she was still in shock, or because she was trying to think of the proper response.

"I don't know," she finally said.

"You've got to help me if I'm to uncover your mole."

"I don't know," she shouted. "I don't know. He never told me."

"You never discussed his past? His Washington days?"

She nodded. "We talked about his parents, and about Boston mostly, but he did tell me once that he thought being a newspaperman was for little boys. Chasing ambulances and going to fires and all that. He said it was a good way to find out about the world in a hurry, but it was just like school. You did it for a while, graduated, then went on with your life."

"Did he ever mention any friends in the States?"

"Mostly newspaper cronies. But he was never close with anyone," Sonja said. She glanced over at Mahoney again. "He still isn't close to anyone except for me."

"Does the name Per Larsen mean anything to you?" Mahoney asked after a few moments.

"No," Sonja said, shaking her head. "I don't think so. Has he got something to do with this?"

"Perhaps. But I don't want you to mention his name to anyone."

"Not even Chaim?"

Mahoney nodded.

They came a few minutes later to the outskirts of Palmahim, and Sonja pulled over to the side of the road and turned the car around. Before she headed back into Tel Aviv she pulled a cigarette from her purse and lit it.

"If it's Chaim . . . I mean if you find out that he's involved in this . . . you'll tell me, won't you?" she asked.

Mahoney knew damned well that she was involved somehow in this thing, and yet he found himself feeling sorry for her. She seemed like a lost little girl trying desperately to find her own niche.

"He's a lonely man, Mr. Mahoney," she said finally. "It's one of the reasons I love him so. He needs me."

"I know," Mahoney said gently.

Sonja had dropped Mahoney back at the house around 1:30, and he let himself in through the front gate. Wasserman was waiting for him in the vestibule, a strained, nervous look about him.

"How did she know you were here?" he said.

"She told me she guessed," Mahoney said, closing the front door behind him and coming across the entry hall. "Ben Abel's ADC, Kominski, has to be picked up."

"Why?"

"Someone tried to kill Malecki this morning. Shots were fired from a university dormitory. It was probably Kominski."

"Is that what she came here to tell you?"

Mahoney nodded. "We're going to have to work very fast now, Ezra."

"Does she know Malecki is the traitor?"

"Not for sure. But she knows that we suspect him."

"She'll tell him—" Wasserman started to say, but Mahoney cut him off.

"Not yet. He's in danger now, and she'll do everything within her power to protect him, including coming to me for help."

"I almost wish he had nailed the bastard," Wasserman said. Forty-eight hours ago Malecki was the fair-haired boy. Now he was the Devil.

"Have you any idea where Kominski is at the moment?"

"On leave. He went down to Hebron to stay with friends."

"It's a safe bet he's not there, but check it out anyway, and then have him picked up and put under wraps somewhere. But quietly."

"And then what, Mahoney?" Wasserman snapped. "Mr. Begin gave you the three days you asked for. You have forty-eight hours left. Did you come up with anything last night?"

"Nothing but questions," Mahoney had to admit. "I'm going to have to see Malecki's operational files. The entire works."

"There's too many there. Even if I could bring them by the truckload, you wouldn't have the time."

Mahoney had expected that. "Then you're going to get me into Mossad archives, and between the two of us we'll go through the pile."

The house was totally silent for a long time, and Mahoney found himself wondering where Ezra's wife was, and what she was doing.

"I can hear it now," Wasserman finally spoke.

"Hear what, Ezra?"

"The entire mess falling down around our ears. Mr. Begin's government is in trouble, serious trouble. If the opposition party got wind . . . even a hint that I had taken a foreigner, a former CIA agent, into Mossad archives, we'd all be lined up against the wall and shot."

"So you arrest Malecki and inform my government that he passed bogus nuclear strike documents to the chief of ININ."

"That's right."

"Why weren't your bosom buddies the Americans told in the first place that you had a traitor at high levels? Why didn't you scream and shout when your Paris legman was murdered in Berlin . . . apparently by the CIA? Why hadn't Mr. Begin called earlier with the suspicion that one of America's former finest was your traitor? Have you the answers, Ezra?"

Wasserman seemed battered.

"Every American schoolchild knows about the Holocaust and the fact that your enemies today are threatening the very same thing. Ben Abel told me that the threat of the ultimate bloodbath is never far from any Israeli's mind."

"What are you driving at?"

"Operation Wrath, Ezra. Is it so farfetched?"

"The place is staffed twenty-four hours a day. There are literally dozens of people coming and going at any given time. Malecki would find out that you had been there."

"He'd come to you, and you could tell him anything you wanted."

"He'd run."

"I don't think so, Ezra. If you can get Kominski out of the way, I think Malecki will have to stick around at least long enough to confirm the validity of the Operation Wrath files he passed to Larsen. It's too big for him to pass up. Besides, he's nervous about me. He'll have to make sure what I'm up to."

"What would you be looking for in Malecki's operational jackets?"

"I don't know," Mahoney admitted. "Except that I want to know if Malecki has had other dealings with Per Larsen."

TEL AVIV . . . MONDAY NIGHT

The Mossad's Records Keeping Center was through a

heavy steel door down one flight of cement stairs from the main Finance Annex entrance. It was a rat's maze of dimly lit rooms and corridors that honeycombed the entire area beneath the courtyard and shops.

Just inside the door Wasserman signed in with the duty desk sergeant posted in a tiny alcove. A faded poster on the wall next to the entryway door read LOCK YOUR BRIEFCASE AND YOUR LIPS. Another poster directly beneath it showed a crude drawing of an Arab soldier and advised THE ENEMY IS LISTENING. They were in English, and from the looks of them Mahoney guessed they had been up since the War of Independence.

"How's the weather out there, sir," the sergeant asked, speaking to Wasserman but eyeing Mahoney.

"Hot," Wasserman said, writing Mahoney's name behind his own in the book.

"Then we have the advantage down here, sir," the sergeant said. "Shall I call Mr. Breitlow for you?"

"It's not necessary," Wasserman said. "Who's the duty clerk this afternoon?"

"It's Grace today, sir," the sergeant said as he pulled two plastic badges from a rack behind him and handed them across.

Mahoney followed Wasserman across the alcove, the sergeant buzzed the inner door, and Wasserman pulled it open. Before they went inside, however, he turned back to the duty desk man.

"No one is to look at the book," he said. "And as far as you're concerned, you haven't seen me all day."

The sergeant smiled. "Got you, sir. Mum's the word."

They went inside, the door automatically closing and latching behind them, then went down a narrow corridor, through a wide archway, and into Customer Service. The room was small, like a miniature rendition of a library reading room. Several tables were set up in rows. Along two walls were floor to ceiling steel shelving that contained world atlases, telephone directories for major capital cities, transportation timetables, foreign-language dictionaries, and a plethora of day-to-day non-classified information useful in mission preplanning sessions.

At the far end of the room was a long counter staffed by two clerks who had at their service a half dozen runners, young people mostly, whose job it was to do the actual fetching of the files from the stacks and then hand deliver them either there or upstairs.

The two clerks were busy behind the counter as Wasserman and Mahoney approached, but the runners were all off somewhere, and the only other person in the room at the moment was a younger man seated at a table piled high with files.

"Good afternoon, sir," he said, looking up.

Wasserman nodded but said nothing, and then they were at the counter looking into the unsmiling eyes of a tall, very gaunt woman who was probably in her mid to late sixties.

"What brings you down here, Ezra?" the woman said softly, without whispering. "I thought we had passed with flying colors."

"Work this time, Grace," Wasserman said, leaning forward slightly. "Thought I'd save us all some time by coming down in person. We may have to pull a lot of jackets."

"We?" the woman said, her right eyebrow arching. She did not look at Mahoney.

"I'll need a runner at my disposal," Wasserman said, ignoring the question. "Someone who can stay late. We may be here for several hours."

The woman seemed to hesitate a moment, then sighed

deeply and turned to the other clerk who was watching
the exchange wide-eyed. Wasserman's presence here was
somewhat odd, but the presence of a stranger was
unheard-of.

"You're running the show, sweetie. If you get
swamped, call the night clerk in."

She turned back. "What's first on the agenda, Ezra?"

"We're going to want to see a number of Chaim
Malecki's operational jackets. But we'd better start with
the index—since January, I suppose."

"Are the indexes in yearly volumes?" Mahoney asked.

"In this case, yes," Wasserman answered.

"Let's have last year's as well, then."

For a moment it seemed as if the woman was going to
resist the request, but then she sighed deeply again, came
around the corner, and indicated one of the empty
tables. "Have a seat, I'll be with you in a moment." she
said, and then she quickly crossed the room and disappeared through a doorway into the file rooms themselves.

By the time Mahoney and Wasserman were seated,
the woman was back, carrying two large, bound volumes against her bosom. Before she handed them to
Wasserman she had him initial two requisition slips, and
then she went back behind the counter.

Stamped in red letters on the spine of each volume
was Malecki's name, behind which was the year, 1980
for the first volume, 1981 for the second.

Mahoney opened the first book and scanned a couple
of pages before he looked up. "It's in English."

"The individual operational files will be in Hebrew,"
Wasserman said. "If you could tell me what you're looking for, this might go a little faster."

"I don't know what I'm looking for, Ezra," he said.
He pulled off his jacket and draped it over the back of

his chair, then loosened his tie as Wasserman went over
to the counter and got a thick pad of paper and a half
dozen pencils.

The index volume had its own week-by-week index
which filled the first few pages. And at first Mahoney
merely sampled a few of the entries to determine exactly
what the book contained.

For the week of February third through the ninth,
Malecki was in Berlin, the volume's index read. Behind
that entry were a series of intials and codes—authorization data, Mahoney supposed—and then page reference numbers.

He turned to the indicated pages and quickly scanned
the neatly handwritten account of Malecki's visit to Berlin, which was capped off with a long series of seven-
digit alpha-numeric codes.

He held the book for Wasserman to see and pointed
at the numbers. "Actual file references?"

Wasserman nodded. "Do you want those?"

"No," Mahoney said, pulling the book back and
opening it again to the index. During the next fifteen
minutes he quickly jotted down the appropriate page
numbers for each of the eleven times Malecki visited
Washington, D.C., in 1980.

Next he turned to the appropriate pages in the volume
for each visit and made note of the kinds of things
Malecki had done.

The volume was even more than an operational index;
it was a day-by-day personal diary on the man. On one
of his trips to Washington he had given a press briefing
on several new kibbutzim in the Golan Heights. On another occasion he drove up to Boston to visit with his
father who was now living in an exclusive nursing home.

On four of his trips, however, Malecki had attended
cocktail parties and dinners of various sorts, among

them two political fund-raisers, one embassy get-together, and in October, the birthday party for a prominent U.S. senator's daughter.

"How about the file reference numbers?" he asked, looking up at Wasserman who had been thumbing through the 1981 volume.

"What about them?"

"How do I know what they refer to . . . specifically?"

Wasserman looked at the book. "The birthday party he attended generated a half dozen files, most of them three-hundred-A series, which report the results of personal contacts."

"All three-hundred-A files are Malecki's written reports on the kinds of things he learned from various people at the gatherings he attended?"

"Something like that," Wasserman said.

"How about the other references? There is a nine-hundred-B for every party he's gone to."

"That's the nuts and bolts file. Guest lists . . . even though he might not have had a chance to speak with them all. Menus. Timetables. Things like that."

Mahoney glanced down at the list of file indexes for the birthday party. "And the one-hundred-A?"

Wasserman seemed suddenly uncomfortable. "Specific objectives with results."

Mahoney had to smile. "Malecki went to the girl's birthday party for a specific operational purpose?"

"I don't remember all the details, but I think it had to do with the fact that her father was campaigning for a reduction in military aid to us. He was at the party, of course. We had to know what his thinking was. And that's as honest as I can be with you."

"I appreciate it, Ezra," Mahoney said, and he turned back to the entries for the four trips and jotted down several file reference numbers that he wanted to see. For each party he had included the 900B . . . the guest list file.

It took the clerk less than ten minutes to return with the dozen or so folders, some of them quite thick, and lay them down on the table. Again Wasserman had to sign the requisition slips.

Mahoney had reasoned that Malecki was the one man who best knew of Sonja's movements and could very well be the "diplomat" who had flagged her when she left Tel Aviv to come to Minnesota. If that was the case, there was a possibility his contact in Washington would be among the people he regularly met with during his visits.

The meetings would probably be out in the open, Mahoney figured. Malecki was apparently too visible a personage on the Washington scene to engage in dark alley or quiet restaurant meetings. And blind postal drops, although convenient in some instances, would be too unwieldy if Malecki was passing a large volume of information.

They had been working on this first series of files for nearly two hours—Wasserman translating the bits and pieces as Mahoney requested them—when they finally came to the series 900B jackets that Mahoney especially wanted to see.

"Guest lists, menus, and physical layouts," Wasserman said. "Most of it self-explanatory."

Mahoney opened the first of the four files and began thumbing through it. It was the party held in early March at the Mexican embassy way out on 16th Street. The guest list started on the fourth page, and near the bottom a name fairly leaped up at him.

Not trusting his own reactions, Mahoney continued flipping pages, as if he had seen nothing of importance, until he was through the file, and then in quick succession he leafed through the other three files. The same name was included on each guest list.

"Anything?" Wasserman asked.

Mahoney looked up out of his thoughts and shook his head. His heart was pounding, and he felt somewhat light-headed. He wanted a cigar and a drink at that moment, and yet he had to dig deeper.

Per Larsen, chief of ININ, was Malecki's contact in Brussels. Robert McBundy, chief of Clandestine Operations for the Central Intelligence Agency, was apparently his contact in Washington. McBundy's name had appeared on the guest list for every party Malecki had attended in Washington. Yet Malecki had never filed a report that he had spoken with the man.

Washington and Brussels. Both members of NATO. So why report to two people? Why double the risk?

Wasserman was watching him, and Mahoney managed a slight smile. "It's going to be a long night, Ezra. Can you round up some coffee or something while I order up the next batch?"

Wasserman signaled for the clerk, who came from around the counter and gathered up the files. When she was gone, Wasserman got to his feet. "How about a little brandy?"

"Sounds good," Mahoney said, and when Wasserman had left, he reopened the index book for 1980 and began delving in earnest into the whirlwind social life that Chaim Malecki led.

Like a drowning man clutching at straws, Mahoney knew that he would never find the connecting link that would tie all of this together in these files. He knew that now for certain. Malecki was too smart for that. And yet he could not help himself from following the man from party to party, and endless chain of affairs, events, and soirées

XX

HEBRON . . . TUESDAY

Zepharim Kominski had done a lot of drinking during the past two days, and this morning as he gradually came awake he felt like hell.

It had been the same yesterday morning. The pain was there when he awoke. The anguish. The uncertainty about the decision he was trying to make. And over all of that was the total disbelief that the sonofabitch Malecki was walking around free. A traitor to Israel, the man responsible for General Ben Abel's murder was walking around free. Dinner with friends. Cocktails. Screwing the Margraff broad.

It was incredible.

As it had been yesterday morning, Kominski's pain was almost blinding in its intensity, and he reached down for the vodka bottle on the floor beside his bug-infested cot, but it wasn't there.

Slowly, he opened his eyes and rolled over on his side and looked down. Two bottles were halfway across the tiny room, empty, and the third, the one he had just opened late last night, was lying on its side in a drying pool of liquor, a dead cockroach at the edge of it.

For a long time he stared at the bottle, which was just outside his reach, his eyes flicking from the roach back to the few precious drops still remaining. For a time he imagined he could see a model ship in the bottle, and for a time he was certain the roach was moving, was edging its way to the bottle to drink the rest of the liquor.

Finally, though, he pulled himself out of those delusions and very carefully sat up, swinging his legs over the edge of the bed, holding himself as if he had a serious head wound that would tear open if he jerked or strained himself.

His breath came in short gasps, and he could feel his heart hammering in his chest, his brain throbbing in time with the beat.

As if he were a man rising from the dead, he got to his feet, fell back on the bed, got to his feet again, and stumbled across the room to the chest of drawers with its shard of filthy, fly-specked mirror, and tried to focus on his image.

"Can't escape," he told his reflection, the words slurred and indistinct.

He laid his head on his arms atop the bureau and closed his eyes for a moment, the room instantly beginning to tilt on him. He had to open his eyes to stop himself from being sick, and he straightened up.

His room was on the third floor of a dingy hotel in Hebron's Arab quarter. He had signed himself out on leave Sunday evening, had taken the bus down, and had checked in here under a false name. The houseboy had been his runner, fetching his vodka, a three-quarter liter bottle at a time, and sometime—yesterday, perhaps, but now Kominski wasn't sure—the boy had brought him something to eat. Something with curry in it, and he had thrown it up an hour after he had eaten it.

"Boy," he tried to shout, but the word only came out

as a croak. "Damn," he whispered, leaning against the doorframe for a moment before he turned and lurched back into the room.

He picked up the vodka bottle from the floor, brought it to his lips and poured what little was left into his mouth, swilling it around before swallowing it, and then he went back to the door.

"Boy!" he bellowed. "Move! Now! Let's go!"

Something clattered on the ground floor, and then he could hear someone racing up the stairs as he turned back into his room and peeled his filthy shirt off and tossed it aside.

"Today," he said, looking sideways at his reflection in the mirror.

The houseboy, out of breath, appeared in the doorway, his hand outstretched, palm up. "More vodka, more money," he said.

Kominski pulled out a couple of pounds and gave them to the boy. "No vodka. I want a large basin of water. Hot, clean water. And soap. and some clean towels."

The boy was nodding, and he sprinted down the hall.

"And coffee!" Kominski shouted after him.

"Coffee," the boy's voice came from the stairs.

Kominski grabbed his small overnight bag from the corner and opened it on the bed. From inside he pulled out a clean shirt and his razor and set them aside. From beneath the other things, he pulled out his 9mm Luger, snapped out the clip to make sure it was full, then rammed it home, levered a round into the firing chamber, and made sure the safety was on. The gun was in perfect condition, well oiled, well used. And he was an expert marksman with it.

Action, Ben Abel's motto had been. "Action,"

Kominski mumbled, stuffing the gun back into the bag.

He sat down on the edge of the narrow bed, his knees suddenly weak, his stomach hollow, and he clasped his hands tightly between his knees.

Malecki was a traitor. A murderer. An eye for an eye. A tooth for a tooth. A life for a life.

Cracow was lovely in the spring, his mother had told him once. At Easter, with the weather becoming warm, the girls would wear their new bonnets to church, their dresses frilly and starched, while the young men would all be wearing their clean, high collars, their hair neatly combed.

"And then later, if the day was especially nice, we would all go for something sweet along the river. You remember, don't you?"

He remembered. At times, like this morning, his memories were crystal clear. But he also remembered wanting so desperately to grow up, to leave, to be on his own. Yet now that he was there, he longed for the simpler days.

Kominski had not thought much beyond the murder of Malecki because in his mind what happened afterward really didn't make much difference. He would be arrested, of course, and tried for murder. But his parents were not alive to suffer the embarrassment and grief, nor would Ben Abel be there to worry about him.

Something touched his shoulder after a time, and he looked up into the eyes of the young houseboy and then beyond him to where a basin of steaming water had been set atop the bureau. Alongside it was a pile of clean towels.

"Thanks," Kominski mumbled, and the boy held out a fresh bottle of vodka.

"This too," the boy said. "Enough money for this too."

Kominski tried to shake his head, but he reached out

for the bottle anyway, broke the seal, opened it, and drank deeply.

"You sleep now," the boy said, and he helped Kominski lie back on the bed.

There was a commotion outside, down on the street in front of the hotel, and the houseboy went to the window and looked down.

Kominski was thinking about Malecki, seeing him coming out of Base Operations with the general's briefcase.

The houseboy was back at his side, shaking him and pulling him up. "Soldiers are here. Soldiers are here," the boy was shouting urgently.

Kominski focused on his face again. "What?"

"Soldiers are here. You have to go now or they will arrest you."

"I didn't do anything . . ." Kominski mumbled, but then he understood everything clearly. European Jews did not hide in Arab hotels unless they were in trouble. And either Wasserman or Mahoney must have figured that he was going to make a try for Malecki.

With the boy's help Kominski got to his feet and pulled on his shirt, but before he left the room he grabbed his Luger from his overnight bag.

When the boy saw the gun he backed off. They could hear the tromp of boots coming up the stairs. "The roof," the houseboy said. "Hurry now."

Kominski stumbled out into the corridor and hurried as best he could away from the stairs toward the back of the building, while the houseboy went to intercept the soldiers.

The corridor was narrow and very dark, so that Kominski missed the wooden ladder that led up to the roof door, and moments later he found himself at the end of the hall where a window overlooked the alley three stories below.

Someone was shouting something, and seconds later he could hear several people hurrying down the corridor.

Malecki could not be left alive. There could be no deals. No plea bargaining.

He tried to open the window, but the rotten frame would not move, so he smashed the glass out with his elbow.

"Kominski!" someone shouted from behind him.

He stuck his head and shoulders out the window and looked up. The lip of the roof was only four or five feet above him.

The soldiers were racing down the corridor toward him as he climbed out the window, holding onto the frame with one hand while trying to straighten up and catch the edge of the roof with his other.

"Zeph!" a familiar voice shouted nearly on top of him, and Kominski lunged up and out trying for the roof as the windowframe came loose in his hand.

As he pitched out away from the building he felt a hand brushing his leg, and then he was falling, the stone blocks of the alley coming up at his face with incredible speed.

JERUSALEM . . . TUESDAY AFTERNOON

"He was killed trying to escape," Wasserman said. "Fell out a third-story window in an Arab hotel in Hebron."

Drinks were laid out on the table they were seated around. The garden patio was pleasantly shaded by a number of cedar trees, and although the afternoon was warm, it was not unbearable here.

"Has the rifle been found?" Defense Minister Gezira asked, reaching for his drink.

"No," Wasserman said. "He probably hid it somewhere. Most likely we'll never find it."

Besides Gezira, at whose home in the Mahanavim section of Jerusalem they were meeting, also present were Foreign Minister Shapiro and the majority party leader Zvi Andabo. Begin's chosen trio, Wasserman thought of them.

"Frankly, I'm finding this very difficult to believe," Andabo said. He had lost his petulance somewhere along the line, and now he was angry, like the others, if somewhat subdued.

"I know," Wasserman replied tiredly. "But I saw Malecki take the briefcase with my own eyes."

"I don't mean that. I mean your handling of this entire affair. Why hasn't Malecki been arrested?"

Operation Joshua it was being called. And now the entire incredible mess was very nearly over. Begin's promise to let Mahoney have his own hand had less than twenty-four hours to run, and by this time tomorrow afternoon Malecki would be under lock and key. It would then be up to Begin and his advisers to deal with the ININ chief Per Larsen and the Operation Wrath documents.

"As I explained earlier, Mr. Mahoney asked for and was granted seventy-two hours to tie up the loose ends."

"What loose ends, Ezra?" Gezira asked.

"Who killed General Ben Abel, for one."

"Obviously Captain Kominski believed it was Malecki."

Wasserman shook his head. "That's what he believed, but at that time Malecki was out of the country. He couldn't possibly have done it."

"Has that been confirmed?" Shapiro asked, leaning forward.

Wasserman turned to him. "Yes, it has."

"Then Malecki had help."

Wasserman nodded but said nothing, thinking about Ben Abel slumped over his desk, the back of his head blown away, and then about Kominski splattered all over a back alley.

"What other loose ends, Ezra?" Gezira prompted. "What else is Mahoney trying to uncover?"

"Why Malecki reports to Per Larsen, and in turn who does Larsen report to?"

"The Soviets," Gezira said. "I think we've pretty well established that in our minds. NATO has had its own troubles in dealing with the Warsaw Pact countries, just as we have had with the Jordanians, Syrians, and Lebanese. Larsen is obviously reporting everything to the Russians . . . NATO business as well as what Malecki has been feeding him. Naturally it all comes back from Moscow to Beirut, Amman, and Damascus. No mystery there."

"I agree," Wasserman said. "But why has Malecki been selling us out? It's still hard for me to believe."

"Money?" Shapiro asked.

"Perhaps," Wasserman said pensively. He wanted to believe that. He wanted desperately to believe that Malecki was motivated by money. It would make things so much easier to digest, and yet he was having trouble swallowing that pill.

If it was for money, then Malecki was a traitor who wore two hats. One beneath which he had been selling out Israel for a number of years. And another beneath which he had been using the money to help develop his country. It didn't make much sense.

"What about Sonja?" Shapiro asked gently.

"The only bright spot," Wasserman said. "Malecki obviously has help, but I no longer believe it's her."

"Soviet agents here in Israel?" Andabo asked.

"Most likely."

The four men fell silent for a time as they listened to the sharp commands of evening drill across the way at the police barracks. It was the only incongruous note in an otherwise peaceful setting.

"There is one other thing we're going to have to settle this afternoon," Shapiro said at last. His manner seemed distant.

Wasserman focused on him but said nothing. The others were uncomfortable, though. He could see that.

"I've made some inquiries, Ezra. Very quietly with some friends in Washington."

"About Mahoney?"

Shapiro nodded. "We're in a rather delicate position here with him. It's my understanding that his government has no knowledge of the fact he has been working for us."

"I think they may have guessed by now," Wasserman said.

Shapiro disagreed. "I don't think so. Sonja was spotted coming into the States, but that was only natural. She worked for them, and it's common knowledge over there that she's working for you now. They would have had her on a list. They'd have to follow her."

"To Mahoney," Wasserman said.

"To Mahoney," Shapiro agreed. "From which does not necessarily follow his working for us."

"It's a moot point . . ." Wasserman started to say, but Shapiro, tamping his pipe, persisted.

"On the contrary, it's a very valid, delicate point now that the Operation Wrath documents have gotten loose. We're going to have to admit their existence, as well as the fact that they are fakes."

Wasserman was beginning to see what the man was getting at and he suddenly felt ill. "If you tell the Americans we ourselves came up with the documents to catch our mole, Mahoney will have to lie for us if he's ever questioned. Is that what has you worried?"

"He won't lie to his own government."

"He broke his country's espionage laws by coming to work for us." Wasserman said. "I think we can count on him to be discreet."

"I . . . we disagree," Shapiro said.

Wasserman got to his feet. "I'm going to leave before I hear any more of this."

"The situation is going to have to be dealt with," Andabo said.

Wasserman leaned forward, his knuckles on the tabletop. "I'm just a government employee, Mr. Andabo, nothing more. Whereas you *are* the government. Now, do you want to give me some specific order this afternoon? Would you like to put something to me in front of witnesses, or perhaps in writing?"

"Dammit, Ezra," Gezira, who had been mostly silent all this time, flared. "Mahoney cannot be trusted."

"We're going to have to trust him," Wasserman said, straightening up. "Or you're going to have to do whatever it is you think is necessary. I will not do it."

Wasserman turned and strode across the garden and let himself out through a side gate to the street where his car was parked.

Behind the wheel he started the engine but sat there thinking for a few moments, trying to understand and deal with his own feelings. He had come to the same conclusion about Mahoney more than a week ago but had been no more ready then to pull the trigger on the American than he was now.

What would happen once Malecki was in custody and they could question him, was anyone's guess. But Wasserman suspected it would turn out like the Israel Beer situation had.

Although they knew Malecki was a traitor, and although they knew he was sending his information to Per Larsen in Brussels, Malecki would undoubtedly remain silent. They would get nothing from him, just as they had gotten nothing from Israel Beer.

It would not be tidy. The loose ends Mahoney seemed so concerned about at this moment would remain loose. Most of their questions would remain unanswered.

When it was over, however, Wasserman thought as he put his car in gear and pulled away from the curb, he was going to retire from the Mossad.

"Any time you've had your fill of Tel Aviv and Jerusalem, you can come down here and help me," Carl Margraff had told him on more than one occasion.

And now he could do it. He could go down to Gan Haifiz bearing a gift. Sonja's innocence.

XXI

TEL AVIV . . . TUESDAY EVENING

Mahoney had gone to the Kfar Saba apartment after they had finished up in Records, to sleep and to wait word from Wasserman who said he would be meeting with Begin's cabinet.

It was a question of noninterference, Wasserman had explained. Malecki had been identified as the mole, he was being watched, and his arrest was imminent.

"So they want me out of Israel, despite Begin's promise that I would be allowed another twenty-four hours," Mahoney had said.

"Very likely. But until I meet with them I'll want you to stay here. Agreed?"

Mahoney had agreed. And now, several hours later, he could hear Wasserman's familiar step on the stairway.

During those hours he had had plenty of time to think, but none of his conclusions gave him any consolation. He felt no triumph in his accomplishment of ferreting out the mole. Malecki, the golden boy of Tel Aviv, would be in custody by this time tomorrow, if not sooner. But it was a hollow, incomplete victory as far as he was concerned.

Malecki was nothing more than one link in what was appearing to be some kind of a network. Or rather from what Mahoney had seen, Malecki was the hub of a wheel with spokes radiating outward to Per Larsen in Brussels, Bob McBundy in Washington, and two other names that had fairly leaped off the pages of Malecki's operational files.

There were others, Mahoney was certain. Others whose names would come to light . . . or could come to light under further study. Yet none of them seemed to fit in any logical pattern. They had nothing in common. Among them there seemed to be no overriding principle or concern for Israel's secrets. So why had Malecki been recruited and sent here to spy in 1966?

And that, he had to admit to himself as he waited for Wasserman to reach the second-floor landing, was only one of a number of disturbing questions that led to even worse conclusions.

McBundy was Malecki's CIA contact. It must have been he who had set up the bombing at the Athens airport. Evidently Sonja had let something slip with Malecki who in turn passed the information on to his contacts. Malecki had then watched very closely the preparations the Mossad was making, somehow spotting the airport locker in Athens where Wasserman's instructions had been placed.

McBundy's people had followed Sonja to Minnesota on her recruitment mission, and the word had spread from there: Mahoney is on his way. Eliminate him.

But why? Why run such a sophisticated network operation against Israel? And why go to such lengths to protect it? Could it have something to do with the spy satellite receiving station that had been destroyed at al Qaryut?

If McBundy had come to him and said, "I want you

to back off on this one, Wallace. We're running a pretty tight ship. Delicate operations," he would have naturally told Sonja he was not interested. He was retired.

He looked up as a key grated in the lock, the door swung open, and Wasserman stepped quickly into the apartment, closing the door behind him.

The Mossad chief seemed out of breath, but there was a determined, almost fatalistic expression in his eyes as he stood by the door looking across the room at Mahoney who was seated in one of the window chairs.

For several seconds both men just stared at each other, and briefly Mahoney felt sorry for Wasserman, who had obviously made some kind of difficult decision and was here to bring the bad news.

"I've just come from Jerusalem," he said finally.

"No one knows you've come here?"

"No," he said. "I mean that's correct. And now there isn't much time."

"For what, Ezra?"

"You're going to have to leave Israel. Tonight. I've come to escort you to the airport."

"How about Malecki?"

"He'll probably be arrested sometime tomorrow afternoon or evening unless he tries to jump before then."

"Kominski is under wraps?"

"He's dead."

Mahoney felt very old at that moment. Old and burned out. Nearly forty years of intelligence service work had dulled his senses to tragedy, and he could see it was the same with Wasserman.

"Who killed him?" Mahoney asked softly. "Was it Malecki?"

"No," the Mossad chief said, making no move to come any farther into the room. "He was trying to escape from a hotel in Hebron. I sent a couple of his own people after him." A little shudder seemed to run through Wasserman. "He was trying for the roof. Third story above a cobblestoned alley. He fell out the window."

"Was the rifle found?"

"No," Wasserman said. "He was carrying a Luger, nothing more. The hotel people swear that he was there during the time the shots were fired at Malecki."

"Reliable?" Mahoney asked, sitting forward, another line of thought momentarily crossing his mind.

"Not very," Wasserman said.

"Kominski is dead, for God's sake. What the hell have they to be loyal about?"

"Arabs can be quite stubborn. I pulled our people out from Hebron anyway. I didn't want it to turn into a bigger mess than it already was."

"You know that Malecki didn't kill Ben Abel."

Wasserman nodded but said nothing.

"Don't you want to find his murderer?"

"Desperately," Wasserman said, something flashing in his eyes. "But we'll probably never find it out. Malecki had help here in Israel. He had to have help. Probably Soviets."

For a moment Mahoney thought about his wife Marge, and there was a deep-seated ache in his gut from the knowledge that she was not at home waiting for him.

"Have you set up an interrogation team?"

"Not yet," Wasserman said. "This has been kept pretty quiet so far. I've put four of my people in rotating teams on him. But even they don't know the full story."

"I'd like to question him when he is arrested."

"You're leaving Israel tonight, Mahoney. Tonight."

"If I refuse—" Mahoney started.

"You can't," Wasserman cut him off.

Again the two men stared at each other for a long time, until at long last Mahoney got up from the chair, took off his coat, and undid the shoulder holster. He laid the gun on the table and then pulled his jacket on again.

"What about Per Larsen, how are you going to handle that situation with the Operation Wrath documents?"

"That depends upon what Malecki tells us, if anything," Wasserman said, watching Mahoney cross the room to his small overnight bag on the table. "I'm sure Mr. Begin will be in personal contact with your president."

"But my name won't be mentioned?" Mahoney asked, turning back.

"No," Wasserman said. "And I'm going to hold you to your promise that you will never discuss this with your government."

How much more to tell the man, Mahoney briefly wondered. "You haven't been honest with me, Ezra. Not from the beginning."

"Nor have you been with me," Wasserman said. "The nature of the business, I suppose."

"There is much more to this than you suspect," Mahoney said.

Wasserman had to smile tiredly. "I'm sure there is. I'm sure my country is crawling with Soviets. Per Larsen is the link. The Soviets run the distribution network."

Mahoney crossed the room to the Mossad chief who handed him a fat envelope.

"Ten thousand American. Is it sufficient?"

"More than sufficient," Mahoney said, pocketing the money. "But there's only one reason I can think of why you'd want me out of the country so fast. Am I correct?"

Wasserman barely nodded, but it was enough, and it

was no less than Mahoney had expected. He himself was marked for assassination by the Israelis themselves. It was a chilling thought, and yet it would give him a little more time.

Malecki would be arrested tomorrow, and then would be interrogated. All that would take additional time. Forty-eight hours, perhaps a bit more. It didn't give him much room to maneuver, he thought, but at least at this stage of the game he no longer had to cover his own moves. He could work very quickly, and the hell with delicacy.

Mahoney stuck out his hand and Wasserman took it.

"I hope this all works out for you in the end, Ezra."

Wasserman's eyebrows rose.

"I mean about Sonja. I hope she turns out to be innocent."

"She is," Wasserman said stubbornly. "And I hope you find what you're looking for."

"Other than the truth," Mahoney said, "what I want is unobtainable."

PARIS . . . WEDNESDAY MORNING

In the main terminal at Charles de Gaulle Airport just north of the city, the lights seemed garish after the subdued atmosphere of the El Al 727. And at two in the morning the people all seemed wan and somewhat detached, as if they were sleepwalkers, not at all certain why they were here or where they were going.

Mahoney's connecting flight to Washington, D.C., did not leave until 7:00 A.M., which gave him slightly less than five hours to do what he had come to Paris for. Plenty of time, he figured, if he was lucky.

After he had confirmed his ticket with the sleepy airline clerk at the TWA counter, he crossed the mezzanine to a newspaper stand where he purchased two large manila envelopes and sufficient postage for an airmail package back to the States, then he crossed to a coffee shop still open.

When he was settled in a small booth at the end of the counter and his coffee and a croissant with butter had come, he took out the notes he had worked on during the flight from Tel Aviv, stuffed them in one of the envelopes, and sealed it.

He wrote a name and a Washington, D.C., address on the front of the envelope and then stuffed it in the second envelope.

Next he scribbled a quick note saying that the inner envelope was not to be opened and was to be delivered only if something should happen to him.

When he had the note sealed in the outer envelope, he hesitated a moment, his pen in hand, not at all certain he was doing the right thing. This next step, in many ways, was even more frightening than everything else that had happened. But in the end he understood that he had no real choice in the matter, and he addressed the envelope to his son John in California, and affixed the stamps he had purchased.

The notes would be a week, perhaps ten days in transit, so that long before they arrived at his son's home in Los Angeles, this thing would be resolved. It would be over with before John became involved unless something happened.

He dawdled for a few minutes over his coffee and roll, the only customer in the restaurant at this hour. He still had the choice, he knew, of remaining here at the airport until his flight was called. And in a few weeks or months it would all settle down, and he could return to his comfortable security at the lake.

Even thinking about that option, however, was nothing more than an exercise in futility. The delusions of a sick old woman, McBundy had said of the Russian's story a thousand years ago. Maybe it had been a catchy malady. Maybe his were the delusions of a tired old man.

At length he got up from the booth, paid his bill at the cash register near the door, and went back out onto the mezzanine where he took an escalator down to the main level, ambled across the terminal and out the front doors into the cool breezy French morning.

There were only a few people outside, and Mahoney paid close attention to them as he went to a taxi and climbed in the back seat.

"The Ritz," he told the driver, and as the cab pulled away from the curb and headed away from the airport, Mahoney looked over his shoulder out the rear window. No one had paid the slightest attention to him. No car had pulled out. Nothing.

Maybe he hadn't been followed. Maybe they—whoever *they* were—had finished with him.

He settled back in his seat and closed his eyes as the taxi sped the fifteen miles south into the city, and for a while he was back in Mossad Records, Malecki's files spread out in front of him.

Per Larsen's name had not been mentioned in any of the files he had seen that night, but references to McBundy ran through the case histories like the strands of a spider web. There were other names that also appeared consistently through the files, among them two that Mahoney had recognized: McNiel Henrys and Armand Arlemont.

Although he had never met either of them, he knew their names well. At one time or another both men had served as duty liaison officers to the CIA, Henrys from the British Secret Service MI9, and Arlemont from the *Service de Documentation Exterieure et de Contre-Es-*

pionage (the SDECE) which was the French Secret Service.

Henrys was an important name in England, and although Mahoney wasn't certain, he thought he remembered some mention of the Henrys name in connection with the gigantic conglomerate ComSat, Ltd, the firm that had built Israel's spy satellite system.

Reserved, aloof, and something of a tough nut to crack, were terms Mahoney had heard in reference to the Englishman, but Arlemont was a totally different story.

The Frenchman, in many respects, was much like McBundy; pompous and puffed up with a sense of self-importance. Arlemont had once helped to thwart a plot on de Gaulle's life, and because of it had been elevated to one position of importance after another within the SDECE. As of a couple of years ago, Mahoney recalled, Arlemont had been deputy director of the Communist Counter-Intelligence Department of Service II within the organization.

But Mahoney also recalled a very terse in-service memo that had come across his desk when he worked in the Western European Division saying that Arlemont was a man of little consequence. A buffoon, Mahoney remembered reading.

A weak link?

Traffic was almost nonexistent within the city, although the streets were brightly lit as always, and the taxi driver shut off his headlights. The Ritz, one of the more famous hotels in Paris, was a magnificent structure on the Place Vendôme at the opposite end of the Champs Elysées from the Arc De Triomphe, and even at this early hour of the morning the doorman who helped Mahoney out of the taxi seemed very much awake and crisp, just as if he had been freshly laundered and pressed.

"No luggage," Mahoney said, and then he paid the driver, tipped the doorman, and entered the lobby where he went immediately to the bar.

There were only a half dozen people seated at the bar, and when he was seated the barman came down to him.

"Monsieur?"

"Cognac," Mahoney said in a subdued voice, and when his drink came he paid the man and then handed the envelope across to him with a twenty dollar bill. "Could you see that this gets in the morning mail?"

"Of course," the man said, taking the envelope and money, and Mahoney drank the cognac. "Another, monsieur?"

"No," Mahoney said. He got off the barstool, left the bar, crossed the lobby, and outside on the street turned left toward Place de LaConcorde, and beyond it, the Seine, his hands stuffed deeply in his pockets.

An occasional car passed him, and at the Louvre he looked up toward the Rue St. Antoine for a moment where there was more traffic, but then he turned right, crossed the river, and three blocks later was standing across from a three-story town house, in a row of similar expensive homes.

The street was narrow and tree-lined, dim lights only at the corners. The houses all were dark, and Mahoney stood awhile contemplating his next move from the shadows.

There were only two cars parked farther up the block, and as far as he could tell they were empty. No watchers. No guards. Would they expect him to show up here? Would they suspect he knew of Arlemont's connection with Malecki?

After a few minutes Mahoney crossed the street, opened the iron gate that led off the sidewalk, and mounted the half dozen stairs to the front door of the house.

He looked both ways down the street, then reached out and rang the bell, the noise startlingly shrill at this hour.

A light came on in the vestibule half a minute later, and a face was peering at him from a window.

"Qui es Là? monsieur?" an angry voice came from a tiny speaker next to the bell.

Mahoney pushed the button. "I must see Monsieur Arlemont."

"It is very late. The Arlemonts are asleep. Come back in the morning, monsieur."

"I must see him now," Mahoney insisted. "Tell him Monsieur Malecki has sent me."

"Moment," the voice said, and the face was gone from the window.

A minute and a half, Mahoney figured. If Arlemont had not come to the door in that time, it would mean he had summoned someone to help him. If Malecki, Larsen, Arlemont, and Henrys had formed some kind of a network to spy on Israel, Mahoney wanted to keep them off-balance for as long as he could. If he could hit and run, first here, then Washington, and finally London, he might uncover their purpose before they would have a chance to fully react and strike back.

In less than a minute the door swung open, and a short, rotund little man wearing pince-nez atop a bulbous nose was standing there. He was dressed in pajamas and a silk dressing gown.

He stood aside. "Come in, don't just stand out there for everyone to see you," he hissed half under his breath.

Mahoney stepped into the vestibule and Arlemont shut and locked the door.

"In my study," he said, still keeping his voice low.

Mahoney followed him through a drawing room, down a short, wide corridor, and then into a huge book-lined room that was dominated by a massive, leather-topped desk on one side facing a huge fireplace on the other.

A door slammed somewhere at the back of the house, and then Arlemont was closing and locking the study doors behind him.

"You said Chaim has sent you?" Arlemont asked, turning to face Mahoney. He had a small-caliber pistol in his hand. "To tell me what, Mr. Mahoney?"

Mahoney started to raise his hands, but Arlemont waved them down.

"That won't be necessary. I am an expert with this thing. If you try anything at all I will shoot you through the heart. Do I make myself clear?"

Mahoney nodded. Whatever this man was, he was not a buffoon.

Arlemont moved sideways away from the door and motioned Mahoney toward a thick leather chair in front of the desk. "Have a seat. I'll pour us a drink, and then you can tell me what message you have brought from Chaim."

"If you know who I am, then you know I have brought no message from Chaim Malecki," Mahoney said.

"Sit down," Arlemont snapped harshly. "Don't force me into killing you. Yet."

Mahoney turned and went across the room where he sat in the chair by the desk. When he was settled Arlemont poured them both a drink from a decanter set on a small library table and then took a seat across the desk. He laid the pistol down in front of him and passed Mahoney's drink across.

"How did you get my name?" he asked.

Mahoney said nothing, sipping at his drink. It was a very fine cognac.

Arlemont stared at him for several long seconds, apparently trying to come to some decision. Finally he set his glass down, picked up the telephone, and dialed for the operator.

Mahoney hadn't known exactly what to expect by coming here and confronting this man, but Arlemont's actions confirmed that he worked for or with Malecki. Which meant his name in Malecki's files had been no coincidence after all, a possibility that had been bothersome.

Arelemont had given the operator a number in England, and a few moments later it was ringing.

"Mongoose, this is Colombe," Arlemont spoke softly.

Mahoney could hear a man's voice from the other end, but he could not make out what was being said.

"Yes,' Arlemont said. "He is here now."

Mahoney took another sip of his drink.

"No, he does not say."

There was a pause from the other end, and then Mahoney could hear something being said, and Arlemont was nodding his head. "Yes, I understand. Yes. By afternoon. Yes. Good-bye."

He hung up the telephone and started to reach for his pistol when Mahoney threw the cognac in his face and sprung up from the chair, lunging across the desk.

Arlemont shouted something in desperation as he fumbled for the gun, but Mahoney had him by the collar of his robe and dragged him across the desk onto the floor, pulling the telephone and lamp with him.

The Frenchman was like a wild animal, kicking and clawing, so that Mahoney had to hit him in the face with his fist.

Arlemont's head bounced hard against the leg of the chair, but still he continued to struggle as Mahoney hit him again as hard as he could, breaking the man's glasses, blood splattering from a broken nose and a split lip.

Mahoney rolled away and managed to struggle up to his feet, but Arlemont scrambled around on his hands and knees, grabbing Mahoney's legs in a bear hug.

Both men crashed sideways into the chair, causing it to overturn, and Arlemont began to shake and jerk spasmodically, his head and shoulders wedged at an odd angle behind one of the legs.

Again Mahoney rolled away, but this time Arlemont did not come after him, the twitching in his body gradually subsiding, and finally stopping.

XXII

WASHINGTON, D.C. . . . WEDNESDAY

The knuckles on Mahoney's right hand were raw and swollen, and he rubbed absently at them as the TWA 747 came majestically in for a landing at Washington's National Airport.

Sunny, light south-to-southeast winds, with an expected high of 75 degrees, the pilot had told his passengers earlier over the intercom. And Mahoney was looking forward to the pleasant change from Israel's oppressive heat.

The weather in Paris, like everything else that had happened there, was mostly an indistinct blur to Mahoney this morning. He kept seeing Arlemont's face erupting in a mass of blood, kept feeling the impact of his fist on the man's flesh and bone.

Arlemont's neck had broken when he and Mahoney had fallen over the thick leather chair, probably severing the spinal cord.

For several minutes Mahoney lay where he had fallen, his gaze alternating from Arlemont's body to the study door, expecting at any moment for someone to come knocking, for someone to ask if everything was all right.

But the knock never came, and after a while Mahoney had gotten to his feet, checked Arlemont's pulse to make sure he was dead, and then had somehow mustered his wits enough to make a reasonably thorough search of the man's study.

He had come up with nothing from his search, and after he had taken a stiff drink of cognac, and had straightened up his clothing, he took the study door key from Arlemont's robe. He exited the study, relocking the door from the outside and then, taking great pains to make absolutely no noise, let himself out to the street.

He hurried back the way he had come until he reached the Louvre, where he continued away from the river to the Rue St. Antoine. Within twenty minutes he was in a cab heading back out to the airport to await his morning flight to the States.

The 747's tires barked on the pavement once, then again, and they were bumping down the runway, the flaps grinding back up into the wing, and the jets reversing with a roar.

Arlemont's name in Malecki's files had been no coincidence after all, nor had he worked only with Per Larsen and Malecki. There was at least one other person, code name Mongoose, in the network. Arlemont's telephone call had been to England, so it was a fairly safe bet that Mongoose was McNiel Henrys.

McBundy was another matter. Mahoney hoped against hope that his name in Malecki's operational files was nothing more than coincidence. Bob was a regular partygoer on the Washington scene, so his appearance at the affairs Malecki had also attended could have been routine. It was something he had been kidded about during the years Mahoney had known him.

McBundy would do practically anything for a free meal and a couple of free drinks, the agency wags said.

And McBundy always took the bait. Each time he heard such a remark, either directly or indirectly, he would puff up and explain that the parties were a part of his job. He didn't like them one bit, but someone around the agency had to keep his ear to the local pavement. Now that Hoover was gone, the FBI could not be depended upon for much of anything other than pap.

Coincidence, Mahoney wondered, or did McBundy have a code name in the network?

Mahoney had only the single overnight bag, so he was one of the first in line at the customs hall. When his turn came he placed the bag on a counter and handed over his passport.

"Mr. Mahoney?" the customs officer asked, an odd expression on his face. Then he opened the passport and glanced at the identification page facing the photograph.

Mahoney stepped back half a pace and the officer stiffened.

The customs hall was contained in a long, narrow room. Along one wall was a single door from the international debarking gates, and along the opposite wall were several doors that led to a corridor up to the main terminal. In between were a dozen customs counters. There were at least two hundred people in the hall.

It was easily eighty or ninety feet from where Mahoney stood to the terminal doors. From there he would have to race down a long corridor, up the escalators, and across the mezzanine itself before he would be able to get outside. There wasn't a chance in hell of him making it.

"Yes, I'm Wallace Mahoney," he said after only a slight hesitation.

"There is a gentleman here who would like to speak with you, sir. If you'll just follow me."

It was probably one of two things, Mahoney thought,

his mind racing. Either he had been identified as Arlemont's murderer, and he would be arrested now. Or the British contact whom Arlemont had telephoned had contacted McBundy. If that was the case, McBundy had probably arranged for his assassination.

But not here, he thought as he hefted his overnight case and followed the officer past the customs gates to the far end of the hall.

They stopped at an unmarked door. The customs officer knocked once, then opened the door and stuck his head inside.

"He's here, sir," the man said.

"Send him in," McBundy's voice came from within, and the customs officer stepped aside.

"Go right in, Mr. Mahoney," he said.

Mahoney steeled himself, managed to put on a tired smile, and entered the tiny office that was furnished with nothing more than a gray steel table, around which were grouped four chairs.

McBundy, wearing a light gray pin-striped suit with a vest, white shirt, and correctly knotted tie, was just taking his feet off the table, and he stood up. He smiled.

"Good morning, Wallace. I trust that you had a good flight over?"

The customs officer had closed the door on them, and Mahoney crossed the room where he set his overnight bag down on the floor and shook McBundy's hand.

"Good to see you, Bob. Do you welcome all your former agents home from vacation like this?"

McBundy laughed heartily. "Have a seat, Wallace," he said, and when they were seated across the table from each other, the smile gradually left his features.

The man was either innocent—a possibility Mahoney firmly wanted to believe—or he was a magnificent actor.

He shook a cigarette out of a pack for himself, not

bothering to offer one to Mahoney. When he had it lit he leaned forward. "Do you want to tell me what the hell has been going on over the past few weeks, Wallace?" he said, his voice low. "Strictly off the record for the moment."

"What are you talking about, Bob? I've been on vacation—" Mahoney started, but McBundy waved if off.

"Cut the bullshit," he snapped angrily. "Darrel came to me when the Margraff woman came to see you. Said he was sure you were up to something." McBundy waved his cigarette. "The kid was worried half out of his mind about you."

"And?" Mahoney asked. Whatever he had expected from McBundy, it wasn't this.

"Come on, Wallace. For chrissake, we've worked together now for more than twenty years. What the hell have you been up to?"

"How did you know I'd be coming in on this flight?"

For a moment it looked as if McBundy was going to blow his stack, but then he calmed down, flicked the ash from his cigarette into an ashtray on the table, and leaned back.

"Let me lay it out for you, all right?"

Mahoney nodded.

"Sonja Margraff comes to see you. We watched her come in, we watched her go out. Neat. Simple. Quick. But then you hand Darrel a line of horseshit about your little chat. Talk over old times, I think he said. Which would have been fine and dandy if it had been left at that." He puffed on his cigarette again. "We picked you up on a one-way into Athens, of all places—which was Darrel's doing, by the way—and a few days later you show up in Tel Aviv. So I asked myself: Bob, what the hell could the Mossad want with one of my former people?"

"What did the sage tell you, Bob?" Mahoney asked. He needed time to think. Did McBundy know about Arlemont's death?

A pained expression crossed McBundy's features. "You were one of the best the agency ever had. They're still talking about you. The good old days and all that."

Mahoney had to smile. "It's only been a year or two."

"Time passes," McBundy said. "What I want to know is why the hell you went mucking around with the Mossad. Besides the fact that it's illegal as hell, it's just plain stupid."

"You seemed to have the answers, Bob. Assuming I was working on something for the Mossad, what might it have been?"

"Don't play games with me, Wallace," McBundy said, vexed. "Just don't play your games with me. You're in serious trouble this time."

"I see," Mahoney said.

"You see," McBundy said, thumping his fist on the table. "For Christ's living sake, all you can say for yourself is, I see?"

"You were telling me about my itinerary," Mahoney said, wondering what McBundy's code name was.

"We had you pegged on and off in Tel Aviv for most of the time, although Interpol Net had you placed in Brussels very briefly. You were following someone."

Mahoney was startled by that bit of news, but apparently it didn't show, because McBundy continued.

"A couple of days later you show up at the airport escorted by Ezra Wasserman, of all people," McBundy said. He seemed to study Mahoney for a moment. "Need I go on?"

"Please do," Mahoney said, still not one hundred percent sure about McBundy.

"Paris next, which really threw us for a loop."

"Did you have me followed from Tel Aviv, Bob? Is that what you're trying to tell me?"

McBundy shook his head. "No, but I should have sent a legman after you. I just alerted our Paris office that you were coming. They were mad as hell, but they sent one of their people out. Said you hung around the terminal for a half hour, and then got up and took a cab —presumably into town."

"He hung around until I came back to the airport?"

McBundy nodded. "He was told to sit tight."

"Not very inventive. I would have thought you'd have someone with a little more pizzazz out there."

"He said you looked fagged."

"Exact words?"

McBundy chuckled. "Fagged, he said. And then our little friend Armand Arlemont turned up dead this morning. Why, Wallace?" he asked reprovingly.

"I didn't kill Arlemont."

"You were placed at his house."

"By whom?" Mahoney asked, a little more sure now about McBundy. The man was digging his own grave.

"By Arlemont's butler," McBundy said. "Not by name, of course, but your description is pretty distinctive. My uninventive legman out there kept one eye on the police wire to see if you had created any waves. As soon as Arlemont's murder came over, he matched descriptions."

Had McBundy told him this story twenty-four hours from now, or even twelve hours hence, Mahoney supposed he would have believed it. But Arlemont's death would not have been placed on the Paris police wires so soon. Someone else's murder perhaps. But not the killing of a high-ranking SDECE officer. It would have been a matter handled internally to the department.

"What do you want from me, Bob?" Mahoney asked,

sick at heart. Twenty years was a very long time to work with and for someone only to discover you didn't know him.

"Did you kill Arlemont for the Israelis?"

"No," Mahoney said, looking directly into McBundy's eyes. "I did not."

McBundy held Mahoney's gaze for a long time, but then he shook his head. "I want you to go back to your little lake in Minnesota, Wallace. Retire."

"Am I getting too old for this business?"

"You're too good for us, Wallace. You've got us all at an unfair advantage. And that's a dangerous position for an operative to find himself in. Control. Remember the operative word? Control is all-important."

Mahoney got slowly to his feet and picked up his overnight bag, sad now that he was almost completely sure that McBundy was a part of the network.

He went to the door, but before he could reach for the doorknob McBundy was on his feet with a parting shot.

"There's enough circumstantial evidence in France to hang you for Arlemont's murder, Wallace."

Without turning around, Mahoney said, "I'm sorry you said that, Bob."

"I'm sorry I had to say it, Wallace. But I want you to go home now. Rest. You've earned it."

"If I don't? If I continue to muck around?"

"The extradition will be honored."

Mahoney turned for a brief look at him, then he opened the door and went back out into the customs hall, where he quickly crossed to the terminal doors, shuffled down the corridor, and took an escalator up to the mezzanine.

Slowly, as if he was a man resigned to his fate, which in a way felt he was, he crossed over to the Republic Airlines ticket counter. When his turn came he purchased a one-way ticket to Duluth, Minnesota, on tomorrow's early-bird flight west.

One day in Washington was an acceptable level of defiance, Mahoney figured. That is if there was still any doubt in McBundy's mind.

It was like the nightfall of a very long, overcast day in which a cold wind that had steadily howled through the eaves began to increase in pitch. The answers were there; he could feel them all around him. But like the wind there was a certain elusive quality about everything he had learned, and the answers had brought no comfort.

It was nearly noon by the time he had caught an airport limousine to the Marriott Two Bridges Motel across the Memorial Highway cloverleaf from the Pentagon, and he was tired not only from his lack of sleep but from the mental battering he had been giving himself.

He felt that the answers were finally starting to fall into place, and yet he was like a thirsty man; having had a sip of cool water, he wanted the entire jug—immediately—in large gulps.

He ate a small breakfast, the first solid food he had had in what seemed like months, and then went directly to his room in the huge motel complex. He lay down for a few hours, the door locked, the chain in place, but he could not sleep. His mind refused to shut down.

He kept seeing Malecki and hearing his lies; he kept envisioning Sonja Margraff as she had first appeared to him at the cabin in Minnesota; and he kept contrasting that image with the things her father had told him. He also had the recurring picture of Arlemont's bloody face.

Other images crossed his mind as well as he lay there. Images of the young boy being killed at the Athens airport, of General Ben Abel's body sprawled across his desk.

"Why? The question hammered in his brain. What were they up to?

Obviously a fairly sophisticated network was being run. That much he knew. But what he did not yet know was legion.

Who formed the network and who was running it, for starters? Who else was involved besides Malecki, Larsen, Arlemont, McBundy, and Henrys? How long had the network been in existence? And what damage had already been done?

After a time Mahoney got out of bed, went into the bathroom, and took a long, liesurely shower, then got dressed again, changing into the one clean shirt he had brought with him.

He had leaned on Malecki, and the man had made mistakes. He had gotten to Arlemont, and he had made mistakes as well.

What was McBundy going to do? How sure of himself was he? Sure enough to expect that Mahoney was going to return docilely to Minnesota? If that was so, then all McBundy would have to do would be to sit tight, and everything would blow over, unless Malecki cracked under interrogation, or unless something else happened . . . something to upset the applecart.

Hares and hounds, Mahoney thought. It had worked so far, perhaps it would work a little longer. Just a little longer.

For a few seconds, then, he stood in the middle of the room deep in thought. If he had this to do all over again he would tell Sonja he was not interested. He would pass the information he got from her on to Darrel Switt, and then would forget about it.

But now it was too late. Far too late for him to simply

pack it in and return to Minnesota. For the rest of his life he would have the young Greek boy's death on his conscience, and he didn't think he could bear that.

Resolved finally to see this thing all the way to its conclusion, wherever that might take him, he went across the room, sat down on the edge of the bed, and picked up the phone.

Hares and hounds it was going to be, he told himself. But this time the game was going to be played with a vengeance.

When the hotel operator came on the line, he gave her his name and room number and asked to be connected with the overseas operator.

"I can make that call for you, sir. To whom would you like to speak?"

"I have two calls to make," Mahoney said pleasantly. "First I'd like to talk with the information operator for London, England."

"Yes, sir, I am dialing that number direct."

Mahoney held the phone in the crook of his neck, and while the operator was placing his first call, he took out a cigar, unwrapped it, and lit it.

"London. Information, please," a female with a very deep Cockney accent came on the line at last.

"Yes," Mahoney said. "I'd like the telephone number of a Mr. McNiel Henrys, please."

"One moment, sir," the London operator said, and Mahoney puffed on his cigar until she was back.

"I'm sorry, sir, there is no listing for a McNiel Henrys in the Greater London area. Do you have his address?"

"No, I don't, but thanks anyway for your help," Mahoney said, and after a moment the connection was broken, and the hotel operator was back on the line.

"Are you ready for your second call, sir?"

"Yes, I am. I'd like to call Tel Aviv, Israel," he said,

and he gave her Wasserman's emergency number.

It took nearly five minutes for the call to go through and when it did the woman's voice that answered was very faint.

"Yes?" she said.

"Larry will be coming home very soon," Mahoney shouted.

There was a silence on the line.

"Larry will be coming home," Mahoney repeated. "Very soon."

There was no answer, and a moment later the connection was broken.

The hotel operator was back. "Are you finished, sir?"

"Yes, thanks," Mahoney said, and he hung up.

McBundy would have had plenty of time to set up a monitor on the hotel's switchboard, and if there had been any doubt in his mind about Mahoney's intentions, it would have been completely dispelled by the two calls.

Mahoney pulled on his coat, let himself out of his room, and hurried down the corridor, taking the stairs instead of the elevator to the ground floor. He left the building by a back entrance.

Whatever he did now, he was going to have to be very careful with himself. The word would have already gone out: Mahoney is still active. Stop him.

XXIII

Mahoney walked around to the front of the motel where he caught a cab just coming into the parking lot. He slipped in the back and kept his body well back so that his face was not visible from the outside.

There was a very good chance that he had been spotted despite his precautions, but there was an equally strong possiblity that whoever McBundy had sent over would be concentrating on the room upstairs.

"Where to, buddy?" the cabby asked as he pulled back out into traffic, and jerked the meter flag down.

"Union Station, I guess," Mahoney mumbled.

"What do you mean, you guess," the cabby said irritably. "You wanna go there or not?"

At the hotel, Mahoney had pulled five hundred dollars from the envelope Wasserman had given him and had stuffed it in a trouser pocket. Now he pulled out a couple of twenty dollar bills and held them up so the cabby could see them.

"Union Station I *guess,* because I don't know for sure," Mahoney said.

"What the hell—"

"There used to be a pawnshop up there. Around the corner from the Sisters of the Poor, I think. You know the place?"

The cabby glanced at Mahoney's reflection in the rearview mirror, then looked at the two twenties Mahoney still held out.

"Not there any more. Cops closed it down."

"I figured that might have happened. What else is up there?"

"I don't know what the hell you mean, mister. What're you lookin' for—a score?"

"A piece," Mahoney said.

"Oh, Jesus," the cabby said. They were already on the Rochambeau Memorial Bridge approach, and there was no place to pull over. "I'm dumpin' you as soon as we get across. I don't want any trouble."

Mahoney pulled out two more twenties and held them up as well. "You're just hauling a fare, that's all. Give me a name. Drop me off at the front door and you can be on you way. We never saw each other before."

Again the cabby eyed the money. "Jesus," he said. "That's eighty bucks."

Mahoney reached in his pocket and pulled out another twenty dollar bill. "Make it an even hundred."

"You a cop or something?" the cabby asked, more nervous, Mahoney suspected, about the money than about being arrested.

"No, I'm not. I'm retired. I'm just tired of being ripped off all the time. I want a little protection."

"Ronald McDonald," the cabby said.

Mahoney didn't say a thing.

"I'm serious. Just like the Golden Arches. Ronald McDonald's his name. I'll drop you off. But I ain't waitin'. No way in hell I'm going to haul you anywhere if you're carrying a piece."

"Fine," Mahoney said, and he let the five twenties fall

down on the front seat, and then he sat back.

Traffic was heavy at this hour of the afternoon, and Mahoney figured if they had picked up a tail, the team would be earning its money trying to keep up with them.

The one thing he did not understand yet was who the network used as legmen. The frontline troops. It was a safe bet that Malecki or the others did not manage stakeouts themselves. And he had seen no indications in the Mossad files that Malecki ever used Wasserman's people for the job.

It was possible that the Mossad chief was right after all, and that this was a Soviet operation. But that would mean that McBundy had had Soviet connections all this time. It was a gloomy thought, and it put Mahoney in a very foul mood.

Perhaps the entire organization did funnel its information through Per Larsen, who in turn passed it on to the Soviets. If that was so it would make the Rosenberg case here in the States and the Israel Beer mess over there seem like child's play by comparison.

There was one anomaly in that line of thinking, however. If Per Larsen was indeed the number-one man, and he operated out of Brussels, then why had Arlemont telephoned London when he was in trouble?

One evening with the computer and a sharp operator down at Langley and he would have the answers. But McBundy was on his guard now, so there wasn't a chance in hell of that being allowed.

No, Mahoney thought as they passed the Museum of Natural History on Constitution Avenue, that definitely was out. The next step would have to be the network's. And it would be an assassination try. Mahoney's only hope was that he would not only survive the attempt, but he would be able to snag his attacker.

All that was needed would be one link—one weak link —and Mahoney was certain that the entire organization would tumble like a line of dominoes. It was one thing to play games with the Komitet; it was an entirely different matter to maintain your loyalty when Rome was tumbling down around your ears.

Past the Capitol building, the cabby turned up Maryland Avenue, coming around Stanton Square, and then he turned north on Sixth, as Mahoney continued his efforts to think this all out.

Even something as mundane as McBundy's promotion jacket would provide invaluable information at this stage of the game. For instance, how had his entry into the service been facilitated.

Wishing for it, however, was like wishing for the moon, and he forced himself to slow down. To think it all out.

He seemed to vaguely remember something being mentioned about the OSS and operations during the war. It had been nothing more than an offhand reference to something. But if McBundy had been in that group, Mahoney was almost certain he would have heard of him. It stood to reason that someone who had climbed as high as McBundy had in the Company—all the way up to chief of Clandestine Operations—would have made some kind of a mark for himself during the war. Any kind of a mark in those days caused ripples, and Mahoney would have heard of him.

He knew that McBundy had been chief of Western European Operations for a while in the early sixties, and later was Reporting and Advising Officer for NATO's Defence Review Committee or something like that.

For a while McBundy was Embassy Assignments and Dispositions Officer; that was during the time when Mahoney himself was in Moscow. And finally McBundy landed the number-two slot in Ops, his promotion to chief coming not long afterward.

The memories were too incomplete, however, to rely

on them for any real conclusions. Which once again brought him back to square one.

"We're comin' up on it in the next block," the cabby said, and Mahoney sat forward in his seat.

The neighborhood was predominantly black and poor. Stripped cars were up on blocks, and near the corner a rusted-out hulk was half up on the sidewalk. It reminded him of the New York tenement neighborhoods the CIA had used as field operations stations during the Korean War.

"Point it out to me, but don't stop," Mahoney said.

"That's fine by me," the cabby said, and in the next block without slowing down, he nodded to the left-hand side of the street. "Mac's Place," he said. "That's it."

Mahoney glanced at the cabby's identification badge and number. "I hope you weren't lying to me, Gil, about Ronald McDonald."

The cabby looked in the rearview mirror at Mahoney. "I wasn't lying," he said. "But if anything happens to you, don't go blaming me. This is a dark neighborhood, if you catch my drift. People here don't care for your kind."

"Pull around the next corner and let me out."

They came around the corner and the cabby pulled to the curb and stopped. "I'll catch the tab outa what you already gave."

"Thanks," Mahoney said, reaching for the door handle.

"You're a cop, ain't you," the cabby said. "Or at least you was a cop once upon a time."

Mahoney smiled. "Sort of."

The cabby nodded. "I knew it. Goddamn, I knew it."

Mahoney got out of the cab and, without looking back, went around the corner and shuffled down the street toward Mac's Place . . . Buy & Sell/New & Used . . . in the middle of the block.

A half dozen black youths were pitching pennies against the curb, and when Mahoney passed they all looked sullenly up at him, hate smoldering in their eyes. But then he was past and he could hear the reassuring, delicate tinkle of the pennies against the pavement.

The windows of the pawnshop were filled with a collection of guitars, typewriters, cameras, and class rings, the windowpanes protected by iron bars and a thick wire mesh. A metallic decal on the door warned that the shop was protected by the Southern States Security Services, Inc.

Mahoney stepped inside and went slowly to the back, where a tiny counter blocked the opening to the rear portions of the building.

A very large black man with a badly broken nose and cauliflower ears shambled from somewhere in the back and stepped up to the counter. For a few moments he simply eyed Mahoney and then looked toward the front door.

"You want something?" he finally asked, his voice surprisingly rich and cultured.

"I'm looking for Ronald McDonald," Mahoney said, feeling faintly foolish.

"Yeah?" the big man behind the counter said disinterestedly.

"I'm not a cop."

"Yeah?"

"I'm looking for a piece. A revolver."

"Get out of here," the black man said, his voice low, menacing.

Mahoney started to reach in his pocket, but the black man held up a big hand. The knuckles were all enlarged and scared.

"Don't want to see your honky money. Don't want your trouble."

No trouble if I get what I'm looking for," Mahoney said softly. "I need protection. Gil Mortenson, a cabby, mentioned your name."

"He's got no call to do that," the black man said, his face totally devoid of expression.

"I can pay you well," Mahoney said. "I just want to buy a pistol and some ammunition, and then get out of here."

The front door opened at that moment, the black man stepped back, and Mahoney turned as Darrel Switt entered and closed the door.

Mahoney's heart clutched in his chest. He had expected McBundy to send someone after him sooner or later, but not Switt. It couldn't be Switt.

The younger man was dressed in a tan suit, his tie loose. His mustache had been trimmed back, and his hair was much shorter than the last time Mahoney had seen him. He no longer looked young and inexperienced, rather he seemed arrived.

"I heard you were coming home," Switt said. "But what are you doing here?"

"I came up to buy a gun."

Switt's eyebrows rose. "I see," he said. "I'll be across the street when you're finished. Dark Chevy."

It seemed to Mahoney as if the moment was suspended in time. Switt turned and went back out the door.

"Do you want the gun?" the shopkeeper asked.

"Yes," Mahoney said, and he hurried to the front of the shop just close enough to the windows so that he could see Switt crossing the street and climbing behind the wheel of a maroon, two-door Chevy. He was alone. There were no other suspicious-looking cars on the street. No windowless vans. Nothing.

How had he known? He must have been at the airport, then the hotel, and he must have followed the cab. But how? Where had his information come from? The network?

"Three hundred bucks," the black man said from the back of the store.

Mahoney turned and went back to the counter where the shopkeeper had placed a small paper bag. He pulled out his money, counted out three hundred dollars, and handed it across. "You've never seen me," he said.

The black nodded, and pocketed the money as Mahoney pulled the gun and half a box of ammunition out of the bag. It was a Smith Wesson snub-nosed .38 most of the bluing gone, the handle grip on the left side cracked.

Mahoney released the cylinder from the breach, looked down the barrel, and checked the firing pin. The weapon was in bad shape, but it would fire.

He looked over his shoulder again toward the windows, but from this deep in the shop he could not see the other side of the street. When he turned back the black man was gone. Which was just as well. The man had sensed trouble from the moment Mahoney had walked in the door, and he was probably correct. There was going to be trouble, and very soon.

Mahoney opened the box of cartridges and slowly loaded the pistol. Then he put a few extras in his left-hand coat pocket.

Resisting arrest. Possession of an illegal weapon. Suspected espionage activities. The litany of his sins, real or imagined, could go on forever. Any one of which was sufficient and just cause for a trigger-happy legman to blow him away.

Gently, he snapped the pistol's cylinder back in place, and with his finger on the trigger stuffed the weapon in his right-hand coat pocket, then turned and shuffled to the door.

Across the street Switt was sitting in the car. He was looking straight ahead. Down the street to the left the group of boys was still hunched down pitching pennies. To the right, a block away, a large canvas-covered delivery truck was rumbling this way.

Mahoney tensed, the muscles in his gut trembling as the truck came nearer.

Not Switt, he thought, almost saying the words out loud.

As the cab of the truck came even with Switt's car, Mahoney jerked open the door, stepped out onto the sidewalk, and raced out into the street, crouching very low as the truck passed, and a second later he had made it to the back of the Chevy without being seen.

Carefully he worked his way around to the passenger side of the car, the duck squat he was doing very hard on his legs.

When he was just below the passenger door window, he took a deep breath and let it out slowly as he pulled the pistol out of his pocket and cocked the hammer.

Slowly he rose up. Switt was staring across at the front door of the pawnshop, and he started to open his door when Mahoney jerked open the passenger door.

When Switt spun around Mahoney had the pistol pointed directly at his face.

"Close your door, Darrel," Mahoney said very evenly.

Switt seemed genuinely hurt, but he complied and then placed both of his hands on the steering wheel. "Are you on the run, Wallace?"

Keeping the pistol leveled on the younger man, Mahoney got into the car and closed the door behind him.

"Is there someone back there, Darrel?" he asked.

"Are you expecting someone?"

"I thought maybe you'd be working in pairs."

Switt's nostrils flared. "What the hell did they do to you in Tel Aviv? Christ, I told you to stay away from that Margraff woman. I knew something like this was going to happen."

"Like what?" Mahoney asked. "Something like what was going to happen?"

"Look at you," Switt flared. "You look like hell. Look like you haven't slept in a month." He turned away momentarily, and when he looked back there was a softening around his eyes. "You look like a hunted man. Burned out. I told you to stay retired."

"You also called me a ruthless sonofabitch."

Switt shook his head. "I should have said stubborn sonofabitch."

Mahoney smiled, and lowered the pistol, but his eyes never left Switt's hands gripping the top of the steering wheel. If they had moved away, Mahoney would have shot him then, but they did not.

"Let's get out of here."

"Where to?" Switt asked. He started the car, put it in gear, and pulled away from the curb.

They passed the boys pitching pennies, and again there were the sullen stares.

Back forty years, Mahoney wanted to say, but Switt was far too young to understand what would be meant by that. Too young and still too idealistic despite his evident desire to come across as an urbane, wordly type.

Back forty years, Mahoney thought, when Marge was a beautiful, willing woman. When he was home on leave they would make love in the daytime on the nine-by-twelve rug they had in their apartment.

"The Lincoln Memorial," he finally said out loud.

Switt glanced over at him as they came around the corner. "You've got it pretty bad, haven't you?"

XXIV

It was approaching midnight. Ezra Wasserman sat in his office, his back to his desk, staring out the window at the Shalom Meir Tower two blocks away. The red aircraft warning lights on the television tower atop the building blinked on and off. An inviting target for incoming enemy aircraft, or for naval spotters far out in the Med. During times of crisis the lights were turned off, of course, but at this moment Israel was ostensibly at peace.

The telephone buzzed. Wasserman turned unhurriedly and picked it up. "Yes?" he said softly.

"He's just arrived, Ezra. He's on his way up."

"Is he alone?"

"Yes, sir."

"Where'd he park his car?"

"He arrived by cab."

"He didn't spot you?"

"No, sir."

"All right," Wasserman said. "Good work. Just stand by out front. If I need anything I'll call."

"Yes, sir," the agent watching the Finance Annex's

front entrance said crisply, and he hung up.

Wasserman replaced his phone on the cradle, got up from his desk, and opened the door to his secretary's office. The corridor door was closed but unlocked.

The strap of his shoulder holster was chafing his left armpit, and he adjusted it as he went back behind his desk and sat down.

What he was doing this evening was exceedingly dangerous. Malecki was a much younger, far quicker man, and it was possible that once he realized he was cornered, he would try to shoot his way out. He wouldn't get far, of course. Besides the two men down in the courtyard, there were an additional four posted on this floor in various offices, and stakeout vehicles were located at the front and rear of the building.

Malecki would not have a chance of getting away. But he could do a lot of damage before he was brought down.

On the telephone earlier that evening Malecki had not seemed overly suspicious when Wasserman had asked him to come up to the office.

"Working a little late, aren't we, Ezra?" he had quipped.

"Something's come up that has me worried, Chaim," Wasserman said, trying to inject just the right note into his voice. "It's Wallace Mahoney. He's disappeared."

"Good riddance," Malecki said.

"It's not quite as simple as that, Chaim. He took something with him that belongs to us. I'm going to need your help getting it back, I think. Or at least your thinking on the subject."

"I've got a dinner party going on here at the moment, Ezra," Malecki said, and Wasserman almost said, I know, but he stifled it in time. "So it may be a bit late before I can break way."

"That's all right. I have a feeling I'll be here most of the night anyway."

"That bad?"

"That bad."

"I'll get there as soon as I can," Malecki said, and he hung up.

Now he was coming. He would be signed in by now, and on his way up in the elevator.

Wasserman felt a deep sadness in his heart for Sonja, and how she was going to take the news that her lover of the past five years was Israel's traitor. And yet he was glad of two things. The first was that Sonja had had nothing to do with this mess. And the second that it was finally over with. Or very nearly so. And yet he knew it was going to be difficult to face Malecki.

The fair-haired boy of Tel Aviv, Mahoney had disparagingly called him. But it had been true. Malecki had been a brightly shining star for so long that even now it was almost impossible for Wasserman to believe he was a traitor . . . *the* traitor.

The corridor door opened, and Chaim Malecki, still wearing his dinner clothes, his bow tie undone and hanging down the front of his ruffled shirt, the collar open, came in.

He spotted Wasserman and smiled as he came across the outer office. "They said at the desk that you were still up here. Haven't you been home yet tonight?"

"Not yet," Wasserman said, shaking his head.

"Couldn't this have kept until morning, Ezra? I'm bushed, and you look all in yourself."

Wasserman motioned for Malecki to take a seat. "No, it can't wait, Chaim," he said softly.

Something flashed briefly across Malecki's eyes as he came all the way into the office and sat down. Wasserman wondered if he had a glimmering of suspicion. But then the look passed, and Malecki gazed across the desk, his eyes open, clear, free of guilt.

"So, what has Mahoney done that has you all upset?" he asked, crossing his legs.

"It's not Mahoney," Wasserman said. "Although he has been directly involved in this."

"I'm not following you."

"I think you are, Chaim," Wasserman said, looking directly into the man's eyes. "I think you've been following this all along."

Malecki leaned forward and Wasserman had become so jumpy he almost pulled out his gun right then, but something stayed his hand.

"What the hell are you talking about, Ezra? Would you mind explaining it to me?"

Wasserman had thought of a dozen different approaches to use on Malecki. A dozen different ways of maneuvering the younger man into inadvertently revealing information. Anything, even a scrap, would help unravel the two big questions in Wasserman's mind: Who was Malecki working for, and why had he done it?

But facing the man now, all that resolve went by the wayside, fueled by the years Wasserman had known, trusted, and respected him.

"Why?" Wasserman asked, his voice barely audible.

Malecki obviously sensed something was drastically wrong here, but he made no overt moves. "Why what?" he asked simply.

"The documents in Ben Abel's briefcase were fake, Chaim. We've known for some time that we've had a mole . . . a traitor in our midst. That's why we brought Mahoney here."

"Sonja was in on it?" Malecki asked, his voice flat, but his eyes still wide.

Wasserman nodded. "Mahoney came up with the files

and David's ADC planted them in Base Ops. We knew the mole would come looking for them. But it was Sonja who suggested Mahoney for the job in the first place."

Malecki said nothing. Wasserman's heart was pounding.

"We were in the parking lot when you arrived on base. We watched you go in, and a minute later watched you coming out with David's briefcase."

"I see," Malecki said.

"Kominski wanted to shoot you then and there, but Mahoney held him off. It was Kominski who fired the shots at you from the university."

Something came into Malecki's eyes at that news, and he pursed his lips. "He's admitted shooting at me?"

"No. He's dead. Fell out a hotel window in Hebron."

"Why in God's name would he want to see me dead?"

"He figures you were Ben Abel's murderer."

For a few seconds both men were silent, but then Malecki spoke.

"For whatever it's worth, I didn't know David had been murdered. But why wasn't I arrested at Base Ops?"

"It was Mahoney's idea," Wasserman said. "He wanted to follow you. See who you delivered the documents to."

"And?"

"He did follow you. To Brussels. He watched Per Larsen pick up the briefcase from the jet."

The color gradually left Malecki's face, and with it had his composure. He uncrossed his legs and got slowly to his feet. Wasserman pulled out his gun and pointed it up at him.

"Don't try to leave, Chaim. Despite everything, I don't want to kill you, but I will try if I must. Besides, I have people posted up here as well as out front and in the back. Just don't make me shoot you."

"Does Sonja know about all of this?"

"Some of it, but I'm sure she's guessed nearly all of the rest. Ironically enough she was our chief suspect for quite some time."

Malecki looked beyond Wasserman out the window. "I've nothing else to say then, Ezra."

Wasserman sat forward, and keeping the pistol trained on Malecki with one hand, he reached with the other to touch the intercom button that would summon the four men posted on this floor. He hesitated for a moment.

"Could you tell me why, Chaim? Was it for money?"

Malecki said nothing as he continued to stare out the window, and Wasserman at last hit the button. Almost immediately he could hear his people out in the corridor.

WASHINGTON, D.C. . . . WEDNESDAY NIGHT

Mahoney and Switt stood within the Lincoln Memorial, looking out beyond the Doric columns across the Reflecting and Rainbow pools. To the east the Washington Monument was stark white against the dark background. Melancholy, almost harsh in its intensity. The loneliness of the scene, as well as the brooding expression on the figure of Lincoln behind them pretty well matched Mahoney's mood.

"What amazes me," Switt said, "was that the stupid fools went along with you. They were playing with fire, they did know that, didn't they?"

Mahoney nodded. "Operation Wrath was, and still is, fire, Darrel. But they were desperate to find out who their mole was."

"And Sonja Margraff was among the chief suspects?"

Again Mahoney nodded. "At least Wasserman had her high on his list."

"So he included her on the list of hunters. Sort of like a wolf in sheep's clothing."

"More like a sheep in wolf's clothing."

"I don't understand."

"You will, Darrel, just bear with me. As soon as Sonja was keyed into the list, she suggested me. Knew I was retired, thought they would do better with an outsider."

"Why, in heaven's name?"

"Begin's government is up for grabs. They figured that any shake-up now would topple him."

"Politics," Switt snapped harshly. Then he looked into Mahoney's eyes. "She came to you, which meant she got the green light from at least Wasserman."

"All the way to the top, from Begin himself. Although reluctantly, from what I was told."

"I'll bet," Switt said cynically. "And you jumped at the chance to keep your hand in."

"No, I didn't. I just agreed to meet with Wasserman on neutral territory. A vacation. A chat over old times. I was curious."

"You were curious. So you went to Athens."

"McBundy told me that you put the trace on me."

"I was worried, you old fool. I had no idea what the hell you were getting yourself into. If I had known how bad it was going to get, I would have physically had you dragged back home."

"Then you know about the explosion at the airport."

Switt's eyes narrowed. "There was an explosion there. We heard about it, but my people said you were clear."

"It was meant for me. Sonja had given me a luggage locker key. Wasserman's instructions for the meet were in the locker. I sent a young shoeshine boy in to fetch it."

"And the locker exploded."

Mahoney nodded.

"Killed the boy?"

Again Mahoney inclined his head.

"And that pissed you off. Not only did they make a try on your life, but it backfired and killed an innocent boy."

"He might have been ten or eleven at the most, Darrel. I couldn't let it go after that."

"What did Wasserman say to you?"

"The usual. Traitor in their service. Wanted to know if I would take on the job."

"No, I mean about the explosion. Obviously someone was on to you already. Sonja was the most likely."

"Sonja didn't have the time to make it to Athens, and the only others who handled the key and instructions were low-level legmen. Someone else had to have been involved."

"The mole," Switt said. "Which told you he was highly enough placed that he could find out about your meet with Wasserman, find out about the luggage locker, and set the bomb before you arrived."

"Exactly," Mahoney said.

"And you accepted, after all that. You went to Tel Aviv. What happened there?"

"An awful lot, Darrel," Mahoney said, and he passed his right hand over his forehead. He wondered about what had been going on here at home in the interim. "How has Bob been acting these past few weeks?"

Switt seemed startled by the question. "What the hell do you mean by that?"

"He knew I went to Athens, and he knew I was in Tel Aviv. He met me this morning at the airport. Knew, or at least guessed that I had been working for the Mossad. How has he been taking it?"

"Trying to cover your ass, Wallace?" Switt asked. "It's a little late for that, you know."

Mahoney said nothing, and after a bit Switt answered his question.

"He didn't believe it at first. Then he got mad. Wanted to shine the light on you, get you back. Then he was worried."

"And when he found out I was coming home?"

"Relieved," Switt said.

"Is that how you knew I'd be coming back, Darrel?" Mahoney said. He had nonchalantly stuffed his right hand in his jacket pocket, and his fingers curled around the grip of the pistol.

"He phoned last night, said you were coming in."

"And?"

"He said you might still be active, and that he was going to try to talk you into returning to Minnesota. But he didn't hold out much hope."

"So you've become McBundy's pitchman."

"Shit," Switt said. "I don't deserve that, Wallace. Not from you." He was angry and hurt.

Mahoney turned away and stared across at the seated figure of Lincoln. He took his hand out of his pocket. There were a few people, including a couple of children at the base of the statue looking up at it. The natural reaction in there was one of silence. It was comforting in some small measure to Mahoney's beleaguered mind.

"Bob knows you came out to see me?" he asked. "He knows we're together now?"

"He wants this handled on a personal level. He doesn't want to prosecute."

Mahoney turned back to him. "You know I did uncover their mole. He's probably in custody now."

"What about the nuclear documents you manufactured?"

"We planted them at Base Operations at Lod. A man by the name of Chaim Malecki picked them up."

Switt was startled. "I know him."

"From where?" Mahoney asked sharply.

"Here in Washington. He used to work for the *Post*, I think. But he's here several times a year looking for money. I've met him."

"He's the mole."

"What did he do with the documents?"

"Took them to Brussels. Per Larsen picked them up."

"ININ," Switt said softly, and he whistled. "What in hell have you gotten yourself into? Jesus. Did you tell Bob?"

"No. Begin is going to contact our government with the entire story, minus my involvement, of course."

"That may not be possible in the end."

Mahoney shrugged.

"Just two questions, Wallace," Switt said.

Mahoney waited.

"What about Arlemont in Paris. Did you kill him?"

"It was an accident. He had a gun. We struggled. I think his neck was broken."

"Was he a part of this thing with Malecki and Larsen?"

"I think so."

"Were they running some kind of a network?"

"That's the third question," Mahoney said pointedly.

"Goddammit, I'm trying to understand what's going on here. What you've gotten yourself into. Evidently you've broken their network; Malecki in Israel, Per Larsen for NATO, and Arlemont for the French. So now you're done with it—" Switt broke off in mid-sentence, his eyes growing wide. "That's not it. You're not done with it, are you? There's more. You're still on the hunt, here in Washington."

Anomalies, Mahoney thought. The world abounded with anomalies, not all of which led to anything significant.

He stepped away from the column and started down the broad stairs to the street level. Switt hurried after him.

"I want you to go home, Wallace. I'll see what I can find out from this end."

"All right," Mahoney said, keeping his eyes straight ahead. The night had turned cool, but the city lights reflected in the long pool that stretched most of the way to the Washington Monument were bright, multicolored, and warm.

"Don't play games with me. Whatever you do, don't play games with me. You could get hurt."

Mahoney had to laugh at that, but he didn't turn to face the younger man until they had reached the bottom of the stairs. And then they stopped.

"Do what you want here in Washington, Darrel, but I'll warn you about two things."

Switt waited for him to continue.

"Go careful. Don't upset the applecart. The Operation Wrath documents are still out there somewhere, and the Israelis are still our friends. If Qaddafi or someone like that got wind that the Isrealis were planning preemptive nuclear strikes in the Mid-East, there'd be hell to pay. There would be a nuclear war out there for sure. And secondly, for both our sakes, I want this conversation between us kept quiet."

"I can't do—"

"Just for a day or two, Darrel. That's all I'm asking."

Switt stared at him for a moment. "You have no intention of returning to Minnesota, do you?"

Mahoney shook his head. "No."

They crossed the sidewalk and climbed into Switt's car. The younger man started it, flipped on the headlights, and then lit himself a cigarette.

"Back to your hotel?" he asked.

Mahoney nodded. "My flight leaves in the morning

and I'm dead tired. I'm going to take a shower, have a drink and some dinner, and then get some sleep."

"I thought you weren't going back?"

"I'm going to head that way," Mahoney said, a slight smile on his face. He had always admired Switt as a capable, albeit somewhat over idealistic, young man. "Will Bob put a baby-sitter on me to make sure I make it home all right?"

"I'll handle it," Switt said. "Only because I know damned well you're not going to listen to any of the good advice you've been given."

They drove across the Arlington Memorial Bridge and then turned south along the George Washington Memorial Parkway, mostly in silence, Switt apparently concentrating on his driving, and Mahoney admiring the city across the Potomac River.

When they came within sight of the Marriott, however, Switt glanced over at Mahoney. "I've always had a great deal of respect for you, Wallace. I want you to know that."

"That's a comfort."

"Don't make fun of me. I meant what I said. You were the best."

Mahoney chuckled. "You're the second one to tell me that today. I almost feel like I should be dead and buried."

They turned into the parking lot and Switt drove around to the back of the building.

"Bob has probably stationed someone out front to watch for you," Switt said. "Might as well keep him guessing."

Mahoney was watching the signs with the room numbers at each entryway, and when they came to his he pointed it out to Switt who pulled into a vacant parking slot.

"Be careful, Wallace," Switt said.

"Thanks," Mahoney replied, and they shook hands.

Mahoney climbed out of the car, went to the motel entrance, then turned and watched as Switt backed out of the parking slot and drove away.

For a couple of seconds he stood where he was, watching the car's taillights disappear around the corner, and then he opened the door and stepped inside.

The stairwell light was out, and the entryway was in almost complete darkness. Instantly Mahoney knew something was wrong. Very wrong. He started to reach for the pistol in his pocket. At that instant something sharp slammed into his chest causing him to reel back, and the pistol got caught in the pocket lining.

A numbness spread rapidly from a point above his left breast, and within a couple of seconds he could feel his knees giving out, and what little light that filtered in from the outside faded. He had forgotten to explain to Switt what he had meant when he said that Sonja was like a "sheep in wolf's clothing," and that worried him. But that was his last conscious thought.

XXV

GENEVA . . . THURSDAY

The first things Mahoney became aware of as he gradually awakened from a very deep, dreamless sleep, were the odor of cut flowers and the bright sunlight streaming through tall windows. He had no idea whether it was morning or afternoon, or even what day it was. He did have a feeling, however, that many hours had elapsed since he had been struck down at the motel entryway.

His hand went to his chest where he had been shot, and his fingertips encountered a small bandage.

He remembered weakening and falling to the floor, but nothing more.

The room he was in was large and very well decorated; tall ceilings, what appeared to be silk wallpaper, and obviously expensive furniture.

He lay nude beneath the covers in a wide, comfortable bed, and for a few moments he was content to remain where he was. The drug, whatever it was that had been injected into his bloodstream, probably by a dart, had afforded him the first solid rest in several weeks. Despite everything that had happened to him and around him, he felt good. Better than he had in a long time.

Gradually, however, his mind went back to McBundy who had evidently stationed his people at the motel. Yet logically, Mahoney supposed that McBundy would have ordered his death, not an elaborate kidnapping. And unless he was mistaken, he had the very distinct impression he was no longer in the United States. The furniture, the room itself, and the lamps and light fixtures all seemed to be European.

France. The thought crossed his mind, and he flipped back the covers, sat up, and swung his legs over the edge of the bed.

It was possible that McBundy had sent him back to France to stand trial for Arlemont's murder. And yet, even if that were the case, Mahoney suspected he would have awakened in a jail cell, not here.

Clothing was laid out on a valet chair, and across the room from the bed, a mirrored door stood open, revealing a very large bathroom beyond.

Mahoney got out of bed, slowly padded across the room to the windows, and looked outside.

The room he was in was on the second floor of what appeared to be a very large house in a row of similar structures that all fronted on a narrow mews. The buildings across the way blocked off any view of the city, but Mahoney now knew for certain that he was in Europe, although it didn't seem like Paris to him. The architecture looked more Germanic than anything else.

After a time, Mahoney turned and went into the bathroom where he ran water in the large tub, cleaned his teeth, and shaved with the things that had been laid out for him. Then he took a long, leisurely bath, after which he went back into his bedroom and dressed in the clothing that fit him quite well.

This was very possibly Brussels, and Per Larsen would be waiting for him. Possibly with the Operation

Wrath documents for confirmation.

Or it could be London, and downstairs would be McNiel Henrys.

At the door he hesitated for a moment. Whoever had brought him here could have killed him at any time. They had not, which meant they very probably wanted something from him. There was a network, of at least that much Mahoney was reasonably certain. There also could be an opposition operation being run by another group. Perhaps he was being recruited. Perhaps it had not been McBundy's people after all who had snatched him.

The corridor was wide, richly paneled in dark woods, with paintings hung at respectable intervals. As Mahoney headed away from his room, his step light on the carpeted floor, he had the distinct impression that he was in a museum. A table between his room and the next one down held a beautifully wrought marble piece that looked Greek. The table was flanked by a pair of massive wing-backed chairs. Beyond that, to the left, the corridor opened to a wide staircase, the massive banisters ornately carved.

The house was quiet, and again Mahoney hesitated before he continued. The staircase faced three gigantic stained-glass windows that admitted the sunlight in soft, multicolored patterns, heightening the impression that this was either a museum or the home of a very wealthy person. Old money wealthy.

A young, very beautiful woman, dressed in a brown blazer, riding trousers, and tall boots, came bounding up the stairs just as Mahoney was about to start down.

She spotted him standing there when she was halfway up, and she stopped in her tracks.

"Oh," she said in a small voice. Mahoney guessed her to be in her mid to late twenties.

"Good morning," he said. "Or is it afternoon?"

"It's afternoon, Mr. Mahoney," the young woman said, smoothly regaining her poise. "My father is waiting for you on the patio." She spoke with a cultured British accent.

Mahoney came down the stairs toward her, and she turned and preceeded him.

"We didn't expect you up quite so soon," she said. over her shoulder. "You had an enjoyable rest?"

"Lovely," Mahoney mumbled. He had not expected anything like her.

She turned and looked at him as she reached the bottom of the staircase. "You certainly look much better now than when you came in."

He managed a slight smile as he joined her. "Where are we, Miss—"

"You may call me Caroline," she said. "And this is Eaux Vives."

Mahoney looked blankly at her.

"The South Bank. Geneva, Switzerland," she said.

"And the day?"

"You *did* sleep soundly," she said. "It's Thursday."

"Of course."

For a moment she just stared at him as if she was waiting for him to ask another equally silly question. But then she shrugged, turned, and continued across a wide reception hall, down a corridor, and out a rear door that opened onto a patio overlooking a magnificent rose garden of at least an acre. A half dozen thickly padded outdoor chairs were grouped around a glass-topped wrought iron table, next to which was a serving cart laden with bottles and glasses. To the right a staircase led down to the garden.

A tall, impeccably dressed man, with his back to the house, was seated at the table sipping a drink as he stared down at the wild profusion of flowers. The young woman went immediately across to him, and he looked up at her and accepted a kiss on the cheek. Then he stood up and turned.

"Ah, Mr. Mahoney," he said, his voice rich and very cultured. He was a handsome, distinguished-looking man in his mid to late fifties, a touch of gray at the temples, flecks of it in his neatly trimmed mustache.

Mahoney crossed to where they stood and shook hands with the man. "McNiel Henrys?"

"Quite right," Henrys said. "Really quite clever of you to have come this far, you know." He turned to his daughter. "What are your plans this evening, my dear?"

"Just as soon as I change I'm going into town. Roger will be meeting me around six for dinner. After that, who knows?"

"Have a good time," Henrys said, and his daughter turned to Mahoney.

"A pleasure meeting you, Mr. Mahoney. Perhaps we'll have the time to go riding."

"Perhaps," Mahoney said, and the young woman went back into the house.

"A lovely young woman," Mahoney said, looking after her, and then he turned to Henrys who was beaming.

"Yes, she is. I'm rather proud of the girl, although she is a bit headstrong at times. Do you have children?"

Mahoney had to smile. "No need for pretense any longer, I don't think."

"Quite right," Henrys said. "Have a seat. Something to drink before dinner?"

"A bourbon would be nice," Mahoney said.

Henrys unhurriedly poured him a drink, neat, no ice, just as Mahoney liked it, then poured himself a glass of white wine.

When they were both settled at the table, Henrys gazed wistfully at Mahoney for a time, but then he said, "Are you at all interested in gardening, Mr. Mahoney?"

Mahoney looked down at the rose garden. "Not especially," he said. "My wife was, however."

"Then she would have appreciated my collection," Henrys replied fondly. "Do you realize there are more than four hundred horticultural varieties of the rose?"

"No," Mahoney mumbled indistinctly. Henrys had the same kind of emptiness, the same offhand arrogance in his personsality that Malecki had exhibited. The similarity was somehow discomforting.

"Of course there are only forty-three major races, of which I have twenty-seven, but the numbers are rather staggering, don't you agree?"

"Lovely house," Mahoney said.

Henrys smiled. "I do tend to ramble on a bit about my flowers," he said, and he glanced over his shoulder at the house. "It's been in the family for years, actually. I use it as a retreat. My daughter loves it. Loves the city." He looked back into Mahoney's eyes. "The Swiss are a wonderfully stoic people. In this century at least they've somehow managed to keep themselves out of the fray, so to speak."

"But you haven't," Mahoney said sharply, not intending that his comment come out quite so harsh.

Henrys seemed genuinely pained. "No, I haven't."

"What do you do with yourself these days . . . aside from your rose gardening? Last I heard you were liaison to the CIA."

"I rather enjoyed those days," Henrys said. "But now I'm no longer with the service. I'm what you might call an ex-officio member."

"But privy to everything?"

"You might say that. I've been making my small contribution as foreign intelligence adviser to Ten Downing Street."

Mahoney took a drink of his bourbon. It was very good, and it warmed his insides, filling the hollow space there with a pleasant feeling. He sighed.

"I get that way at times, as well," Henrys said, staring down at the garden. "I wonder if any of it is worth the effort."

Mahoney set his glass down on the table, suddenly weary of the little game of pleasantries they were playing. "The Israeli nuclear strike documents are fakes."

Henrys turned to him. "We know," he said. "We suspected the bundle as soon as we had confirmed that you had followed Malecki to Brussels."

"We?" Mahoney asked.

Henrys smiled again. "There's so terribly much to tell you, and so little time in which to make our position clear."

"Why go through all the bother? Your people tried to kill me in Athens and again in Asha. Why wasn't I killed in Washington? Why did you bring me here?"

"Yes, we did try to eliminate you in Athens, or at the very least, discourage you. But I'm afraid we rather bungled that one."

"Rather," Mahoney said dryly.

"We need your help, Mahoney," Henrys said, and Mahoney nearly laughed out loud, except for the fact the man was deadly serious.

"With what?"

"To clear up the mess you've created for us. You've placed us in a deucedly difficult position with your meddling in Tel Aviv. Malecki is under arrest at this moment so, as I say, there isn't much time."

"And if he breaks, your entire network will come tumbling down around your ears."

"He won't break. The Israelis aren't that crude."

"But if there was a chance of it, you'd kill him, wouldn't you?"

Henrys didn't say a thing for a moment. His right eyebrow was arched. But when he did speak, his words came as softly as a gentle wind sighing through a wheat field.

"Yes, we would."

"But that still wouldn't clear up your problems."

"No."

For just the briefest of instants Mahoney had a terrible premonition that he was not going to be able to deal with what the smug Britisher was going to tell him. That somehow what he was going to be asked to do would be much too large for him. Too large, perhaps for anyone. Yet he could not more demur from listening, from taking an active part in the exchange, than he could demur from breathing.

"Why me?"

"Because you chose to involve yourself in our affairs."

"*Our* affairs," Mahoney said. "I've identified Malecki with the Mossad, Larsen with ININ, Arlemont with the SDECE, McBundy with the CIA, and of course yourself with MI 9. Are there others?"

Henrys smiled almost indulgently, and Mahoney had to control himself not to lunge across the table, as he had with Arlemont, and drag the man to the ground, and pound him into insensibility.

"There are others," Henrys said. "The KGB, the Chinese, Bonn, Rome."

"The Soviets are involved?" Mahoney said, slightly disappointed. "But why pick on Israel?"

"Why pick on Israel . . . " Henrys started to ask, but then understanding dawned in his eyes, and he sat back, a new expression on his face as he regarded Mahoney. "My dear fellow, no one is picking on Israel, as you say, any more than anyone is aiding the Soviets or the Americans or anyone else exclusively."

"I don't understand."

"Evidently not. We're not working for the benefit of any one nation . . . or I should say, we've not become involved to the detriment of any country."

"You operate a network," Mahoney said, slowly, carefully.

"You could call it that," Henrys said. "But it isn't one of those cold war operations. Ours started with the Manhattan Project. Almost *because* of the project."

"World War Two?"

"Actually 1943. October, to be exact."

"And you've been operating all the time?"

Henrys nodded. "We have as a group. Of course at that time, I was not involved."

"The CIA wasn't even in existence then."

"The OSS was," Henrys said, and Mahoney immediately thought of McBundy's OSS background.

"Who started it and why?"

"That I'm not at liberty to say at the moment," Henrys said. "At least not until you've straightened out the mess you've created."

"If I refuse?" Mahoney asked.

"You won't," Henrys said confidently. "Not after I've told you what I brought you here to tell you."

Below, in the garden, a series of white stone pathways meandered throug the various species of rose plantings. Some of the flower beds were raised above the general level of the garden, held there by stone retaining walls, other beds were sunken, some were surrounded by lovely, shimmering pools of water, and still others were kept under glass in miniature greenhouses.

Mahoney and Henrys had finished their drinks in silence and then had descended into the garden, into the humid atmosphere that smelled of rose scent, rich dark earth, and from time to time the sharp odor of fertilizer.

They followed the pathways and were deep into the garden before Henrys spoke again.

"When you first became involved in our affairs a couple of years ago, you were lucky. And afterward, after your wife had died and you went into retirement, it was felt that you could be left alone. That you would do no further harm."

"Your people killed Lovelace and the Russian woman in San Antonio?" Mahoney asked incredulously. He had always supposed it had been the Russians.

"Yes."

"And yet telling me that now, you still expect me to help you?"

Henrys stopped a moment to face Mahoney. "When I've finished explaining it all to you—or at least as much of it as I can—I believe you will come to see that you have no choice in the matter."

"Expediency evidently is your philosophy," Mahoney said as they continued their stroll. "Malecki spouted the same doctrine."

"Not expediency," Henrys countered in a schoolteacherish fashion, "but peace."

"By assassination?"

"Several hundred thousand men, women, and children incinerated at Hiroshima and Nagasaki is expediency, Mr. Mahoney. Assassinating an old man and a dying woman who could have embroiled the entire world in nuclear holocaust is not. It's nothing more than common sense."

"Does your daughter Caroline share your philosophy?" Mahoney asked, not able to keep himself from taking that shot.

"Yes, she does," Henrys said with a straight face. "But I've never involved her in the details."

"Thoughtful of you."

Again Henrys stopped and faced Mahoney. "World War Two. Your government, by all the accounts my people could gather at the time, was almost certain to be successful in the development of the atomic bomb. It was a coming fact. The terrible weapon was a fact that no one could deny. So its secret was shared voluntarily with my government, and by our organization with the Soviets."

"Balance of power you're telling me?"

"Indeed. But it came too late to save the Japanese."

"The casualties would have been five times the number there were, had we been forced into invading the mainland."

"Such an invasion would never have taken place."

"You advocated a test shot of the bomb with Japanese witnesses?"

"That, Mr. Mahoney, and an understanding by your government of the Japanese mentality. Put simply, the Japanese people were afraid that their king, descended from the sun, would have been dethroned ignobly. They were willing to fight to the death to avoid that. They were even willing to submit to your nuclear attack."

"So giving the bomb to the Soviets was your answer," Mahoney said disparagingly. "Bullshit, Mr. Henrys. There's more to it than that, and you damned well know it."

Henrys didn't reply immediately, and Mahoney moved farther down the path until he came to one of the stone retaining walls for a raised flower bed, and he sat down. Henrys followed a few moments later and sat down beside him.

"You're a stubborn old man," he said.

"I can't abide lies. I can't abide murder. Yes, I am stubborn."

Henrys looked fondly at his flowers across the

pathway from where they sat. "How would you rank your service, the Central Intelligence Agency, in efficiency or in effectiveness?"

"The service has had its moments."

Henrys chuckled. "As we all have had," he said. "What I'm trying to ask, is simply this: Do you believe your agency—or any other agency anywhere else, for that matter—provides sufficient intelligence to counteract a war?"

Mahoney flared. "What the hell kind of a question is that?"

"A perfectly valid question—considering nuclear proliferation."

"A proliferation of your own doing."

"Only for the balance of power, just as your own government has proliferated its surplus food, its vaccine for polio."

"So your people formed a supra-intelligence service," Mahoney said. He could not quite believe he was hearing what he was hearing. He could not quite believe that he was calmly seated in a lovely rose garden listening to what Henrys was telling him.

"Close but not quite," Henrys said. "What we maintain is an old boy network. You're of course familiar with the term."

Mahoney nodded, but he too looked across at the roses. "Why was al Qaryūt destroyed?"

"The Israelis do have tactical nuclear weapons and the means to deliver them. If ever they did gain the clear edge in intelligence gathering, if ever they learned that their enemies were either unwilling or incapable of immediate retaliation, they will strike."

Mahoney looked back. "Do you honestly believe that?"

Henrys nodded.

"How about Ataruz? Did your people kill everyone there?"

"Yes, we did," Henrys said glibly.

"Who supplied the Labun nerve gas?"

"It was Soman gas, actually, but at this point in time I'm not able to discuss its source or method of on-site delivery. That will come later."

Mahoney could taste the bile, bitter at the back of his throat. "You share everyone's secrets, and eliminate anyone who opposes you."

"In the name of peace," Henrys said softly.

Mahoney turned to him. "You've murdered a lot of people in the name of peace."

"Good heavens, man," Henrys said, "it's either that or an all-out nuclear war. Which would you rather face?"

XXVI

GENEVA . . . THURSDAY EVENING

Mahoney and Henrys had dinner alone in a huge dining room that could have, and probably had, seated more than thirty people. During their meal of sole amandine with a very good Dom Perignon, they spoke of nothing of consequence. But afterward, sated with food and drink, they retired to Henrys's magnificent book-lined study, with its leather-topped desk, soft, glove-leather furniture, and antique Oriental rugs on the floor.

Mahoney sat in one of the easy chairs, letting the deep cushions and soft leather enfold his body, almost as if he were retreating into a protective cocoon, and waited for Henrys, who poured him an after-dinner brandy and then, almost on cue, offered him a cigar.

When they were both settled, Henrys, a few feet away on the couch, his legs crossed delicately as he sipped at his drink and smoked a cigarette in a bone holder, took up where they had left off in the garden.

"Violence is a part of the human condition," he began with no preamble. "Either it's a war, or a series of skirmishes somewhere, or it's the assassination of a world

313

leader like your president, or even a Pope. But we can't escape the fact of violence, Mahoney. Not and remain human."

"Then why do you advocate a balance of power? Why not let the bombs rain down?"

"Ah," Henrys said, setting his drink down on a low table in front of the couch. "That's just the point, don't you see. Assassination, skirmishes, war . . . on a limited scale, all those are acceptable. But now we've been placed in such a position that an all-out global war may not—*must* not—occur, else all life on this planet would either cease to exist or cease to have any meaning in our sense of civilization."

"So you proliferate nuclear knowledge—"

"Not any longer. We won't give the bomb to Qaddafi, or Khomeini, or their ilk. That would be suicide. But by the same token, we must carefully watch that those countries do not of themselves get the bomb, and then decide to use it."

"It sounds like you *advocate* violence," Mahoney said, finding this all increasingly difficult to swallow.

"Exactly," Henrys said triumphantly. "But channeled violence. We cannot allow, let's say, the trouble between Israel and Syria and Lebanon to escalate beyond a conventional war. We cannot allow the introduction of nuclear weapons into the fighting."

"So you destroy al Qaryūt," Mahoney said.

Henrys nodded. "To eliminate Israel's very clear advantage."

"El Salvador?" Mahoney asked, taking a random stab in the dark.

Henrys smiled. "You're catching on. We managed to supply some of the weapons to the rebels."

"Iran?"

"That was a much more delicate operation. In 1975

and again in 1978 we stopped CIA liquidation attempts on Khomeini while he was still in Paris in exile."

"You knew then that the Shah would be ousted?"

"We suspected as much, although we couldn't be certain. We had to cover every contingency, however. We could not allow Khomeini's assassination, not at that time. He was the only man who could hold Iran together if and when the Shah was deposed."

"You must have been involved in the Cuban missile crisis as well," Mahoney said, marveling despite himself at the apparently world-girding efficiency of the network.

"That one gave us a fright," Henrys said angrily. "Our contact in Moscow told us that the Soviets were building missile installations in Cuba. The information was passed on to your government, and the sites under construction were 'discovered' during a photo recon mission over the island. But the entire operation nearly backfired on us. Kennedy wanted to play cowboys and Indians. Your president very nearly got us into a global war that time."

Kennedy. Even after all these years since his assassination, the memories were still electric. Were still dark and frightening. It was as if something you had always believed to be true was probably false. Yet Mahoney could not bring himself to ask Henrys what part, if any, the network had played in the president's assassination. Violence, the man had said, was a part of the human condition. Controlling that violence was the network's apparent aim.

"If the war is to come," Henrys was saying, "it will come because of a president like Kennedy trying to overstep his power, or because of a country like Israel actually making a nuclear strike in the Middle East. The Arabs would have to retaliate with Soviet-supplied

weapons, and soon we would all be pulled into it. Or
perhaps some madman will sell nuclear weapons to an
Idi Amin, or an Ayatollah Khomeini or a Muammar
Qaddafi. Or perhaps the next time the Soviets will be
successful in their placement of offensive nukes in
Cuba, or your own government in its placement of
nukes in Turkey."

Henrys stood up, went across to the sideboard, and
brought back the brandy bottle. He poured some more
in Mahoney's glass, then his own.

"We've been more or less successful in our efforts
these past thirty-eight years, Mahoney. We've managed
to weather some serious storms, managed to avert some
devastating moves by politicians, yet you're the first to
really hurt us."

He put the bottle on the table, and then sat down
again.

"Unless you help us now, everything we've worked
for will, as you have said, come tumbling down around
our ears. Ezra Wasserman is a bright man. He's worried
about you and what you came up with. He won't be
satisfied merely with Malecki's arrest and Per Larsen's
exposure. Sooner or later this all could go public."

"Maybe that wouldn't be such a bad thing,"
Mahoney said.

"It would be ruinous," Henrys disagreed. "The first
effect would be that the general public the world over,
who have little if any respect or trust for their own intelligence services or their leaders, would revolt. And the
second obvious effect is that we would be at war,
Mahoney, world war within a year."

"Is that your best estimate?"

"It's our best estimate, and I think you believe I'm
right."

"You want me to return to Tel Aviv and assassinate
Wasserman?"

Henrys looked horrified. "Good heavens, no!" he said.

"What then?"

"I want you to go back to Tel Aviv and convince Wasserman that Malecki and Larsen worked together. I want you to convince him not to look any farther. Malecki was selling Israel's secrets to Larsen who in turn was selling them to the Russians."

"You're leaving two of your people out in the cold?" Mahoney asked. "Just like that?"

"They understood the risks when they agreed to take on the job. We all do."

"What will happen to Larsen?"

"He'll be arrested unless he can make his escape and go underground."

"He won't be warned?"

Henrys shook his head. "No. Nor was Malecki warned."

Mahoney seemed to sink farther back into the soft chair as his thoughts flitted randomly from Marge, to his early days with the Agency, when he was naive and idealistic. Quite a contrast, he thought morosely, to his present state of cynicism. And yet, in practical terms, he could see that what Henrys was telling him—the raison d'être of the network—made it seem as if the organization was a necessary adjunct of modern society. Pollution had been the by-product of the industrial revolution. Dehumanization of the average man the by-product of the present-day technological revolution. Yet in each case it would have been impossible, unthinkable, to change what had happened. To alter the course of history with an eye to eliminating the problems inherent in progress was not possible.

The network began with the atomic bomb. A by-product as insidious and as deadly, and yet as necessary, as radiation. Yet Mahoney felt like a caveman; having discovered fire, he was burning his fingers in the flames so that it was very difficult for him to see the benefit of the heat.

"Did your people kill Max Rheinhardt?"

"Yes," Henrys said. He had been waiting for Mahoney to speak, but the question about the Israeli operative who had followed Sonja Margraff on Wasserman's orders apparently had not surprised him.

"How was Malecki recruited? Was it someone from the CIA while he was working for the *Post* in Washington?"

"Actually, no," Henrys said, a hint of sadness or regret at the corners of his eyes. "I recruited him while he was at Oxford as a Rhodes scholar."

"Why him?" Mahoney asked, not quite understanding, but suspecting there was something more to it than that.

"He was bright, very young, idealistic, and angry, of course, at the treatment his parents received at the hands of Boston society."

"I meant how did he come to your attention in the first place? Or have you made it a practice to recruit on college compuses just like any big business?"

Something flashed in Henrys's eyes, but then he looked away. "I knew that Chaim was destined to do big things, to become involved in society, to travel the world."

"How did you know that?" Mahoney persisted. "He was just another bright young man in school."

Henrys turned back. "Henrys is an old, well-established, and honored name in England, Mahoney. It is a name that carries with it certain obligations and responsibilities."

Mahoney said nothing, waiting for the man to continue.

"Two hundred years ago, however, that wasn't the case. The family was hated and reviled. We were the money-lending Jews, the sheenies, the filth of the earth."

"Good Lord," Mahoney said softly. "Your original family name was Malecki."

"Yes," Henrys said. "Levi Malecki is my brother. Before he left England his name was Leonard Dennis Henrys."

"Chaim is your nephew, and you just couldn't see him remain as a newspaperman for the rest of his life."

"He would have eventually run his father's string of papers, and probably would have expanded on them."

"Perhaps you should have left him be."

"No," Henrys said firmly. "Almost more than anyone else, Chaim has helped keep the lid on the ultimate war in the Middle East."

"You're telling me that as soon as the dust settles out there you're going to put someone else in the Mossad?"

Henrys didn't say anything at first, his gaze blank, but Mahoney supposed he was thinking about his nephew who would at the very least be spending a long time in an Israeli prison. The network was powerless to help him, because if they did arrange his escape from the prison, Wasserman would know for certain that Malecki had had help, and he would continue looking.

"We can't do that until Ezra Wasserman is convinced that Chaim worked alone."

Mahoney took a deep drink of the brandy. He would have preferred bourbon, but this was nice. "Wasserman is a stubborn man," he said. "He's pretty well got everything he needs to put it all together. How do you suggest I convince him to stop?"

"He and Ben Abel were very close—"

"Why did you kill that old man?" Mahoney snapped angrily.

Henrys shook his head. "We did not kill him," he said. "There was no reason for us to kill him."

"Even after Ataruz?"

"Especially not after Ataruz. He was an ineffectual old fool. Begin was on the verge of retiring him anyway."

On the one hand Mahoney was having difficulty in believing Henrys. Yet on the other, he could see no logical reason for the man to lie to him about this detail now. But that led him to some very troublesome thoughts.

"Who killed him then, and why?"

"We don't know, Mahoney," Henrys said. "But if you return to Tel Aviv and find his murderer, and hand that person over to Wasserman on a silver platter, any idea that Malecki had help beyond Larsen and the Russians will die."

Find Ben Abel's murderer, Mahoney thought. Wasserman had as much as told him outright that he was a marked man. Yet he knew firmly that he could not turn this down.

"And if I do?" he asked. "If I do return to Tel Aviv, expose Ben Abel's murderer, and sidetrack Wasserman, what then?"

"Return here and I'll tell you everything else."

Marge used to tell him that there never was any need to worry about things. In her view a person always had the choice of either doing something about a bothersome situation, or accepting the fact that action was beyond any control. Yet it made Mahoney angry now that Henrys had maneuvered him solidly into a position from which retreat was totally impossible.

TEL AVIV . . . FRIDAY

It was shortly past two o'clock in the afternoon, local time, when Mahoney deplaned at Lod Airport outside of Tel Aviv, and was passed without a hitch through Israeli customs.

He was tired despite the couple of days of enforced rest that he had enjoyed courtesy of McNeil Henrys and the network, and he put it down to the fact that although his aging bones had been at ease, his mind had not.

The American OSS officer Michael Lovelace, and the Soviet defector Jada Yatsyna had been correct in their suspicion that there had been collusion between the Soviet and American governments during the war. Atomic bomb secrets had been freely passed back and forth at fairly high levels. McBundy had probably been in on the entire deal from the beginning.

So Stalin's move to sabotage the bomb, according to the Russian, had been nothing more than a double-cross. When this was over, Mahoney meant to ask Henrys about that, and how it had affected the network.

Yet Mahoney was still deeply troubled by a number of aspects in the situation, among them who were the network's legmen, and who did the dirty work. Although its motives were noble, its methods were anything but.

During his stay at Henrys's home, and again during the plane ride over the Mediterranean, Mahoney's resolve to expose the network had strengthened. The ends did not justify the means, he kept telling himself. Malecki and Arlemont and McBundy and very certainly Henrys were empty, hollow men, for whom the philosophy of expediency, with all of its ramifications, transcended mere human considerations. People were nothing more or less than insignificant little pawns to be pushed and maneuvered from one square to another. But for what purpose, Mahoney wondered. There had to be a purpose behind it all. A reasoning. Henrys had refused to touch on that gray area for the moment, promising only that Mahoney would know everything when his work was completed. It was a promise that Mahoney intended to hold the man to.

The sun was shining with a furnacelike intensity in a perfectly clear blue sky, there was little or no wind, and the temperature was nearly a hundred degrees when Mahoney emerged, blinking from the terminal building, crossed the wide walk, and slid into the back seat of a waiting cab. He gave the driver Malecki's address in Ramat Aviv, then sat back and closed his eyes.

During the past twenty-four hours or so, he had managed for the most part to blank out of his mind the logical conclusion from Henrys's statement that the network had *not* killed General Ben Abel. Sadly now, as the cab raced into the city, he turned his mind to that problem. All the clues were there. Some of them blatant, others not so obvious, but all there for anyone to unravel, nevertheless.

Much of Mahoney's professional life had been spent relatively insulated from the grimy details of the operations he had analyzed and ordered. The greatest portion of his workaday existence had been spent in an intelligence service ivory tower. Data from a myriad of sources flowed into his office, and out the other end came his assessments and, in some cases, his action orders.

Once in Germany during the end of World War II, a couple of times later during the German occupation, and again a few years ago in Moscow, and finally in San Antonio, Texas, he had found himself directly involved in the dirty side of the business.

Each time the results had been far less than satisfying, far less than neat and clean. Nothing had been wrapped up, nothing had been really gained.

And this incident promised to be more of the same. He would see it to the end, but the end would come to no one's satisfaction.

They had passed through Ramat Gan, and were crossing the Hayarkon River when Mahoney finally opened his misty eyes and looked outside. Traffic was moderately heavy at that time of the day, yet everything seemed old and very dusty to him.

"Earth to earth; ashes to ashes; dust to dust." Death, he thought. The city smelled of death. Soon, and very messy. Unlovely.

Then they were turning off the throughway and onto a residential street, and Mahoney sat forward in his seat. Parked in front of Malecki's house was an Army jeep and two civilian police cars. Three men were leaning against the hood of one of the squad cars, and as the cab approached they all looked up.

"I've changed my mind," Mahoney told the driver. "Take me downtown."

"Sir?" the driver asked, confused, but knowing something was going on because of the police vehicles in front of the house.

"Downtown," Mahoney said. "The Central Railway Station."

"You don't want to stop here?"

"No," Mahoney said, sitting back in his seat so that he would be slightly less visible from the outside. "I've changed my mind."

"Very good, sir," the cabby said, but he did not speed up until they had passed Malecki's house, and Mahoney could almost feel the officers' eyes boring through the steel and glass of the car.

XXVII

GAN HAIFIZ . . . FRIDAY

From the Central Railway Station Mahoney took another cab back out to the airport where he rented a car, then picked up the main highway heading south to Beersheba.

He was sick at heart about his own conclusions, yet for the time being at least his mind was preoccupied with staying alive long enough to do some good here.

The heat shimmered off the highway as he raced south, past irrigated farm fields that stood in stark green contrast to the softer browns and grays of the surrounding desert.

The policemen posted in front of Malecki's house had probably spotted him in the cab, and the news that he was back would get to Wasserman very quickly. But it would take a while before they figured out that he had left Tel Aviv. They'd expect him to remain in the city, at the center of the activity.

He needed just a little time. Twenty-four hours would be a luxury for him to complete his work, but a few hours would probably be sufficient.

He had suspected that Wasserman would have posted

a guard on Malecki's home, although he thought there might be a chance that Sonja would have remained there to oversee everything. But he had had to make sure, even at the risk of being spotted.

The students who worked for Malecki no doubt had been sent back to the university without an explanation, and the rumors would be falling like autumn leaves in a windstorm. It would further confuse things for a while, yet once Wasserman began to sort things out, the answers would come very quickly. Wasserman would have to be sidetracked. Ben Abel's murderer would have to be handed to him.

There was no guarantee, of course, that Sonja had gone to the kibbutz near Beersheba where her father lived, but Mahoney suspected that she had. As soon as Chaim had been arrested and she banished from the operation, she would have run home to try to get her head together. It was the one fatal flaw in her character that Mahoney had spotted almost from the beginning. She always needed a strong father figure nearby for her own survival. At first it had been her brother, but when he had been killed her need had been transferred to Chaim Malecki. Now that he had been exposed as the traitor, she would have to get close to her father. There was no one else left for her.

But there was even more to it than that, and Mahoney began to turn his mind to the other problem.

Sonja had signed in at the Records Center at Lod Airport the afternoon that Ben Abel had been murdered. It had made her the chief suspect in Wasserman's mind for some time, until the Mossad chief had finally accepted Mahoney's supposition that the general had been shot from a distance. The bullet had been a 9mm, but had been so distorted that it had been impossible to tell if it had been fired from a handgun or a rifle. But Mahoney had smelled the odor of perfu   or after shave lotion in the general's office when he had arrived.

Wasserman had never questioned her about her conversation with Ben Abel that afternoon, at first because he had been afraid of what he would learn, and later after he had discounted the possibility that Sonja was the mole and therefore the murderer, he had not thought it necessary.

But Mahoney was very interested. Not only in what she would have to say about that afternoon, but how she was taking the fact that her lover had been exposed as the mole.

It was shortly after three o'clock by the time Mahoney had passed through the town of Beersheba and drove out to the kibbutz on the secondary highway. This was the hottest part of the day, and although the rental car's air conditioning unit was going full blast, Mahoney was beginning to sweat by the time he topped the rise and entered the kibbutz gates.

He had seen no one below in the fields nor was there much outside activity in the compound itself. In part he supposed the quiet was due to the intense heat that afternoon, and in part because in a few hours the Sabbath would begin.

After he had pulled up and parked in front of the Community Center building, he let the car idle for a few moments while he gathered his thoughts. Hares and hounds it had been from the beginning; from the moment Sonja had been flagged and had come to Minnesota to see him. And somehow her involvement with Chaim and this entire mess was linked with her brother's untimely death, or more accurately, how she had been affected by his violent end. As distasteful as it was, Mahoney knew that pressing on that nerve end would provide the key to unlocking whatever dark secrets she possessed.

Finally he shut off the engine and climbed out of the

car, the heat instantly crashing down on him; overwhelmingly thick. He hurried up the gravel walk and entered the air-conditioned building, his shirt already plastered to his back.

A half dozen young people were lounging around the day room, and when he came in, the young girl who had met him there the first time jmped up and came across to him.

"Mr. Mahoney, isn't it?" she said. She was a lovely young girl in her teens.

Mahoney smiled. "You have a good memory."

"May I tell Carl that you've come to visit again?"

"I'd like to speak with his daughter Sonja," Mahoney said. "She is here, isn't she?"

The girl nodded, and the other young people were watching him. "Yes, she is," she said. "She's in the kitchen. I'll get her."

"Please," Mahoney said, and the girl turned on her heel, crossed the day room, and went through another door, deeper into the building, leaving Mahoney standing by himself, the other young people still staring at him. There was trouble here, and it was obvious that they sensed it. They knew that Mahoney had not brought good news, and like people everywhere who run to the scene of an accident or to a burning building, they too were curious about him.

The door beyond the day room opened, and Sonja appeared. She was wearing sandals, very short shorts, and a white T-shirt but no bra. She had a lovely body, and now seeing her dressed like this, Mahoney could not help but think of how she had look that night in the library while she and Malecki were making love.

Her hair was disheveled, and she wore no makeup; her eyes were puffy and somewhat red-rimmed. For several long seconds she stood just within the day room staring across at Mahoney, a range of emotions crossing her face, from fear to dull acceptance of his presence. But finally she moved across the room to him.

"Welcome to Gan Haifiz, Mr. Mahoney," she said, her voice soft and lovely.

"I've been here before," he said, his eyes locked into hers. She was frightened. Deeply frightened.

"I know," she said. "Why did you come now? You aren't supposed to be in Israel. Uncle Ezra said you had finished what you came here to do, and had left."

"I'm not quite finished," he said, and she flinched. "Is there someplace we can talk?"

She glanced over at the others, then back at Mahoney. "My father is in town; we can use his office."

"That would be nice," Mahoney said, and he followed her out of the building into the oppressive heat. She quickly crossed the square and Mahoney was sweating hard again by the time they entered a building marked KIBBUTZ OFFICE.

An attractive woman was typing a letter, and when they came in she looked up and smiled. "Oh, hello, Sonja," she said. "Your father isn't back yet."

"I know," Sonja said, crossing the reception area. "We need to use his office for a little while."

"You can't . . ." the woman said, starting to rise, but then she sat back down as Sonja opened the door to her father's office and went inside. Mahoney followed her, closing the door behind them.

"His secretary?" he asked.

"His new wife," Sonja said disgustedly.

"How long has your mother been dead?"

She glared at him. "Ten years," she spat. "But that woman out there is only two years older than me." She turned away, unable for the moment to handle her emotions, and she went across the room where she looked out the window toward the edge of the compound and down to the fields.

Carl Margraff had been here for several years, and it was reflected in his office, crammed with an accumulation of books, papers, and maps, as well as dozens of framed photographs on the walls. There were pictures of Margraff with Ben-Gurion, Rabin, Begin, Moshe Dayan, and dozens of other men and women important in Israel's history. There were also a number of testimonial certificates on the walls. The man had led a rich, varied life, and was obviously proud of his accomplishments.

Low on the wall to the right of the desk was a small frame that contained a battered identity card of some sort. Mahoney went across the room and bent down to examine it, intrigued by its incongruity among the other mementos.

"It was his first Israeli citizenship card," Sonja said. Mahoney straightened up and looked at her.

"It's dated 1947. Israel wasn't an independent state then."

She smiled. "The cards were illegal, but they were issued anyway. My father is very proud of it."

"He loves his country."

"Yes," she said. "Many men do."

"But not Chaim."

Her nostrils flared. "You knew all along, didn't you."

Mahoney shook his head. "No, I didn't. He was a suspect, but I didn't know for sure until I watched him take Ben Abel's briefcase from Base Ops."

Sonja turned away again, tears suddenly welling up in her eyes. "It's not fair," she said. "Dammit, it's just not fair! I loved him with all my soul."

"Enough to kill for him?" Mahoney asked softly.

Sonja spun around. "What?"

"Why did you kill Ben Abel?"

Her eyes widened. "Are you crazy? He was like family to me. Why would I want to kill him?"

"Because he somehow managed to find out that Chaim was the mole."

"You *are* crazy," she said in amazement. "He called me to his office and told me that both you and Uncle Ezra suspected me of being the mole. He wanted me to stick around and talk to you."

"But you couldn't."

"No, I couldn't."

"And you couldn't face Ezra."

Sonja lowered her head. "I couldn't stand the possibility of knowing for sure that he thought I could be a traitor."

"He suspected you from the beginning," Mahoney said, hating himself for it.

Sonja looked up almost defiantly. "I don't believe that. Why don't you go home? Leave us be. You've caused enough damage."

"It was you who selected me for this job," he reminded her.

"I'm sorry I did. You've ruined everything."

"I've uncovered your traitor."

Once again she turned away. "There's been a mistake. It can't be true."

"Have you seen him since he's been arrested?"

"I can't," she said in a small voice.

"Why?"

"I can't!" she shouted. "Don't you see that I can't face him now? Don't you see, Mahoney?"

And now it was coming, Mahoney thought. He had done what he considered to be a number of miserable things in his career. Said things that had been designed to maneuver people into acting the way he wanted them to act. But standing before this young woman now he felt despicable. Yet he knew he had no choice.

"You're going to have to see him, Sonja," he said very carefully.

"I can't."

"Have you read his background files?"

She shook her head. "No. Uncle Ezra wanted me on the interrogation team, but I couldn't."

"Chaim has been a traitor to more then Israel."

"I don't understand," she said miserably.

"He sold out the United States before he ever came to Israel," Mahoney said, hating himself for the lie. "He was stationed in Berlin for the Washington *Post* at the same time you and I were stationed there with the Company. The same time your brother Peter was stationed there."

"No," she said.

"He was almost certainly working for the East Germans then. And he had ties with our embassy. A young cipher clerk, I believe it was."

"Don't tell me that," she said, and she held up her right hand, palm out, as if she were trying to ward off an attacker.

"He left Berlin after that—shortly after Peter was killed, I mean—and he showed up next in Moscow. A coincidence, do you suppose?"

Her eyes glistened. "Peter was spotted by the border patrol when he tried to come over."

"They were waiting for him," Mahoney said. "They knew he was coming."

"If you knew that, why didn't you arrest him then?" she said.

"Don't be a fool," Mahoney snapped, the bile bitter at the back of his throat. "Of course we didn't know it at the time. I didn't know for sure until a couple of days ago."

"Why?" she asked. She sounded worn-out.

"Money, I suppose," Mahoney said. "But he probably didn't even connect Peter with you. At least not at first." He wondered why he was bothering to soften the blow.

"Have you told my father?"

Mahoney shook his head. "There's no need."

She went around the desk and slumped down in the chair. For a time she stared down at the desk calendar and pencils, but when she looked up there was a thinly disguised hate in her eyes.

"Why did you come back?"

"To find Ben Abel's murderer."

"It was Chaim."

"He was out of the country. He couldn't have done it."

"Then he had help. Possibly a Russian here in Tel Aviv."

"Possibly," Mahoney said, staring at her. "But what about you now, Sonja? What are your plans."

"I'll get over it, if that's what you mean," she said. "I'll go back to work in a month or so. Maybe sooner. Who knows?"

Between the anger and the sadness, it seemed to Mahoney that Sonja was like a tightrope walker on a badly swinging wire. Her balance was precarious at best, and it was very likely she would fall soon. He wondered which way she would go.

He turned then without another word, opened the door, and stepped out into the reception area. Carl Margraff was standing by his wife, and he looked past Mahoney into his own office, spotting Sonja who had buried her face in her arms on the desk.

Mahoney softly closed the door, went across to the man, and shook his hand.

"Is she all right?" Margraff asked.

"Leave her be for a few minutes," Mahoney said gently. He genuinely liked the man. "Walk me to my car."

Margraff looked down at his wife who was obviously confused and somewhat frightened. "It's all right," he said to her. "I'll be right back."

He turned and went outside. Mahoney followed him, this time the heat not so noticeable. They walked slowly across the square toward the Community Center.

"I thought you had left the country," Margraff said. He didn't walk so fast this time, and Mahoney had no trouble keeping up with him.

"I came back earlier today. There are a couple of things I had to wrap up."

"Involving Sonja?" Margraff asked. He looked up at Mahoney. "It came as quite a shock to all of us when Chaim was arrested."

"I wanted to see how she was handling it."

Margraff stopped. "I'm afraid for her sanity, Mr. Mahoney," he said. "She's not been herself. She's holding it all inside. I can't get close to her."

"Has she any friends up here?"

"No," her father said. "There's no one here for her except me. And she's shut me out."

They started walking again. "Has Ezra been out to see her?"

"Yesterday," Margraff said. "He wanted her in on the interrogation team. I thought it was a bad idea, but now I'm not so sure. Maybe it's what she needs. Maybe instead of burying her head in the sand, she needs to confront him face-to-face." He shook his head. "I couldn't believe it when I heard the news. I still can't."

"It's what made him so effective."

"Did he hurt us badly?"

"Not the country," Mahoney said. "Not really. But the people around him have been pretty well battered."

They had reached Mahoney's car, and he was bathed in sweat now but didn't notice it. "Were you involved in the Israel Beer thing?"

Margraff nodded. "I knew him. But it was different that time. Beer was well respected by a lot of people, but he had his detractors. There were a lot of people then who were not surprised at all when he was exposed. But Chaim . . ." He paused. "Everyone liked and respected him. He did so much for Israel."

"I know," Mahoney said. He opened his car door, the metal very hot.

"What can I do for her?" Margraff asked, almost pleading, and Mahoney found it difficult to look him in the eye.

"Don't crowd her. Give her a little room."

Margraff's eyes narrowed. "I don't understand."

"I think I might have talked her into helping Ezra see this thing through. But don't say anything to her about it. She'll have to make that decision herself."

For several moments both men stared at each other until Margraff spoke, his words soft, emotionless.

"If I asked you, is there more to this business? Would you give me an answer?"

"No," Mahoney said. "I wouldn't."

XXVIII

In Beersheba the lack of outdoor activity was even more pronounced than at Gan Haifiz. It was nearly six o'clock, and Mahoney had been seated for the past two hours at a window table in a tourist restaurant at the edge of town. From his vantage point he could look down on the empty road that led in from the kibbutz. Anyone driving from the compound and then heading north to Tel Aviv would have to pass this spot. He had noticed it on the way up earlier in the day.

About ten years ago he had been nicked for a ninety-day TDY stint as Tradecraft Adviser to the school at Langley. He had fussed and fumed over the assignment, but in the end he had given his chosen few students the best of the knowledge he had gleaned over the years . . . mostly through making mistakes, he admitted.

Tradecraft, he had told them more than once, is nothing more or less than patience. Patience for detail, for instance. Notice the look in her eyes. Notice how she held her head, what she did with her hands; was she tapping her foot or chewing on her lower lip?

Tradecraft was patience for other kinds of details as

well, like the patience to make one last fail-safe switch just to make sure a secondary tail hadn't picked you up. Patience to scout the territory even before your planned operation went into effect. Patience for the kinds of details that would never catch you short. That could save your life.

But, and Mahoney had cautioned at the time that this was the biggest and least glamorous in a long string of *buts*, tradecraft was the ordinary, garden variety patience that any big-city cop on stakeout understands. Sitting down on position for hours, or days if need be, to prove a point. But sitting down in such a fashion that you never lost the edge to your vigil. If you're caught napping, he had told his people, as likely or not you'll end up with the short end of the stick.

A French couple with three children had come into the restaurant around 4:30, and now they departed noisily, leaving Mahoney the only customer in the place.

He glanced apologetically at the waiter, the man's white apron stained with coffee and wine. He suspected they wanted to close the place, but he could not leave just yet. He turned away, sipped at his tea, and continued staring out the window down at the road.

If Sonja had taken his bait, there were really only four courses of action open to her. She could go see Wasserman and ask him about Chaim's Berlin background. She could go see Chaim himself at the prison and confront him directly with it. She could try to get into Chaim's house and pry through his files, looking for something that would verify what Mahoney had told her. Or she could run.

The last option, of course, would be the easiest to handle. The least messy and certainly the most conclusive. But Mahoney thought the likelihood of that happening was as slight as the possibility that she would sit tight up at the kibbutz, the fifth option.

No, he told himself, going over the options for the tenth time in as many minutes, she could not sit tight, nor would she jump. She'd do something. But . . . .

A thin, yellow cloud of dust became faintly visible, south in the distance beyond the last whitewashed buildings at the edge of town. Mahoney stiffened inwardly but turned languidly in his chair and motioned for the waiter.

The young man hurried over. "More tea, perhaps?" he asked, not really meaning it.

"The check," Mahoney said, and the waiter pulled the slip from his pocket and laid it gently on the table.

Mahoney placed an American twenty dollar bill on top of the check. "Keep the change," he said, and he glanced idly out the window as the small dust cloud materialized into a plain gray four-door Fiat of the kind the Mossad and dozens of other Israeli government agencies used as staff cars.

The waiter scooped up the money and the check as Mahoney got slowly to his feet.

The Fiat passed the highway sign at the edge of the town and then slowed down, moments later passing within twenty feet of where Mahoney was standing. He had gotten a clear view of Sonja behind the wheel, a very intense expression on her face.

TEL AVIV . . . FRIDAY

It was still light by the time Sonja reached Tel Aviv, skirting the Hatikva Quarter, then heading downtown past the Great Synagogue and the Shalom Meir Tower.

She had been easy to follow, her driving straightforward and single-minded. She had tried no tricks. She had not doubled back, or slowed down, or even pulled off to the side of the road, which were all maneuvers designed to catch a tail off-balance. Instead, like a lemming heading down to the sea, Sonja made a direct line to Mossad headquarters off Allenby Street.

Mahoney found a parking spot half a block away from the parking ramp into which Sonja had pulled. He barely had the time to shut off the engine and roll down his window when she emerged from the ramp and passed across the street from him, ducking into the Finance Annex entryway almost as if she were a woman possessed, which in a way she was.

Lights began coming on in the city, one by one, here and there, as twilight began to deepen. Although the sun was down, and the heat wasn't as intense as it had been, it was still oppressively warm, and the car was like a sauna.

For a while, sitting there, Mahoney wondered about men like Carl Margraff. When they had first come to places like the site of Gan Haifiz, they had been faced with nothing more than the bleak, forbidding desert where temperatures in midsummer would often reach 125 degrees, where some wells had to be drilled to five hundred feet and deeper before potable water was found, where the struggle was never ending.

In one respect men like Margraff were very similar to those like McNiel Henrys. Both types had very intense desires and the driving power to match. But unlike Henrys, Margraff had a sense of gentle purpose. He and his kind were not looking for stasis. They worked for progress. They did not believe that violence was a necessary part of the human condition. Margraff and his people were the gentlemen. Henrys and his network were the hollow men.

A half hour after Sonja had entered the Finance Annex, a cab pulled up and Ezra Wasserman climbed out of it, paid the driver, and went inside.

The call had evidently gone out to him when Sonja had shown up at the front door, and he had answered the summons. He was worried about her, as her father was, and now probably curious as to why she had suddenly shown up here. What would he say to her? How would he react when she asked him about Chaim's background in Berlin? He would deny that Chaim was connected with her brother's death, of course, because it simply was not true. At least on a bureaucratically superficial level, Wasserman was aware of Chaim's background.

But, and this was one of the big tradecraft *buts,* if all went well, the seed would be planted in Wasserman's mind that if it was *untrue* that Malecki had been a spy for the Russians in Berlin, then it was very likely he had become a spy for them only after he had come to Israel. And he had done his spying for money, and money alone.

It was a thin line of reasoning, Mahoney thought, but such was the stuff of implanting the impressions you wanted in other people's minds.

The scene would be emotional in there, he suspected, which was also good. In this instance Wasserman's love for his friend's daughter would temporarily blind him. Hopefully, enough so that his better judgment would be suspended.

Sonja was on the verge of cracking. Mahoney had pulled her one way with his story about Malecki's involvement in her brother's death. Wasserman would pull her the other way by denying it. Which, if Mahoney's hypothesis was correct, would leave her only one choice. She would have to confront Malecki. She would have to go to him that night and face him. Malecki, of course, would deny it. And the final wedge would have been jammed beneath her line of resistance.

Mahoney was a disinterested party; his story would carry weight with her. Wasserman loved her like an uncle, so she had to believe that he would lie to protect her feelings. And Malecki was behind bars. A proven traitor. Anything he said would be suspect in her mind.

It was nearly ten o'clock by the time Sonja emerged from the Mossad headquarters and headed down the street toward the parking ramp. From his vantage point, Mahoney could see that her shoulders were squared, and she held her head high as if she was now a woman with a purpose. To Mahoney she seemed proud, almost haughty, and the stark change in her apparent attitude from when she had come to see Wasserman was bothersome. It didn't immediately fit into Mahoney's prediction of her reactions. For the first time since he had returned to Israel he had a slight doubt whether he had guessed correctly, whether he was doing the right thing.

But then she disappeared into the parking ramp, and he started his car. A few minutes later the plain gray Fiat came out of the ramp, swung south on Allenby Street, and shot past Mahoney, going in the opposite direction his car was pointed.

With some difficulty he made the U-turn from where he was parked, catching up with her a couple of blocks away.

Like before, her driving was straightforward, no tricks of any kind. Mahoney doubted if she was even aware of any of the traffic around her as she drove south through the city and into Jaffa, the old section.

Mahoney lagged back in the last few blocks, not because he had given up the chase, but because at that point he knew where she was going. Although her destination came as no surprise, it gave him no satisfaction.

It would have been nice, he mused as he watched the taillights of her car turn a corner ahead of him, if she had done something totally unexpected. She could have returned to Gan Haifiz. But she hadn't.

Mahoney came around the corner moments later, in time to see Sonja parking across the street from one of the side gates of the old Military Garrison Prison where Malecki was being held. He pulled over to the side of the street and immediately doused his headlights as she got out of the car and without looking back crossed to the heavy wooden door set in the tall, yellow brick wall.

A strong light at an angle above the door cast Sonja's elongated shadow halfway across the street as she pushed the buzzer, and a second later the door was opened for her and she disappeared inside.

Wasserman, believing her to be totally innocent, had probably called ahead to authorize her admittance to the prison despite the late hour. They would probably escort her to a secured interrogation room where Malecki would be brought, and the two of them would be left alone.

It would be another of Wasserman's strategies designed to dislodge a few answers from Malecki. And the Mossad chief's thinking was sound on that point, considering what information he possessed. But tonight, Mahoney hoped that the opposite would happen. That seeing her lover face-to-face would dislodge something inside of her. Would make her vulnerable for one last attack.

Mahoney slid over to the passenger side of his car and got out. He moved immediately into the deeper shadows close to the buildings, and keeping his attention on the prison across the street, he made his way down the block to a spot just opposite the Fiat, where he stepped into the doorway of a shop, its windows covered with metal security shutters.

A hundred yards farther along the wall was a glassed

in tower perched above the corner. The guards' attention would be directed inward toward the prisoners, not toward traffic on the outside, so Mahoney figured he had a fair chance of escaping detection.

It was absolutely quiet here. What traffic did flow at this hour was far away in the livelier sections of the city. Inside the prison the inmates would be bedded down for the evening, and the second-shift guards would already be looking at their watches as their duty tours neared the end.

Mahoney was tired. The combination of mental stress, too much sun, and too many hours in this day, made him slightly depressed. The only reasonably bright spot on his horizon was the fact that very soon he would be finished with what he set out to do. Or at least he would have completed the distasteful parts. What he was going to do afterward depended a great deal upon what happened tonight. But at the back of Mahoney's mind he knew that once he finished here in Israel he was going to give it up. He was going to turn it all over to Switt, who was younger and much better equipped to handle what would probably turn out to be a very long and messy fight.

Sonja had been in the prison less than half an hour when she emerged from the doorway and moved fast across the street to her car, nearly catching Mahoney off guard.

He waited until she had her door open and the dome light came on inside, momentarily blinding her from seeing anything in the dark, before he stepped out of the shadows, yanked open the passenger door, and got in.

Her face was white and tears were streaming down her cheeks. "Oh, my God," she said, half in and half out of the car.

"Close the door, Sonja, and let's go," Mahoney said.

She glanced back at the prison, her motions jerky, and

then got in behind the wheel, and slammed the door shut. Her hands were shaking so badly she had a difficult time inserting the key into the ignition, and when she had the car started she jerked the clutch, forgot at first to switch on the headlights, and nearly hit a parked car at the corner.

Once they were clear of the prison area, however, she began to calm down, although she had the same bothersome look in her eyes.

"What did he say to you?" Mahoney asked, feeling somehow that it was the wrong question, and yet one that had to be asked to open her up.

"You followed me," she said, her voice tremulous. It was a start.

"I waited for you in Beersheba. I thought you might come in to see him. Evidently Ezra still believes in you."

"He doesn't believe in anything except the service," she snapped, her reaction surprising to Mahoney.

They stopped for a traffic light, and then Sonja turned down a side street that led a few blocks later to the seacoast highway running south toward Ashdod. As she drove she kept looking back in her rearview mirror, as if she was fearful that she was being followed.

"Do you want to tell me what happened in there?" Mahoney asked at last.

"With Chaim?" she asked, glancing over at him. "I knew all along that he was spying for the Russians. I knew it."

"Then why did you suggest my name? Did you want him exposed?"

"I thought he was too good for that. I thought he would kill you first. And he nearly did."

"Athens?"

Sonja laughed. "He had help with that. But I'm sure he ordered it."

"But why, Sonja?" Mahoney asked, sick at heart that

his worst suspicions were all true. "What about your father, and the work your brother did?"

"Don't talk to me about my brother!" she screeched. "Chaim may have engineered his death, but you were responsible for it! He didn't have a chance out there, and you all knew it. Even if no one had blown him, he wouldn't have had a chance. And yet you sent him out there."

"Did Chaim admit it?"

"No," she said. "Even now he couldn't face me and tell me the truth."

"Did he know that you were spying as well?"

Sonja didn't answer him at first; instead she slowed the car as if she was looking for something. They were well south of the city now, its lights raising a glow on the northern horizon. To their right, a few hundred yards away, was the Mediterranean. A mile or so farther down the two-lane highway they came upon a dirt road that led toward the sea, and Sonja turned down it, the car's headlights bouncing across the sand dunes ahead of them.

"He guessed," she said offhandedly. She was concentrating on her driving. The road was deeply rutted, and at several spots the car bottomed out.

"Ben Abel made the same guess, didn't he," Mahoney said.

They topped a rise, and below them was the sea. Sonja pulled off the road, doused the headlights, but left the engine running.

"Chaim was the mole we were all looking for, but you were spying as well. Probably sending your information to the Syrians. It was your department. And it was you whom Ben Abel figured was the traitor within the service, which is why your dossier was in the stack he was studying, and not Chaim's."

Sonja stared straight ahead out the windshield, a narrow, pinched expression on her lips.

"It was also why the general called you up to his office that afternoon. He was going to confront you with what he knew. You went directly up to see the old man, and you killed him, then mixed up the files and took his notes."

Still Sonja maintained her silence. Mahoney took a cigar out of his pocket and lit it. There was a pleasantly cool, fresh breeze coming from the sea, and it dragged the cigar smoke out the window.

"You shot him from behind. Probably with a Luger," he said. "What about the muzzle flash burn? How did you avoid that?"

"I was wearing a jacket," she said softly. "I wrapped it up into a bundle and shot him through that."

"Did Chaim suspect that you had killed the general?" Mahoney asked. Even though he had figured out most of it himself, he was having a difficult time dealing with the reality of her admission. He had thought Malecki was an empty, expedient man, but Sonja was worse, yet he felt sorry for her.

"Yes," she said. "But he thought I did it to protect him. He thought the general suspected him." She gave a little laugh and then turned to Mahoney. "But even now he couldn't tell me the truth about Peter. Neither could Uncle Ezra. Both of them lied." She reached for her purse beside her near the gearshift lever. Mahoney grabbed her wrist.

"I'd like a cigarette," she said.

Mahoney picked up the purse with his other hand before he let go of her wrist, and he opened it. Inside were a wallet, some cosmetics, a few keys, and a cigarette case and matches, but no weapon. He looked up. Sonja was holding a 9mm Luger on him.

"To the left of my seat," she said.

"You knew I was coming?" He was still holding her purse open.

She shook her head. "I thought I would have to get out of the prison in a hurry. Once I made it to my car, I didn't want to have to fumble around in my purse in case I needed this."

"I see," Mahoney said, everything else falling into place for him. "You killed Chaim tonight."

"Yes," she said. "They will have discovered his body by now. I told them that I had to go to my car to get a tape recorder and some notes. They believed me."

"How did you kill him?"

"I stuck a knife in his heart," she said, her voice shaky, tears welling up in her eyes as she went through another mood swing. "They taught us that in Langley, you know."

"Why, Sonja?" Mahoney asked. "Why betray your own country?"

"It's not my country," she said. "It's my father's country. Uncle Ezra's, General Ben Abel's. Not mine. Israel killed my brother."

"The East Germans killed him."

"Peter was a product of this place. A product of my father and people like him. Israel killed him."

"Why didn't you kill your father, then?"

"My father?" she asked in a tiny voice, and then she shook her head. "It has to end, don't you see? It has to end. When Israel is wiped off the map, it will be over. Don't you see that too?"

Mahoney let her purse tip upside down, spilling its contents on the floor. His eyes never left hers. She instinctively lunged forward grabbing for it, and at that moment Mahoney lashed out, hitting her gun hand, forcing the weapon upward.

The Luger went off, and Sonja's head was thrown violently backward, bouncing off the doorframe, and then she slumped forward against the steering wheel, blood oozing from a small bullet hole at her temple.

For a long time Mahoney sat there in stunned silence. It had been an accident. He had meant to disarm her. It wasn't supposed to end this way, for her.

But then he thought of Ben Abel and especially of the little boy at Athens airport. They were mistakes too. All monstrous results of McNiel Henrys' terrible arrogance. And just thinking about that and the man's empty philosophy was enought to set Mahoney back in motion to finish, finally, what he had set out to do.

XXIX

TEL AVIV . . . SATURDAY MORNING

More than once during the past few weeks Mahoney had felt a sense of unreality about what he was doing; a feeling that all the daylight in the world had slowly faded, leaving in its wake an eternal twilight. The bright clean light on a mountain peak, the sparkling sunshine on the ripples of a pond, and the glorious multicolored sunsets were all lost forever.

He had placed Sonja's body in the trunk of the Fiat, careful not to get any of her blood on him, then had climbed in behind the wheel. It was just a few minutes past midnight, by the time he had made it back into Tel Aviv, had crossed the city, and had parked in a dormitory lot on the campus in Ramat Aviv.

From here he could look across a wide field toward the back of Malecki's home, partially screened by a line of sycamore and cedar trees.

And now, more than at any other time in the past weeks, he felt a heightened sense of unreality. He felt that none of this was really happening to him. That none of this was possible. There were no such people as McNiel Henrys, or Chaim Malecki, or Sonja Margraff.

Such things were impossible in the real world.

Yet all of that was at an emotional level. In his mind, in the rational areas of his consciousness, Mahoney knew exactly what was and what had happened. He also knew what he still had to accomplish that night.

He had been careful to park in the shadows very close to the building so that someone from within would not easily be able to look out their window down at him. He had made a mistake with Sonja and the gun, which had very nearly cost him his life. He did not want to make another.

For a full ten minutes he had waited, listening to the errant sounds of the campus. Somewhere in the distance he could hear a siren, and somewhere deeper within the university campus he could hear the thrumming of some kind of machinery. Air conditioning. Perhaps water pumps. It didn't really matter. The sound was just there. Impersonal in the night.

Finally Mahoney got stiffly out of the car, and leaving the door open, he went around to the back and unlocked the trunk.

Carefully he lifted Sonja's body out, carried it back to the driver's seat, and sat it inside. Then he closed the door and went around to the passenger side from where he arranged her body so that it lay slumped against the steering wheel. Using his handkerchief he laid the Luger on the floor near her feet and replaced the keys in the ignition.

If they checked very closely they might find his own fingerprints on the steering wheel, he thought as he went back to the open trunk. He took out his handkerchief again and wiped a small smudge of blood from the floor of the trunk. But they would not look any closer. They had no reason to look any closer. In a fit of grief over the fact she imagined her lover had had something to do with her brother's death, she had killed him. Then she had driven away from the prison and, later in the evening, had killed herself.

Wasserman, especially Wasserman, would never question it. He had spoken with her shortly before she had killed Malecki. He, almost more than anyone else, knew that she was distraught. Mahoney, he might think, had provided the push, but Mahoney would have no reason to kill her.

After he had closed the trunk lid he went back to the car and took a cigarette and a book of matches from Sonja's purse. For a few seconds longer he stared at her body. But then he shook his head and resolutely walked across the parking lot to the edge of the grassy field where the line of trees made a bend from Malecki's house toward the university, and he started across along a narrow footpath, his hands stuffed deeply in his pockets, head bowed, as if he was a professor out for a midnight stroll.

If they were watching the back of the house, his job would be difficult if not impossible, he thought as his shoes crunched on the loose gravel. But he didn't believe Wasserman would have posted that tight a guard. Malecki was under arrest, and it was not very likely that he kept anything of importance at his house anyway. There had always been too many people around for that. A few men out front would keep the curiosity-seekers away until a proper team could be sent over to begin sifting through his files just in case something might turn up.

It was very dark. There was no moon, and by the time he had made it halfway across the field he was completely in the shadows, invisible either from the university or from the back of Malecki's house. He pulled his hands out of his pockets and, careful to make as little noise as possible, hurried alongside the path, dodging in and out of the line of trees.

He was out of breath by the time he reached the low brick wall that separated Malecki's property from the field, and he rested behind it on one knee for a few minutes.

There were no noises here except for the night insects in the field and in the trees and his own heartbeat, which seemed as loud as a bass drum.

At length, he stood up slowly and studied the back of the house. The place was large, built in two wings that jutted off a central core. Upstairs were the bedrooms, and on the first floor rear were the library, the work-room where Malecki's student helpers had managed the paperwork for his fund-raising activities, and the large kitchen. In the front was the living room and dining room.

All the windows were dark, and from his vantage point he could see no guards. No one lurking in the shadows. No one seated on the patio furniture. No one waiting for an assault from this side.

He sat up on the brick wall, swung his legs over, and stepped lightly down to the patio, where he waited a few seconds longer, holding his breath, listening for something, anything.

Finally he crossed the patio to a set of French doors that opened onto a corridor which ran from the rear to the front of the house. He took his penknife from his pocket, opened it to the smallest blade, and in a few seconds managed to pick the simple tumbler lock. He eased the door open, slipped inside, and closed it softly behind him.

Still no alarm was raised, and although there was a possibility that someone was stationed inside the house, Mahoney doubted it.

He bent down and took off his shoes, and leaving them by the door, he noiselessly moved down the corridor to the front of the house.

Absolutely nothing had been disturbed as far as Mahoney could tell in the dim light that filtered in from the outside.

In the front vestibule he stepped carefully up to the narrow windows that framed the front door, and he peered outside. Parked on the street was a single civilian police radio unit, and as he watched he could see a brief point of light glow and then die down, illuminating for just that moment the figures of two men.

They weren't expecting trouble. They had no reason to expect trouble.

Mahoney turned and hurried to the back of the house where across the hall from the library he entered Malecki's workroom. It was a very large room that took up most of the back of the house. Laid out like any big office, there were a half dozen rows of desks in the middle, surrounded on three sides by dozens of file cabinets. To the left were several large flat tables at which, Malecki had explained to him, his student helpers clipped three dozen different daily newspapers in fifteen languages, and nearly as many national and international newsletters and news magazines.

Malecki had described his work as that of a vulture. "We look first in the society columns to find out what families have the money this year, and then match that up with the obituary columns to see who has died."

With that information Malecki ingratiated himself with the families, and sooner or later managed to talk them out of a memorial gift of one sort or another for kibbutzim.

Gruesome, Malecki had admitted at the time. But it worked.

Across the back wall, above the file cabinets, was a long row of windows that admitted just enough light so that Mahoney could see what he was doing.

He went immediately across the room to the first of the cabinets, opened the top drawer of one, and began pulling out the files, crumpling up the paper and dumping it on the floor in a heap.

At first he had thought he would be able to come in here and search through Malecki's files for any information that might tie the man to the network. But when he thought about it, he knew the job would be impossible in the time he had left.

One by one he opened each of the file drawers, removed its contents, and dumped the papers on the floor. It was mindless work, and Mahoney fell into a relatively quiet but steady motion from one file drawer to the next, gradually working his way completely around the room, not bothering to look at any of the files he was pulling out.

Every now and then he had to stop and rest, his forehead wet with sweat, his arms aching, and when he did he would look back at what he had accomplished so far.

The crumpled files were piled in hip-deep mounds all along the fronts of the cabinets, and in some places spilled over the tops of the desks, almost completely covering them.

He would shake his head then and turn back to his task of dumping the results of eight years of work that had raised more than fifty million dollars for Israel.

Once, around 3:30 A.M., Mahoney thought he heard a noise from the front of the house, and he stopped what he was doing long enough to slip out of the workroom and pad softly to the front door. But the two officers were still seated in the front seat of the squad car, and as far as he could tell there was no one else out there.

He had gone back to his work then, finishing with the file cabinets around 4:30 or so, and then dumping the contents of the two dozen desks in the impressive heap, finishing with that just at 5:00.

It would be light soon, and he would have to be away by then. But finally he was very nearly finished.

Again at the front door he looked outside, and still the two officers were seated in their unit. Then he hurried upstairs to the bedroom that Malecki and Sonja had shared.

This room was at the front of the house, so Mahoney was very careful to keep well away from the windows as he pulled clothes out of bureau drawers and dumped them on the floor. Then he went into the closet and yanked Malecki's clothes off their hangers, tearing sleeves off coats, pulling trousers apart, and ripping his expensive silk shirts into shreds.

As one last gesture in this room, Mahoney went to the nightstand next to the bed on which was a framed photograph of Malecki and Sonja. They were arm in arm, smiling, at a restaurant.

Mahoney looked at the photograph for a few moments in the dim light, and it was strange to realize that both of them were dead, their smiles now meaningless.

Finally he pulled the frame apart, ripped the photograph into little pieces, and let them scatter on the floor before he turned and went back downstairs.

Moving quickly now, Mahoney went past the workroom and entered the kitchen, which was set up to accommodate the large number of guests who always stayed at the house.

A massive eight-burner stove squatted next to a tall baking oven. Mahoney quickly went over to them and opened the oven doors. He stuck his head inside, located the pilot light, and blew it out. Next he opened the front door of the stove, located its master pilot light, and blew it out as well.

Finally he turned on all eight of the stove's burners as well as the oven controls full blast, the kitchen almost immediately filling with the nauseating reek of escaping natural gas.

Back out in the corridor Mahoney left the kitchen doors open, then hurried back to the workroom where he pulled out the cigarette and matches he had taken from Sonja's purse.

He lit the cigarette, took a couple of deep drags on it to make sure it was going well, and then wedged the unlit end inside the book of matches. In ten minutes or so when the cigarette had burned down, the tip would ignite the matchbook.

At the center of the room he cleared a spot on the floor, set down the matchbook fuse, and then made a tent of crumpled paper a couple of inches above it. When the matchbook ignited, the paper would catch and within minutes the workroom would be a blazing inferno.

By that time, Mahoney thought as he left the room and headed back down the corridor to the French doors, the level of the gas in the house would be sufficient to cause a tremendous explosion, setting the entire place on fire from which very little of any intelligence value would be salvaged.

The odor of gas was already very strong in the house by the time Mahoney had put his shoes back on, let himself outside, and relocked the doors.

For a minute he stood there looking across the patio toward the university. The sky to the east had lightened perceptibly, and before too terribly long he would not be able to get away without almost certain detection.

He glanced back inside the house, and for one insane moment, an almost overwhelming urge came over him to go back inside, find the liquor cabinet, pour himself a drink, and sit down. If there was a god, and an afterlife, it would be pleasant to rejoin Marge. He missed her at that moment more than he had in months.

But then he turned, crossed the patio, and quickly climbed over the brick wall, and made his way along the line of trees back onto the campus.

Within five minutes he passed the dormitory parking lot where the Fiat with Sonja's body was parked, and a few minutes later he was calmly seated at a bus stop on the Ha'universita.

The explosion, when it came, was nothing more than a gentle thump a half dozen blocks to the south, and a few minutes later a bus came along and Mahoney got on. Neither the driver nor his half dozen sleepy passengers evidently were aware that a house had exploded nearby, because none of them looked up. Within a half hour Mahoney was getting off downtown near the Central Post Office.

Tel Aviv was coming alive with the sun. Traffic was already starting to build up despite the fact that it was a Saturday, some street vendors were out to take advantage of any early-morning tourists, and the sun glinted off the upper windows in the taller buildings.

Mahoney felt almost like a sleepwalker as he shuffled across to the Central Telegraph Office, where he was given a chit and assigned a telephone in a long row of booths.

As soon as he made his call, he was going to retrieve his rental car from where he had parked it the night before near the prison, and then openly check into the Dan Hotel. It would take several hours before

Wasserman's people would finally track him down, and in the meantime he would be able to take a hot shower, and get a few hours of much needed sleep.

The operator had his call to Geneva ready by the time he reached the booth, sat down, and picked up the instrument.

"Yes?" McNiel Henrys's voice came over the line.

"It is done," Mahoney said, and he hung up the phone.

It is done, he thought, sitting there. The only links were Per Larsen and the Operation Wrath documents. But that now was totally out of his control. Larsen was out in the cold, and at least the network understood that the nuclear strike documents were fakes.

The danger was past. All that could be done had been done. Now it was time for him to go home, as empty as it was.

XXX

TEL AVIV . . . SATURDAY

Mahoney was unceremoniously arrested at his hotel room shortly after two in the afternoon. There was no telephone call, no knock on the door, nothing but four burly, unsmiling men standing over his bed as he woke up.

"Are you Wallace Mahoney?" one of the men said. They all were dressed in baggy, dark suits. They looked ludicrously out of place for Tel Aviv.

"Is Wasserman here?" Mahoney mumbled, the sleep slowly leaving his brain.

"We don't know any Wasserman, sir," another of them asked. "Are you Wallace Mahoney?"

Mahoney glanced at his overnight bag on the chair. It had been opened, its contents spread out on the table. "Yes," he said softly. "I'm Wallace Mahoney."

"You're under arrest, sir," the first one said. He had a perfectly round face, and he wore thick glasses, but he must have been at least six-four with a football player's frame.

"What's the charge?"

"No charge has been specified, sir," the football

player said. "You have been declared persona non grata. We're here simply to insure that you make your flight this afternoon. It leaves at three-thirty sharp."

Mahoney flipped back the covers and sat up, swinging his legs over the edge of the bed. He had a dull, throbbing headache that pounded at the back of his skull, and his mouth tasted foul.

"It's a long drive, sir," the football player said. "If you could get ready now . . ."

Mahoney looked up at him and nodded. "Sure," he said, and he got carefully to his feet, wobbled there a moment, and then went into the bathroom where he brushed his teeth and then shaved, nicking himself twice on the chin.

One of the men stood at the bathroom door watching him all the time, and Mahoney wondered if they expected him to cut his own throat with a safety razor.

When he was done he went back into the bedroom and got dressed. One of the others had already stuffed his things back into his overnight bag.

"My passport is down at the front desk," Mahoney.

"We have it, sir," the football player, who seemed to be in charge, said. "You also had an envelope that contained eight thousand seven hundred dollars. We picked that up for you as well. It will be returned to you just before you get on the airplane."

"Thank you," Mahoney said, and then flanked by his escorts they moved across the room where one of them opened the door and peered out into the corridor.

"Let's go," he said a moment later, and the five of them stepped out into the corridor and walked briskly to the elevator which they took down to the lobby.

"How about my bill here?" Mahoney asked.

"It's been taken care of, sir," the man nearest him said without breaking stride, and within seconds they were outside, climbing into a large Mercedes sedan, one man on either side of Mahoney in the back seat, the other two up front.

The car had been left running, its air conditioner on, so that it was pleasantly cool despite the heat of the afternoon, and Mahoney settled back for the long drive out to Lod Airport.

It was finally over. No pomp or ceremony. No thank you's, or, on the other side of the coin, no accusations He had been hired to ferret out a mole at high levels within the Israeli Secret Service, and he had done just that. Wasserman would be satisfied if not happy. But now that his usefulness here in Israel had run its course, his continued presence would be an embarrassment. They'd have to get him out of the way as quickly as possible. No medals for service well done here.

It was just as well, Mahoney mused as the driver raced expertly through the city, and then southeast toward the airport, because he didn't think he had the stomach to face anyone in the government. They couldn't keep their own service clean, and they certainly wouldn't want to talk about it.

As they passed irrigated farm fields, Mahoney stared out the window, but he was not really seeing anything outside. Instead his thoughts kept coming back to the little boy at the Athens airport, to Ben Abel slumped over his desk, to Malecki lying dead in the prison, a knife in his heart, and Sonja, a beautiful woman with a lovely body. All those people dead. For what?

"We've booked you on a flight direct to Washington, D.C., sir," the man to his right said and Mahoney blinked.

"That's fine," he said. "Will there be time for me to get something to eat?"

"No, sir, but they serve dinner on those flights."

"Fine," Mahoney said again, and he went back to his thoughts.

They arrived at Lod just at three, and Mahoney was immediately escorted to the VIP lounge in the terminal. A half dozen other passengers, cocktails in hand, were waiting there for the flight. At the door Mahoney was handed his overnight bag, the envelope containing what was left of the money Wasserman had paid him, his passport, and a boarding pass envelope that contained his ticket.

"You'll not be allowed to leave the lounge," the football player said. "Someone will be stationed at this door as well as at the boarding gate."

Mahoney nodded.

"We thought it would be best this way. We don't want to create an embarrassing scene for you."

Mahoney was touched by the attempt at decency, and he told him so, then turned, and entered the lounge where he showed the airline clerk his ticket.

Ezra Wasserman was seated by himself near one of the large plate glass windows that overlooked the airport. When Mahoney spotted him, he wasn't surprised, merely sad that he was going to have to discuss Sonja's death with him.

He stopped at the bar first, and when he had a glass of bourbon, neat, he ambled slowly across the room and sat down next to the Mossad chief, placing his overnight bag on the seat next to him.

For a while both men just stared out at the activity on the field. Mahoney sipped his drink; it wasn't a very good bourbon.

"Why did you come back?" Wasserman said, his voice low.

"I had to find out who killed Ben Abel. It wasn't Chaim."

Wasserman looked at him, his eyes moist. "Carl told me that you came down to see Sonja. He was worried that something like this was going to happen."

Mahoney's headache was much worse, and his gut was tied up in knots. "Something like what?"

"Where were you yesterday evening and then early this morning?"

"Driving, and thinking," Mahoney said. "I hung around Beersheba. I was trying to decide to go back out there to talk again with Sonja and her father."

Wasserman stared at him for several seconds. "Shortly after you left the kibbutz, she came up to see me."

Mahoney said nothing, waiting for the man to continue.

"She said she wanted to talk to Chaim, alone. She had this idea—at least that's what she told me—that she could get him to open up. Said she felt he may have been involved in her brother Peter's death in East Germany."

"Where did she get that idea?" Mahoney asked, hating himself for the deception at this late date but hating McNiel Henrys with an even greater passion for making it necessary.

Wasserman shook his head sadly. "I don't know. I told her to come with me down to Records, and I could show her in black and white that he was nowhere near Berlin at that time, but she wouldn't listen. Said she wanted to see him face-to-face."

"And you agreed?" Mahoney asked.

Wasserman seemed completely worn-out. "We'd gotten nothing out of him. Not one scrap. And I thought perhaps she would unlock him. They were lovers for a long time."

"What happened then?" Mahoney asked. "Did she go see him?"

"She went to the prison last night and killed him. She

was with him for just a few minutes when she came back out and told the guards she needed something from her car. When she didn't come back they got worried and checked on Malecki. He was dead. She stabbed him to death with a plastic letter opener."

Mahoney looked away, unable to face the man. "Where is she now?"

"Dead," Wasserman said. "She set fire to Chaim's house, then shot herself in the head."

"I had no idea," Mahoney said.

"You pushed her to it."

"I only pushed because I believed she was the one who murdered Ben Abel."

"The Soviets murdered him!" Wasserman said sharply.

"No, Ezra. Sonja did. She went to see him that afternoon, you know that. Her name was in the log."

"I know that. She told me herself. It's very likely he wanted to ask her something about Chaim."

"It wasn't Chaim," Mahoney said again. "Ben Abel discovered that Sonja was a spy. It was she who passed information to the Syrians and the Lebanese. It was her department. Ben Abel confronted her with what he knew, and she killed him for it."

Wasserman was just staring at him, his mouth half open.

"You say Sonja shot herself? With what caliber weapon?"

"Nine millimeter," Wasserman said.

"The same that killed Ben Abel."

"The shot would have been heard."

"She probably muffled it through a pillow, or perhaps she was wearing a jacket and she took it off and bundled it up. It would explain why there wasn't a muzzle flash burn on his head."

A woman's voice blared over the public address system, first in English then in Hebrew: "El Al flight five-oh-one, direct service to Washington, D.C., is now accepting passengers for boarding at gate seven. All passengers please have your boarding passes ready for inspection."

The others in the lounge began gathering at the door which led to the first class boarding tunnel to the airplane.

"It's over anyway," Wasserman said, and he got slowly to his feet.

"What about you, Ezra?" Mahoney asked.

A slight smile crossed the man's face. "I'm getting out. My wife and I will be moving down to Gan Haifiz. I'm going to work for Carl."

"Soon?"

"Immediately," Wasserman said.

The other passengers from the VIP lounge had already gone, and the ticket clerks were waiting for Mahoney.

"What about Per Larsen and the Operation Wrath files?" Mahoney asked. "Surely you're going to see that through?"

"No need; it's already been taken care of," Wasserman said.

Mahoney had picked up his overnight bag. "What?"

"Two of my people went to Brussels yesterday to talk with him. That's all I wanted them to do, just talk with Larsen."

"I thought you were going to turn it over to my government to handle."

"That would have been too dangerous. I was told to handle it myself."

"Because of me?"

Wasserman nodded. "Your government would have

put the pressure on you about the documents. You couldn't lie to your own people."

"Have your people talked to Larsen yet?" Mahoney asked. It was very possible that the entire thing would blow up in their faces now. If Per Larsen had cracked, Wasserman would soon know enough to pursue the network in full force. Yet he had said he was retiring. Mahoney was confused.

"No," Wasserman said. "When they got to him he was dead. Heart attack, they think; there were no marks on his body."

"Dead?" Mahoney snapped, stepping forward.

Wasserman ignored the outburst. "Amazingly enough the Operation Wrath files were found intact in his safe. Apparently he hadn't had the time to make his contact and pass them over. There was evidence that he had been working on a translation. It was just an incredible stroke of luck."

Mahoney couldn't believe what he was hearing. Henrys said Larsen and Malecki would both be left out in the cold, and now they were both dead. They had killed their own man in order to protect the network. But protect it from what? Larsen could have left the documents intact in his safe, and then drop out of sight. Why had they killed him?

Wasserman held out his hand and Mahoney shook it.

"It's over, Mahoney," the Mossad chief said. "It's finally over. Return to your lake in Minnesota and enjoy your retirement. I'm going to enjoy mine."

And then truly it was finished as the El Al jetliner lifted off the main north-south runway at Lod Airport and accelerated up into a perfectly clear blue sky, the Mediterranean in the distance dotted with boats, and spread along the coast like a sugar and cream fairy-tale city, was Tel Aviv-Jaffa.

Leaving the VIP lounge, Mahoney had looked over his shoulder, expecting to see Wasserman standing there, but the Mossad chief had already gone, certain in his own mind that this incredible business was over.

The airplane banked gently to the right, and then straightened out as it continued its ascent to cruise altitude. Mahoney laid his head back on his seat.

If the aircraft crew had been notified that he was being kicked out of Israel, none of them showed it. The stewardess and steward had both treated him pleasantly. He had been given a window seat with no one next to him, his bag had been stowed for him in the overhead locker, and the seat belt and seat controls had been explained.

A chime sounded and he opened his eyes. The no smoking sign had been switched off, and the first class stewardess appeared around the corner from the forward galley, a telephone handset to her lips. She began explaining about the aircraft's emergency systems, while the steward, a young, handsome man, demonstrated the oxygen mask system, the seat bottom flotation devices, and pointed out the emergency exits.

In a way Mahoney felt sorry that he had not gotten to know Malecki and Sonja much better than he had. He had a sort of grandiose notion that he somehow might have redeemed them. They had struck him as being empty, lost souls, ripe for salvation. And yet he knew in his heart that it could never have happened that way.

Marge would have laughed and called him a romantic old fool.

McNiel Henrys, on the other hand, had struck Mahoney as a man of such huge arrogance that he felt it was his duty to operate the world according to his own twisted philosophy, for his own strange pleasure. Sort of like the Crusaders versus the infidels. Sort of like Hitler and the Jews.

The steward was standing over him, and Mahoney looked up.

"Would you care for a drink before dinner, sir?"

"Bourbon plain, no ice," Mahoney said, and the young man wrote it down on his order pad, then turned to the passengers across the aisle.

They were already well over the Mediterranean, and very high so that there was nothing to see out the window except the blue sky and the deeper blue water far below.

He would retrieve the notes he had sent to John and hand them over to Darrel Switt himself. In that way he would be able to insulate his son completely from any repercussions that Henrys might want to inflict. Once Switt was apprised of everything that had happened, he would be able to take care of himself, especially after McBundy was neutralized.

McBundy, Mahoney thought. His was the one name in the entire bunch that didn't seem to fit.

McBundy had been a friend, a confidant, a mentor in some respects. And among all the other bitter pills Mahoney had had to swallow in this mess, McBundy's complicity was among the worst.

The steward was back and he set Mahoney's drink on the table that separated the seats. Mahoney opened the little bottle, poured the whiskey in his glass, then sat back again as he sipped the drink. It too was bad bourbon, even worse than the drink he had had in the VIP lounge.

He wished, now that he was going home, that Marge could be there waiting for him.

It would have been so much better if he had been able to explain the entire thing to Wasserman and to Carl Margraff. Because of what they had suffered, both men deserved to know the entire story.

He was sipping at his drink again when the first pain,

sharp and very hot, stitched across his chest, making his gasp.

It passed, and for a few moments he was confused about what had happened. Perhaps it had been a gas bubble, he thought, but then the second pain, massive and exceedingly sharp, caused his vision to dim, and he realized only vaguely that he had either spilled his drink on his lap or he had wet himself.

He started to reach, trying to catch his breath so that he could call for help, when a third pain wracked his body with unbelievable strength, and before his vision went totally dark, he was looking into the face of his steward.

The man was smiling.

It was late evening in Washington, D.C., when Darrel Switt finally looked up from his reading. He was still dressed in his dark suit from the funeral, his tie loose, and his shirt sleeves rolled up.

"You say that you've read this?" he asked.

John Mahoney nodded his head very slowly, almost as if he was afraid he might break something. "What do you make of it?"

"I don't know what the hell to make of it," Switt said. He stood up and laid the thick bundle of notes on the coffee table, then stretched.

"My father was a very pragmatic man. He wasn't given to flights of fancy."

"Were you aware that he had worked for the Agency?"

"We all knew it," John Mahoney said. "So did our mother, but we all loved him for his attempts to keep us insulated from it."

"Have you discussed this with anyone?"

"No."

"Not even your wife?"

"No one," John Mahoney said. "My father evidently

*trusted you. In his letter he told me to make absolutely
sure no one but you was to get his package.''*

Switt seemed lost in thought, and he said nothing.

"What are you going to do about it?'' Mahoney asked.

*"I don't know . . . yet,'' Switt said. "When are you
going back?''*

*"We're not going directly home. We'll be leaving Wash-
ington the day after tomorrow for Minnesota. We have to
close down his cabin. We'll probably be there for a few
days.''*

*Switt seemed to draw inward again for a moment, but
then he said, "Are you staying at the Marriott?''*

Mahoney nodded.

*"Fine. I'll call you there before you leave. I'm going to
have to think about this for a day or two. I need some
time.''*

*"Good enough,'' Mahoney said, rising. "Thanks again
for your help.''*

"I don't know if I will be able to help,'' Switt said.

"My father evidently thought you were the man for it.''

*"I'll call you before you leave,'' Switt said, walking the
young Mahoney to the door and shaking his hand.*

*"Please do,'' Mahoney said, and then he left the apart-
ment.*

*For a full five minutes Switt paced the room, every now
and then glancing down at the bundle of notes that he had
been given shortly after the funeral, until finally he went to
the phone, dialed for the operator, and asked for an
overseas line.*

*It took ten minutes for his call to go through to Geneva,
and by the time it did, he was sweating.*

*"Yes?'' a long-familiar voice came over the trans-
atlantic line.*

*"This is Ferret,'' Switt said. "The Mahoney business
isn't finished yet,''*